Gordon Hardwick heard footsteps behind him. His legs did not seem to be responding as they should and he stumbled and almost fell. He knew he was finished. By sheer power of will he forced himself to keep moving for another fifty yards but it was no use. His body had deserted him.

He stopped and struggled around to face his pursuer.

Chameleon, gun in hand, circled his prey warily from a safe distance. He approached Gordon and stood over him. "Gordie," he said, "I want you to know it was me."

Gordon's eyes widened in recognition and he struggled to pull himself to his feet. As he did, Chameleon took one step forward, held the pistol an inch behind Gordon's ear, and pulled the trigger. . .

RED CHAMELEON
by
Charles Robertson

Bantam Books by Charles Robertson

THE OMEGA DECEPTION
RED CHAMELEON

RED CHAMELEON

Charles Robertson

BANTAM BOOKS
TORONTO • NEW YORK • LONDON • SYDNEY • AUCKLAND

RED CHAMELEON

A Bantam Book / November 1985

ISBN 0-553-25246-1

Published simultaneously in the United States and Canada

Bantam Books are published by Bantam Books, Inc. Its trademark,
consisting of the words ''Bantam Books'' and the portrayal of a
rooster, is Registered in U.S. Patent and Trademark Office and in
other countries. Marca Registrada. Bantam Books, Inc., 666 Fifth
Avenue, New York, New York 10103.

PRINTED IN THE UNITED STATES OF AMERICA

O   0 9 8 7 6 5 4 3 2 1

For Ann,
whose hard work made it possible.

Toronto, June 1972

Fist pounding on the door he called, "Robert, are you in there?" He pounded again. "Open up, Robert. I know you're in there."

The door shook, rattled on its hinges from the pounding, but there was no response.

The landlord came, mumbling, "Easy—easy. You'll break the damn door. Let me open it."

The key slipped in the lock and the landlord jiggled it a little to make it catch, then he turned the key and pushed open the door. They both stood in the hallway as if afraid to enter.

Somehow they knew.

The basement room was dark, lifeless. It had the smell of old socks and yesterday's dinner. In a far corner an unmade bed, gray sheets pulled back, gestured uninvitingly. Below the lone window dirty dishes cluttered the sink. In the center of the room, above a faded oriental rug and a knocked-over kitchen chair, a body swung gently in the rhythm of an imperceptible breeze.

"Oh, sweet Jesus," said the landlord.

The one who had been pounding on the door said nothing.

Staring at the face of the dead man the landlord swallowed, hard. The dead man's eyes were wide open, and he seemed incredibly surprised, as if death had sneaked up on him and caught him unawares.

"Don't touch anything," the landlord said unnecessarily, "I'll call the police." He ran back to his apartment, one flight up, even though there was a phone plainly visible in the dead man's room.

The other man waited. Hands thrust deep in his pockets, he leaned against the wall in the hall. He was already think-

1

ing about whom he would have to call and how he would tell them.

He dared one more look. The body, rotating on its axis, twisted to face him for just a moment before spinning slowly back away. He watched in ghoulish fascination as it circled sluggishly toward him again. The staring eyes seemed to accuse him, to demand some response, but before he could frame a rejoinder it turned away again in a deathly gesture of ultimate disdain.

He reached out and slowly swung the door shut so that he did not have to look or be looked at.

One

New York City, April 1973

Karpenkov had been following the middle-aged man for the better part of Friday afternoon waiting for the perfect opportunity to kill him.

The man, Harold Miller, was obviously on a shopping expedition of some kind. Karpenkov, who had been following him for more than a week, knew that Miller would normally have returned to work by now.

Miller was a man of set habits. He left his Fifth Avenue office at precisely twelve noon each day and returned to the office at precisely three minutes before one. Those three minutes placed him at his desk before everyone else in the office returned from lunch. It didn't mean much, but Miller thought that it made him look good.

Each day Karpenkov had followed Miller to a succession of restaurants in the midtown area. Sometimes Miller lunched alone, sometimes with others in his office. Even if he left the office in a group he usually returned alone, but the streets of New York and the elevators in Miller's office building were too crowded for Karpenkov to contemplate murdering Miller at that time.

So Karpenkov had followed Miller everywhere, learning his habits and idiosyncrasies. It hadn't taken long to discover that Miller had a mistress in the city, whom he visited regularly before taking the train home to his wife in Greenwich, Connecticut. It wasn't the same mistress that he had had last year when Karpenkov had followed him for a week. On the first day of his "tail" Karpenkov had followed Miller to the woman's apartment and waited outside for over an hour until Miller emerged, smiling happily, obviously pleased with himself.

And Karpenkov hated him more than he had ever hated anyone in his life.

The next day Miller took a cab to a small restaurant on the Upper East Side where he met the woman for lunch. Karpenkov, who entered the restaurant a few minutes after Miller, sat at a small table where he could watch their every move.

The woman was half Miller's age and quite attractive, thought Karpenkov. An actress or a model perhaps who found a dalliance with an older married man an easier way to make ends meet than working as a waitress.

But Karpenkov's focus was really on Miller. He was middle-aged, hair thinning and thick-waisted, but still the remnants of his former youthful macho attractiveness were with him Karpenkov hated him.

Watching the woman laugh at some probably stupidly inane remark Miller made, Karpenkov steeled his resolve to do this thing and do it soon.

Friday would be a good day he thought. And he would do it so that Miller's relationship with the girl would be exposed. He would have preferred to do it while Miller was naked in the girl's bed, but that would mean killing the girl too and that had been strictly forbidden. He had to find some way to link them so that everyone would know what kind of a man his father was.

That's when he thought of the elevator in the woman's building. Perfect.

She lived in a five-story building in the East Eighties that she obviously could not afford. Karpenkov went to the building at different times during the day to familiarize himself with the layout and with the security procedures. A doorman was on duty from early morning until early evening. After that, admittance was gained by calling the desired tenant on a

3

call box in the foyer. Then, a buzzer would announce when the tenant was unlocking the front door. But the security procedures were easily breached. If he pressed one call button for each floor someone was sure to allow him entry. He memorized a few names from the call box so that if he were questioned he could claim to be visiting someone in the building.

The single elevator was paneled in mahogany with brass trim in a moderately successful attempt to emulate the elegant elevators of a bygone era. Karpenkov touched the paneling. It reminded him of a brightly polished coffin.

Perfect, he thought. On Friday.

On Friday he waited for Miller, but on this day, instead of going for lunch, Miller went shopping. He purchased a gold chain at B. Altman's on Fifth Avenue as Karpenkov watched him with thinly disguised disgust. What Karpenkov did not know was that the chain was for Miller's wife. At Bloomingdale's he bought a lacy negligee that both Karpenkov and the saleswoman who waited on Miller were sure was for his mistress.

Karpenkov was so filled with fury that he even contemplated killing his target right there in the store. He watched him go up the escalator and considered waiting for him to descend. As Miller came down Karpenkov could pass him on the way up and he would do it then. But before Miller reappeared Karpenkov had regained his composure. Better to stick with his original plan: the elevator at the apartment.

He followed Miller back to his office and then went to the library on Fifty-third Street to wait for five o'clock and the expected trip to the woman's apartment.

His full name was Aleksei Gregorevich Karpenkov, and he had waited many years for this day to arrive.

His mother's name was Raya Karpenkov, and in her youth she had been one of the most beautiful women in Moscow. Tiny and delicate as a flower, Raya Karpenkov had been thrust by her uncommon beauty into political situations of which she had no knowledge and which were beyond her limited powers of comprehension.

In 1947, this beautiful child-woman, then just eighteen, had applied for a position as a clerk in the Ministry of Internal Affairs. She was accepted and proved to be competent in her work. Because of her attractiveness and the men she came to know she found fairly rapid advancement in the ponderous bureaucracy of the Soviet machine. In less than a year she was a Grade 7 clerk and offered a position with the commercial section of the Soviet embassy in East Berlin. Unbeknownst to her, officials at the KGB had ordered this promotion hoping to exploit her beauty and her apparent willingness to dispense her favors to those who were in a position to help her. Even the KGB could not have been expected to know that such willingness was more an indication of innocence than it was a sign that Raya Karpenkov was the woman of the world others believed her to be.

In the dangerously fluctuating political situation of Berlin in the late 1940's, such a combination of innocence and corruption would inevitably lead to disaster.

Enter Harold Miller, colonel, U.S. Army. He met Raya Karpenkov at an embassy function in 1949 and was instantly smitten. Although somewhat older than she, he pursued the young Russian fervently. She, for the most part, rebuffed his advances but was flattered to have gained the attention of this dashing American, who was the chief aide to General William Hotspur, the man in charge of American military operations in Berlin. Sensing a possible advantage, the KGB approached Raya and persuaded her that it was her patriotic duty to encourage Colonel Miller to tell her everything he knew about the American military intentions in Berlin.

She knew only one way to get a man to tell her such things and soon she was spending much of her time in various hotels around the city with the American colonel.

In return for her favors Harold Miller told her everything he knew, which turned out not to be very much or of any great importance. The KGB was disappointed in her performance, although Raya could not imagine what more she could do to elicit information from the American.

Upon the discovery that she was pregnant Miller made what the KGB told her was a great show of wanting to marry her and take her back to America. Frightened and confused Raya did not know what or whom to believe, but when the KGB ordered the Ministry of the Interior to send her back to Moscow she obeyed.

Back in Moscow she found her once promising career stalled. No more promotions, no more parties. Instead she found only whispers and sidelong glances. When she walked into a room all conversation stopped. She wanted to scream,

"I did it for my country," but the absurdity of that remark prevented the attempt.

When the child was born things became worse. The KGB tried to elicit her cooperation in another, similar escapade with a diplomat at the American embassy; when she refused she found herself demoted from her present position and even more a pariah than ever.

So she raised the boy alone, never once saying anything unkind about his father. But it was not so in the schools and at the playgrounds. Young Aleksei was taunted unmercifully by his schoolmates. "American," they called him, "American bastard."

His mother married when Aleksei was nine. The man was a laborer in the tractor factory at Podolsk outside of Moscow. He drank heavily and when drunk he beat both Aleksei and his mother. "American bastard," he called the boy. "American whore," he called the mother. In the strangely accepting way of children Aleksei felt that for some unknown reason he deserved to be abused and despised; he wasn't precisely sure what it was he had done, but he sensed that it must have been terrible and therefore demanded perpetual punishment.

In a perverse defensive manifestation, perhaps to ally herself with her drunken husband and save herself from his temper, even his mother turned against him. She too began to drink heavily and abuse her son. At other times she lived in the throes of deep depression.

Although a brilliant student the boy was always in trouble. He did not lash out at his tormentors, but he was often discovered in mindless acts of vandalism and sometimes outrageous cruelties to animals.

During what was called the Cuban Missile Crisis as Russia and the United States stood on the brink of nuclear holocaust, the abuse from all quarters reached a high-water mark. And while he was taunted by his classmates and battered by his vicious stepfather, Aleksei felt sure that he was somehow responsible for the struggle between the two superpowers.

In December of 1962, harassed at work and hounded at home, unable to rise above the deep depression caused by both real and imagined injuries, Raya Karpenkov committed suicide.

Aleksei was now more alone than ever. His stepfather

alternately ignored and abused him until after one particularly violent incident when the boy was beaten almost to death. At last he was removed from the stepfather's care and placed in a home for children. But in six months he was back again, and one night, after his drunken stepfather had beaten him and then passed out in the living room, the boy had stabbed him twelve times with a kitchen knife.

Remanded by the courts to the custody of the state, Aleksei began a long and intricate series of psychological evaluations. Two years later, when he was fourteen, the boy's file came to the attention of the Committee for State Security. A psychologist at the Serbsky Institute, who was assigned to look for such cases, turned his file over to the KGB; what had interested the doctor and ultimately the KGB was Aleksei Karpenkov's unrelenting hatred. Not of his stepfather who had abused him or of his mother who had abandoned him or even of his playmates who had tormented him, but for his American father and all things American.

After evaluating his file and personally interviewing the young man, the KGB removed him from the state institution and placed him in a private school for boys where children of KGB agents and other government officials sent their children. He was assigned to a childless couple who raised him competently if not lovingly.

Aleksei was overwhelmed by the largess of the Soviet state. Rescued from life in an institution he pledged eternal fealty to the kindly souls who had brought him deliverance.

In school he was a dedicated student. His courses selected for him by his KGB mentors, he became fluent in English and German. Science and mathematics were his strong suits and he soon surpassed the wildest expectations of his instructors in these disciplines.

When he was fifteen his course of study was subtly altered: Aleksei soon found himself immersed, along with his science and his mathematics, in the study of that which he despised most—America. When he demurred to his foster family he was told that these orders had come from higher up and that he was ordered on this path of discovery.

When he seemed morose it was decided that he had reached a critical juncture in his development and that for the first time he should be allowed some knowledge of his purpose. He received a visit from a KGB officer who told him that he had been among those chosen to study all there was to know about America. If he were diligent and patient he might be among the lucky few who would be allowed to perform a great service, not just for his own country, but for all of the oppressed peoples of the world. If he were fortunate it would be his privilege to strike a blow against the hated United States.

So at sixteen Aleksei was filled with pride and for the first time a sense of his own worth and power. He flung himself headlong into his studies with an almost obsessive fury. He perfected his already near-flawless English until he could converse easily with English-speaking diplomats who marveled at an educational system that could produce such apt pupils.

In 1966 he was sent to New York with a family, the father being the KGB agent on the Russian delegation to the United Nations' Food for Peace Committee. By this time he was well aware that the KGB had some vitally important assignment awaiting him. He was enrolled as a special student at Columbia University taking math and science courses, but his primary purpose was the study of American idiom.

He returned to Moscow in 1968—eighteen years old and expert in things American. Now it was time, the KGB decided, to bring some of their hard work to fruition.

He met with a major in the KGB, Vladimir Gorsky, who took him to the Gastronom Restaurant in Moscow where privileged *nomenklatura* often dined. Over a lunch of finely smoked salmon, Gorsky explained why Aleksei had been so fortunate.

"We," said Gorsky, "think that you are a special individual. One who deserves the opportunity to show his gratitude to Mother Russia."

Karpenkov's face was moved slightly into the approximation of a smile. "I would do anything for my country," he said.

Now it was Gorsky's turn to smile. "There are many who say that, but few who really mean it."

"I mean it," said Karpenkov flatly. "What do you want me to do?"

Gorsky looked around the dining room, then leaned forward. "We want you to live in America. We will provide you with false identification and documentation. You will attend college there—studying mathematics and computer

8

sciences. Something for which you have already displayed great aptitude."

Karpenkov nodded, eagerly waiting to hear the assignment.

Gorsky went on, "Tremendous studies are being made in the computer sciences. We cannot permit the Americans to get ahead of us. Your job will be to gain employment in the computer industry and report back any new developments to the KGB."

Gorsky smiled and dabbed at his lips with a napkin.

Karpenkov's face, like a melting glacier, began to slide. "That's it?" he asked. "Report about computers?"

Gorsky nodded. "You may not realize it, but this is vitally important. What did you expect?"

Karpenkov's head was shaking. "I was expecting something more dramatic."

"Like what?"

Karpenkov shrugged. He did not want to say it.

"Like murder? Assassination?"

Karpenkov was beginning to feel foolish. He nodded reluctantly.

"We didn't invest all of this time and training to turn you into a common thug, Aleksei."

Karpenkov nodded sadly.

"Besides," Gorsky went on, "we don't do that sort of thing"—he paused and when he continued his voice had dropped in pitch—"very much."

He studied Aleksei, who seemed saddened, subdued, disappointed. He studied the boy's face and began to think about the opportunities afforded by this very special individual. Only rarely did he come across someone who looked like Karpenkov and who had the instinct of a predator. The boy was handsome, intelligent and could be quite charming when he wanted to. If he had not known the boy's psychological history he would have been fooled by him himself. He made a quick evaluation and decided to go farther.

"Being involved in this type of operation," he said slowly, choosing his words carefully, "does not necessarily negate the possibility of other—shall we say more adventurous—assignments."

Aleksei raised his eyebrows.

"Imagine the possibilities," said Gorsky. "Living in America as an American. Freedom to go wherever you want without interference from the police. We could easily provide an occasional operational opportunity. Your cover would make the possibilities endless."

Aleksei smiled.

"Are we agreed then?" Gorsky asked. "You will be trained by our organization. You will work for us?"

"Yes," said Aleksei immediately. "But there is one condition."

Gorsky frowned. "What condition?"

Aleksei's eyes were like glacial ice and for a moment even Gorsky wondered what he was dealing with. "When I return to America," said Aleksei. "The first thing I want to do is kill my father."

Gorsky's face was expressionless.

"I have thought about it for years," said Aleksei. "It would be done so that no one could possibly suspect I was involved."

Gorsky was silent for a moment then nodded. "As long as it does not jeopardize our operation and you are willing to let us judge when and where, I think that that would be an acceptable condition."

Aleksei's smile moved muscles that had not moved in years.

Gorsky watched him carefully, noting the sheer joy that bounced like reflected sunlight from Aleksei's normally placid face. We have here, he thought, a very rare and potentially dangerous piece of equipment.

At five o'clock on that Friday, Karpenkov, a rolled newspaper in his hand, waited outside the apartment building, and when Miller appeared at 5:22 Karpenkov crossed the street to enter the building just behind him. He let Miller press a button and then he too pressed one.

The voice box crackled and Miller said, "It's me," and almost immediately the door buzzed and Miller opened it.

The box crackled again and Karpenkov responded with, "It's me, Ron. I'll be right up."

He walked through the door with Miller without waiting for a response.

They entered the elevator together, Miller pressing the button for the fourth floor, Karpenkov for the fifth. They stood silently, not two feet apart, Miller watching the lights that indicated the floor numbers, Karpenkov breathing easily, watching the face of the man he had come to kill.

"I bring you greetings from Moscow," he said.

"What?" said Miller, startled that the other man, a perfect stranger, had spoken.

"Greetings from Raya Karpenkov."

Miller's face screwed up into a knot of puzzlement. "What are you talking about?"

Karpenkov smiled. "Moscow? Berlin?" he said pressing the stop button and the elevator rumbled to a halt between the third and fourth floors.

"Now see here," Miller said, a slight note of panic creeping into his voice, "what's this all about?"

"Surely you remember Raya Karpenkov?"

Miller's face fell in a rush of remembrance. "What does she have to do with you?"

"I am her son."

Miller's eyes widened.

"I am your son, Colonel Miller."

In some inner recess of his mind, Miller knew enough to be afraid. "What do you want with me?"

Karpenkov looked away. "Nothing," he said releasing the stop button. The elevator began to move.

"I don't understand what you are doing here," Miller whined as the elevator glided to a stop at the fourth floor.

Just before the doors opened, Karpenkov took a deep breath and raised the rolled newspaper which contained a narrow cylinder of prussic acid. In one fluid motion he aimed the open end of the newspaper just below Miller's chin and released the spring mechanism that propelled the gas directly into Miller's startled face.

Miller gasped as the sharp acrid smell hit his nostrils, and then his eyes shot wide open as the first hammer blows thumped inside his chest.

The door opened and Karpenkov helped Miller out into the hallway and gave him a shove in the direction of the woman's apartment. He watched for a moment as Miller staggered forward, then, certain that his target was finished, he walked toward the stairwell exit door.

He turned at the doorway and watched Miller, left hand clutching at his chest, right hand steadying himself against the wall, stagger the few feet to the apartment and somehow manage to fumble with the door buzzer. When the girl opened the door her bright smile turned instantly to panic.

Miller slumped, crashing forward into the foyer of the apartment. He was dead before he hit the floor.

Karpenkov let the door to the stairwell close, shutting out the girl's screams. He found himself whistling as he made his way down to the ground floor.

Perfect, he thought. Absolutely perfect!

Outside he looked cautiously up and down the street before proceeding, but there was no sign yet that anyone had noticed anything amiss. Whistling happily and feeling better than he had in years, he walked quickly across the street, turned a corner and disappeared into the fabric of American society.

1985

WASHINGTON (AP)—The Congressional Office of Technology Assessment concluded, in a report released today, that the President's "Star Wars" antimissile system is not technologically feasible.

The report went on to say that "the prospect for success of such a system is too remote to ever consider the commitment of the vast sums of money required for testing and development."

The report, coauthored by Walter Gibbons and Robert Riley, research fellows at the Massachusetts Institute of Technology's Center for International Studies, says that such a system "is technologically unattainable" and that "its testing would violate the 1972 ABM treaty with the Soviet Union."

House Speaker Thomas Carrigan waved the report before reporters in his congressional office suite and said, "There is no hope that the President's pie-in-the-sky defense will work and I, for one, am not going to approve hundreds of billions of dollars of taxpayers' hard-earned money for what is surely a technological dead end."

TWO

Vandenberg Air Force Base, California, 1985

"We have ignition!"

The earth shook. It began as a slight, almost imperceptible trembling, but within seconds of ignition, like concentric circles radiating outward in a pond, the sound of the great engines and the shuddering blast of the inferno that was the exhaust from two hundred thousand pounds of monstrous thrusting rockets reverberated for miles from the Air Force testing facility at Vandenberg in Southern California.

"We have liftoff," the launch officer announced to the tense assembly of high-ranking military and government officials who were clustered in the underground command capsule two miles from the launch site.

The strain on the faces was evident as every eye fixed on the video monitors that showed great billows of smoke and flame escaping from the vent ports of testing silo number seven.

"Here she comes," said one of the military men who stood next to the President's National Security Adviser. His voice was low, controlled, but a slight wavering betrayed his anxiety.

Like some sleek predator the Minuteman ICBM emerged from its lair, moving slowly at first but already gaining momentum as its huge engines gulped fuel at an incredible rate. The tail emerged, spouting fire; the great missile had cleared the eighty-foot-deep silo.

"Go, baby, go," someone whispered, echoing the silent thoughts of all the others.

Straight up and still gaining speed, the monster rose, standing on its great glowing tail, lighting the predawn California sky like another sunrise. Then, as if sensing its prey, the monster seemed to veer slightly west, out over the Pacific, its exhaust arcing across the sky in a great curving trail.

In minutes even the long-range telephoto lenses on the video cameras could detect only a bright, fiery glare fifty miles up and seventy miles downrange as the monster headed for the upper reaches of the atmosphere. A small puff of distant fire announced—and all instruments confirmed—that the first stage had disengaged and the second stage had begun its burn. Now all that remained in view was the long, sweeping vapor trail, already dissipating and made ragged by the strong high-altitude winds.

The National Security Adviser took a deep breath and released it as a long, soft sigh. He was a tall, slender man with gray hair and sharp blue eyes. His patrician bearing belied his humble origins in the fruit fields of California. His name was Webster Connolly and he had been a political adviser and close friend for over thirty years to the man who was now President of the United States.

Connolly turned to the man at his side. "Do you realize, General Thompson, what this event will mean if this test is successful?"

Thompson's beefy face cracked into a wide grin. "You bet," he said gleefully. "It'll mean we have the Rooskies right by the balls again."

Connolly smiled condescendingly. General Thompson was not exactly his idea of the enlightened military man. "Of course, General, but it will also mean an end to our worries about nuclear war. An end to our fears of annihilation. It will mean peace—real peace—at last."

Thompson furrowed his brow, trying to reconcile Connolly's remarks with his own conceptions. To him this event meant the rightful regaining of American nuclear superiority from the Russians. But if this was how the National Security Adviser wanted to phrase it, that was fine with him.

What it also meant, thought Connolly, was that his friend, his President, could keep his promise to the American people. In his first campaign the President had promised the electorate "peace through strength." In the second campaign the promise was "freedom from the tyranny of nuclear weapons." Connolly smiled; he had thought of that phrase himself. The President's detractors and Democratic opponents had ridiculed his "Star Wars Folly," his "pie-in-the-sky defense" but the American people failed to find anything ludicrous in a

14

defensive strategy that promised to "make America safe again" —that was another one of Connolly's campaign phrases.

The President wanted to be remembered as a peacemaker—to laugh in the face of those who had derided him as "the cowboy President" or "John Wayne in the White House." He had, at least for the moment, gotten his word across to the American people, but those Eastern liberal intellectuals had refused to lessen the tenor of their criticism. Connolly wondered why the President—any President—cared so much about what these people felt, but it was enough to know that he did.

The President had survived a bad scare in the last election. A coalition of traditional Democrats, along with an influx of feminists, gays, nuclear-freeze proponents, teachers and others, had almost combined to force him out of office. By the thinnest of margins the President had managed to hang on. Postelection polls showed that what had carried the day was the President's campaign pledge to "make America safe again."

Now the President was almost desperate to make good on that promise. His greatest fear was that some other President—or as he sometimes put it, "some goddamned Democrat"—would be in office when his grand defensive strategy came to fruition. "If Jack Kennedy had been alive in 1969," the President had said many times, "how do you think he would have felt watching Nixon greeting the astronauts returning from the moon? It was his program—and Nixon just happened to be in office when it all came together."

What he wanted of course was his place in history. What only a year ago had seemed to be just another empty campaign promise had with surprising suddenness become a startling possibility. A research breakthrough had turned a vague, distant goal into an attainable objective. The President had leaped on his opportunity like a hungry cat on a mouse.

"How long before we know?" Connolly asked Thompson, who had remained at his side. He knew the answer before he asked the question. It was just something to say.

General Thompson looked at his watch. "In about ten minutes we should hear from downrange tracking, seven minutes after that the missile should begin reentry, three minutes after reentry the nose cone will separate and in fifty-five seconds the three warheads will eject and independently pursue target objectives."

15

As usual, thought Connolly, the general was thorough in his response. "And when will we know if all of this works?"

"The warheads will have to be recovered by the Navy helicopters and returned to the carriers. Preliminary examination will take place on board the *Nimitz*. Later, the warheads will be returned to the nuclear testing facility in Nevada for more definitive examination," Thompson replied.

"What if it doesn't work?"

Thompson seemed unsure of what he meant.

"There's no chance of accidental detonation, is there?"

Thompson smiled, seeing what Connolly meant. Civilians were paranoid about nuclear weapons. "No. The warhead is a dummy. Only the firing mechanism is real. There's no chance for any kind of nuclear explosion."

Connolly breathed a sigh of relief. Although this had been explained to him several times, he still felt a sense of relief each time he heard it.

"And the recovery ships—"

"On station."

"The helicopters—"

"At the ready." Thompson was filled with confidence. "Don't worry," he said. "The helicopters will be right on top of the payload at splashdown. Although this isn't our most accurate missile it has a guidance package upgrade which will achieve a CEP"—he saw Connolly's face go blank—"a Circular Error Probability—of about three and a half kilometers." He grinned and for a moment considered slapping Connolly on the back. Wisely, he did not. "We've got our end covered. Let's just hope Professor Kincaid can cover his!"

At that moment the tracking station on Oahu was following the path of the rapidly approaching ICBM. Two hundred miles above the atmosphere and still over a thousand miles from its targets the monster's inertial guidance system was fixed on a star and the onboard computers were busily calculating the correct flight path to the target. During the descent trajectory the Advanced Ballistic Reentry System program would maneuver the payload package into position, then release the warheads from the MIRV dispenser in the appropriate sequence.

Fifty miles above the missile, a Synod II tracking satellite was examining the Minuteman's every move and relaying the information to the ground-based tracking facility.

As the missile's angle of attack increased and it began its plunge through the atmosphere, a small group of men— scientists—flanked by another, larger group—soldiers—stood around three men who sat at three identical computer terminals. In the middle was Professor Jonathan Kincaid, bushy-haired with thick glasses, and in his early fifties. He was generally regarded as one of the world's foremost authorities on computer design.

"Reentry begun," said the man to his left.

Kincaid nodded. He could see the figures on his computer screen.

"Reentry angle of deflection is 52.006 degrees," said the third man.

Kincaid spoke for the first time. His eyes were fixed on the screen. "Speed sixteen thousand, height seventy-eight miles . . . distance from targets two-zero-six miles on A, two-four-three on B, and two-six-two on C."

"Deflection alteration is one-point-zero-seven, bringing angle of deflection to 53.076."

Kincaid pushed a single button and his screen changed to show a small green blip descending at an increasingly sharp angle. "Computer locked on target. Weapon coming up to power," then, "Weapon armed and ready."

"Twenty-six seconds to nose-cone ejection."

"Still tracking," said Kincaid. "Still locked on."

Sixty-six miles above the surface of the Pacific and almost four thousand miles from the launch site, the bullet-shaped nose shroud that protected the final stage and the MIRV dispenser glowed a dull red like dragon's breath before flames. As the plunge through the atmosphere continued, a small charge blasted the base of the nose shroud and like petals on a deadly flower the two-sectioned cone opened up and tumbled away in the slipstream. For the first time the MIRV dispenser, and its three-warhead package, was revealed.

"Shroud ejected!"

"Still tracking." Kincaid turned to his right. "No change in deflection?"

"Still constant."

"Package A ejected," said the man on the left, a tiny note of excitement creeping into his voice for the first time.

Forty-one miles high and already more than six hundred miles west of the tracking station, the first warhead began its descent.

Kincaid leaned closer to the screen as if to block all distraction. The screen was alive with data. "Selecting target," he said punching keys. As he did, the lines of data on the screen that depicted the missile, nose shroud and miscellaneous debris the computer was tracking disappeared, leaving only the reentry vehicle and the one ejected warhead to contend with.

"Package B ejected."

Another blip appeared on the screen.

"Warhead A, twenty-seven miles high, 147 miles from impact in . . . three minutes, fifteen seconds." The speed had decreased dramatically. "Warhead B, thirty-one miles high—"

Kincaid interrupted. "Trajectory on reentry vehicle seems off a bit. Verify." There was a noticeable note of tension in his voice.

"Trajectory variation four percent and increasing rapidly. Package C, ejection imminent."

"Any information on the variation?"

The man on the right punched in the question on the computer. Almost instantaneously the computer flashed back and he read aloud from his screen, "Probable retro-rocket malfunction in GEMK-12 reentry vehicle. Possible guidance system malfunction."

"Package C must have ejected by now," the third man added, "but I'm not getting anything on my screen."

Behind them, there was a nervous murmur from the gathering.

"Angle of error increasing."

Kincaid's voice was still in control. "Enter error correction and lock into Package A."

"Error correction entered—locking on to Package A."

"Still seeking C."

Kincaid stole a glance at the man on his left but was unable to get his attention.

"Firing range—fifteen seconds."

"Locked on target," said Kincaid.

"Still seeking C."

"On my command. 10-9-8-7-6-5-4-3-2-1. Activate."

"Tracking B. Still seeking C."

Above a promontory at the United States Navy facility, overlooking the Pacific Ocean, on the roof of a recently constructed concrete-block building that resembled something a child would construct with Legos, was a radar direc-

18

tional disk with a long, hollow rod protruding from its center. At the word "activate" the rod began to hum, and as Kincaid called, "Fire," an incandescent stream of charged particles like a steady flow of bullets streaked off into the atmosphere.

Warhead A was now less than thirty seconds from impact and almost seven hundred miles from the particle beam weapon, traveling at more than five thousand miles per hour. The energized stream of electrons struck the descending warhead with the force of a trillion electron volts, moving just below the speed of light. Like a gigantic lightning bolt the beam punched a hole in the outer casing of the warhead, devastated everything in its path and exited through the other side.

"On target and holding for three seconds," announced Kincaid.

The warhead was starting to tumble now as the beam raked it from stem to stern.

"Switching to Package B at my count of 5-4-3-2-1. Now."

The beam stopped as instantaneously as it had begun and the tracking computers locked on the next target. On Kincaid's command, the directional disk moved almost imperceptibly and again the beam blossomed into the atmosphere.

"On target."

"We have Package C on the screen. Target overflight two miles, plus or minus one thousand yards. Impact in fifteen seconds."

Kincaid shot him a dirty look, as if the man were responsible for his problems. "Lock on Target C. I am switching on my count—3-2-1. Now!"

Kincaid wiped his brow with the back of his hand. "It's going to be close," he whispered to himself.

"On target and ready."

"Fire."

Three miles up and less than ten seconds from what would have been a 200-kiloton thermonuclear explosion, Package C was bombarded and sliced almost in two by the man-made thunderbolt that struck it from 750 miles away. Penetration had been instantaneous, devastation total. So Package C, its firing mechanism fused, its dummy warhead punctured and fractured from thermal stress, tumbled harmlessly into the ocean.

"Shut down power," Kincaid said and slumped back in his chair.

The gathering of high-ranking military men who formed

an almost perfect semicircle behind Kincaid and his two associates stole glances at each other, unsure of what they had witnessed. There were mumbled questions and a few embarrassed shrugs. The air was charged with agitation, but Kincaid's workmanlike demeanor, his lack of exuberance, served to diminish the excitement.

Finally one man in the semicircle, General Chester Moreland, stepped forward. "Well, Professor Kincaid? Don't keep us in suspense. Do we have a success here?"

Kincaid swiveled in his chair to face his questioner and the others. "It's too early to tell with any degree of certainty"—he saw the general's face begin to crumble—"but I can tell you this." He stood up and put his hands into his trouser pockets. "We successfully tracked the reentry vehicle and were able to locate and lock onto the payload packages on ejection—even though I'm sure you saw what happened with Package C. We were then able to track and successfully fire the particle beam weapon at each individual target. We were able to direct the beam at the targets for at least the minimum of three seconds' firing time." Feet still planted, he twisted and looked back over his shoulder at his computer screen. "The instrumentation shows that the warheads and the firing mechanisms were severely damaged."

The buzz of excitement from the semicircle grew in intensity and Moreland raised his hand to quiet the growing sound. "What does all that mean, Professor? Do we have a successful test or what?"

"It means," said Kincaid patiently, "that as far as we can tell from here, the tracking and firing of the weapon worked as planned"—he held his hand up as a cautionary gesture as the buzzing threatened to break out again—"Now we'll have to wait for the recovery teams to inspect the warheads."

General Moreland could hardly contain himself. "Professor," he said, his smile threatening to slice his face in two, "the combination of the particle beam and the Kincaid Computer Assisted Guidance System just might be the greatest advance in weaponry the world has ever seen."

The professor winced at the name the military seemed to be using for his device. "I hope, General, that it will be a force for peace." His voice was calm and almost sad, with no trace of the excitement Moreland would have expected and which had already infected the others in the room.

Moreland eyed Kincaid carefully, trying to read what

was on the professor's mind. There was something there that he wasn't saying.

After a moment Moreland spoke to the professor, but in a voice loud enough so that it was obviously intended for everyone in the room. "You and I are leaving for Washington within the hour, Professor. Before we arrive we should receive news from the recovery teams, which I am sure will verify the effectiveness of the technique demonstrated here today." He smiled and his eyes were twinkling. "If this Kincaid System works as well as I think it does, I want to personally deliver the word to the Chairman of the Joint Chiefs and to the Secretary of Defense."

Kincaid's eyes held the general's firmly. "And if it doesn't?"

"Then you and I will sneak quietly out of town, Professor, and let someone else tell the Joint Chiefs what we did with a coupla billion dollars of Uncle Sam's money."

Five hours later, when the KC-135A transport landed at Vandenberg Air Force Base, there was still no word from any of the recovery teams. General Moreland, who had spent most of the flight from Hawaii pacing in the aisle of the aircraft, transferred his nervous pacing to the VIP lounge while they waited for their plane to be refueled.

Kincaid sat quietly reading, trying to avoid the anxious glances of the pacing general.

Just before takeoff they were joined by Webster Connolly, who was to accompany them on the trip back to Washington. Connolly greeted Kincaid and congratulated him on the apparently successful test. Kincaid thought the National Security Adviser seemed as nervous as General Moreland.

Twenty minutes into the flight the copilot came back with a coded message for Moreland. Tension was high; the general fumbled with his codebook and decoded the message.

The general sighed and Connolly felt his heart sink. "It's only notification that they have recovered A and B and are still looking for Package C."

"What the hell is taking so long?" Connolly snapped, and was immediately embarrassed that his impatience was showing. "I'm sorry, General," he said, forcing a smile. "I realize that everyone is just as anxious as I am."

Kincaid said nothing. He turned his head away and watched the landscape slide by below.

General Moreland's voice displayed more patience than

he really felt. "The third warhead malfunctioned and went down outside the target area. It's taking a little longer to recover it, that's all."

Connolly nodded appreciatively and tried to read some papers he had brought in his briefcase, but found it impossible to concentrate on anything but the day's events.

Less than an hour later a second message arrived and was relayed to Moreland. He read, "All recovered. A and B on carrier. C on way." Then he looked dramatically around at the men, who seemed poised on his every word. "It won't be long now."

The wait seemed forever but in actuality the final message arrived a little more than two hours later. Below them, as they raced toward the darkness, the first lights of early evening began to twinkle in Kansas City.

General Moreland read as he decoded. "Packages . . . A . . . B . . . and C . . . delivered and inspected." He looked up and wiped perspiration from his upper lip. "Extensive . . . damage . . . nuclear devices." His eyes danced. "Firing . . . mechanisms . . . damaged . . . beyond . . . function."

Connolly burst into spontaneous applause. He couldn't help himself.

Moreland giggled nervously and continued decoding while Connolly vented his tension. When Connolly was finished he could have sworn there were tears in Moreland's eyes. "There's more?" he asked.

Moreland nodded. "Yes. The warheads are being prepared for shipment back to the United States." Moreland handed Connolly his notepad so Connolly could finish reading what he had just decoded.

Connolly read aloud. "Nuclear devices totally inoperable—test complete success. Congratulations." Connolly sank back in his seat. He read the message again then looked at Kincaid. "It works," he said gently. "Holy Mother of God—the goddamned thing works."

General Moreland leaned forward. "Could I have that message back, Mr. Connolly? I'd like to keep it as a souvenir."

Connolly was about to hand it back when suddenly he snatched it back. "Y'know, General, I think the President might like to have this." He saw Moreland's face sag a little. "Someday this piece of paper might have historic implications. I think we should—all three of us—sign it and I'll give

22

it to the President. Perhaps in time this might be displayed in the Smithsonian along with other historic American documents."

"Let's have a drink," said General Moreland. "This calls for a celebration." He laughed. "I'd love to see the look on the President's face when you hand him that message."

Connolly smiled. He knew what the general was asking but that was a privilege he wanted to keep for himself. "Yes," he said, "let's celebrate." He left Moreland's subtle request dangling in the air.

For the first time in hours Kincaid spoke. "I wouldn't celebrate too enthusiastically," he said softly.

The smile drifted slowly from General Moreland's face. "What in hell are you talking about, Kincaid? This is the greatest day since . . . since creation. You should be dancing in the aisles. What you've done is nothing short of a miracle— it's a God-send."

Connolly's eyes narrowed as he watched Kincaid's face. He had been increasingly concerned over the scientist's silence and general lack of enthusiasm; he knew he wasn't going to like what Kincaid had to say.

"I haven't done anything yet," said Kincaid.

"What do you mean?" Moreland squealed, his voice rising in pitch. "You made it work!"

Now it was Connolly's turn to be silent. He waited for Kincaid to explain.

Kincaid sighed. "The success of this test is predicated upon the combining of two advanced research projects. We've known for a long time that a particle-beam weapon was feasible—that a beam of charged particles could blast its way through any kind of metal casing and cause catastrophic damage to whatever was contained within. The problem has been to achieve sufficient energy levels."

"And that," said Connolly hopefully, "has been achieved."

Kincaid nodded. "Which brings us to the second part of the problem—my part. How do you aim such a weapon at targets hundreds—thousands—of miles away, traveling at thousands of miles per hour?" He paused, and when Connolly made no response he went on. "The answer obviously is a computer-directed aiming system. I've developed many such systems before. But never one with so many critical problems." His shoulders sagged. "I'm afraid I've failed."

"Before your proposal, Professor, we were looking at

ten—perhaps twenty—years before this beam weapon could become a reality."

"Yes," said Kincaid. "So now the beam technology is here but we're still ten years behind in the computer technology to make it work." Kincaid shook his head in frustration. "Look, the original concept for this missile defense system was multilayered. A space-based system of laser and particle-beam weapons that would pick off Soviet missiles shortly after launch, and a secondary system to pick off missiles in the upper atmosphere. As a final barrier, a ground-based particle-beam system would destroy whatever warheads got through the primary barriers."

Connolly sighed. "You know as well as I do, Professor, that the space-based system is—from a technical standpoint—decades in the future. It's prohibitively expensive, so much so that it might never be built and, I might add, exceptionally vulnerable to presently available antisatellite technology. That's what makes *this* system so attractive. It's ground-based and unassailable."

"Yes, but it's only part of the system—and it won't work alone."

General Moreland was losing patience. "What the hell do you mean it won't work," he hissed. "It does work." He pointed to the decoded message that Connolly still held in his hand. "It says so right there."

Kincaid shook his head. "I don't want to be a wet blanket—after all, this was my idea—but . . ." His words drifted off to nothing.

Moreland began to sputter incoherently but Connolly interrupted him and said, in the calmest voice he could muster, "Maybe you'd better explain to us, Professor, what you mean. In view of today's success how can you say your weapon doesn't work?"

Kincaid nodded. "What you saw today was a test—only a test. It was conducted under the most controlled circumstances. It demonstrated that the particle-beam weapon can indeed render a nuclear device impotent. But we knew that anyway."

"Go on."

"You also saw that we were fed information from the launch site—velocity, exit, separation, reentry, anticipated angle of deflection, point of impact." He looked searchingly at Connolly. "I mean we knew where the damn things were

24

coming down. We knew where the warheads were supposed to impact. All the information was fed into the computer in advance. We were ready for the attack. You saw what happened with the third warhead. There was a slight malfunction and we almost blew it."

"But you did it. You got all three."

"We were lucky. We had all the data going in and we got lucky. What if there had been five missiles and fifteen warheads? Or ten with thirty? The problem with the land-based system is that we are unable to destroy the missiles themselves the way a space-based system could. We can only hit the warheads. We may have to hit ten warheads for every missile launched and if the Russians launch a first strike they'll send hundreds of missiles with thousands of warheads. Such a massive strike would simply overwhelm the capabilities of the computer-directed aiming system." He laughed. "Three warheads almost overwhelmed it today."

Connolly knew the near miss had had a profound effect on Kincaid. "Couldn't we just use more computers?"

"More missiles," said Kincaid sadly. "One can't keep up with exponential growth simply by lining up thousands of computers. The simple truth is that the generation of computers available to us today—even the fastest, most powerful—are totally inadequate for the task."

"You mean this has all been for nothing?" said Moreland.

He was about to launch into a diatribe but Connolly shut him off with a wave of his hand. Something Kincaid said had left him with a glimmer of hope. "You said that today's computers were inadequate. What about the next generation?"

Kincaid's eyes were fixed on the cabin floor. "Perhaps not the next, but the one after that or"—he gave a helpless shrug—"the one after that."

Connolly sighed. Trying to get information from a scientist was like trying to get an admission of failure from a politician. "We have super-fast computers available today."

Kincaid tried to explain. "Today's machines might have as much as a billion logical inferences per second, but they 'think' almost exclusively in a sequential manner—a single task at a time—no matter how fast. What we *need* is a machine that can carry out many parallel operations. In other words a computer that can almost instantaneously calculate the velocities, orbits, flight paths, descent trajectories and impact points of a thousand warheads *at the same time*, and then relay that information to the computers that guide, aim and fire the particle-beam system."

"How far away are we from the development of such a computer?" Connolly asked.

"At the present rate of development—five years, maybe more."

"What would it take to accelerate that timetable?"

"Money and commitment. Lots of money." Kincaid nodded slowly.

"I can guarantee the commitment, and if you say that this can be done in two years I can guarantee the money." He thought of saying, but did not—"more than two years and I guarantee nothing."

Kincaid looked at him, his eyes rapidly calculating the earnestness of Connolly's proposal. "It could take several billion dollars."

"Can it be done in two years?"

"Perhaps."

"Perhaps isn't good enough."

"I'd need the best people in the country."

"You'll get everything you need. Can it be done in two years?"

Kincaid thought for a moment, but he had already made up his mind. "Yes. It can be done."

Connolly nodded. "I'll speak with the President tonight," he said, then added quickly, "After consulting with the Secretary of Defense, of course. I feel confident you'll get everything you need, Professor."

General Moreland breathed a great sigh of relief. He felt as though he had been falling from a great height, only to be saved at the last minute. "I think I'll have that damn drink anyway," he said. "Anybody join me?"

Neither man answered. Both were too lost in their own thoughts.

Professor Kincaid was imagining the scope and difficulty of the work ahead of him. Had he overcommitted himself? Had he promised too much? A slow smile spread across his features. Dammit no, he hadn't. His life was dedicated to the creation and development of the most advanced computer the world had ever seen, and the only way to get the money needed for a project of this size was to tie it into a weapon procurement proposal. His money problems were over. It could be done. Such a computer could be built and he would be the one to build it.

Connolly sat back, his eyes closed, his head back on the headrest. His thoughts were on the last two successful presidential campaigns he had run for the current President. Now it seemed he was running a third—not for the votes of the electorate but for the approval of posterity. The electorate, he reflected sadly, had turned carnivore. Voters, spurred by the media, demanded instant gratification. If a President could not satisfy all of their disparate whims he would be cast aside for the next pretender, who in turn would be cast aside for the next. What was worse, once out of office, ex-Presidents became the objects of scorn and ridicule to press and public alike.

This would not happen to his President. The one thing the public wanted more than anything else, the one thing that would satisfy them—bring them joy even—was the elimination of fear. Elimination of the burning dread of instant incineration in a nuclear conflagration. They wanted peace—at any price. His President was prepared to give them that. Then he thought, a thin smile forming, his President's place in history would be secure.

Carrying the hopes and disparate dreams of its three passengers, the KC-135 began the slow descent toward Washington. To Professor Kincaid the weapon meant the fulfillment of his life's work. To Connolly it meant the culmination of his political career, and to General Moreland it meant being able to tell the Russians to kiss his ass.

WASHINGTON—A Pentagon spokesman announced today the first successful test of the new American anti-ballistic-missile system. The spokesman said, "The test demonstrated the reliability of the system and its incredible defensive potential."

Although classified, the system is believed to be a ground-based, computer-guided laser device that tracks and destroys incoming strategic ballistic missiles before they enter the atmosphere. "We are on the verge," said the spokesman, "of ridding ourselves of the threat of nuclear attack."

Defensive experts, who were present at the briefing, were mildly skeptical about the effective

27

ness of such a system, saying that only full-fledged testing with independent verification of success could prove the Pentagon's claim. Furthermore, said some experts, any such defensive system could be defeated by relatively minor modifications on the part of the Soviet missile-firing procedures, or quite simply by overwhelming any defensive system through the addition of multiple warhead launchers to existing missiles.

Dr. Robert Quinn, an expert on military affairs who covers the Defense Department for *Aviation Week*, said that "any defensive system is bound to cost billions and is doomed to failure before it begins."

The Pentagon denied Dr. Quinn's allegation but refused further comment on the potential cost of further research and development of the ABM system.

Three

Bethesda, Maryland

The phone rang while they were at dinner and K.C. Hardwick watched the expression on his sister-in-law's face crumble.

"Can't we even have one dinner in peace," she said, "without that damn phone?"

Her husband, Gordon Hardwick, sighed. "I'm sorry, Carol," he said getting up. "Maybe it's nothing."

When he had gone into the kitchen, Carol turned to her brother-in-law. "It's like this almost every night"—she made a face of dismay—"if he manages to make it home for dinner."

K.C. smiled sympathetically. "Must be rough having a husband who's important."

She caught his drift. "I know I shouldn't complain—but dammit, the CIA can run alone for one night. You know how many times that phone has rung while we're in bed making love?" Her eyes went to the ceiling. "I used to laugh and call it 'phonus interruptus.' But it's not funny anymore."

Carol Hardwick was thirty-five years old and K.C. found her just as devastatingly attractive now as he had fifteen years ago when his brother had married her. K.C. was fourteen years old then, and his first look at her had started him on what was to be a lifelong crush.

Carol was long and lean and athletic and well aware of her power over her brother-in-law. She pushed her long dark hair out of her eyes and winked. "Speaking of love life—how's yours lately?"

K.C. groaned. "Terrible."

He sprinkled his food with salt.

Carol reached across the table and gently slapped the back of his hand. "Enough," she said. "It's not good for you. What about that girl in the admissions office—Martha what's-her-name?"

"Marjorie," K.C. corrected.

"Yeah, Marjorie. Gordon told me she was supposed to be really hot."

K.C. laughed. "She got married. An old boyfriend showed up and popped the question. So she called, told me he'd asked her and asked me what she should tell him."

"You were supposed to say, 'Marry me instead.'"

"I guess so."

"What did you tell her?"

"I told her to do whatever would make her happy."

Carol chuckled.

K.C. nodded. "She hung up the phone and the next thing I heard she got married and left the university."

Kevin Collin Hardwick was, at twenty-nine, a professor of electrical engineering and computer science at Columbia. He had dark hair and brown eyes, with a small V-shaped scar under his left eye. In contrast to his brother, Gordon, who seemed larger than life in almost everything, K.C.'s slight build and reserved demeanor made him seem less than his measured height of five-feet-ten. Except for their attraction to Carol Hardwick, the brothers had little in common. Someone had once remarked that the two were as much alike as John Wayne and Dustin Hoffman. Gordon had bellowed his approval and for almost two years afterward had dubbed his brother "Dusty." K.C. had resisted the implied suggestion to call his brother "Duke."

Gordon was ten years older than his brother and although only a few inches taller, he towered over K.C. in almost every way. Ruggedly handsome and glib, Gordon was the epitome of a man to whom everything comes easily. His athletic prowess in high school, where he had also been the senior-class president and valedictorian, was legendary. K.C. was forever known as Gordon Hardwick's kid brother.

Some might have excused or even expected that K.C., living for so long in Gordon's shadow, would resent and ultimately despise this loud and boisterous mountain of a man who had for so long dominated his life, but K.C. had only to think back to when he was eight years old—the day when Gordon Hardwick Senior had been killed in an automobile accident. The boys' mother had died only three months earlier after a long struggle with cancer. She was forty-one. Their father, always a heavy drinker, had sought solace for his loss in the oblivion of booze and on this particular evening had wrapped his car and himself around a tree.

At the gathering of friends and relatives, K.C. had felt every eye on him. In the strange way people have of talking about children as if they aren't there, or are deaf, or unable to understand their own language, K.C. heard the murmured conversations and saw the long soulful looks in his direction. "What about the young one? . . . Who will take take care of him? . . . Gordon's too young . . . Besides Gordon's off to college in the fall. . . . We'll have to make some arrangements for the child somewhere. . . ."

K.C. had begun to weep silently. His world had been shattered in ways that he could barely begin to comprehend, and he began to feel the terror of being absolutely alone.

Gordon, himself little more than a boy, had sensed his brother's fear. He had scooped him up and in a voice loud enough for all to hear had announced, "Don't worry, squirt. Nobody's breaking us up. From now on it's just you and me."

And Gordon had kept his word. He had given up his recently acquired and much-heralded full athletic scholarship to Michigan State to attend a small local college and work full-time.

Gone were the dreams of big-time football and the glory that would come with it. But later, even when K.C. had disappointed him so, Gordon never once, even in anger, reminded him what he had given up.

K.C. had needed no reminder.

When he was older K.C. idolized his brother, although

he had always found it difficult to reconcile Gordon's anti-quated political beliefs with his own. Gordon had an almost absolute and unshakable faith in the inherent decency of American policymakers. Even after Vietnam and Watergate, Gordon remained a true believer.

Gradually though, K.C. and his brother grew farther and farther apart on the political spectrum and their differences became a wedge between them that sometimes resulted in harsh verbal confrontations. K.C., for his part, could not understand how someone as bright as Gordon could cling to such shopworn "good-guy/bad-guy" or "us-against-them" ideas. Gordon on the other hand could never understand how K.C. could fail to see the nature of what he called "the enemy."

"Communism," Gordon had said during several of their discussions, "is a quasi-religious political creed, and communists believe that anything that helps promulgate their faith is a moral act. Their faith is like the Christianity of the Inquisition or the fundamental Islam of the ayatollahs. Those who do not embrace the faith are infidels and can be considered less than human. Those nonbelievers are vermin who can be lied to, cheated, deceived or even destroyed, and there is no moral implication in the act.

"You mustn't forget that Western civilization has barely touched the Russians; their cultural heritage is closer to the East than it is to us. They play in a different ballpark and have little regard for our Western concepts of morality and fair play."

"Such as it is," K.C. would add, which would usually precipitate an argument.

Over the years, mostly due to Carol's influence, the brothers had learned to avoid political topics as much as possible. They had both come to regard the other as intransigent in this one area and had decided that discretion required avoidance of such topics.

Gordon Hardwick returned from the kitchen and from the wide grin on his face it was obvious that the phone call had been good news.

"So is the Cheshire cat going to tell us all about it?" Carol asked.

"Classified," Gordon said, mock serious.

Carol sighed. "Probably one of his girlfriends."

The grin slipped from Gordon's face.

"I'm sorry," said Carol. "I meant that to be funny."

K.C. looked down and began aimlessly to move food around on his plate. To avoid looking at them he sprinkled more salt on his food.

"Go ahead with your story, Gordon," Carol said softly. "I'm really sorry. I shouldn't have said that."

But Gordon's discomfort was only momentary. The grin returned.

"Not a word to anyone," he said.

Laughing together Carol and K.C. simultaneously crossed their hearts and made Boy Scout salutes.

"Very funny, very funny," said Gordon. "Just make sure you say nothing to anyone." He grew serious. "Got that?"

Both nodded.

"That was DDO Hanson on the phone. I'm being transferred temporarily to the Technology Transfer Assessment Center."

"Doing what?" asked Carol.

"Trying to keep the Russians from stealing every high-tech secret we've got."

"I know what it is," she said. "But what will you be doing and"—her voice got serious—"where will you be doing it?"

Gordon smiled. "I can't keep anything from you, can I?"

Carol wasn't smiling. "Where?"

"California. Silicon Valley area."

"Shit," said Carol. "We're just getting settled here."

"California's nice, baby," Gordon said. "San Francisco, Carmel"—he grinned lecherously—"remember the beach at Carmel."

She would not be placated. "I thought this latest assignment at Langley would last for a while."

Gordon shrugged, dismissing her concerns. "I've been assigned as the security liaison officer at the TMK Corporation in Mountain View."

"TMK?" said K.C. "Computers."

"Yeah," Gordon said enthusiastically, turning to his brother. "They just got a huge Defense Department contract to develop a very-big-deal computer. They're bringing in top people from all over the country to work on this one. Top priority—hush, hush—rush, rush."

"Isn't TMK a subsidiary of Ameronics Corporation?" asked K.C., the hint of a frown beginning to cloud his face.

Gordon nodded. "Yeah."

"And isn't the Secretary of Defense a former president of Ameronics?"

Gordon nodded again, but this time said nothing.

"So the secretary maneuvers a big-bucks contract to his old buddies at Ameronics. Some things never change."

"Look," said Gordon. "You don't know shit."

This time it was Carol's turn to interrupt. "Don't you two get started again." She turned to Gordon. "We've got enough to worry about with this move." They both fell into silence. "When does this all come about?"

Gordon looked up sheepishly. "I leave day after tomorrow."

Carol's mouth dropped open. "You're kidding."

"You can follow in a week—or a couple of weeks. As soon as you get straightened out here."

Carol fought to hide her disappointment. "When you got this job I thought we'd get to spend more time together, settle down a little."

Gordon nodded. "I know, baby," he said. "And we will—I promise. But this is really important."

"I know it is," she said. "That's the problem with your job. Everything is important."

They finished their meal in near silence, and as soon as they'd had their coffee Gordon excused himself and went to the phone in his den.

"Everything okay with you two?" asked K.C.

Carol smiled. "Better."

"You sure?"

She nodded. "He gave up drinking."

"I noticed."

"You know Gordon. He decided it wasn't good for him anymore so he just stopped. He hasn't had anything—not even a glass of wine—for weeks."

"There was never a middle ground with Gordon."

She laughed. "All, or nothing at all."

"What about . . ." He hesitated, unsure of how to phrase it.

"Other women?" Carol asked, helping him out.

K.C. nodded sheepishly.

"I think that's over too," she said. "He promised me after the last one."

"I don't know how he can do it . . ."

"Stop," she said gently. "It's just the way he is. He's

33

wild and a bit reckless—you know that." She laughed sadly. "That's what I loved about him. I just wish it didn't have to hurt so much."

"He's always been crazy about you."

"I know." She grew thoughtful.

"What is it?"

"I'm worried about him."

K.C. let her go on.

"He's always been a field officer. Bringing him back to Langley has really taken a lot of the fire out of him. He seems"—she paused groping for the right word—"depressed."

K.C. laughed off her concerns. "He'll be fine, Carol. Gordon is always fine."

She eyed her brother-in-law carefully. She knew that he idolized his older brother. "You're right, K.C.," she said. "Gordon is always fine."

She rose to clear the table.

If K.C. had suspected then what was ahead for all of them, he would have begged his brother not to go.

WASHINGTON—A subcommittee of the Democrat controlled House of Representatives today challenged the President's assertion that there is a need for a defensive system to thwart the growing arsenal of Soviet nuclear weaponry.

The report from the Foreign Affairs subcommittee on international security and scientific affairs said that the President had not demonstrated to the satisfaction of the committee members that such a system is required or even that such a system is technically feasible.

Committee chairman Bill Parsons, Democrat of Massachusetts, said that "the U.S. should be seeking an arms-control agreement with the Soviet Union that would eliminate any need for such unrealistic and unproven and incredibly expensive technologies."

Four

Two days later, Gordon Hardwick was in California preparing for his first visit to the TMK Corporation headquarters in Mountain View. Carol was still in Bethesda clearing up some last-minute problems with furniture storage and rental agents. Gordon, having promised to let Carol pick out their apartment when she arrived, had moved into a small motel near Route 101.

The TMK Corporation headquarters was in the center of the twenty-five-mile corridor south of San Francisco that had come to be known as the Silicon Valley. The Valley was home to hundreds of companies—small and large—that served the rapidly burgeoning computer and electronics industries. Every year another hundred or so small companies sprang up in the Valley like mushrooms after a spring rain. Some would survive, some would make it big, but just as many would disappear in a year or two.

TMK was one of the winners.

Gordon Hardwick's first view of the headquarters came only a few hours after his morning arrival in San Francisco. He stopped at his motel, had a quick shower and a change of clothes, and then drove out to TMK.

The building was a two-story, rectangular figure-eight with a flat roof that made it seem low and squat. Inside the figure-eight were two beautifully landscaped courtyards that provided natural light to the inner core of the building.

A high fence surrounded the entire complex. At the entrance to the parking lot Gordon reported to a security guard who politely directed him to the visitors' parking area and then to the security guard at the front entrance of the building. There, Gordon was led across the large, open entrance foyer and past the modern sculpture that dominated the entire lower section of the building. The guard accompanied him to the top of the stairs and then pointed to a group of offices down the hall.

"Mr. Lawson's office is that way," he said and turned to leave. "Have a nice lunch," he added.

Gordon smiled to himself. Either the guard was exceptionally polite or he knew that this particular visitor would very soon be his boss. Probably the latter, Gordon thought. Very little in this world is secret.

Reid Lawson, company president, was waiting for him. He stood up from behind his desk when Gordon entered his office, gave him a vigorous handshake and offered Gordon a seat. He himself did not sit down. "So you," he said, "are our new security man."

Gordon had the immediate impression of an engine running on all cylinders. Reid Lawson was a man in perpetual motion. He was tall, with dark wavy hair and fine, chiseled features. He wore a blue button-down shirt with a maroon tie. His jacket was draped over the chair behind his desk, and his waist was trim and his stomach flat. He was obviously a man in excellent physical shape, Gordon thought. It was difficult to categorize his age but Gordon estimated he could be anywhere from middle thirties to early forties.

"I want you to meet a few people before we go off to lunch," Lawson said. He looked at his watch. "They should be here soon. I also want to apologize in advance. I have to cut our lunch short. I'm expected at corporate headquarters in San Francisco in a few hours."

Gordon nodded. "No problem."

"You'll be meeting Bill Donovan. He's in charge of the uniformed security people and I suppose, technically, he's your next in command. He can show you around this afternoon."

"That'll be fine." Gordon paused slightly. "Should I expect any resentment from him?"

Lawson seemed puzzled. "Pardon?"

"I mean, did Donovan expect the top job for himself."

Lawson shook his head. "No. Donovan has been here for two years. He knows the situation. The government wants their own people here to run security. You'll also meet Ted Nichols. He's the project director for the SP group."

"SP?" Gordon asked.

"Special Projects. The SP program is probably where

your primary interest will be. That's where most of our government work is developed. Although there are lots of other things going on here that we don't want to let loose."

There was a knock at the door. "That'll be them," Lawson said. "C'mon in."

The door opened and two men walked in and were introduced to Gordon Hardwick. Both were in their late thirties, tanned, and obviously physically fit.

"Looking at all three of you," Gordon said, patting his bulging stomach, "I get the feeling I've been letting myself go."

"Company fitness policy," said Lawson. "We have a gym in the building and a jogging track on the property."

"Good body—good mind," said Ted Nichols. He smiled when he said it, as if it were a joke, and Gordon could imagine that it was a company slogan that no one paid much attention to.

Nichols wore a tennis shirt, khaki trousers and sneakers. He was a walking testament to California living. Donovan, on the other hand, wore a rumpled suit that might have been ironed with a hammer.

All four sat around Lawson's desk for a while chatting amiably. Lawson looked at his watch several times. He was obviously in a hurry.

"Tell you what," he said. "Gordon and I will have lunch together, and then he can pick up where he left off with you both this afternoon. Ted and Bill, you'll both make yourselves available to answer any of Gordon's questions."

Donovan nodded agreeably; Nichols looked at his watch before doing the same. Gordon decided that here was another man without much time on his hands.

Gordon and Lawson ate in the company cafeteria. At TMK everyone used the same facilities. There wasn't exactly an executive dining area, but Gordon noted that Lawson's table was separated from the others and no one thought to join them.

"So what do you know about computers, Gordon?" Lawson asked after they had helped themselves at the salad bar. From the smile on his face it was obvious he expected the answer to be, "Nothing."

Gordon put down his fork. "My degree is in electrical

37

engineering, with a minor in math. I'm reasonably conversant with most of the latest developments in the field."

Lawson raised his eyebrows in surprise. "Well, well," he said. "The CIA is hiring a higher class of people these days."

Gordon ignored the remark. "How about you?" he asked.

The smile disappeared. "Not much," Lawson said. "Actually I'm only acting as president of TMK on a temporary basis—perhaps a year or two. We're presently conducting a nationwide talent search for the right man for this job. My commitment is to the parent company, Ameronics. TMK is only part of that corporate structure. I leave the computer decisions to others. My field is sales and marketing."

Gordon Hardwick smiled. "My field is intelligence—acquiring it and preventing others from doing the same."

Lawson seemed uninterested. He looked at his salad plate, pushed around the contents with his fork.

"I also know a great deal about security," said Gordon. "And I know you've had your share of problems here at TMK."

Lawson looked up from his plate. "That's true. We've had one major security problem and a few minor ones." He put down his fork. "In order to satisfy the government that we're capable of taking on a project as important as this, we've had to revamp our entire security system."

"Apparently against your better judgment."

Lawson said nothing at first. Then, "I'll level with you, Mr. Hardwick. I think our security precautions are adequate. You are here merely to satisfy the bureaucrats in Washington."

"I'll level with you too, Mr. Lawson. I think you're right. I don't think I should be here either."

Lawson seemed puzzled.

"But," Gordon went on, "I also think this project should not be developed at a private company. It should be pursued at Livermore or one of the other government weapons laboratories."

"This project was conceived here by Alan Kincaid, who happens to be the K in TMK."

"I know that. And I also know that Professor Kincaid insisted that the project be completed here."

"Everything is here—the best people, the best research facility, the best—"

Gordon interrupted him, "—security man."

Lawson stopped, then smiled. "Apparently so."

"There will probably be quite a few changes around here. I'll need a free hand."

"You've got it," Lawson said. "When do you start?"

"I already have." Gordon looked around the room and then back to Lawson. "Tell me something about TMK," he said.

"Tolbert, Morton, Kincaid: TMK. Tolbert started an electronics company out here, Tolbert Electronics, almost twenty-five years ago. It was moderately successful. Five years after that Tolbert hooked up with Kincaid, who was one of the brains behind UNIVAC and wanted to start his own computer company. They did and have done well ever since."

"What about Morton?"

"He's dead. Drowned in a boating accident sixteen years ago. You might say he was the money behind TMK. Kincaid was the brains."

"And Tolbert?"

"Organizational genius. He was the one who kept everything going during the lean years. He also has a talent for attracting the right people, so we have some of the best computer men in the country right here at TMK. Tolbert also organized the buyout of the company by Ameronics Multinational. It was really Tolbert's team that Ameronics wanted."

"So the big fish swallowed up the little fish?"

Lawson laughed. "Yes, but in this case there was a big difference. One of the little fish—Michael Tolbert—wound up running the big fish—Ameronics."

"I read about that. Married the boss's daughter, then moved over to the parent company."

"It's worked out well. TMK has become an important part of Ameronics and the parent company's contacts have enabled TMK to acquire some very lucrative government contracts." Lawson paused and looked around the room as if he were finished.

"And that," said Gordon, "is where the trouble started."

Lawson turned back to look at him with a mixture of dismay and understanding in his face. "I suppose you could say that. One of our biggest sales was an advanced computer guidance system intended for medium-range ballistic missiles. It was a grand success. Everyone was elated by the project. The Defense Department said it was one of the cleanest, most error-free jobs they had ever contracted."

"Yes," said Gordon, his voice expressionless. "I understand the Russians liked it too."

Lawson suddenly looked very tired. His shoulders sagged and his eyes seemed unable to meet Gordon's. "Yes. One of our employees—a young man with an access to security areas, named Carl Burns—managed to smuggle out most of the documentation. He sold it to the Russians. The next thing we know, the Russians are equipping their missiles with our technology. For a lousy few thousand dollars they bought a million-dollar system."

Gordon knew the story well. It had already become part of United States intelligence lore. What made the story doubly demoralizing was that the American-designed system was actually operational on Soviet missiles before it came into use on American missiles. There had been an appropriations battle in Congress and funds for the project had been delayed. Six months after acquiring the technology, the Russian medium-range missiles that were aimed at all major European cities had been fully operational with the new guidance system installed. American missiles would wait almost another year.

"After that," said Lawson, "we had trouble getting another government contract."

"But they've changed their minds."

"They had to."

Gordon looked puzzled.

"Kincaid is the best there is. His research is already well along on a computer that surpasses anything ever developed before. With the weapon already developed and lacking only the brain to make it operational, they would have been foolish to start from scratch with someone else." Lawson sat back and pushed his almost untouched plate away. "We are determined to perfect the necessary components that will make this project a success."

"And I am determined to make sure that information goes only to the United States."

Lawson looked at his watch. "We are certainly in agreement on that." He stood up. "I've got to run. I'm due in San Francisco in a very short time. Finish your lunch and then talk with Donovan. He'll fill you in on all you have to know."

With that he was gone. Gordon watched him until he had disappeared through the glass cafeteria doors before he pushed his salad aside and started thinking about getting something solid to eat.

WASHINGTON—In a scathing response to a House committee's report on the feasibility of his "Star Wars Defense," the President today blamed the Democratic leadership in the House for "failing to provide the country with either the offensive weaponry the military requires or to fund the defensive system that would make nuclear weapons a forgotten nightmare."

"The Democrats," said the President, "cannot continue to say no to every move the U.S. makes to defend itself without having to answer to the voters of the U.S."

The President said he wanted to "leave behind the unacceptable doctrine of mutually assured destruction and embrace a doctrine of mutually assured survival."

Five

From his office high atop the Ameronics Corporation Building in San Francisco, Board Chairman Mason Whitaker could look out across the city that in his younger days he had helped to build. His corner office faced northeast, giving him a panoramic view of the bay with the San Francisco–Oakland Bay Bridge on the right and the Golden Gate Bridge to his extreme left. Almost in the center of his view sat Alcatraz, the former prison that in other times had served as a remembrance that all was not glory and grandeur.

Nowadays he hardly noticed such reminders. During his increasingly less frequent visits to his office he rarely bothered to admire the panorama that had once so captivated him.

Mason Whitaker was seventy-one and the years had left the taste of ashes on his tongue.

The Ameronics Corporation had been founded in 1903 by Mason Whitaker's father, Cyrus Whitaker, Sr., a San Francisco toolmaker. The company had gradually grown in size until it became the largest manufacturer of tools and heavy construction equipment on the west coast. During World War II the company moved into the defense contracting field and built several large military installations in California. In the late forties and early fifties the company began the process of acquisition that was to make Ameronics one of the largest private, family-owned corporations in the United States.

Until the death of Cyrus Whitaker in 1955 at the age of seventy-five the Ameronics Corporation had primarily concentrated its energies in the fields of tools, machinery, and oil-drilling equipment. But under the aggressive direction of Mason Whitaker, its new president, Ameronics had embarked on a program of diversification that led the company to acquire several other businesses, smaller companies active in electronics, telecommunications and in the aerospace industry.

Mason Whitaker's eldest child, Alice, was married in 1965 and divorced soon after. In 1970 she had remarried Michael Tolbert, founder and majority stockholder in the TMK Corporation, then a small but well-established computer company. Tolbert had sold to Ameronics part of his interest in TMK, which then became a partly owned subsidiary.

TMK flourished under the protective wing of Ameronics. In 1973 Tolbert sold the remainder of his interest to the parent company and joined Ameronics as a vice president of sales and marketing.

Mason's son, Cyrus II, graduated from Harvard Business School and became executive vice-president of the company. He aggressively expanded the company's mining interests and moved into oil exploration and refineries. By 1975 forty percent of Ameronics's revenues came from its growing foreign operations, which included joint ventures with companies in Spain, France, and South Africa.

Mason Whitaker seemed master of all he surveyed. In 1975, with his company more successful than he or his father had ever dreamed, he prepared himself to step down from the everyday operation of his far-flung empire and turn the reins over to the capable hands of his son. It was at this point, with Mason Whitaker at the absolute pinnacle of his career, that disaster struck. Cyrus II, along with his wife and two sons, Mason and Cyrus III, was killed in the crash of one of the company's private jets. The family had been on their way to a brief vacation in Mexico.

Mason was shattered by the loss. He did not appear in public for more than six months after the funeral, and, had it not been for Michael Tolbert, the company might have come apart. Tolbert assumed command of the company during Mason's long bereavement and won the grudging respect of the board of directors who had only reluctantly approved the appointment.

When Mason returned it was soon evident that he had lost heart, and the company's fortunes began to wither like a flower in an early frost. To the great relief of the board of directors, three years after Cyrus II's death, Mason Whitaker moved up to the position of board chairman and left the day-to-day operation of the company to his son-in-law, Michael Tolbert.

The company, which for three years had seemed to advance only by the weight of its own momentum, shook itself free of its imposed lethargy and under Tolbert's direction once again began to assume its preeminent position in a wide variety of fields. Tolbert brought in his own people— young, bright and aggressive—and together they began to reshape the company in his image. Ameronics, once basically conservative and a company that conducted its business primarily within those nations that might be classified as pro-Western, became a company that did business wherever there was business to do.

Ameronics built a refinery for Qaddafi in Lybia, sold drilling equipment and related technology to the Soviet Union, and helped finance and construct a truck factory in China.

Michael Tolbert was quoted in *Business Week* after the deal with China was made public, "This contract is in the best interests of Ameronics and in the best interests of America. We do not expect to change the world through trade. Nor do we judge other countries as good or bad. Our business is to provide goods and services to those who need them. If we don't, someone else will."

In a profile in *Forbes Magazine*, Tolbert was pictured at his desk surrounded by what the magazine called "the group of young turks with whom Tolbert has transformed a formerly stodgy monolith." One of the "young turks," Reid Lawson, when asked about government interference in the marketplace, was quoted as saying that "the government should stand aside and let us get on with the business of doing business."

Ameronics was described as "a company with over sixty major projects in more than ten countries, determined to make itself a force to be reckoned with." The company had excellent contacts in the government: former executive officers served as Undersecretaries of State and Commerce, and several former high-ranking Defense Department officials were on the payroll as consultants.

This then was the company, owned and operated by Mason Whitaker and, through Alice Whitaker, Michael Tolbert. And it was Tolbert who in fact ran the far-flung operations of the company. Whitaker had long since abandoned that role and the company executives had long ago ceased looking to his office for direction. His was a ceremonial role, one in which he participated only reluctantly. Mason Whitaker seemed content to live out his life in comparative luxury, far removed from the hectic pace that had driven him since boyhood. He rarely involved himself in the multimillion-dollar decisions of the company of which he was still the majority stockholder, contenting himself with rubber-stamping the decisions of his son-in-law.

There were those who said Mason Whitaker's spirit had died in that fiery plane crash in Mexico almost twelve years ago.

On this day he busied himself with signing the half dozen or so contracts that every once in a while came across his desk. His limousine was waiting in the street below, motor running, to take him to the Olympic Country Club where he would have lunch, play his customary nine holes, and then play bridge for the rest of the afternoon.

At the same time, in the office directly below Whitaker's, his son-in-law, Michael Tolbert, was deep in the business of the day. Hands clasped behind his head, feet up on his desk, he listened in rapt attention while one of his project directors described to him and four members of his executive committee the financing arrangements for a billion-dollar construction project in South Korea.

"The South Korean government is willing to put up at least twenty-five percent of the required capital for the project and we feel certain that substantial credits can be arranged through the U.S. Export-Import Bank."

"Substantial?" asked Tolbert.

"At least fifty percent."

Tolbert nodded, apparently satisfied. "Go on."

"Which means that our degree of financial involvement—as an absolute maximum—would be in the area of two-fifty to three hundred million. It might be considerably less."

"Don't count on it," said Tolbert. "The Pearson Group is also bidding on this project. If we want it, we'll have to be prepared to be heavily involved in the financing."

Before anyone could comment, Tolbert stood up and looked at his watch. "Let's mull this one over at lunch. I've got a meeting right now that I can't possibly avoid. We'll gather our thoughts and get together this afternoon . . . let's say in two hours."

There was a general nodding of agreement as the group rose and began to leave the office. Tolbert turned to the young man who had prepared the report and who was now gathering up his charts and papers as the others filed out the door.

"Tom," said Tolbert and the young man looked up. "You've done a good job. I feel good about this project. We'll talk later."

Tom beamed. This was high praise indeed and with a hint that perhaps there was more to come. "Thanks, Mr. Tolbert."

When Tolbert was alone he sighed and ran his fingers through what was left of his dark hair. It always surprised him when he felt how thin his hair had become. When he thought of himself it was always with the thick, curly head of hair he had had as a boy. But at fifty-seven, Michael Tolbert still projected the aggressive image of a young man on the way up. He was lean and hard and his craggy face was drawn with what might have been battle lines. Teeth clenched, strong chin, and always with a slight scowl across his face that made others reluctant to question his decisions, he was a man very much in charge.

Tolbert sat in his leather chair, straightened his tie and swiveled so that he was facing the window and the marvelous view of San Francisco. He pushed a button on his intercom. "Please send in Mr. Hanson and Mr. Birdwell."

Hanson and Birdwell were ushered into Tolbert's office and stood for a moment or two staring at the back of Tolbert's chair, waiting for him to turn and acknowledge their presence. When he did swivel back around his face showed a calculated surprise as if he had not known they were there.

The whole exercise took less than five seconds, but it served to establish who was in charge.

"Gentlemen, gentlemen," said Tolbert warmly. "It's so good to see you."

Thomas Hanson was in his middle fifties, tall, clean-cut, and handsome. He wore a gray three-piece suit and striped tie. He might have been an investment banker but was in fact the Deputy Director of Operations of the CIA. As DDO, Hanson headed one of the two large departments of the CIA—the Operations Department, in charge of all covert activities.

They shook hands and Hanson introduced Birdwell.

"Mr. Tolbert, this is Robert Birdwell, who is head of the Technology Transfer Assessment Center at the Agency."

Birdwell was a younger version of Hanson—three-piece suit, striped tie, same clean-cut, Ivy League look. He was lean and muscular with a firm jaw and a firmer handshake.

Tolbert wore a wry smile during the introductions. He offered both men seats in front of his desk, then sat down himself, his eyes still on Birdwell. "Technology Transfer?" he asked. "I hope this isn't going to be one of those 'let's not let our technology slip away to the Russians' talks."

Birdwell, unable to meet Tolbert's stare, looked uncomfortably at his boss.

"I'm afraid it is," said Hanson.

Tolbert sighed. "Let's see, in the last four months I've talked with representatives of the Commerce Department's Office of Export Enforcement two or three times, at least several times with representatives of the Customs Service and now apparently I am to do the same with representatives of the CIA." He eyed them both sternly. "Why don't you government types get together and appoint one agency to handle this situation? It would eliminate a great deal of duplication of time and effort."

"We'd like to do that, Mr. Tolbert," said Hanson. "But unfortunately it is a matter that concerns all three agencies. Customs has the facilities, Commerce has the overseas contacts and we at the CIA have the intelligence apparatus that allows us to hear about impending technology thefts or transfers. We realize that there is duplication of effort but there is also a great deal of cooperation on this very serious concern."

Tolbert shrugged but his attitude seemed to soften. "Very well, what can I do for you?"

Hanson nodded to Birdwell, who opened his notes and began, "Mr. Tolbert, as you I am sure are well aware the United States defensive posture consists of what is referred to as the Triad System: long-range bombers of the Air Force capable of penetration of Soviet air space and delivery of nuclear weapons to specific targets; ICBM's placed at several locations in the United States and which are pretargeted on Soviet cities and military installations; and finally, the Navy's nuclear-powered strategic missile submarines." He paused, waiting for some acknowledgment from Tolbert that he was following the discussion.

Tolbert sighed and said, "Go on please," as if he were in a hurry.

"Because of several well-known and understood factors— the aging of the bomber force, the unwillingness of Congress to fund the revitalization of the strategic missile program— the submarine has become the linchpin of the Triad."

Tolbert nodded, unimpressed with Birdwell's monologue.

"If the Russians ever made a breakthrough in Anti-Submarine Warfare technology—the kind of breakthrough that we have made—the whole Triad System could collapse."

Tolbert leaned forward, his elbows on his desk. "I can see that, Mr. . . . uh . . ."

"—Birdwell—"

"Mr. Birdwell. And your concern is admirable. Now perhaps you can tell me what all this has to do with me?"

Birdwell cleared his throat. "The ASW capacity of the U.S. is based on a combination of technological advances. Several of these advances are operated from spy satellites— high-resolution cameras that can track Soviet subs on the surface as they leave their home bases, a laser-detection system that can 'see' the subs underwater, and a heat-sensing system that can actually detect the minute changes in water temperature as a submarine passes through the oceans. On the ocean floor we have banks of hydrophones that listen to the sounds of passing submarines and then feed the data to computer centers which are linked by communications satellite.

"The computers take all of this data and tell us if we're looking at a whale or an attack submarine, a thermal layer or a missile-launching submarine. The computer pinpoints the locations and also targets our own attack submarines . . ."

Tolbert impatiently began shuffling papers on his desk. "I'd appreciate it if you could come to the point of this talk about our military superiority over the Russians."

Birdwell looked beseechingly to Hanson for help but none was forthcoming.

Birdwell plowed on. "The problem is, we're afraid that our technological superiority in this area is being quickly eroded."

Tolbert raised an eyebrow and motioned as if he wished to interrupt, but Birdwell went on quickly.

"A few months ago a Navy frigate plucked a canister out of the ocean near Block Island Sound. It turned out to be a hydrophone the Soviets use to track our subs as they leave New London. It had somehow broken loose from the ocean floor and was bobbing around on the surface. The startling thing was that the circuiting of the sonar device was an exact copy of the RCA design that's used in our hydrophones. This is an item that was never approved for export but still the Russians got their hands on it.

"Last month—through an agent in an Eastern-bloc country—we acquired a Russian satellite photo taken of the New Siberian Islands. The Russians are particularly interested in this area as a potentially vast oil field. We, of course, are interested in determining the extent of their oil resources. What turned out to be most interesting about this photograph, however, was the high degree of resolution of the image. The Russians have obviously developed—or in some other way acquired—optical lenses that are at least the equal of our own. It seems our technological advantage is shrinking in leaps and bounds."

Birdwell sat back in his chair and took a deep breath, his spiel apparently over.

Tolbert turned to look at Hanson.

"And now," he said, "I suppose you, Mr. Hanson, are going to tell me what my company has to do with all this."

"Yes, Mr. Tolbert," said Hanson. "I'm going to try." Hanson sat forward on the edge of his seat. "Several of your companies are involved in computer research. The TMK Corporation has just begun work on the computer that is an integral part of the new defensive system which is being developed by the Defense Department."

"Yes," said Tolbert, "and we at Ameronics are very

48

proud of the part our company is playing in the development of this system."

"You have every right to be proud, Mr. Tolbert," said Birdwell. "Your company has been in the forefront of new technological development. But our main concern is to ensure that none of this technology winds up in the wrong hands."

Tolbert's eyes narrowed. "I can assure you that you need have no worries on our end. Our security at TMK is excellent. One of your own men has been appointed chief of security . . ."

"We're not here to talk about security at TMK—or about theft, Mr. Tolbert," said Hanson.

Tolbert seemed baffled. "About what then?"

Hanson seemed uncomfortable. He turned to Birdwell. "Bob here knows a lot more about this stuff than I do. Go ahead, Bob."

"Two years ago, TMK developed a computer which you call XED 37/86," said Birdwell.

Tolbert shrugged. "You may be right. I don't familiarize myself with every product made or used by my companies."

Birdwell, undaunted, went on. "This XED 37/86 is what is sometimes referred to as an expert system. It stores knowledge rather than data and can actually make judgments based on outside information. It's a remarkable machine, Mr. Tolbert. It approaches the area of artificial intelligence."

"I'm quite familiar with the kind of work Professor Kincaid does at TMK. It's that kind of work incidentally that brought the government to us for the ABM system, rather than going to Livermore or some other government lab."

"Quite true," Birdwell said. "The XED 37/86 is used in your mining operations. It evaluates geological information fed to it by a reconnaissance satellite and points out the likely locations of mineral deposits."

Tolbert nodded but said nothing.

"The success rate of the 37/86 is nothing short of remarkable. You should be very pleased with the performance of those who developed such an incredible machine."

Tolbert did not smile. "You're beginning to try my patience, Mr. Birdwell. You didn't come out here to give me or my company a pat on the back. Get on with it."

Hanson jumped in between them. "Your company has applied for an export license for the XED 37/86."

"My company is in the business of selling products."

"The problem is, Mr. Tolbert," said Birdwell, "the circuitry in the 37/86 is almost identical to that in the 37/93 which was also developed by TMK and is the prime computer used by the Navy in its ASW systems. If the 37/86 fell into the hands of the Russians they would need only make minor modification to upgrade its capability. If that happened their ASW capabilities would equal ours." Birdwell's face was grim. "That would be disastrous."

Tolbert made a dismissive gesture with his hands. "Ameronics would never sell that or any other sophisticated computer to the Eastern bloc."

"One of the companies that has applied for the 37/86 under license from you is Swiss Minerale Ltd."

"Swiss Minerale is one of the oldest mining concerns in Europe."

"Swiss Minerale also does business with the Soviet Union. They have had multimillion-dollar contracts with the Soviets in several mining operations. Additionally, they are believed to have assisted in the transfer of millions of dollars' worth of American equipment to the Russians—equipment that is prohibited to the Soviets by the Export Administration Act of 1979."

Tolbert was beginning to show his frustration. "This particular piece of equipment has been approved for sale to friendly governments. We would like to expand that to include companies within friendly countries. Why talk with me? Talk to the United States Congress."

"You're right, Mr. Tolbert. Congress has a responsibility in this area, but right now there's a real battle between those in Congress who believe we should be able to trade with anyone we choose and those who don't want us to sell products with possible military applications to our potential adversaries. I'm afraid the free-traders are winning."

"What do you want with me?"

"Withdraw your application for an export license. This could be a real hot potato—it's hard for a congressman to go back home and tell his constituents that he voted against a bill that would provide jobs or relieve the balance-of-payments deficit."

"So you want me to take the pressure off them?"

"Exactly," said Birdwell, and Hanson nodded his agreement.

"You're talking about millions in sales here."

Hanson nodded. "We know."

Birdwell chimed in. "We're appealing to you as a patriot, Mr. Tolbert."

Tolbert's look might have felled another man. "I'll ask my board of directors," he said. "I can't make this kind of decision without consulting them."

Hanson realized the meeting was over. He stood up and Birdwell followed. "That's all we ask, Mr. Tolbert. That's all that we ask."

Six

Michael Tolbert sat silently in his chair for a long time after the two visitors had left.

Damn them! he thought. Damn government types gave him a pain in the ass. To them everything was a matter of national security. He was in business and his business was selling—to any and all customers. Obviously he wasn't going to sell the Russians technology that was vital to American national interests. But according to the CIA and Commerce and Customs *everything* was vital to American interests. These government types knew how to spend money—damn did they know how to do that!—they just didn't know how to make it.

He could still picture Hanson and Birdwell stammering and stuttering, pleading their case. They knew they didn't have the votes in Congress to block the sale of his computer, so they came whimpering to him, playing on his patriotism. Patriotism! What a laugh. That was too many years and too many nightmares ago to mean much to him now.

It was probably government agents much like the two who had just left who had hounded his son to death in

Canada. Poor misguided Robert who had wanted nothing more than to be left alone.

At first Tolbert had been disappointed when Robert had told him he was going to Canada to avoid the draft. Robert and a few of his college friends were leaving the country. "We're going to sit this one out, Dad," Robert had said. "We don't want any part of this war."

Tolbert had been disappointed, but he was glad his son was safe. He was also glad, in a way, that Robert was out of his hair, and a monthly check had been enough to soothe his conscience.

Robert had not taken too well to his father's second marriage. When Tolbert had married Alice Whitaker, granddaughter of the founder of the Ameronics Corporation, his son and his new wife had been unable to find common ground for their relationship. Alice had tried to be a mother to the boy and that had proved to be a mistake. Robert grew sullen and resentful and somehow managed to reacquire the nasty traits of adolescence. Things were much less strained when Robert was away at college, and his Canadian sojourn seemed at the time to be a welcome delay in his homecoming.

Things had started to go wrong about six months after Robert arrived in Canada. The phone calls home became more frequent and more hysterical. Sometimes Robert would call in the middle of the night to announce that the FBI or the CIA was after him. He had been told, he said, by anonymous callers that the FBI had concocted a plan to kidnap him and bring him back across the border, then arrest him and put him in jail. So he changed apartments often, but the harassment continued. Robert began to live the life of a fugitive, but wherever he went they were able to find him and the harassment continued.

Finally it was too much for him to take. Driven to the edge of despair, he hanged himself one winter night in Toronto. His friends, who had been calling him for several days, grew worried, went to his new apartment and found him dangling from an overhead pipe in his one-room apartment.

Robert had typed a letter to his father describing the torment and harassment he had suffered. He could never live in a country that treated people the way he had been treated. He could no longer withstand the abuse, the midnight phone calls, the threats. He could never, he wrote, come home again. He had suffered too much and the wounds were too deep.

His final words were, "I want to be where I can be left in peace."

Michael Tolbert was almost destroyed by guilt. He had been too glad to have his son run off to Canada, he realized. Glad to have him three thousand miles away. When Robert had called with his problems, Tolbert had sent him more money. At first Tolbert had refused to believe that the FBI could possibly spend so much time hounding one hapless individual, but as the calls and harassment continued, he began to realize that his son might indeed be a target. Keep moving, he had told his son. They'll never find you.

Tolbert was already an executive vice-president of his father-in-law's company and too involved in his own concerns to be overly concerned about the hysterical rantings of a son who had always been an annoyance to him. Too many drugs, too much pot, he had thought. College had turned his son into a real freak. Long hair, LSD, filthy clothing. He was glad he wasn't around. But now the boy was dead and the guilt and sadness had been like a crushing weight that threatened to drag him down.

But that was long ago. He was over that now. . . . Maybe.

He pushed the button on his office intercom. "Find out if Reid Lawson is here yet. If he is I want to see him right away."

Tolbert began working his way through a pile of papers waiting for his signature. Anything to get his mind off the past and onto the present. The two CIA men had upset him more than he wanted to admit.

Five minutes after his call, Reid Lawson entered the office.

"You looking for me, boss?" he asked. Lawson was the only one at Ameronics who called Michael Tolbert anything but Mr. Tolbert.

"Yes, Reid. I have to talk to you about an important matter that has just been brought to my attention." Michael Tolbert had almost gotten over the hurt that used to attack him whenever Reid Lawson walked into a room. Reid had been Robert's college roommate and closest friend. They had gone to Canada together to avoid the draft and it had been Reid who had found Robert and called Michael Tolbert with the awful news.

After returning from Canada, Reid had gone to work for Ameronics, and even though Tolbert had been responsible for bringing his son's friend into the company, for the longest time he could not bear to see this constant reminder of what his son might have been. Lawson was bright and aggressive. His forte was sales, and watched carefully and from a distance by Michael Tolbert he soon began a rapid climb up the corporate ladder. Gradually it became apparent to most observers at Ameronics that Tolbert had chosen Reid Lawson to take on the mantle that he had hoped his son would wear. At age thirty-seven Reid Lawson was president of the electronics division of Ameronics and of the several companies that fell under that umbrella. Keen observers noted that the electronics division of the corporation was the part of Ameronics that had been started by Michael Tolbert and then brought into the company fold when he had married Alice Whitaker.

As always Tolbert looked at Reid Lawson with an odd mixture of pride and sadness. Lawson wore a bright and easy smile and Tolbert could not help but be reminded of his son. This is what my son might have been like if he had lived, he thought. Reid had gone through all that long-haired rebellion nonsense, just like Robert, and look at him now. He had protested his country's involvement in Vietnam, he had gone off to Canada, but he had come back into the mainstream. He was now the perfect picture of corporate America.

Lawson's smile faded. "Problem?"

"Maybe. I just had a couple of CIA men in here."

Lawson raised an eyebrow. "Export sales?"

"Yes," said Tolbert with a sad smile. "They were particularly concerned about the export license application for the . . . uh . . ."

"XED 37/86?" said Lawson helpfully.

"Exactly. According to them the circuitry is remarkably similar to the"—he looked at his notes but once again Lawson was quicker.

"The 37/93."

"Right again."

"What do they want from us?"

"That we withdraw the application."

Lawson blew a long, noisy exhalation. "We're talking about a sales potential of several million dollars here. Every major mining corporation in the world wants to use that system."

"According to our friends at the CIA, so do the Russians."

Lawson waved the remark aside with a casual motion of

his hand. "They say that about everything. If they had their way, we'd sell nothing. Why should we spend millions to develop a product and then have the government tell us we can't sell it?"

"You don't have to convince me," said Tolbert. "We're in agreement on that one. I've been telling Washington to get off our backs for years. Let us do what we do best and let them do what they do best"—he chortled without humor. "Whatever that is."

Lawson smiled. "So what do you want me to do?"

"I'm not sure."

"We've already put a lot of pressure in Washington to get this license approved. Senator Cranston has been working hard with the Permanent Subcommittee on Investigation of the Government Affairs Committee. We've got people lobbying at Commerce, at State—"

Both smiled involuntarily at the mention of the State Department. Randall Baldridge, a former executive vice-president at Ameronics, was now an Undersecretary of State.

"People are working for us at almost every level to get this one okayed."

Tolbert turned away and for a long time he stared at the view of the city. Finally he spoke. "Is it true that this system could easily be modified and used for military purposes?"

Lawson sighed. "That's true of just about any advanced system. But in order for the Russians to turn this system into the 37/93 they'd have to have a complete circuitry schematic of the 93, and new super chips. They'd also have to have the people to put it together. They have none of these."

Tolbert thought for a moment. "So you'd recommend we go ahead?"

"Absolutely. Unless you feel like throwing away five or ten million in sales."

A quick smile flashed across Tolbert's lips. "Not likely," he said. "Not likely at all."

Seven

Gordon spent the rest of the afternoon with Bill Donovan, who showed him around the facility and discussed the security situation as he saw it at TMK.

"Looks like a pretty nice place to work," said Gordon as they walked past a glassed-in area that permitted a view of one of the landscaped courtyards on one side and the outside on the other.

"It really is," said Donovan. "Trouble with California living is that you tend to forget that everything here—underneath the laid-back facade—is just as dog-eat-dog as anyplace else. Maybe more so."

"I can see how that could happen," Gordon said, looking out to the green rolling hills that sat like resting animals in the distance.

They left the main building and crossed the grounds to a smaller concrete block building.

"This," said Donovan, "is the S.P. building."

"Special Projects?"

"Yes. You'll notice it's completely enclosed by fencing so that access is limited to this one main gate area."

They stopped at the gate and the uniformed guard signed them in, entering their time of entry.

"Everyone is signed in and out," said Donovan. "Nothing goes in or out without inspection."

"What about Carl Burns?" asked Gordon, referring to the TMK employee who had stolen company secrets and sold them to the Russians.

"That happened before I came here," said Donovan quickly. "Things have been tightened up considerably since then."

"I can see that, Bill," said Gordon reassuringly. "I'm not

here to condemn anything that's happened in the past. I'm here to see that nothing jeopardizes the security of this project." He put a hand on Donovan's shoulder. "I want you to understand that, Bill. We'll be working together and I'll need your full cooperation. I want to know everything that goes on here. Security precautions, who has access, who doesn't. Strong areas, weak areas. Personnel problems, physical problems. Anything else you can think of. Educated guesses, pure hunches—anything."

Donovan nodded. "No problem there. I'm on your side—one hundred percent."

They were stopped halfway between the gate and the entrance to the building. Donovan thrust his hands deep into his jacket pockets and looked around as if to assure himself that they were alone. "So you want to know about Burns? I'll tell you what I know. You might want to ask some of the others who were here when it happened."

"Like who?"

"Most of the research people. Nichols was here."

"Lawson?"

"He was here. Not as president. He was a v.p. in charge of sales. After that he moved back to Ameronics for a while. Now he's back here, at least for now."

Gordon nodded. "I'll talk to them and to the others."

"Don't expect much cooperation from the research people," said Donovan.

"Why not?"

"These people are mostly scientific types. They don't really like government or any kind of official intrusion in their lives. They think we're here to get in the way of free interchange of ideas or something. They have an inherent distrust of anyone who tries to interfere with their work."

Gordon thought about his brother, K.C. Donovan's words could apply to him just as much as they did to anyone here at TMK. They had had this same argument a hundred times. "I know what you mean," he said to Donovan.

Donovan motioned toward a group of picnic tables clustered near a shady tree. "Let's sit," he said. "Let me start with Carl Burns."

What Gordon Hardwick found was that TMK's security system had been defeated for the usual reasons—complacency and stupidity. The security system seemed foolproof so everyone assumed that it was. There were so many checkpoints, sign-ins and sign-outs that the security personnel figured their job was automatic. But a young man, less than a year out of college, hired as a courier, had figured out a way to beat them.

The young man, Carl Burns, for reasons that few had ever understood, claimed to be disenchanted with the foreign policy of his own government. His belief was that the world would be a much safer place if we all shared information with each other. He was willing to do his part and the Russians were willing to pay for the information he provided. For twenty-five thousand dollars, Carl Burns sold technical secrets about a new computerized guidance system developed at TMK. Without this knowledge it would have taken the Russians perhaps five years of research and one hundred million dollars to develop their own system.

How had he gotten the information out of TMK, past all the elaborate checkpoints? Simple. One of his jobs was to make copies of classified and top-secret documents and distribute them to those offices of the company and the CIA and NSA operatives assigned to the various projects who had a "right-to-see" classification. He was permitted to make only the required number of copies and each one had to be accounted for. He would take the documents to the woman in charge of copies and state the number of copies required. She would sign an authorization for that many and he would countersign. Together they set the number of copies and waited for the machine to produce them.

He was then supposed to distribute the copies and file the original in the master file where all such documents were kept for a year. What he did, however, was take the original and mail it to himself from inside the plant. When the mail arrived he made copies at a local library, then returned the originals to the master file the next morning. No one ever checked what people brought in—only what went out.

Burns might still have been able to get away with what he had done if a British agent hadn't been able to find out through a Moscow contact that the Russians were obtaining priceless information from a source within TMK.

It would not have been a secret much longer, thought Gordon Hardwick. As soon as the new guidance systems were installed the United States certainly would have realized something was up.

That was the part of the story that intrigued Gordon

Hardwick. The theft that would soon have been discovered was revealed a few months early by the British agent through what was described only as "a source in Moscow." Gordon Hardwick didn't like the smell of this one.

Donovan shrugged, signaling that his story was at an end. "That's pretty much it," he said. "Burns was caught and sentenced to forty years to life for espionage."

"Shoulda hanged the bastard," said Gordon getting up from his bench.

They went inside the S.P. building, down a flight of stairs and into a large, high-ceilinged space that seemed eerily quiet. On the perimeter of the area were at least a dozen glass-enclosed offices where men sat around computer screens. No one looked up. In the center of the room stood a contraption that looked like a cylinder standing on its end. It was over eight feet tall and wires and cables ran to and from every square inch. The cylinder was surrounded by a scaffolding and technicians swarmed all over it.

Ted Nichols saw them and approached. "What you're looking at," he said, "is the fastest computer ever created by man."

"How fast is fast?" asked Gordon.

Nichols shrugged. "We're not sure yet. Certainly a billion instructions per second." He smiled. "Once we get the kinks out and turn her loose, we'll have a better idea."

"What do you call it?"

"Alice," said Nichols, laughing, and when Gordon did not seem amused, added, "The government, however, prefers to call it Prometheus II. This is the ultimate fourth-generation machine. The next step will be a machine that thinks for itself." He smiled. "Then all of us will be obsolete."

"Oh happy day," said Gordon Hardwick grimly.

"You ready for a quick tour of the S.P. building?"

"Yes," said Gordon looking around. "I'm impressed by all the activity."

"We're working hard to complete this project," said Nichols. "Everybody is working as hard as possible."

Nichols led them around the room, stopping at several offices to introduce Gordon to the generally young computer scientists seated there. Most gave a brief nod and a smile and went back to work.

"Not enough time in the day," said Nichols by way of explanation.

They followed him upstairs and into several smaller rooms where others were busily engaged over printouts and calculations.

"The classified documents section is also on this floor," Nichols said as he walked ahead of them down a hallway. "Bill has probably told you that no one is allowed in or out without proper authorization."

"Yes," said Gordon, not saying that that didn't seem to be much of a deterrent.

The classified section was at the end of the hallway. A secretary sat at a desk outside the door. Nichols signed a list and the woman gave him a key. He held it up with a smile. "This is it. The dark cavern where we keep all our secrets."

They entered, and Gordon was surprised to find the room so small. There was a row of filing cabinets on either side and a double row back to back down the center. Space was so cramped that anyone opening a file drawer would have to stand to the side in order to extend it fully.

Gordon looked at the ceiling. There were no closed-circuit cameras and only two fluorescent tubes for illumination. The place had the look of a damp cellar.

Gordon looked at Donovan, who shrugged in what might have been embarrassed resignation. "This is it?" said Gordon in amazement.

Nichols smiled, apparently unaware of Gordon's displeasure, but Donovan felt compelled to answer. "The idea is to keep all classified documents in one location and to severely restrict access."

Gordon shook his head and sighed. "Well, at least I know where I have to start." He looked at Donovan but the security officer looked away. Dammit! Gordon thought. He knows what a crummy setup this is. Why hasn't he done something? "The problem with a setup like this," he said, "is that you have to trust the people with clearance."

"Of course," said Nichols. "If you can't trust the people with clearance—who can you trust?"

Gordon's face was grim. "Only people with clearance have opportunity. I don't trust anyone."

All three were silent as Gordon Hardwick continued to inspect the room. Finally he said, "Let's get out of here."

They were signed out and returned the key. Nichols, in somewhat more subdued tones, was resuming his tour. He stopped in front of an open door. "Someone you should meet," he said and went inside. The others followed.

The room was about the same size as the classified documents room, but without the files and with a large window to the outside it seemed spacious. At a long table in the middle of the room two men were engaged in discussion over a stack of printout sheets. The room was littered with electronic components, wires, and two large computer terminals. Neither man looked up as the others entered.

"Jimmy," said Nichols and one of the men, with a full beard and a dark serious face, looked in their direction. "I want you to meet Gordon Hardwick. He's the new security man from the CIA. Gordon, this is Jim Progano."

Progano gave an audible sigh and a brief nod of recognition before returning to his work. Nichols did not bother to introduce the second man, who never looked up from his stack of printouts.

Back in the hall, Nichols explained. "Progano is Professor Kincaid's number-one programmer. He's absolutely brilliant. Kincaid brought him aboard two years ago when they had the big shake-up at Atari."

"Atari?"

"Yes," said Nichols laughing. "His big thing was games. Now he's the one who tells 'Alice' how to respond to every possible situation. Next to Kincaid he's probably the most important man on the project."

"What about you?"

"Me?" Nichols shook his head. "I'm project director, but that means I organize and schedule. When these guys start doing their thing, I feel like I should go out for coffee." He shook his head sadly. "Most of them are light-years over my head."

"I'm sure you're exaggerating," Gordon said.

Nichols's laugh reverberated down the hallway. "I sure as hell hope so."

They were back where they started, looking down into the main room where work on Prometheus II seemed most hectic. Gordon watched for a while, his eyes riveted to the machine in the center of the room. It seemed incredible that so much hope—so much promise—had been invested in this somewhat unimposing-looking conglomeration of wires and panels.

As Gordon turned back to thank Nichols for the tour, an

older man hustled by and Nichols grabbed him by the sleeve and pulled him to an abrupt halt. "Professor Kincaid, this is Gordon Hardwick. He's the new security liaison man from the government."

Kincaid eyed Gordon with thinly disguised distaste. He shook Gordon's extended hand and mumbled a greeting. As he was about to step away, he stopped. "One thing, Mr. Hancock," he said.

"Hardwick," corrected Gordon.

"Hardwick. Try not to get in our way. We're very busy here."

"I'll do my best, Professor," Gordon said, but Kincaid was already moving quickly away.

"That," said Nichols with a quick smile, "is our resident genius. The man knows more about computers than anyone alive." He noticed Gordon's expression. "Doesn't know much about the social graces though. Don't let him bother you. We've had people here for over a year and he doesn't know their names."

"I understand," said Gordon. "People like Kincaid aren't like the rest of us."

"The others here are pretty friendly," said Nichols. "Most of us get together at one of the local watering holes on Friday nights. You're welcome to join us."

"Maybe I'll do that sometime," Gordon said. "Right now I'm just trying to acclimate myself to this new environment. I've got a lot to think about."

"Anytime you're ready, just say the word." He looked at his watch. "Gotta get back to work. See you later."

Then he was gone, leaving Gordon and Donovan standing watching him as he descended the flight of stairs and walked toward the cylindrical device on the main floor.

Gordon shook his head in resignation and Donovan smiled. "That's how everyone is around here. Very busy."

Gordon sighed. "Well, let's get back to the main building. I've got some ideas and I want to get busy too."

The first thing Gordon Hardwick did at TMK was to institute a computerized check-in system similar to the one used by the CIA at Langley. Every employee received an I.D. card that looked similar to a credit card. This card was to be inserted in an electronic slot when entering and leaving the building, and also at strategic locations within the complex. The computer could list the locations where anyone was in the building at any given time and store the information for later use if needed.

Another change made was the relocation of the "classified documents section." Gordon Hardwick had decided that the reason Burns had been able to get to the documents so easily was that they were enclosed in a small room with access restricted to only a few people. Consequently Burns was able to spend a lot of time alone in the documents room doing whatever he wished. So Gordon moved the classified documents storage area to a larger open room. The secretaries who had previously sat in the outer office merely confirming the clearance of those who wished to enter the closed area, now sat inside the filing area, where anyone in the classified section could be watched at any time. Four video cameras, similar to bank cameras, were placed at strategic locations in the room and kept a record of everything that went on.

Some of the employees grumbled about the "Big Brother" mentality of the new security chief but it was generally agreed that the new precautions made document theft highly unlikely.

Nothing left or entered the building without being checked. All incoming packages, briefcases, plants—anything—had to be left at the security office upon arrival in the building. After inspection the item would be delivered to its owner within one hour by security personnel. All classified documents were treated with a special powder that would set off an alarm triggered by sensors at the doors. Those who carried briefcases also had to leave them at the security office at the front desk one hour before leaving, and anything else had to be personally inspected and approved by Gordon Hardwick himself.

Once again there was much grumbling. Some employees complained that the security precautions were interfering with their work. The precautions were too time-consuming and constituted what some felt was an undue invasion of their privacy. Some even took their complaints to the president of the company, but Reid Lawson's reply was always the same. "This is the price we have to pay to do work for the Defense Department. We have to be able to convince them that our security is foolproof."

It was generally regarded as true that no one could beat the system. Everyone agreed—everyone except Gordon

Hardwick. "If someone wants to beat the system," he said, "he'll beat it. But he's got to be awfully clever and awfully daring. He's got to be willing to take chances, and if he makes one mistake I'll catch him."

Carol arrived in California two weeks after Gordon, and by that time Gordon had already established his procedures and was working toward their implementation. His work had the approval of the Defense Department and of the CIA. Everything was going smoothly.

Gordon worked long hours but was soon able to establish a routine that for him was somewhat predictable and boring but for Carol was heaven on earth. For the first time in almost fifteen years she had a husband who was home every night for dinner. His Sundays were free, so they took advantage of the California weather to travel around what was surely one of the world's most beautiful areas. They did the wine country, the redwood country, the Monterey Peninsula, the beach. Gordon even talked about buying a boat. Carol was ecstatic.

But it didn't last.

After about six months Gordon started getting home later and later. He talked about working late but Carol was sure he had been drinking. Even their idyllic Sundays became less frequent and more unpleasant. Gordon seemed harried and sullen. He was quick to anger and often verbally abusive.

Carol kept this to herself until she could bear it no longer. Finally she appealed to K.C. to talk with Gordon, to find out what was troubling him.

The brothers did talk but the results were negligible. Gordon Hardwick was on a long spiral downward, and he seemed bent on taking his marriage with him.

MOSCOW—The American decision to continue with the development of its so called "Star Wars" defense program is a detriment to world peace and poses a dangerous dilemma to the Soviet Union, said a leading Soviet scientist in an address to the Soviet Academy of Sciences today.

Professor Vladimir Yasnev said that the Soviet Union would have no choice but to match any U.S.

developments in this area. "To do any less," said Yasnev, "is to doom the Soviet Union and the rest of the world to second-class status and would usher in a period of American dominance that would rival the dominance of the Roman Empire."

Professor Yasnev dismissed U.S. claims that this weapons system is purely defensive in nature by saying, "Any weapon that renders one's adversaries impotent is offensive in nature and must be regarded as a threat to freedom-loving peoples everywhere."

Eight

Moscow, June 1987

The thirteen men sat around a long green felt table. On opposite walls of the large, high-ceilinged room, portraits of Lenin and Marx stared grimly down at the gathered members of the Politburo, reminding them of the gravity of their responsibilities.

These were old men. Only three of them were less than sixty years old—and two of those three were fifty-nine. The average age of these men who ruled one of the world's two most powerful countries was in the seventies.

They sat in straight-backed wooden chairs with brown leather cushions, listening intently as Defense Minister Dimitri Ushenko continued to rail about American provocations in Europe and elsewhere. Foreign Minister Andrei Gromyko stifled a yawn and General Party Secretary Nikolai Chernetsov gave him a small smile of understanding.

"This is *our* sphere of influence," Ushenko said vehemently. "The Americans have no right to install their missiles in our backyard. Perhaps if we threatened to place a few SS-20's in Nicaragua or Cuba we would impress upon them the severity of their provocative actions."

None of the others said anything. They were used to Ushenko's tirades. Some were staring at the crystal chandeliers that were suspended over the table, or at the porcelain urn with the portraits of Andropov and Brezhnev that sat on a nearby table. There wasn't much else to look at in the room itself. Like the men of the Politburo the room was Spartan and austere. Those fortunate enough to be seated opposite one of the three tall windows in the room were able to catch a glimpse of the gray, early morning sky. It was June in Moscow and the temperature promised to move into the sixties today.

"And what about this antiballistic missile system the Americans are developing? I've said it before and I'll say it again—if this becomes reality and we are unable to match their technology, we are finished as a major military power. We might as well give up."

Chernetsov looked up from his notepad. "And does the Defense Minister have a suggestion as to how we might prevent this catastrophe?"

Ushenko was short and stocky with the full beefy face of a well-fed farmer. "I say that we can never allow that to happen. We must take all possible steps to prevent it."

"Yes, Comrade Defense Minister," said Mikhail Gorbachev. "But short of a catastrophic nuclear war, how can we prevent it from happening?"

"Perhaps," said Ushenko, "there is no other way."

"Then we must hope, Comrade," said Chernetsov, "that we can find another way."

Ushenko continued his harangue while the others sighed and glanced furtively at each other.

"Thank you, Comrade Defense Minister," said Chernetsov when Ushenko had droned to a conclusion. The others gave a collective sigh of relief and Ushenko looked around sharply at the culprits, though few dared meet his eyes.

"Do we have any questions for the Defense Minister?" asked Chernetsov.

No one said a word.

Chernetsov smiled gently. "Then, gentlemen," he said, placing his palms on the table and rising slowly from his chair, "I would say that our meeting is concluded."

Gratefully the others rose, their chairs clattering on the parquet floors. As the men filed toward the doorway at the far end of the room, Chernetsov called out in his soft voice to the last man in the line.

"Vitali. A word with you please."

Vitali Fedorchuk, chief of the Ministry of Internal Affairs, stopped and slowly turned to face the General Secretary. He nodded slowly, grumbling to himself as he realized that Chernetsov would not after all allow him to leave without asking the inevitable question.

Chernetsov gestured and Fedorchuk slumped into a chair across from the General Secretary, wondering if he should have mentioned the problem earlier, or if he should mention it now before Chernetsov did. He decided to say nothing.

Chernetsov began innocently. "It is unfortunate that Comrade Chebrikov could not be with us this morning."

Fedorchuk sighed. The old bastard knows, he thought.

"I understand there is a small problem at Dzerzhinsky," said Chernetsov, using the address of KGB headquarters as its name.

Fedorchuk nodded. "I talked with Chebrikov earlier this morning."

Chebrikov was the Chairman of the KGB and a member of the Politburo.

"And?"

Fedorchuk looked at his watch. "At this moment he is probably meeting with the Moscow Station Chief to ascertain the potential damage." He coughed nervously. "I am meeting with him as soon as I leave here."

The General Secretary's droopy eyes bored in on the Internal Affairs Minister. "Then it is certain that there has been a defection?"

Fedorchuk seemed noncommittal. "There have been no announcements by the other side yet."

Chernetsov's eyes betrayed his displeasure with the inadequacy of that response.

Fedorchuk cleared his throat. "No one had heard from him in seventy-two hours. He disappeared in London three days ago. So far we have said nothing, hoping he might have a change of heart."

"Who is he?"

"Mikhail Belenkov. He was the—"

Chernetsov cut him off with a wave of his hand. "I know of him," he said sharply. "He is—was—the deputy director of the American bureau at the office in Moscow."

Fedorchuk nodded grimly. There wasn't much Chernetsov

didn't know about any of the apparatus of the Party—including the KGB. Four years ago, when Chernetsov had been elevated to the post of General Secretary, it had generally been assumed that he would merely be a transitional leader until the new, younger leadership was ready to take over. Chernetsov knew he was regarded merely as a Party hack, the man who had licked Leonid Brezhnev's boots. He also knew that until Andropov's death he had been on his way out of power. Andropov and his cronies at the KGB had slowly but surely been consolidating their power at the highest levels of government. But when Andropov died after only fifteen months in office, his appointees were not yet firmly entrenched enough to take over—they needed more time. In order to gain that time and to prevent one of the younger members of the Politburo, Gorbachev or Romanov, from taking the reins of power, the KGB clique had rallied behind Chernetsov. They knew that Gorbachev or Romanov, if elected, could rule for twenty years. They wanted someone for a year or two, so they had voted as a block for the sick and apparently hapless Chernetsov.

Chernetsov had fooled them. The one thing they had not counted on was that he had connections at every level of government. From village Party organizations to the Council of Ministers, Chernetsov had quickly consolidated his power. Within two months of his elevation to the post of Party Leader he also became President, or Chairman of the Presidium, acquiring in two months the power it had taken Andropov seven months and Brezhnev thirteen years to acquire. The man thought to be a hack now held the reins of power in both the Communist Party and in the elected government.

"What we are trying to discover now," said Fedorchuk, who, before moving to his post as Minister of Internal Affairs, in effect, the national police chief, had been the head of the KGB for a short time, "is how much this Belenkov knows."

Chernetsov made a choking sound in his throat that was almost a chuckle. "You can be certain he knows a great deal."

Fedorchuk looked away. Chernetsov seemed to be enjoying the KGB's distress. As a Party man he had made no secret of his desire to block the KGB's grab for power in the government.

Fedorchuk looked at his watch. "Chebrikov is probably waiting for me right now."

"Perhaps I should join you at that meeting."

Fedorchuk could not keep the surprise from his face. "This is a matter you need not concern yourself with, Comrade General Secretary."

Chernetsov's dour face remained expressionless. "My information tells me I *should* be concerned."

Fedorchuk shrugged in apparent acquiescence. The old bastard didn't miss a trick, but he had a few tricks up his sleeve, too. "Then perhaps I should call Viktor and have him meet us here in your office."

Chernetsov gave a sly smile. He would not take the bait. "You are right, Vitali. It would be better if this remained KGB business. I wish to avoid linking the Politburo or my office in this matter." He smiled pleasantly. "You may go."

"But—" began Fedorchuk.

The General Secretary raised his hand, dismissing the feigned protest, and Fedorchuk fell silent.

Fedorchuk rose and gave a short nod of his head that was not quite a bow. "As you wish, Comrade General Secretary."

When he was alone Chernetsov poured himself a glass of water with trembling hands. His performance had taken a lot out of him and now his breath came in short, wheezing gasps. It was becoming difficult to hide these increasingly frequent spells. The General Party Secretary knew that those who had elected him to his present position in hopes that he would hold it only briefly would someday very soon get their wish.

He knew that Andropov's crowd, as he and the others had come to call them, were up to something and were worried that this defection could upset those plans. Let's let them stew in their own juices for a while, he thought. There is still time to see what they're up to.

The thought of "time" made him stop, drinking glass halfway to his lips. Time, he repeated to himself as he shakily placed the glass on the table. How much time do I have left?

Nine

As was his usual practice, Captain Vladimir Gorsky of Directorate S of the First Chief Directorate, KGB, spent the first hour at his desk each morning carefully reading the summaries of his reports from his agents in the field. He sat behind a large, plain metal desk in a small and sparsely decorated office that was little more than a cubicle in the huge KGB complex on the outskirts of Moscow.

He was a small man in his late forties, with dark intense eyes and lips that seemed paralyzed in a tight-lipped sneer.

This morning his mind did not give its usual attention to the minute details of the reports before him. He had always taken pride in his ability to detect the nuance as well as the substance of a communication from a just cursory examination, and sometimes he was able to detect subtle shifts in meaning that others had missed. In that way he was able to keep on top of his agents, never letting the chain of his authority get too loose.

But this morning he could think of little other than the apparent defection of Mikhail Belenkov. Belenkov, who was second in command at the First Department of the First Chief Directorate, had not been heard from in seventy-two hours. He had accompanied a trade delegation to London and disappeared shortly after arrival. With his knowledge of American affairs his loss would be a tremendous blow. Rumors of the defection had raced around the building like a fire out of control and although the rumors had not yet been confirmed, Gorsky knew that such attention only meant one thing—Belenkov had gone over to the other side.

He also knew that sometime today, as soon as his superiors saw fit to admit the loss, the word would go out to all departments: "Find Belenkov." Department 8 would be given the job of silencing—if possible—the defector, while Service A, disinformation, would create some sort of cover story to discredit anything Belenkov might reveal.

But Gorsky knew it was already too late for any of that. Belenkov knew the score. He would be so well protected that it would be impossible to get to him, and the other side would of course be expecting the onslaught of disinformation. In some ways the attempts at discrediting Belenkov's knowledge would only serve to prove his value to the other side. Gorsky shook his head and sighed. The fools at the top would go ahead and do it anyway.

He pictured Belenkov's face and tried to imagine if there had been any clues to the departure. He could think of nothing. Belenkov had done a good job of disguising his intentions. Gorsky admired and despised him at the same time.

With a sigh he returned to his reports, flipping through them absently until one of them caught his eye. The report was from the controlling *rezident* in the San Francisco mission, whose reports were always of great interest to Gorsky and many others at KGB headquarters because of the mission's proximity to what had become the heartland of American technology, Silicon Valley.

The San Francisco report always filled Gorsky with a strange sense of pride and resentment. It was here that he had been able to place his best and most productive agent— Aleksei Karpenkov—and for several years Gorsky had been able to bask in the reflected glory of that agent's success. Five years ago, however, Gorsky had been removed as controlling officer of that agent and Karpenkov had been transferred to the control of the Director of Department 8, called the Executive Action Department. Department 8 was responsible for sabotage, kidnappings, and political murders, the kind of operations that the KGB called "wet affairs." It was the most secretive of all the secret departments in the KGB.

Many reasons had been given for the transfer, all of them logical and reasonable: Karpenkov was too valuable to remain under the control of the "Illegals Directorate"; his skills were too great to confine him solely to infiltration; Karpenkov had already shown an aptitude for the kind of work carried out by Department 8.

But even though the reasons for Karpenkov's transfer were logical—and Gorsky often had to admit glumly that much of what was said was true—Gorsky knew that the real reasons were much simpler: a man of Karpenkov's immense talents was incredibly valuable to the political aspirations of his controlling officer. Once that fact was acknowledged and Karpenkov's value ascertained, it had been only a matter of time before some higher-up with political connections decided that Karpenkov was too valuable to let someone else take the credit for his work.

Such a man was Anton Melekh, Director of Department 8 and close personal friend to Viktor Chebrikov, Director of the KGB.

And so Gorsky had lost Karpenkov to the machinations of Melekh. What hurt more than the loss, and a quick look around the tiny office showed what a loss it had been, was the fact that Gorsky believed that Karpenkov was ill-suited for his work with Department 8. Perhaps "ill-suited" was the wrong term—"overqualified" was closer to the mark. There were many men—and some women—who had the ruthlessness and dedication for the kind of "wet affairs" required in Department 8, but very few in the field combined these qualities with the intelligence necessary to perpetrate the sophisticated infiltrations that Karpenkov was capable of. In addition to his skills and intelligence Karpenkov also possessed a single-minded determination, an instinctive, almost diabolical hatred for America, which spurred him on to sometimes incredible achievement.

Gorsky thought back to that first meeting with Karpenkov, then only a boy, when he, Gorsky, had first persuaded Karpenkov to work for him. At that time Karpenkov's only desire was to strike a blow against his American father, who had made his life a living hell. Perhaps, Gorsky thought, by destroying his father Karpenkov thought that he could destroy the part of himself he most despised.

Gorsky had used that hatred well. For several years he had refused Karpenkov's constant requests to be allowed to "terminate Columbus," as his father had been known in their personal code. Karpenkov's requests had been refused because Gorsky had feared that once this goal had been achieved, Karpenkov would lose the white-hot spark of hatred that made him such an effective agent.

What had made Gorsky change his mind, in addition to the persistent requests, was the fact that Karpenkov's value was growing; Gorsky began to fear that his pathological hatred of his father might force him into some spontaneous action that might jeopardize that value. Adding to Gorsky's fear was the knowledge that several times Karpenkov had followed his target for days on end, against orders. Some action was imperative, or one way or the other, the KGB might lose a potentially valuable agent.

Gorsky had ordered an investigation of Karpenkov's father, William Miller, and found that like many American military men, Miller had returned to the mundane life of a civilian after leaving the Army. He was employed with an advertising agency in New York City selling soap powder or some such nonsense. And so, reluctantly and with great trepidation, Gorsky had finally given the order—"terminate Columbus."

Gorsky's fear had proved groundless. After killing Miller Karpenkov had maintained his zeal. He had continued his training and methodical attempts at infiltration. And the infiltration had been a total success. One of Karpenkov's earliest achievements was the acquisition of the latest generation of microchips used in airborne navigation systems. Following that there had been many other "acquisitions" as they were called at the KGB. Several years later, Karpenkov had been responsible for the theft and delivery of the United States spy satellite technology, called TRISAT, which had saved the Soviet Union at least ten years of research and perhaps billions of rubles in development costs. Such an espionage coup by the man whom Gorsky had personally recruited for the KGB had been a great boost to Gorsky's career, and Gorsky began to imagine even greater rewards.

That spectacular success, however, had been the beginning of the end for Gorsky's involvement with Karpenkov. It had become too obvious that Karpenkov was an extremely valuable commodity, and shortly thereafter Gorsky found himself minus his top recruit. There was, it seemed, an inordinate amount of political infighting and back-stabbing at KGB headquarters, but, thought Gorsky, what could you expect from an organization that had a history of removing its leaders by execution? He tried not to let his disappointment show, but it was a bitter blow and he had vowed to get even.

The KGB was so compartmentalized that very few knew what anyone in any other department was doing. So Karpenkov, quite naturally, was unknown to all but those intimately involved in his operations. Now that Gorsky was no longer involved he was supposed to forget that Karpenkov had ever existed. He was able, however, through contacts in Department 13, where all foreign communications were decoded, to keep abreast of Karpenkov's activities.

Gorsky took a perverse pleasure in noting that Karpenkov's triumphs were not as frequent now as they had been several years ago. He imagined that his own removal as controlling agent had had something to do with Karpenkov's lack of success, but was objective enough to realize that it could also be because the Americans were putting greater effort into their security procedures.

After the TRISAT fiasco the U.S. had tightened up on security at many of the companies that produced high-tech products for the government, and Karpenkov's reports showed an increasing frustration. He seemed unable to break the new security procedures established by the CIA liaison man at the TMK Corporation, Gordon Hardwick.

Uninvolved but still interested, Gorsky checked the files on CIA agents and found that Gordon Hardwick was a Soviet expert who had worked extensively in Europe. He spoke fluent Russian and was regarded as a formidable opponent.

As usual, when an obstacle was placed in his path Karpenkov's first reaction was elimination, but so far that request had been denied as too dangerous and perhaps counterproductive.

Each month, Gorsky read in the reports some new method advocated by Karpenkov for the elimination of Hardwick. The termination would be made to look like an accident. Denied! The termination would be accomplished by introducing some chemical agent into Hardwick's food and the American would suffer a terminal kidney malfunction. Denied! Then Karpenkov suggested another technique. He would slowly, over the course of several months, spike Hardwick's food with the chemical Aminazin. Gorsky smiled. This was a technique he favored and one that he had taught Karpenkov at the Dietskoye Selo Training Center. He also noted with some pleasure that that particular request had not been denied, but listed as "under consideration."

Aminazin was a chemical frequently used by the KGB in mental hospitals where Soviet dissidents were treated. In small quantities the chemical caused mental confusion, disorientation, and even hallucinations. In larger quantities it could kill.

For several months there had been little or nothing of interest in Karpenkov's reports. Through a third party he had identified a potential recruit at TMK and was in the process of ascertaining the possibility of acquiring classified documents. As usual, the initial attempt would be only a test to see if penetration were possible. If failure occurred there was no possibility that Karpenkov's position would be jeopardized. Karpenkov did not hold out much hope for success in this particular endeavor.

As Gorsky opened the latest San Francisco *rezident* report he noted the usual references to "contacts" and "security probes." Nothing seemed out of the ordinary. Then he read the classified Karpenkov report he had obtained that morning. He liked to read it in conjunction with the other reports from San Francisco.

Much of it was still in code. Only someone who knew the code names for Karpenkov and the companies in Silicon Valley would have been able to make anything at all of it. The only thing of any interest in the report was at the end, where Chameleon (Karpenkov) reported that Clyde (Hardwick) had been rather abruptly ordered back to Washington. No one at Zebra (TMK Corporation) knew why, only that the recall was abrupt and was to be for an indeterminate period. To the best of Karpenkov's information, Hardwick would be gone for a week, perhaps two.

Karpenkov, it seemed, had returned to his old carping about eliminating Hardwick. His plan was to follow Gordon Hardwick to Washington and there, far from California, where no possibility of his involvement could ever be proved, eliminate Hardwick at the first opportunity.

Gorsky shook his head. The man had a one-track mind. He was like a bulldog, tenacious to the point of stupidity. If anything happened to Hardwick, it was possible that Karpenkov's absence would be noted. It was unlikely that he could be linked to the death, but one could never tell, and Karpenkov was far too valuable to be placed at such risk. Gorsky was confident that Melekh would not permit such foolishness.

He was about to put the folder away when suddenly a thought occurred to him. Why was Hardwick being recalled? He was a Soviet expert with a fluency in Russian. Did this have anything to do with the Belenkov defection? Had the two ever met?

He pushed a buzzer and his aide, Lieutenant Sakov, appeared in the doorway.

"I need some information on Colonel Belenkov," said Gorsky.

Sakov raised a discreet eyebrow. Everyone was interested in Belenkov today.

"I want to know to what foreign posts he has been assigned over the past twenty years. Also bring me the file on CIA staff officer Gordon Hardwick."

Sakov nodded and quickly left the room.

Gorsky, hands behind his back, paced back and forth in his small space until Sakov returned. The aide placed the files on his desk.

"They made me sign for it," he said.

Gorsky shrugged and waved a curt dismissal in his aide's direction.

As soon as he was alone Gorsky sat down with Belenkov's file. He flipped through it until he found the listing of assigned stations where Belenkov had worked. Then, holding the file open to that page, he opened the file on Hardwick and found the corresponding information. He quickly noted that both had worked in Berlin in 1974, and both had been assigned to duty in Sweden in 1980. Belenkov had, of course, been assigned a long tour of duty in Washington from 1982 to 1984. For part of that time Hardwick had also been in Washington. It was entirely possible that the two had established some contact, and as was often the case, had found some area of mutual respect. It was also possible that Hardwick was being recalled to Washington to meet with Belenkov!

Gorsky closed the file and sat silently for a moment pondering the possibilities. If he was right, and Hardwick was heading for a meeting with Belenkov, then Karpenkov, by following the American, might be led right to the defector.

Gorsky's sneer spread to a smile. This could be his chance for redemption, his chance to get his career back in gear again. After a moment's hesitation, he picked up his phone and dialed. The sweat was beginning to form on the back of his neck. What he was about to do was very risky.

He identified himself to the voice on the other end. "I would like to speak—for a very brief moment—to Comrade Director Chebrikov, please."

"Quite impossible," said the voice.

"This is in regard to the whereabouts of Deputy Director Belenkov of the—"

He was cut off. "I am quite aware, Comrade Captain, of the position of Deputy Director Belenkov. You may give me your information and I will pass it along to the Director— along with the other fifty messages about the same subject."

Gorsky was daunted but remained firm. "I would prefer to pass along this piece of information personally. There is some explanation required."

There was the sound of a lengthy sigh on the other end and after a brief pause the voice returned. "You may have five minutes with First Deputy Chairman Kalmykov at noon. Be here promptly."

"I'll be there," said Gorsky but the line was already dead.

Ten

Colonel-General Kalmykov, Deputy Chairman, KGB, carefully stoked the smoldering embers in his office fireplace. He was on one knee, his back to Captain Gorsky, whom he had managed to ignore since the man had been ushered into his office several minutes ago.

Gorsky gave a nervous cough and Kalmykov stopped his poking long enough to look back over his shoulder. His look was enough to raise goose pimples on Gorsky's flesh.

Kalmykov was almost seventy, short, squat, and with a face that was frozen in a perpetual scowl. As a political commissar during the war against the Nazis, one of Kalmykov's jobs had been to prevent desertion at the front. It was said, although Gorsky had believed the story to be an exaggeration, that in one day in the terrible winter of 1941, Kalmykov had personally executed more than one hundred Soviet soldiers during the German assault on Kiev.

Looking at that face now, Gorsky was not so sure the stories were exaggerated.

"Taking a chance, aren't we, Captain?" said Kalmykov in a surprisingly high-pitched voice.

"A chance, Comrade General?"

"Going outside of channels. Going over your own director's head."

Gorsky gulped noticeably. "I was convinced, Comrade General, that this information was so important that any delay in its—"

Kalmykov cut him off. "I hope so," he said. The general struggled to his feet and straightened out his double-breasted tunic. On the left breast of the jacket he wore the Star of a Hero of the Soviet Union, two Orders of Lenin, and the Leningrad campaign medal. On the right he wore the Orders of Suvorov First Class, the Red Star, and the War for the Fatherland.

Gorsky gulped again, his Adam's apple bobbing nervously in his throat.

Kalmykov sized him up carefully, noting the tense posture and the eyes that could not seem to find a comfortable resting place. His lips moved in what was for him a smile. Another weak sister, he thought. The KGB was full of them. It wasn't like the old days. We had balls then.

He kept the poker in his hand. "So tell me what you came to say, Captain. I'm a busy man."

Gorsky began his story. His mouth was incredibly dry and he would have given a day's pay for a glass of water, but Kalmykov offered nothing.

When he was finished Kalmykov was silent. The general went to his desk and sat down heavily. He drummed his fingers on the table for a moment before he spoke. "Sit down, Captain," he said, picking up the phone. He waited only a fraction of a second for his aide. "Tell Director Melekh that I want to see him in my office—right away."

Gorsky's eyes widened and his heart thumped in his chest. He had not planned on Melekh.

Kalmykov's eyes were dark, distant pools. "I think Melekh should hear what you have to say, don't you?" He did not wait for an answer. "After all, one of his men seems to be involved in this . . . this suggestion of yours."

Gorsky felt himself sink deeper into his chair. "May I have some water, Comrade General?"

Kalmykov nodded his assent and busied himself with some paperwork on his desk. Gorsky had the strange feeling that the general was signing death warrants.

After ten excruciating, silent minutes, there was a sharp rap on the door. Kalmykov looked up at Gorsky and bared his teeth in that savage approximation of a smile. "Enter," he said.

Anton Melekh came in, the smile on his face fading when he noticed Gorsky, who had leaped to his feet. Melekh was in his middle forties, with the body of a ferret and the sly, inquisitive face of a fox.

Kalmykov dispensed with any pleasantries. "Captain Gorsky here, from S, has an interesting theory, Comrade Director, about your departed friend Belenkov and one of your 'illegals.' "

Melekh turned to Gorsky. The smile was completely gone now. "I'd love to hear it." His words were like icicles that shattered and fell to the floor as soon as they were spoken.

Gorsky felt faint. His career was as good as over. Of that he was certain. He had hoped to go over everyone's head with this but realized now that that had been a grievous miscalculation. He plunged into the icy waters, once again relating his story, this time for Melekh, of the possibility of Belenkov and Hardwick having some association

When he was finished Melekh said nothing. Melekh seemed only to have eyes for the file folder that Gorsky had brought with him and which had by now grown limp in his sweating palms.

Kalmykov broke the ugly silence. "I still don't see what makes you think that this"—his eyes closed as he tried to recall the name—"Hardwick is going to Washington to meet with Belenkov."

"It is only a guess, Comrade General," said Gorsky. "It may only be a series of coincidences, but we know several things to be true. One, Belenkov is gone"—he waited for someone to dispute him on this, but both men were stonily silent—"and we know that if he is not already in Washington, he will soon be there."

Kalmykov nodded. Melekh gave no sign of assent.

Gorsky went on, praying that this interrogation would soon be over. "Is it only a coincidence that a Soviet expert

who speaks Russian, and who might have an acquaintance-
ship with Belenkov, is suddenly recalled to Washington?"

Melekh's hungry eyes were still fixed on the file.

Gorsky's inner voice screamed at him, Why have I done
this to myself? How could I be so stupid to think I'd get away
with it? He struggled to remain calm. "It has been my
experience that those who defect feel a certain sense of
isolation and even loneliness."

"As well they should," said Kalmykov brusquely.

"Of course, of course," Gorsky added quickly. "Even
those who defect from the West feel this loss of place—this
sense of having burned all their bridges behind them."

Kalmykov was not one for psychoanalysis. "Get to the
point," he said, looking at his watch.

"In my experience with defectors I have found that they
very often want to speak with someone they knew before . . .
before they decided to make such a drastic change."

One of Kalmykov's bushy eyebrows went up—the other
went down. He was beginning to see what Gorsky was driving at.

"It is my guess that Belenkov and Hardwick knew each
other, at one of their pervious posts perhaps, and that Belenkov
trusts this American and supposes that the American trusts
him. This Hardwick is being brought in to make Belenkov
more comfortable during the debriefing period."

Kalmykov was drumming his fingers again. "It is not
impossible, I suppose." He turned to Melekh. "What do you
think, Comrade Director?"

Melekh was blunt and to the point. "Nonsense. Absolute
nonsense. The invention of an obviously idle mind. The first
thing that my department did was, of course, to check on the
possible association between Belenkov and Hardwick. There
is absolutely no evidence to support the contention that the
two men have ever laid eyes on each other. Never mind that
they have formed some sort of mutual admiration society. If
Comrade Gorsky had paid more attention to his duties and
less to peeking into classified documents of other departments, he would not be free to waste the Deputy Chairman's
valuable time."

Kalmykov's yellow teeth were showing again. "What do
you have to say for yourself, Captain?"

Gorsky stood. "I am terribly sorry that I have wasted
your time, Comrade General, with this foolish tale. Obviously

if I had been careful enough to check with Comrade Director Melekh I would have known just how ridiculous my supposition was."

"I want a reprimand in this man's file," said Melekh, taking the folder from Gorsky's hands. "And I will speak with his supervisor about his prying into other departments. Perhaps a reduction in rank would teach him respect for authority."

Kalmykov made a clucking noise with his tongue. "I think we can excuse Comrade Gorsky for his excess of zeal. I'm quite confident that a severe reprimand and a talk with his director will be sufficient to keep his nose out of the business of others. Don't you agree, Captain?"

"Yes, Comrade General. Thank you."

"Then you are dismissed."

Gorsky turned to leave, but Kalmykov held him with a word. "And don't forget, Comrade, I'll be keeping an eye on you. I want no repetition of this business."

Gorsky's face was bright red as he backed toward the door, bowing as he went. "Thank you, Comrade General." He slipped through the narrowest of openings in the door, and gasping for breath, rushed for the exit.

Kalmykov lit one of his smelly cigarettes. "Well," he said, putting the match in the ashtray carefully, "what do you think?"

Melekh feigned puzzlement. "About what?"

"Don't bullshit me, Anton Sergeevich. I wasn't fooled by your reaction—and neither, I might add, was that weasel Gorsky. He was just glad to get out of here with his balls intact. The whole idea seemed plausible to me."

"Perhaps," Melekh said, still unwilling to give up the charade. His pointed nose twitched as he sniffed the air.

Kalmykov put out his hand. "If I may see the folder, Comrade."

Melekh shrugged and handed over the folder he had taken from Gorsky. Kalmykov flipped from page to page, grunting as he read to himself. "This man of yours—Chameleon. Is he capable of dealing with the situation?"

Melekh smiled. "More than capable, Comrade General. He is intelligent, ruthless, calculating, and absolutely brilliant. He is the best man I have ever placed."

Kalmykov raised a bushy eyebrow, and Melekh wondered if Gorsky had mentioned that it was he who had recruited and trained Karpenkov. He'd make that bastard pay for the trouble he had caused today.

"I understand that the latest computer acquisition is still impounded in Holland."

"I don't think the situation is Chameleon's fault, General. He was to arrange the sale to a South African firm and its subsequent transfer to one of our companies in Holland, where it was to be rerouted to Switzerland and then on to Czechoslovakia. Somehow the Americans got wind of the transactions and were able to persuade the Dutch to impound the shipment in Rotterdam." He sighed and made a gesture of futility with his hands. "Such things are getting more difficult every day. The Americans are being much more careful."

Kalmykov closed the file folder. "Perhaps. But in the meantime we should at least give *our* new plan a chance for success."

The general's emphasis on the word "our" made Melekh smile. "As you wish, Comrade General. I will begin immediately."

"Nothing ventured, nothing gained."

"I would not want to jeopardize Chameleon's identity unnecessarily," said Melekh. "He is far too valuable."

"Belenkov must be found."

"We have other agents working right now on that problem."

Kalmykov stood up. "I want Belenkov found and I want all available resources used. We have the full authority of the General Secretary in this matter. Belenkov must be stopped at *whatever* cost. Do I make myself clear?"

"Perfectly, Comrade General. I'll see to it immediately."

Melekh stood, made a curt nod of his head, and quickly left the room.

The old executioner of Leningrad thumped down into his chair. Getting old was awful, he thought. Twenty years ago I'd have found this bastard Belenkov and finished him myself.

NEW YORK (AP)—Chanting slogans and wielding placards against the American deployment of its new antiballistic missile system, more than 200,000 marchers paraded down New York's Fifth Avenue today in a demonstration of solidarity with peace groups marching today in several of the world's capital cities.

82

Crowds in excess of 300,000 were reported in London and Paris, and in perhaps the biggest march of the day, organizers estimated the number of demonstrators at 500,000 in Bonn, West Germany.

The theme everywhere was the same—"Support the Freeze: Ban ABM"—as the demonstrators pressed their demands for an end to what one called "the impending nuclear nightmare."

March organizers—U.S. Peace Council, Mobilization for Survival, and Physicians for Social Responsibility—declared the day "a huge success" and an obvious "demonstration of the demands of the people of this planet" that the United States cease and desist from "military madness."

Eleven

Viktor Chebrikov, head of the KGB, was aghast. His mouth was open and his eyes bulged. "Chernetsov wanted to come here?"

"Don't worry, Viktor Mikhailovich," said Vitali Fedorchuk. "I talked him out of it."

"A good thing. All I need is that old donkey snooping around in this mess."

"Don't underestimate him. He's a crafty old bastard."

Chebrikov fell into silence. He was sixty-four, balding, and wore thick tortoiseshell glasses over droopy eyes that masked an intense ambition. He had served as Yuri Andropov's deputy chairman when the former General Secretary had headed the Komitet Gosudarstvennoi Bezopasnost. When Andropov had left the Committee for State Security after fifteen years to serve on the Secretariat of the Party Central Committee, he had maneuvered to have one of his closest friends and advisers, Vitali Fedorchuk, named to succeed him, and to have Chebrikov named as one of two First Deputy Chairmen. A few short months later, after the death of Leonid Brezhnev Andropov was named as General Secretary of the Communist Party. He made Fedorchuk Minister of Internal Affairs, replacing one of Brezhnev's closest friends, General Nikolai Shcholokov, and promoted Chebrikov to Chairman of the KGB. In one swift move the KGB had taken over both the Party leadership and control of the uniformed police forces throughout the Soviet Union, in addition to its traditional role as the nation's secret police force.

Fedorchuk did not interrupt his colleague. He looked around the spacious office and was pleased to note that very little had changed since he had occupied this same office four years ago. It still smelled of fifteen years of Andropov.

Finally he could bear the silence no longer. "How bad is it, Viktor?"

Chebrikov jumped as if startled. "It's bad," he said. "It could be very bad."

"Then they have him for sure?"

Chebrikov nodded reluctantly. "Informants in British intelligence tell us that he is being held at a country estate forty miles outside London . . . and he is talking his fool head off."

"Then," said Fedorchuk, "it is absolutely essential that we know exactly what this *stukach* had access to." He raised an eyebrow and looked pointedly at Chebrikov. "I am particularly concerned that he might have access to any information that could lead him to Chameleon. This is a very critical time for that operation."

Chebrikov spoke positively. "Absolutely not. Only three men have had complete access to the file on Chameleon—one, our dear friend Yuri Vladimirovich Andropov, is dead, and the other two are in this room right now." He glanced at the portrait of the first secret police chief, Felix Dzerzhinsky, which hung on the far wall. "That file is kept in the safe in this office, where Yuri Vladimirovich placed it more than thirteen years ago. There are no other copies and the file has not left here since the day it was created. First Deputy Chairman Kalmykov and Department 8 Director Melekh are the only others who know of the existence of Chameleon. Even the San Francisco *rezident* is unaware of what he has in his backyard."

"Such secrets are hard to keep, Viktor. What about

Chameleon's first controlling officer, the man who recruited and trained him?"

Chebrikov gave a dismissive shake of his head. "Control of Chameleon was switched from the Illegals Directorate more than five years ago. No one knows if Chameleon is alive or dead."

Fedorchuk shook his head sadly. "A word here, a whisper there . . ." He let his words trail off.

Chebrikov was anxious to change the subject. "I've asked General Kalmykov to gather whatever operations Belenkov might have had access to. We might have to get some people home in a hurry."

Fedorchuk was unwilling to drop the matter. "We should pay particular attention to anything—*anything*—that might lead Belenkov to suspect the existence of Chameleon."

"Well," said Chebrikov with a show of indifference, "let's not worry about that until we talk with Kalmykov."

Kalmykov had just finished his meeting with Melekh when his aide informed him that Chairman Chebrikov was waiting for him. The general straightened his tunic, brushing away the cigarette ash that had accumulated on the front, picked up the files the aide had brought to him, and rushed off to meet with the Chairman.

Chebrikov greeted Kalmykov warmly. "You of course know Internal Affairs Minister Fedorchuk." He nodded toward Fedorchuk, who remained seated by the fireplace. "I have asked him, as a former chief of this office, to assist us in this matter."

Kalmykov nodded agreeably. "Of course, of course."

Kalmykov dropped heavily into a chair in front of Chebrikov's desk. He reached forward and placed the file folders he had brought with him on the edge of the desk and then took out a *papirosy*, the thin cardboard tube filled with strong Russian tobacco. Kalmykov preferred the foul-smelling Russian brand to the imported cigarettes that were available at the first-floor commissary. As he lit his cigarette, he did not notice the look of displeasure that passed between Chebrikov and Fedorchuk. Had he done so he would have immediately extinguished the *papirosy*. The only thing that frightened the "Assassin of Kiev" was the disapproval of his superiors.

"So tell me, Comrade General," said Chebrikov, patting

the files with his palm, "what does Belenkov know that can hurt us?"

Kalmykov shook his head sadly, sending a small avalanche of ash cascading across his jacket. "As is to be expected, Comrade Chairman, he knows practically everything in his field: agents' names, operations in progress, informants in certain foreign countries. His greatest area of knowledge, of course, is in the American sector."

Chebrikov clenched both fists and silently cursed Belenkov.

Kalmykov went on. "I have taken the liberty, Comrade Chairman, of ordering his Director in the First Department to warn anyone in the field whose cover might be in danger, and to begin recall proceedings of those who are particularly vulnerable."

"You have done well, General Kalmykov."

Kalmykov smiled. He loved to bask in the praise of his superiors. "I think that we can control most of the damage on this," he said. "If not, we can deny much of the rest."

Fedorchuk spoke for the first time, and Kalmykov had to turn in his chair to face him. "If I may be permitted to intrude for just a moment, Comrade General. The Chairman and I were discussing earlier a potentially more dangerous situation."

Kalmykov's eyes narrowed as he listened.

Fedorchuk went on with a nod to Chebrikov. "We were wondering if it were possible that Belenkov might have any knowledge of Chameleon or any of his operations?"

Kalmykov smiled. "That secret is perfectly safe, Comrade Minister. It would be—"

Chebrikov interrupted, forcing Kalmykov to swivel around in his chair again. "No secret of this magnitude is ever completely safe, Comrade General. The right man with access to the right information, and intelligent enough to ask the right questions, might be able to ascertain the existence of Chameleon. Put that man together with the right American, and together they might even venture a guess at the identity of Chameleon." His explanation complete, Chebrikov gave Kalmykov a chilly smile. "That is what concerns us most."

Kalmykov seemed bewildered. "Belenkov has had no access to any information about Chameleon."

Fedorchuk broke in again. "There are peripheral matters

pertaining to Chameleon that might lead a man in Belenkov's position to suspect something."

Just as Kalmykov turned to respond, Chebrikov spoke, forcing him to twist back in his seat again. "Is it remotely possible that Belenkov might have an inkling of Chameleon's existence?"

Kalmykov's head was spinning and the ash from his *papirosy* was like fresh snow falling on his jacket. He reclaimed the file from Chebrikov's desk and opened it. "He knows a great deal, Comrade, but—"

Chebrikov cut him off sharply. "We are concerned only with Chameleon and what, if anything, Belenkov knows about that." He looked straight at Kalmykov. "Does he know anything about any of the related operations?"

Kalmykov looked at Belenkov's file. He sighed. "Yes."

Chebrikov looked at Fedorchuk and shook his head, then leaned back into his chair.

"Which operation?" asked Fedorchuk, sensing that the Chairman would not speak.

"He was part of the TRISAT operation, where we enticed the American to sell us the secrets of the American intelligence satellite."

Chebrikov sat up. "Was he part of the operation to leak the information about that sale back to the Americans?"

Kalmykov looked at the file. "No. But . . ."

"But what?"

"In his capacity as American expert he might have had access to the files of those who were involved in that part of the operation."

Chebrikov closed his eyes. "What else?" he asked softly.

Kalmykov scrutinized the file. "The only other possibility I can see is our acquisition of the computer guidance technology."

"What was his involvement?"

Kalmykov seemed nervous, as if waiting for an explosion from Chebrikov. "He was in charge of the operation that leaked information to the British that we had acquired the American technology. But," he added quickly, "he knew only that we wanted the Americans to be aware that we had equaled their capability. He was given no inkling of the real reason for the leak."

His words oozing sarcasm, Chebrikov said, "It won't take a genius to figure out that we wanted them to know for other reasons. If he talks to the Americans they'll know we're protecting someone."

Fedorchuk spoke for the first time in a long time. "But he doesn't really know any of the details."

"It's enough that he knows this much," said Chebrikov. "Don't underestimate the intelligence of our enemies. With this much information, the Chameleon operation could come tumbling down like a house of cards." He pounded his fist into his palm.

"What do you suggest, Comrade Chairman?" asked Fedorchuk. "I am sure the Comrade General will do everything in his power to minimize the damage."

Kalmykov nodded enthusiastically.

Chebrikov looked carefully from one man to the other. "Can we get to him? Can we eliminate his potential for damage?"

"That," said Kalmykov, "would not be without risk."

Chebrikov's face was in stone. "Chameleon must be protected at all costs."

Kalmykov waited for Chebrikov to elaborate, but the Chairman said nothing more. He merely stared into space as if his work were completed. Kalmykov coughed nervously. "Am I to understand, Comrade Chairman, that I have your full authority to act in this matter?"

Chebrikov nodded. "But not a word of this conversation must ever be traced to me. Those involved must know as little as possible about what is to be done." Chebrikov's eyes rolled skyward. "And for God's sake don't involve the Bulgarians. Their enthusiasm is commendable but this assignment must remain in house and as secret as is humanly possible."

Kalmykov's eyes were twinkling. "I may have the perfect solution to our problems."

Chebrikov leaned forward. "Yes?"

"If Chameleon is the one to be protected at all costs, perhaps he should be the one to take care of Belenkov."

"If we don't know where Belenkov is, how could Chameleon possibly be of assistance?" said Fedorchuk.

Kalmykov's beefy face was split in a sly smile. "I was looking at the latest reports from Chameleon just this morning, and happened to notice something very unusual that just might be of interest."

Chebrikov looked with wary eyes at Fedorchuk. "Tell us."

Kalmykov related to the Chairman of the KGB and to

the Minister of Internal Affairs the story that had only a short time ago been told to him by Captain Gorsky. He did, of course, omit any references to Gorsky, giving the information to his superiors as if he, Colonel-General Kalmykov, First Deputy Chairman, KGB, had conceived the idea himself.

Chebrikov seemed unsure. "It's a possibility," he said. "But definitely a long shot. I think we'll have more success finding Belenkov through regular channels."

"As you wish," said Kalmykov and rose to make his exit. The meeting was obviously at an end.

Chebrikov looked to Fedorchuk. "What do you think?"

Fedorchuk shrugged. "It may be worth a try."

Chebrikov nodded and turned his attention back to Kalmykov, who stood awkwardly, as if he were uncertain whether he should sit back down. Chebrikov gave him no help. "Let's give Chameleon the okay on this plan of yours. Let him follow this American, and perhaps he will be led to Belenkov."

"And if he does not?"

Chebrikov seemed puzzled.

"Chameleon wants permission to eliminate the American," said Kalmykov

"We're interested in Belenkov, not in Chameleon's idiosyncrasies."

"This particular American has been most troublesome to our operation. Since he was assigned to TMK our sources have virtually dried up."

"I don't like it," said Chebrikov. "It's asking for trouble."

"Chameleon thinks it can be handled with an absolute minimum of risk. He has already laid the groundwork for the elimination."

Chebrikov looked to Fedorchuk, but the Internal Affairs Minister looked away. This was one where he would let Chebrikov handle the details himself.

Chebrikov shrugged. "All right. If there is absolutely no risk to Chameleon—and I repeat *absolutely*—he may eliminate the American. But our—and his—first concern must be finding and eliminating Belenkov."

Kalmykov flashed his yellow teeth. "Thank you, Comrade Chairman. I'll get on this right away."

"Do you think it's possible that Chameleon might actually get to Belenkov through this American?" asked Fedorchuk when Kalmykov had gone.

"Sounds too good to be true. If so it is a clever piece of deduction."

"Yes," said Chebrikov. "I wonder who thought of it. Obviously not that ignoramus. His loyalty is unquestionable, but he has the intelligence of a sled dog." He shrugged. "Such beasts of burden are necessary to do the work of the state. Is it not so, Vitali?"

Fedorchuk smiled. "Viktor Mikhailovich," he said warmly, "someday soon you will make a very good General Secretary."

MOSCOW (UPI)—Seven Soviet peace demonstrators were arrested today when they unfurled a banner in front of the Kremlin, asking Soviet leaders to stop the deployment of nuclear missiles in Eastern Europe.

Six of the demonstrators were released shortly after their arrest, but the seventh, said to be the leader of the small group, was removed to a psychiatric hospital in Moscow for what doctors say was "observation of schizophrenic tendencies."

Twelve

London

By nightfall the KGB had swung into high gear. Any astute observer would have noted intense activity emanating from the Russian embassies in London and Washington and in the New York mission to the U.N. More than fifty percent of the diplomats in these delegations were in actuality KGB agents who were able to use their diplomatic immunity to great benefit. As soon as word came from Moscow Center, the Russians scrambled for any scrap of information that would help them find Belenkov.

* * *

Arthur Morris was in his den, reading his evening newspaper, when the phone rang. Morris was forty-five, tall and slim, with dark hair that was thinning rapidly. He was a civilian clerk in Section C of British Secret Intelligence.

"Arthur," said a voice that instantly made his heart race, "I must see you."

"I can't" said Arthur, his voice a whisper. Arthur's wife, Katherine, was in the kitchen cleaning up the dinner dishes.

"Yes you can," said the voice. "You know you want to."

"No. It's impossible."

"I've checked into the Motor Hotel. Arthur, you know which one. I'll only be in town for a day or two."

"I can't."

"I'll give you my number here," said the voice, ignoring Arthur's unwillingness. "Call me back."

"It's quite impossible . . . Not tonight."

"It's very important that we meet, Arthur. I must see you."

As always with Stefan there was only the slightest hint of threat. It was never spoken, but Arthur could hear it, rattling around like a rat in the basement.

Stefan repeated the number. "You must come," he said, and hung up.

Arthur sat holding the dead phone next to his ear, remembering with a mixture of horror and excitement the first time he had met Stefan. He had stopped at a pub on his way home from work. Katherine was visiting her sister, so he had decided to get a bite to eat and have a few pints. A young man with a slight foreign accent had struck up a conversation with him. Stefan was blond and good-looking and had an easygoing pleasant manner. They had a few drinks together and Arthur, who was usually taciturn, found that Stefan was easy to talk to.

Stefan did most of the talking. Mostly he talked about his job as a cosmetics salesman, and the young women he had bedded in the course of his travels.

Arthur had stayed longer than he had intended and drank a bit more than he should have. When it was time to go, Stefan asked if Arthur could drop him off at his apartment.

On the way home Stefan was strangely quiet. Without a word he placed his hand on Arthur's left knee. Arthur's eyes widened and his stomach churned. After a moment's hesitation, Stefan slid his hand up the inside of Arthur's thigh and

Arthur realized that this was where the evening had been heading from the beginning.

Arthur found himself thinking about the bodies of the weight lifters in the magazines he kept hidden in a box in the attic.

Stefan unzipped Arthur's fly and began to masturbate him.

Arthur could barely breathe. His mouth was dry and he had difficulty swallowing. He gripped the steering wheel as if it were a life buoy.

"I'd like to do more than this," said Stefan. "And I think you would too. Would you like to come up to my apartment?"

Arthur struggled to speak. "I have to get home . . . my wife is waiting," he lied.

Stefan bent over him, teasing him with his tongue. "Are you sure you can't come in for a minute?"

This is insane, Arthur thought. But of course he went in.

They met at least once a week for the rest of that month. Then Stefan showed Arthur the pictures of them together.

"Aren't they marvelous?" said Stefan.

"My God, are you crazy?" wailed Arthur. "What did you do this for?"

"Don't worry. No one will ever see them. I just like to have memories of our times together."

Arthur was nervous about the photographs, so Stefan promised to destroy them. But about a month later Stefan burst out a confession. "I lied to you," he said.

Arthur was puzzled. "About what?"

"I told you I was Swiss."

Arthur held his breath.

"I'm a Soviet citizen. I work for the embassy here in London."

"Doing what?"

Stefan ignored the question, but Arthur had already begun to guess the answer.

"The security chief at the embassy searched my apartment yesterday. . . . He found the photographs."

Arthur buried his face in his hands.

"Don't worry," said Stefan. "It's me they will punish."

"Punish? How?"

"By sending me back."

Arthur knew the game. He was supposed to ask what he could do to help, and Stefan would be coy for a while but

92

finally admit there was something. Arthur had seen it before. He couldn't believe he had been so stupid to let it happen to him.

He also knew that if he didn't volunteer his help the next step would be out-and-out blackmail. He thought about that for a while. Russians did not make idle threats.

He swallowed hard. "Is there anything I can do to help?" he asked.

And so Arthur was drawn into the web of spies and informants the KGB had accumulated around the world. Much of the information he turned over to Stefan was innocuous, but once in a while a snippet of information was enough to tip off the Russians that something was going on. Occasionally the information was enough to allow the KGB to thwart some minor British operation already in progress.

After thinking about Stefan and the two years he had supplied classified information to the Russians, Arthur was convinced that he had never really given the Russians anything of any importance. It was all rather harmless. We did it to them, he thought, they did it to us.

His conscience soothed, he picked up the phone again and dialed. "I want to see you," he said.

"I knew you would," said Stefan. "I can't wait."

"You need something, don't you?"

"Must you always be so suspicious, Arthur?"

"What is it? Tell me."

"It's not important. It can wait."

"Tell me."

"There has been a defection. I need to find out anything I can."

Arthur sighed. "I'll do what I can."

"I know you will, Arthur. We'll talk about it when you get here. Please hurry."

Arthur hung up the phone. He hated himself and knew that someday he would get caught. Perhaps he would kill himself if that happened. But at that moment he could think of little other than rushing off to meet Stefan.

That evening in Arlington, Virginia, just outside Washington, D.C., Nancy Cooper's phone rang. She was already in her pajamas, watching television in bed.

At first she was angry that anyone should call her so late, but when she heard the voice on the other end she forgot her irritation.

"Nancy," said the voice, and then without bothering to identify itself, "how have you been?"

She knew the voice. "I've been fine, Eric," she said, trying to keep her voice cool. Her heart was thumping in her chest. "Where have you been?" she said with what she hoped was more than a trace of sarcasm. "I haven't heard from you in . . . months."

The voice hesitated. "I've been away on business. "I'll tell you all about it." There was a long silence. "I'd like to see you."

Nancy had rehearsed what she would say to him the next time he called her. I don't think so, she had practiced saying with the cold disdain she had heard so often from others. I've got better things to do with my life than involve myself with this kind of relationship, she had repeated to herself. Instead, she heard herself say, "When?"

"Now. Tonight," Eric said.

She felt a tightness in her chest, a tingling in her fingertips. "Tonight? Do you know what time it is?"

"I've taken a room at the Hyatt. Why don't you come on over?"

"How can I? I've got work tomorrow."

"Bring a bag. You can go to work from here."

Eric was being his usual assertive, persuasive self. Nancy Cooper felt a tightness in her throat. Instinctively her hand moved as if to loosen her collar, but she was not wearing anything around her neck.

Nancy was plain. She had rather nondescript features, brown lackluster hair, and she was twenty pounds overweight. Her adolescent years had been filled with emotional disappointments and her college years, if anything, had reinforced the idea in her own mind that she was unattractive and undesirable to men. In college, searching for the sense of community that came from being part of a group, Nancy had drifted in and out of liberal and radical causes.

She had taken her law degree at Columbia and then moved to Washington to work at a small, relatively low-profile firm. After two years she moved on. Her new position was as a legislative aide to a congressman from Massachusetts who happened to be a member of the House Select Committee on Intelligence.

Eric Swanson, the man on the phone now, was muscular and handsome in the same way all of her fantasy men had been. Just like all the gorgeous college men who had ignored her for her entire collegiate tenure. Eric was her perfect male—except for two things. One, he was married, and two, he was an agent for the KGB.

She hadn't known either of those things at first. She had only been surprised and somewhat bewildered that this handsome young man, who told her he was a gem merchant from Switzerland, seemed somewhat interested in her.

Before she met Swanson she had had sexual relations with a man only twice and one brief affair with a woman professor in college. She had never been courted, and when Swanson brought her flowers and took her to dinner she was starstruck. She couldn't think of anything but him. On their second date she let him take her to bed and after that they had sex every day. On their first weekend together they went to a motel on the Maryland shore and spent two days in bed. She felt wonderful. A man actually desired her!

She knew of course that he traveled a lot and would spend long periods away from her. She lived for the times when he returned. Her whole world began to revolve around his brief visits.

It wasn't long before he began asking her for information about her work with the congressman, whose committee assignments gave him and his staff access to a great deal of classified information. At first she thought Eric was merely interested in her work. Most of the things he asked about were rather innocuous and consisted of information that any diligent newspaper reporter might have been able to find in an afternoon. But soon the questions became more pointed and the information he requested more classified.

She remembered the morning of their first confrontation. "Why," she had said, "do you want to know all this?"

At first he had been evasive but she had persisted. He sat naked on the edge of the bed hunched over like a small boy discovered naked in the woods. He shrugged in resignation. "I work for Soviet Intelligence," he said. "They want to know these things."

Nancy's mouth fell open in amazement, and then the amazement turned to hurt. "You've been using me?" she said, her words a question, hoping he would disagree.

"Yes," he said simply. "They made me do it."

She began to cry—softly and without sound.

He went on, ignoring her tears. "At first I was only doing what I was told to do." He paused to look up at her. "But that was before . . ."

The tears stopped. "Before what?"

"Before I got to know you. Before I fell in love."

He watched her, knowing she would believe him. Women like this, he thought, live only for someone to tell them lies. Even if they know it's a lie, they believe it. He saw her eyes widen, the first hint of a smile beginning to form. He rushed on with his prepared talk. "Now they want more and more information of me."

"Tell them you can't get it."

He chuckled sadly. "If I don't, they'll send me back to Russia—for good."

That prospect alarmed her. "Defect," she said hopefully.

He shook his head. "And what about my family? My mother and father? My brother is a scientist at Moscow University. He would lose his job if I defected."

Nancy was bewildered. "What can we do?"

"It's up to you," he said.

"Me?"

"You can help me—you can keep me here in this country."

Her eyes narrowed. "How?"

"By supplying me with the information I require to keep my bosses happy."

She shook her head. "I'm not sure I could do that."

He knew a way to help her.

"Look," he said, "I am associated with a group of people in my country who believe that the only way to avoid conflict is the free exchange of information. If your country knows what my country is doing and my country knows what your country is doing, the chances of war are almost eliminated. If both countries would only be honest with each other we would all be safe."

Nancy nodded, wanting to believe.

"At this very moment," he went on, "people in my country are secretly passing information to people in your country. People who believe, as we do, that secrecy is the road to confrontation."

"I'm not sure," said Nancy.

He could tell she needed convincing. He pulled down the covers on the bed, revealing her nakedness. She made a futile attempt to cover herself with her hands. He bent over, kissing her large breasts. Her body reminded him of the stocky Russian women, but it was without their strength. He much preferred the long and lean look of American women, but was willing to sacrifice for his country.

His tongue was in her mouth as she reached for him. He closed his eyes and pretended she was one of the girls he had seen on television. His body began to respond.

"I'll do anything for you," she said, stroking him gently. "Anything."

So Nancy began her life as a spy, or more accurately, the conduit of a spy. Every scrap of information that came across her desk which she felt might be of some importance to him, she copied or committed to memory. Frequently he would ask for specific information, and she would find a way to acquire it. Nancy proved to be the most valuable of the small stable of contacts Eric had serviced in various parts of the country. Nancy knew nothing of these other "contacts." Sometimes he would be gone for weeks at a time. "Taking care of his cover" as he called his gem business. And when he came back it was often only for a day or two. Because they could not be seen together he never took her anywhere other than a hotel room, but she lived only for the ring of her telephone and the sound of his voice.

Soon she was providing more and more classified information from her Massachusetts congressman's Intelligence Committee assignment. The congressman believed that secrecy was anathema in a democratic society and barely tolerated the restrictions his committee assignment placed upon him. He rather casually allowed his trusted staff access to most of the files with which he came in contact. At first Nancy felt pangs of disloyalty, not to her country but to her employer. She had great respect for the congressman and hated to use his confidence and trust in her for such purposes. But in the end her need for Swanson won out.

So when Swanson called to meet with her she could only say, "When?"

She packed an overnight bag and drove to his hotel. Eric greeted her warmly. He fixed her a drink and they sat for a while, he on the bed, she on a chair across from him.

"Would you like another?" he asked as she finished her drink.

"Not yet," she said. "After."

"After?" he said, laughing, and she blushed. She hadn't meant to be so blatant, but it had been a long time since she had seen him.

He stood up and quickly began to undress. She marveled at the strength in his slim body. When he moved, the muscles in his stomach rippled.

When he was naked he walked over to her and stood in front of her. Her eyes were riveted on his growing organ. Involuntarily, she wet her lips with her tongue.

"Go ahead," he said. "You know what you want to do."

She looked up at him for a moment but then her eyes dropped back to her point of focus. Her head moved forward, her mouth opening wide to receive him.

Later in bed she held onto him, savoring the strength in his body. "I missed you," she said.

"And I missed you," he said. Lying was another of the things he did well.

"You don't know how much I need you," Nancy said.

He chuckled. "And you don't know how much I need you." This time he was not lying.

He kissed her and pulled her to him. Her hand found his penis and began to stroke him to life.

"I'll do anything for you," she said. "You know that."

He wondered if she could lose twenty pounds. But realizing that she still would probably not be attractive, he remembered what his boss, the chief of Special Service II, KGB, had told him. "We must seek out those who are dissatisfied with their lot in life—the misfits, the ugly, those defeated by unfavorable circumstances—for it is there that we shall find profit."

"Yes," he said. "I know that. And I need your help again."

Her hand missed a beat but only for a moment. Then she was stroking him again.

"Whatever it is, you can count on my help," she said.

His erection surged in her hand. "There has been a defection. A high-ranking official of my government has gone over to your side. He does not understand the ramifications of his actions."

"And?" she said, holding his throbbing penis. It was like a stallion, bucking and moving beneath her gentle caress.

"Someone must talk to him before he does irreparable damage."

She was silent.

"But we don't know where he is. We must find him before it is too late."

"Will you kill him?" The words just came to her.

His erection wilted for a moment and she speeded up her stroking. "I don't care about that," she said. "I just wondered if you yourself would do it."

"I don't do such things," he protested.

"I'm glad," she said, but she wasn't. There was an excitement to involvement in such things that she found increasingly exhilarating.

He rolled onto her and entered her easily.

"Will you help me?" he said, thrusting deep.

"Yes."

"It must be immediately—tomorrow, no later?"

"Yes."

"Do you think you can do it?"

"I'll do everything I can."

If she felt she was being used, she did not care. She had felt used her whole life. Now at least she had someone who was willing to satisfy her every need. There was, of course, a price to pay, but the price was well within reason. She would have paid any price to have him.

* * *

MOSCOW (AP)—Nikolai Chernetsov, General Secretary of the Soviet Union, urged the President of the United States to relinquish plans for a defensive missile system that he had said "would embroil the two superpowers in another and more dangerous weapons race."

In a statement published by Tass, the Soviet press agency, Mr. Chernetsov said that the Soviet Union had "some time ago" abandoned plans for such a system, because it was believed to be destabilizing and contrary to the terms of the U.S.-Soviet treaty on antiballistic missiles.

Mr. Chernetsov offered to sign immediately an agreement specifically banning "any type of anti-ballistic missile system, including those not specifically banned by the 1972 treaty."

Tass said Mr. Chernetsov's statement was a last-ditch effort to alert the world to the dangerously provocative policies of the United States and to demonstrate that the Soviet Union was willing as always to "show the way to a peaceful path."

Thirteen

Celia Progano woke to find her husband, Jim, sitting on the end of the bed, his elbows on his knees, his chin in his hands, staring vacantly at some spot beyond the bedroom window. She sneaked a look at the bedroom clock—4:53.

"Jim," she whispered and he turned to look at her. "What's wrong?"

"Nothing," he said softly, touching her legs beneath the covers. "Go back to sleep."

Something was wrong and she knew it. He had been awake every morning for a week. Today was Sunday. Usually on Sunday Jim Progano could be counted on to sleep until noon.

She pulled back the covers, got up, and sat next to him. He put an arm around her, she liked that, but still he said nothing

"Is it the job?" she asked.

"It's not the job," he said.

She wasn't so sure. For months he had been upset about his work at TMK. At first he had been extraordinarily happy with the importance of the work and the quality of the people he worked with, but after a few months he had seemed troubled. When Celia had asked him about his change in attitude he had only mumbled something about the government's perversion of his work. When his dour mood continued she had pressed him for an explanation and he had told her—"when you do what you do best and you do it well, it's a good thing. But then someone can come along and take your work and turn it into something terrible—something that can kill people."

She knew then that he was talking about Prometheus II. But that had been a long time ago. For months he had seemed fine; laughing, joking, hardworking, fun to be with. Now whatever it was that had touched him earlier was back.

Celia stood up. "I'll make some coffee," she said. "Maybe if you talk about it you'll feel better."

Progano gave her a sad smile. Maybe she was right. In any event she had to know. Whatever he decided would ultimately affect her as much as it did him. But it was hard to know where to begin.

Progano sat across from his wife at the kitchen table. He watched her sip her coffee. She hardly ever drank coffee.

She gave him her best smile of encouragement. "If it's the job, Jimmy," she said, "why don't you just quit and we'll move on. We can always find work—I'll find some secretarial work until you get settled in something."

He shook his head. "It's not that," he said and then plunged in. "You know how I've felt for a long time about this project we're working on for the Defense Department."

She nodded, but he repeated it anyway.

"I thought it was going to be something good—something fine. I thought I was helping to make the world safe from the nightmare."

"And then they changed it."

"They didn't change it—they never intended to use it that way. To them it was always something else—another weapon in the arsenal—only I didn't realize it."

Celia watched him and, remembering, smiled a little. It hadn't been since college that she had heard him refer to the U.S. government as "them." Back then it had always been "them" and "us," and she had been proud to be part of "us."

"It turned out," Progano went on, "that I wasn't the only one at TMK who felt that way. There were others—only a few—who wanted to do something to stop them."

Celia nodded, not wanting to say anything that would interrupt his words.

"But they needed me. I was the key. I was the only one who could really do anything—other than Kincaid of course, and he's so lost in theory he would never question the application of his design. I was the only one who could alter the programming."

He waited for Celia to question him, or to betray shock or sadness at what he was telling her, but she merely nodded and waited for him to continue.

"So," he said, his throat constricting with the revelation, "I helped them. I wanted to make my work good again."

Celia reached across the table to touch his hand. "I trust you," she said. "I've always trusted you."

He couldn't meet her eyes. "Now," he said, starting slowly but his words gathering momentum, "I'm not sure I've done the right thing. I may have made things worse."

She shook her head as if that were not possible.

He smiled. Her faith in him was boundless. "I'm afraid that I—both of us—may be in for a lot of trouble if I try to make things right again."

"I know you'll do the right thing," Celia said. "No matter what, I'll always love you."

He nodded and they held hands across the table.

"Don't worry," he said. "I'll take care of it. Everything will be all right. I'll talk with the CIA security chief at TMK. He'll know what to do."

Celia looked at the kitchen clock. "It's too early to call anybody," she said, getting up from her chair. "Why don't we go back to bed."

Progano lay awake until 7:30 listening to the steady rhythm of Celia's breathing as he went over and over in his mind what he would say to Gordon Hardwick. He slipped out of bed, careful not to disturb her, and went to the kitchen.

When the phone rang Gordon Hardwick had to struggle to rouse himself. Always a light sleeper, he had found that lately he slept like a dead man. He sat up in bed, groggy and unsure of his surroundings. Even now, after all this time, it still surprised him that he was not at home with Carol sleeping beside him. The girl next to him in bed was definitely not Carol.

Finally he responded to the clamoring phone. "Yes," he managed in an almost narcotic stupor. His head was pounding and he was aware of an unsettled feeling in his stomach. Can't drink like I used to, he thought.

"Hardwick," said a voice that was vaguely familiar.

Gordon grunted something that was close to affirmation.

"This is James Progano," the voice said, and when Hardwick didn't answer, it added, "From TMK."

"What the hell time is it?" Hardwick asked.

"I'm sorry to call so early," said Progano, "but I've got something very important to talk to you about."

The girl next to Gordon was stirring beneath the sheet. She rolled over to face him, blond hair spilling across her face. "Time's it?" she mumbled. She pushed her hair away from her face, one breast peeking out at him from behind the sheets.

Gordon watched her in fascination, remembering her from last night. Christ, she's young, he thought. She looked older last night in the bar.

"Are you there?" asked Progano.

"Yeah, I'm here. What is it?"

The girl was stretching herself, arms straight out over her head, legs rigid, both breasts quivering.

"I've got to talk to you about the project," said Progano.

The girl pulled the sheet up across her breasts and gave Gordon a sly smile. She rolled over onto her side facing him, one arm bent beneath her head. Her free hand touched him lightly on the chest, twirling the hair around her fingers.

"This is a helluva time for a chat," Gordon said into the phone.

"I know," said Progano, "but I've been up all night thinking about this and I decided I had to talk to you."

The girl slipped her hand down across his chest, paused

to circle a finger around his navel, then continued down beneath the sheets.

"Could we meet now?" asked Progano.

"Now?" Gordon said, gasping as the girl's fingers encircled him.

She was enjoying his discomfort, almost giggling as she watched him.

"Now is out of the question," Gordon said.

"Later then," persisted Progano.

"Later?"

The girl was shaking her head. Gordon had promised to take her sailing today. She began stroking him gently.

"I'm not sure," Gordon said.

The girl picked up the pace of her stroke.

"Today is not a good day," Gordon said. "Why don't we meet tomorrow."

"This is important," Progano said. "Very important."

Gordon couldn't think straight. Between the headache and the grogginess and the girl's soft fingers he could not make a simple decision. When he looked at the girl she saw the confusion in his face. She ran her tongue playfully across her lips to help him decide.

"This is definitely not a good day," Gordon said. "Talk to me tomorrow."

For one fleeting moment Gordon thought he might be making a mistake. The old Gordon Hardwick, he thought, would have jumped out of bed and raced off to do his duty. He had left Carol in the middle of dinner, at parties, on vacations, and sometimes waiting in bed. Thinking about it only made his head hurt more. He was sure that this girl—whoever the hell she was—could make him feel better.

"But—" Progano began, but Hardwick was already hanging up the phone.

Progano sat for a few minutes, the dead phone still in his hand. At first he was stunned by Hardwick's reaction. This was a side of the usually serious and conscientious Hardwick he had not expected. Then he began to see it as somewhat humorous in an ironic sense. Here he was, trying to unburden himself, and no one would listen to his confession. Even the CIA, he thought, takes Sundays off.

But he had made his decision, he would not wait until tomorrow. He would talk to someone today.

Progano took the address book where Celia, in her neat,

meticulous hand, had written the names of their friends. He had added a few names in his scratchy, near-illegible scrawl. It was one of those names he looked for now.

Aleksei Karpenkov waited in his parked car off Mt. Eden Road in Stevens Creek County Park. The car was nose-in at a small parking area with a good clear view of the Stevens Creek Reservoir. He drummed his fingers on the steering wheel in what was for him an uncharacteristically nervous motion. He didn't like unexpected surprises and Jim Progano's call had certainly been unexpected. Karpenkov liked to think he could handle almost any unusual occurrence, but this one had been so completely unexpected it had rattled his usually phlegmatic demeanor.

Thinking quickly as always he had told Progano to meet him here, assuming correctly that the early hour would provide the necessary privacy. There was no time to visit his rented garage in San Bruno, where he kept another car and much of the paraphernalia he sometimes required. He rented the garage under an assumed name from an old couple who lived on Social Security and who, he was certain, did not report the income. He paid once a month by certified check and was sure that nothing could be traced back to him. But, ever cautious, he never went there at odd times or if he thought his visit might provoke undue attention.

He would have to make do with what he had available. As he checked the rearview mirror watching for Progano his hand touched the small case in which he had put the hypodermic syringe. He had estimated Progano's weight at around one hundred seventy-five pounds and hoped that the dosage he had selected would not be too strong. Too much of the succinylcholine chloride and Progano would drop dead of apparent heart failure. That, however, would certainly arouse suspicions. Progano was thin and in good physical health, and the circumstances of such a death would provoke investigation. Although succinylcholine chloride rapidly breaks down, once it enters the body, into succinic acid and choline—both of which are found in normal tissues—an excess of either in Progano's body would only add to the mysterious circumstances. Sooner or later someone would ask questions.

That wouldn't do. For Progano there would have to be another way. Then there was the problem of Progano's wife—

what was her name? No matter. He could take care of her later if he had to.

In the rearview mirror he saw a car pause and then pull into the parking area. It was Progano. Karpenkov took a deep breath and looked at his watch. It was ten past eight.

Karpenkov put the case in his jacket pocket and stepped out of his car. He waved as Progano pulled his four-door sedan alongside Karpenkov's two-door Chevy.

"Don't get out," Karpenkov said, opening the rear door of Progano's car and climbing in behind the driver's seat. "Now, what's all this about," he said before Progano could question his seat selection.

Progano watched him in the rearview mirror. "I have to tell someone what's been happening with the project," Progano said. "I can't keep it to myself anymore."

"I'm glad you called me."

"I called Hardwick first. I figured he was the logical person to talk to."

Karpenkov's voice was strained. "And?"

"He didn't even listen. Told me to see him tomorrow."

"But you told him what it was about?"

"I didn't get the chance. He hung up on me."

Karpenkov smiled. This was getting easier by the minute and his worst fears appeared groundless. He took the case from his pocket and removed the syringe. "If you've got a problem with the project, Jim, I want you to tell me about it." He depressed the plunger on the syringe until a small squirt of the drug appeared.

"It's hard to know where to begin," said Progano.

"Have you told your wife about it?"

Progano shook his head. "Not really. She knows I'm upset about something, but she doesn't know about what."

"But you told her you were coming to see me?"

"No. She was still sleeping. I told her I was going to call Hardwick, but when he wouldn't talk to me I thought of you."

Karpenkov almost laughed. It was all going to be so simple. "What time is it?" he asked, and when Progano looked away from the rearview to his watch, Karpenkov plunged the syringe through the shirt into the muscle between Progano's neck and right shoulder.

Progano jumped, more startled than hurt. "What the hell," he cried, his left hand clutching at the spot, but

Karpenkov had already withdrawn the hypodermic. "What was that?" Progano demanded, turning around in his seat.

Karpenkov sat back. "Just a little something to make you relax. You seem so tense."

Progano's eyes bulged in amazement. "You've got no right to do"—here his head bobbled slightly. He was already feeling the effects—"something like that."

He felt hot. "I think you'd better get out of my car," he said. "I'm leaving." He reached for his key in the ignition, missed it twice, and when he did find it he found he was unable to turn it.

"What have you done?" he attempted but it came out more like "Wovooda?"

Karpenkov opened the back door and stepped out of the car. He went to his own car, opened the trunk, threw in the small case and syringe, and removed a roll of tape and a short length of hose that he had cut from his swimming pool vacuum line. He returned to Progano's car and inserted the hose into the exhaust pipe, securing it with the tape. He snaked the hose under the car over to the passenger side and put the free end in through the back window.

Progano was slumped over the steering wheel, his jaw slack, his arms useless, twitching at his sides. His eyes were wide open.

Karpenkov climbed into the passenger seat beside him. "Let me tell you what's happening," he said in a conversational tone as he rolled up all the windows. "I've given you a dose of a synthetic muscle relaxant—not enough to kill you outright but enough so that in about twenty minutes you'd be unable to inflate your lungs enough to breathe."

Progano rolled his eyes wildly and tried to move but was unable to generate more than a weak flopping motion on his left side.

"Don't worry," said Karpenkov, "you don't have twenty minutes." He patted Progano's shoulder. "I'm told that this is not an unpleasant way to die."

Progano mumbled something as saliva began to drool down his chin. His head, too heavy for him to support, was flopped over, his chin on his chest.

Karpenkov locked all the three other doors and opened the one next to him, then reached past the slumping Progano and, left foot on the accelerator, started the car.

He stepped out, depressing the lock button. "I'm sorry

about this," he said matter-of-factly, "but in the long run it's really not very important."

Progano flopped over on his side twitching on the front seat like a beached fish, his eyes wide and staring, fixed on Karpenkov, pleading for mercy.

Karpenkov slammed the door shut, checking the doors and windows. As he walked away he noted that Progano's car was already filling with exhaust fumes.

Fourteen

Even though he had talked with Carol about it, K.C. was not prepared for his next meeting with Gordon.

"He's a different person," Carol had said, which led K.C. to expect some change, but he was totally unprepared for the complete transformation he found in his brother. In little more than a year Gordon seemed to have shrunk in size, his eyes were glazed and sunken, and his face drawn. But more than his appearance had changed. Gordon seemed subdued. He had lost his macho exuberance. It was as if every aspect of his being had been diminished.

"I'm fine," he assured his brother when K.C. expressed his concern. "This is what happens when you're on your own, cooking for yourself."

"I'm sure Carol—"

"I don't want to talk about her," Gordon snapped.

They rode the rest of the way from the airport in almost total silence.

After Carol and Gordon moved from Bethesda to California, K.C. had talked with them perhaps once a month. At first everything seemed fine and the Hardwicks appeared to be adjusting nicely to their new surroundings. Early conversations were filled with talk about the beautiful climate and how exciting San Francisco was. But gradually K.C. noticed that Carol seemed to lose her enthusiasm. Finally, about six months after they had arrived in California, K.C. asked his sister-in-law what was wrong.

"Gordon's drinking again," she said, but in a tone that let him know there was more.

"And?"

"That's it. He's been drinking . . . a lot."

"You've put up with that before," K.C. said. "There's something else you're not telling me."

Her voice was wavering and he could tell she was on the verge of tears. "He's found somebody else."

Carol was not one to exaggerate or to cry over nothing. K.C. knew the situation must be serious. "Is he there? Let me talk to him."

"He's not here. He left."

"That stupid bastard," K.C. said, his anger boiling over. "When is he going to grow up?"

"I thought we were past all this mid-life crisis," Carol said. "How many mid-life crises is one man supposed to have?"

"Tell him to call me when he gets in. I'll straighten him out."

But he couldn't. Gordon seemed hell-bent on destroying his marriage. K.C. flew out to talk with them both but merely managed to arrange a temporary truce.

After that the situation deteriorated rapidly. Gordon became more abusive and more blatant in his infidelities, as if determined to provoke a final confrontation. In the end Carol moved into her own apartment, and after a few months of waiting for some change in Gordon's attitude, she filed for a legal separation.

A few months later she called K.C. "I wanted you to be the first to know," she said. "I've found someone . . . we've been . . . going out for a month or so."

K.C.'s reactions were indescribable. He had always known that an attractive woman like Carol wouldn't be alone forever. He had even hoped that she wouldn't be. But now that she had found someone he felt that he too had lost her.

"That's wonderful," he said without conviction.

"You're upset," she said.

"No, I'm not. Don't be silly. I think it's great."

"I understand how you feel," she said. "I feel the same

way. For some crazy reason I keep thinking that I'm being unfaithful to Gordon—to you, too."

"Me?"

"You've been my little brother since you were fourteen years old," she said. "I've lost Gordon. I don't want to lose you too."

"Don't worry," he said. "Friends forever."

"You mean it?"

"No matter what."

"Thanks, K.C. I needed that."

"So is this thing serious, or what?"

"I don't know how serious it is, but right now we're at the steamy part of the relationship."

K.C. had a sudden flash—a vision of his sister-in-law in bed, naked with another man. He squeezed his eyes shut to block out the picture. "That's terrific," he said, trying to muster some enthusiasm. It wasn't easy. "Does Gordon know?"

She sighed into the phone. "I don't know how he found out, but he did. He called me last night—what you might call an obscene phone call. He accused me of screwing around behind his back. When I reminded him that we no longer were regarded as a couple he said I'd probably been screwing around for years."

K.C. didn't know what to say. "I'm sorry," he offered helplessly.

"Have you talked to him lately?"

"Not for months."

"He needs some help, K.C.—I mean psychiatric help."

K.C. did not want to admit that to himself. "He seems to be functioning fairly well otherwise," he said. "He's still on the job, isn't he?"

"Nothing interferes with Gordon's work. Not even severe mental disturbance. I've talked with people at TMK who think I'm the crazy one. He seems perfectly normal to them. But I'm telling you, K.C., something is seriously wrong with him. He needs help."

"I wish I could do something. He hardly talks to me anymore."

"Can you come out—talk to him?"

K.C. smiled. This was typical Carol. Gordon had hurt her and humiliated her. She had left him but she still cared about him. "It was going to be a surprise, but I'm interviewing at Stanford, first week in June. I'll be there for a few days."

Carol's spirits soared. "You mean you might move out here?"

"Well, I've been asked to do the visiting-professor bit for a year. If it works out, it could become permanent."

"That's great. You'll love it out here."

"That's what they all say." He was thinking about what had happened to Carol and Gordon.

Now, driving with Gordon to his new apartment, K.C. could see what Carol meant. Anyone who hadn't known Gordon Hardwick before would not have noticed anything out of the ordinary, but to K.C. he seemed a different person. He was not the crazy man that Carol had led him to believe, he didn't rant and rave or seem paranoid. He just seemed . . . different.

They arrived and Gordon, always the big brother, grabbed the biggest bag and carried it up the stairs. "Hope you don't mind sleeping on the couch," he said, " 'cause that's all there is."

K.C. looked around the apartment. It was small, with one bedroom and a combination kitchen, living and dining room.

"Never thought I'd be living in a bachelor apartment at this stage," Gordon said with what K.C. thought was a tinge of sadness.

K.C. resisted the temptation to say what he felt like saying. "It's nice," he said instead.

"You hungry?" Gordon asked.

"I ate on the plane."

"Drink?"

"Sure. A light one."

Gordon went to the kitchen and K.C. watched his brother make him a Scotch and water. It would be too strong, he knew. It always was. He watched Gordon make his own drink—a few ice cubes in a glass filled with vodka.

Before coming back with the drinks, Gordon took a long drink from his glass and refilled it. K.C. looked away. He couldn't bring himself to watch.

"How's the job going?" he asked when Gordon returned.

Gordon rolled his eyes to the ceiling. "Bo-o-oring." He took a good long slug on his vodka. "Baby-sitting computer scientists is not my favorite thing."

111

"I thought you liked it."

"I liked establishing the security procedures which were practically nonexistent when I got here. Anybody—you, the Russians, the Queen Mother—could've walked out of there with the latest technological development in a lunch bag."

"But not anymore."

"Damn straight. If Russians are going to get secrets out of TMK they're going to have to come up with a new method."

K.C. raised his glass in mock salute. "Gordon Hardwick, fighting for truth, justice, and the American way, once again does battle with the evil Tartar hordes." He meant it to be funny. He saw immediately that that was a mistake.

Gordon's jaw was clenched, his face turning red as if he had stopped breathing. "You never did think much of what I do."

"That's not true, Gordie. I only—"

"You and your goddamn pinko academic friends think this world would be just fine if people like me didn't go around looking for trouble. If we'd just stop pestering those poor, innocent Russians."

K.C. sighed. They had had this argument many times. "That's not true, Gordon. I just think that if we're going to live together in this world, we're going to have to start trusting each other."

Gordon laughed loudly. "Trust the Russians?" he asked.

K.C. sipped his drink. The Scotch bit at his throat.

Gordon drained his glass and started to get up as if to get another, then slumped back down into his chair. "This whole valley," he said waving his arms as if to encompass the room, "is loaded with the most technologically sophisticated computer equipment on the face of the earth. You—of all people—should know that."

K.C. nodded.

"We've got billions of dollars' worth of research and man-hours devoted to this one small square of the country. From an economic and military viewpoint this may be the most important piece of real estate on the face of the earth. What is done here may decide what America will be like in the next century—or if there will *be* an America in the next century."

"It's important, Gordon. But let's not exaggerate."

Gordon's face was impassive. He got up, went to the kitchen, and came back with a full glass. "Right now the Soviet

112

consulate in San Francisco is staffed with three times as many people as are required to accomplish its normal business. The excess over the required number is composed primarily of KGB agents whose business it is to acquire technological information from any and every source. Anything that's missing in the Valley, you can be sure they have a hand in."

"So some disgruntled programmer sells his company's wares to a competitor or to the Japanese, and you blame the Russians. Very convenient."

Gordon shook his head sadly. "You'll never see how important this is. You'll never change."

K.C. smiled and mimicked his brother's headshake. "Neither of us will ever change, Gordie. You've always had a passion for secrecy that I don't share."

"Some things have to be kept secret. In a free and open society it is very difficult to keep anything secret, and the Russians take advantage of that fact. But if we're to survive, there are some things we must keep secret."

"It always comes back to 'Reds under the bed,' Gordie."

Gordon's face was grim. "Under rocks," he said. "Turn over a rock and what do you find?"

K.C. didn't answer. Instead he fought for a way to change the subject. "Can we get some golf in tomorrow?"

Gordon ignored his question. "Right now," he said, his face deadly serious, his eyes boring into his brother, "the Russians are mounting a massive campaign to steal what may be the most important computer ever created. Quite simply, we can't allow them to do it."

"Professor Kincaid's new super computer?"

"Exactly. The Prometheus II will guide the most important weapons system ever developed. It would be a disaster if the Russians ever acquired that capability."

K.C. put his glass on the table in front of him. He had avidly followed any news of Kincaid's progress in this area. "A lot of people think that it's a disaster that it was ever conceived in the first place."

"People like that don't count."

K.C. sighed. There was little else to say.

Gordon surprised him by abruptly changing the subject. "Will you see Carol while you're here?"

"Yes," said his brother carefully.

"Did you know she's found herself a boyfriend?"

"She told me."

113

"Big shot with TMK and with the parent company, Ameronics."

K.C. raised an eyebrow. "She didn't tell me that."

"Yeah. Reid Lawson, Vice-president in charge of marketing in the computer division." Gordon drained his drink. "She's sleeping with him."

"Gordon," K.C. began, but his brother went on as if he were talking to himself. "I followed them to Carol's about a month ago. He never came out."

"Carol's a big girl, Gordon. She's got a right to build a new life for herself."

"I've been thinking of putting a wire in her bedroom—just to get positive proof." He looked down at the carpet. "But I don't think I could stand to listen to it."

"Don't do that, Gordie. That would be"—he was going to say "crazy" but decided not to—"foolish."

Gordon looked up. "Foolish," he mumbled. "You're right, little brother. As usual, you're right." He stood up on wobbly legs. " 'Nother drink?"

"I'm fine thanks." K.C. watched his brother weave his way to the kitchen. Gordon wasn't holding his liquor as well as he used to, he thought. He tried desperately to find a topic of conversation without emotional mine fields. "Hey," he said. "I see that the Giants and the Mets are at Candlestick this weekend. How about Sunday? We'll get a couple of box seats and do the old ballgame routine."

Gordon paused in mid-pour. A smile of remembrance slid across his face. "I haven't been to a ballgame in years," he said. His eyes took on a faraway look. "Remember that time we went to the Stadium after Munson's funeral? And Murcer hit the home run to win the game?"

K.C. nodded. It had been a home run earlier and a base hit in the ninth that had won the game, but he wasn't about to contradict Gordon's memory.

"That was something, wasn't it? When was that anyway? Seventy-eight? Seventy-nine?"

"Seventy-nine, I think."

Gordon shook his head. "That's almost ten years. Where the hell did it go?" He looked into his glass as if the answer lay there.

"So what about Sunday?" K.C. asked.

Gordon's head snapped up as he was yanked from his reverie. "Can't make it. I won't be here."

"Won't be here? What does that mean?"

Gordon laughed. "Just what I said—I won't be here."

"So where will you be?"

The laughter died and the smile slipped from Gordon's face. It was as if a visor had dropped over his face. "I've been called back to Washington. Agency business. I'm leaving Saturday afternoon."

K.C.'s first thought was that Gordon was being replaced. The thought showed in his worried expression.

Gordon misunderstood. "I'm sorry," he said. "I know you were counting on us spending some time together, but something has come up quite suddenly and I've been called back to help out."

"How long will you be gone?"

Gordon shrugged. "A week, maybe two."

"I'll be back East next week. Maybe we can get together then."

"If I'm on the job, I won't be seeing anybody. If I'm not, I'll be back here." He seemed genuinely apologetic. "I'm sorry."

"That's okay," said K.C., feeling very much the kid brother. "Just bad timing on my part."

There was a long embarrassed silence as the two brothers groped to bridge the distance between them.

Gordon was the first to look away. He jiggled the ice in his glass. "Sure you won't have another?"

"No. No thanks."

Neither had very much else to say.

Fifteen

Friday

As soon as Gordon left for work the next morning, K.C. called Carol.

"I'm dying to see you," she said, her voice filled with

115

excitement. "I'll make you a nice dinner tonight"—she hesitated—"unless you have plans with Gordon."

He laughed. "Gordon leaves for Washington tomorrow. He'll be gone the entire time I'm here. But I'm having dinner with some Stanford people tonight. We can have dinner tomorrow night."

"Okay."

He could sense the disappointment in her voice. "What about this new boyfriend of yours? Do I get to meet him?"

"Reid? He's off on business. Won't be back till next week sometime."

"That's too bad. I was intending to give him the full inspection. Find out if his intentions are honorable and all that."

"I think you'll like him, K.C."

"Gordon tells me he's a big shot at TMK."

"Actually he's a vice-president of the parent company, Ameronics. He's running TMK temporarily until they find someone for the job."

"Sounds pretty important."

"Lots of responsibility, I guess. You know, it's funny. He's away as much as Gordon used to be. No matter who I'm with, I seem to spend most of my time waiting for him to come home." There was a pause and then she said, "How is Gordon?"

"He seems okay. Maybe he's getting better. I don't know. You were right. There is something wrong but . . . maybe it's not too bad. I hope so anyway."

"I hope so too."

The silence hung between them, but just before it reached unbridgeable length, Carol, her voice filled with enthusiasm, said, "Hey! I got a job."

"Terrific."

"Well it's only part-time. For now anyway. I'm working for a local newspaper here in Menlo Park. I do feature articles about cultural activities in the area. I'm enjoying it. I always wanted to do something like this."

"Sounds great."

"What time is your interview this morning?"

"Ten o'clock. It's not an interview really. It's more like a get-together . . . or something."

"Look," she said, "I'm having lunch today in Menlo

116

Park. The restaurant isn't ten minutes from Stanford. Why don't you meet me for lunch?"

"I'm not sure what time I'll be through."

"I'll give you the address. If you can make it—great. But try to make it. I'm having lunch with a friend—a girl I work with."

"I don't want to intrude."

"Don't be silly. Besides I think you'll like her."

"What makes you say that?"

"She looks like me when I was twenty-five."

"You still look twenty-five to me."

"I wish," she said. Her voice took on a sad, pleading sound. "Promise you'll try to make it."

"You're not going to try to fix me up with one of your lonely ladies, are you?" Carol's longtime project had been to find the right woman for her brother-in-law.

"No. I like her—I think she's gorgeous. I like you—I think you're gorgeous. I just think it would be nice if you two got to meet."

"If she's so beautiful how come she has to get fixed up?"

"She doesn't." Carol laughed. "You're the one who has to get fixed up."

"I do all right," he said sheepishly.

"Sure, like that one in New York a few years ago. Melanie? What was she, twelve?"

"She was twenty. But I was only twenty-five myself. You act as if I was cradle-robbing."

They were both laughing. This mock argument was the continuation of a long-standing joke between them. Carol, always anxious to find someone for K.C., was never happy with the women he found for himself. She enjoyed the role of "big sister" and was always ready to pass judgment on K.C.'s selections. They were always "too young" . . . "too dumb" . . . or as a last resort, "not good enough" for him.

"Let's not worry about the mistakes of the past," she said, enjoying herself again, "just say you'll meet me today for lunch."

"I'll try," he said, and when she didn't answer he added, "I promise—I'll try to be there."

It was after one o'clock before K.C. was able to get away from Stanford and head into downtown Menlo Park to meet Carol. He parked his rented car, and following Carol's directions, arrived at the restaurant. He paused outside, fighting the urge to peek through the window to see if Carol was still inside.

The restaurant was typical California—brightly lit and cheerfully decorated with touches of greenery everywhere. K.C. stepped inside and, feeling somehow foolish, looked around at a sea of strangers' faces.

Carol, who sat facing the door, spotted him first and raised her arm in a brief wave. K.C.'s face broke into a smile of recognition as he made his way to her table. He could not help but notice the young woman who sat with Carol. His sister-in-law had been right—she was stunning.

Carol jumped up into his arms. "You made it," she said, hugging him. "It's so good to see you."

"Good to see you," K.C. said, feeling embarrassed to be conducting his reunion in so public a place.

"This is my friend, Diane Rollins," Carol said. "And this is my brother-in-law, K.C. Hardwick."

Diane offered her hand and a brief nod of welcome as K.C. sat down.

"I'm sorry I couldn't get here any sooner," he said. He looked at the plates in front of them. "I'm glad you didn't wait for me."

Carol was apologetic. "Diane has to get back to work."

"That's okay. I'm not really hungry anyway," he lied. "I'll just have coffee."

"You can share my spinach salad," Carol said. "It's really too much for me."

K.C. made a face. "Spinach salad? No thanks. That sounds too much like health food to me."

He meant to be funny, but Diane looked at her own salad and then at him as if she were inspecting overripe fruit.

He smiled apologetically. "I only meant that . . ." His voice trailed off as Diane returned to her salad.

Carol jumped to the rescue. "Diane does free-lance journalism. That's how we met. She did a few articles for my paper."

No one said anything. "She's very good," added Carol.

Diane looked up from her salad with a small, appreciative smile at Carol. Then, as if deciding to make an additional effort at friendliness, she turned to K.C. with a smile. "Carol tells me you're a college professor. Computers or something."

"Yes. Computers. Maybe you'd like to do an article about me."

The smile faded. "Everybody is into computers out here. The subject has been completely overdone. I couldn't sell an article on computers in a million years—unless you were a paraplegic or something."

"I could throw myself in front of a bus and see what happens."

Again, Carol stepped in. "Diane is trying to get into television work."

Diane gave an almost derisive snort. "I haven't quite given up yet. I have an interview with KLFA in San Francisco tomorrow. Maybe I'll get lucky." She was talking exclusively to Carol. K.C. felt left out. "Trouble is," she said, "all the token female jobs are taken. Now they're looking for talent, good looks, *and* experience."

As she talked, K.C. watched her. Her dark hair was pulled away from her face, revealing high cheekbones and expressive eyes. She talked with her hands—pointing, motioning, touching—and K.C. realized that everything about her was animated. Even sitting, she seemed to be in motion.

She and Carol were talking about exercise while K.C. sat, not paying much attention to what they were saying, but watching Diane closely. It gave him pleasure to look at her.

"What do you do?" she asked, and K.C. realized with a start that she was talking to him.

"Pardon?"

"To stay in shape."

He shrugged embarrassedly. "Not much."

"Do you run?"

"No."

"Tennis?"

"No."

"You must do something."

Carol was watching him with what he thought must be helpless discomfort. Here he was, a poor creature who liked neither spinach nor exercise. "I play a little golf," he said.

"Golf? That's not exercise."

"I play some softball in the summer," he said, wondering why he was defending himself. "We have a league that plays in the park."

"You should start running," she said, apparently discounting softball as exercise.

"I'll start tomorrow," he said. "Right after I have my morning salad."

Carol was wearing herself out with rescue attempts. "It's just that Diane is such a nut when it comes to fitness. We work out together in the gym."

"Sweat is such a turn-on," said K.C. sarcastically. "Do you guys lift weights too?"

There was a long pause during which the three of them had a hard time looking at each other.

Diane stood up. "I'll be right back," she said. She took her pocketbook and headed for the ladies' room.

"Probably going to put on her roller skates," said K.C. while she was still dangerously close.

"What's happening here?" Carol whispered. "How could you pick a fight?"

"Me? I didn't say anything. She started in on me like I was a ninety-eight-pound weakling or something."

"You know how people are in California. They're into health foods and exercise."

"And I'm from New York. We're into pastrami and arguing with cabdrivers."

Carol shook her head. "You *could* use a little tightening up, K.C."

"Christ."

Carol put her hand on his arm. "I'm sorry," she said, laughing. "Maybe I've been in California too long."

They were both laughing by the time Diane came back. She did not sit down. "I've got to run." She put some money on the table. "It was nice to meet you," she said to K.C. without actually looking at him. "Have a nice trip back to New York." She put a hand on Carol's shoulder. "I'll call you tomorrow." With a few quick confident strides she was gone.

K.C. watched her go, shaking his head in a mixture of admiration and bewilderment. "I feel like I've been run over by a truck."

Carol's disappointment was visible. "I really thought you two would hit it off famously. It just shows how wrong you can be."

K.C.'s eyes were still fixed on the exit. "You were right about one thing."

"What's that?"

"She is gorgeous."

Carol's face brightened and she reached into her pocketbook. "I wrote down her number for you, thinking that you two would fall into each other's arms."

"If we fell into each other's arms, she'd probably knock me over."

"Maybe it's still worth a try."

He laughed. "You must think I'm a glutton for punishment. It'll be a cold day in Southern California before I call that girl."

But he took the number anyway.

Sixteen

Gordon was at his desk in the security office at TMK. The office was small and cramped but had several large windows that afforded a good view of the courtyard. Lately Gordon had spent a lot of his time staring absently into the courtyard, admiring the foliage. His usually meticulous habits and record-keeping had deteriorated, and his desk was strewn with papers. Even his thought process—normally concise and rational—seemed as disordered as his desk. Although he would admit it to no one, Gordon Hardwick was confused and sometimes frightened by the disturbing things that had happened to him. He was glad to be getting away for a while and hoped that a change of scene would arrest this growing sense of bewilderment.

It was Friday afternoon and Gordon was attempting to clear up some unfinished business when Bill Donovan entered.

"Leaving today?" Donovan asked.

"No," said Gordon absently. "Tomorrow afternoon. I've still got a few things to clear up at this end."

"Don't worry. The place will still be here when you get back."

Gordon mumbled something and went back to his work. "Something you wanted, Bill?" he asked.

Without a word, Donovan placed a computer printout sheet on Gordon's desk. Gordon looked up at him puzzled and Donovan said, "I think you'd better take a look at this."

Gordon picked up the sheet, turned it right side up and took a quick look. "What is it?"

"This is the red-flag sheet from the personnel location computer."

Gordon's eyes widened with renewed interest as he stood up, the sheet in his hand.

The personnel location computer tracked the movements of everyone in the building. If anyone gained or tried to gain entry to a restricted area the computer recorded the number of that person's I.D. card. If that person was not allowed access an alarm was triggered, and if a person who was cleared for access overused that clearance the computer "red-flagged" his number and notified Security.

"This might be nothing, but the computer just red-flagged one of the programmers in the research department."

Gordon looked at the printout. "Jerry Greenwood," he said.

"Yes," said Donovan. "He's the junior man in the department, so he gets to pick up and deliver the documents. He has a 'priority clearance' so he's okay to enter the classified documents section . . ."

"But?" Gordon asked, interrupting him before he could finish.

"*But* his frequency of visits has jumped from once a day to"—he looked at the sheet, reading upside down—"as much as three times in one day."

"Maybe he's got reason," said Gordon.

"Maybe," Donovan said.

Both men grinned without humor and said in unison, "But maybe not."

Gordon picked up his phone and dialed. "Ron," he said, "Gordon Hardwick here. I'd like to take a look at this week's tapes if I could." He listened. "Right now," he said. "I'll be down in two minutes."

He hung up the phone and looked at Donovan. "Let's go."

They went to the lower level and there, in the back room of the security office, Ron Pace was waiting for them.

Pace was young and blond and wore a neatly pressed uniform. He seemed eager to please. "Monday's tapes are already in the machines and ready to go," he said. He tapped a cardboard box with that week's dates printed on the side. "The rest, except of course for today's, are in here."

Donovan and Gordon sat down in large chairs facing four twenty-five-inch television monitors that were hooked up to four video recorders.

"Okay," said Ron Pace. "Where do you want to start?"

Gordon looked at the printout sheet in his hand and read the record of Jerry Greenwood's visits to the documents area. "Let's start with o-nine-fifty."

Pace sat at a console and punched in the time on a computer keyboard, then pressed a single button and all four machines began to whir as the tape raced forward to 9:50 A.M. on Monday. Simultaneously all stopped and the four screens sprang to life. What was shown was the documents room from four different angles. It was large and well lit. The long rows of filing cabinets which might have formed a barrier to a single camera were no obstacle to the four.

At the bottom of the screen the time of the taping was seen in a blinking digital readout. Gordon noted that the left monitor was six seconds behind the others. Pace made a quick adjustment at his keyboard and all four were in synch before Gordon could comment.

"He should be appearing anytime now," said Pace as the digital readout reached 9:50.

Jerry Greenwood appeared. He was short and slim and sported a bushy mustache. He wore a white short-sleeved shirt open at the collar.

The three security men watched the monitors as Jerry Greenwood walked slowly down the aisles.

"What's he supposed to be doing?" Gordon asked.

Donovan looked at the printout sheet. "Returning some documents from Research."

"Let me see that," Hardwick said. Donovan handed him the sheet. Hardwick looked at the list. "Returning F file documents." He looked back at the screen. "If he's going to F file he's taking the long way."

Jerry Greenwood wandered down the aisles as if he were on a shopping expedition. Finally he reached the section marked F, opened a file drawer and inserted the folder he had in his hand. This accomplished, he left quickly.

"Nothing there," suggested Donovan.

"Next item," said Gordon.

Ron Pace punched the time on the keyboard and the tape whirred forward to the designated spot. Once again the same scene appeared and soon Jerry Greenwood made his appearance. He repeated his meandering path down the aisles, then deposited his folder in the drawer and kept going.

"Next item."

And so it went. For the better part of an hour they watched Jerry Greenwood pick up files and drop them off. Although vaguely suspicious his movements were not much out of the ordinary.

When they had finished, the three looked at each other. Donovan spoke first. "Nothing out of order, I guess. He seemed to be wandering around a lot, but he didn't do anything unusual."

Gordon looked to Ron Pace, who shrugged. "I can't figure out what he's up to—or if he's up to anything."

Gordon looked down at the sheet in his lap. "Try this on for size. He makes an average of four trips per week to the documents room. This week he's made thirteen trips so far."

Both listeners nodded.

Gordon went on, "He's picked up files four times and dropped off files nine times. What does that mean?"

Ron Pace spoke. "He's spreading out his visits to the documents room so that he can get in there more often."

Gordon smiled. "Why?"

"He's casing the joint," said Donovan, then smiled at his antiquated police reference.

"It would seem so," Gordon said.

"And more than that, he's getting everybody used to the fact that he's in and out of there a lot," said Donovan.

"Familiarity breeds inattentiveness," said Gordon. "He's up to something."

The phone rang and Pace answered. He made a face, then said, "Okay, we'll take a look." He hung up and turned to Gordon and Donovan. "That was Security. Jerry Greenwood has just gone into the documents area again."

"Let's see," Gordon said. Pace punched in the correct numbers and a live picture appeared on the screens.

Greenwood appeared, carrying several file folders. Casually he walked down the aisles in full view of the cameras. He stopped in front of a file cabinet, opened the top drawer, leafed through the row of files until he found the appropriate spot, then inserted one of the folders into the stack. He moved on to another cabinet and did the same with a second folder. Moved on again and repeated the process with the third and last. Empty-handed, he walked toward the exit. They watched him sign out and leave the area.

"Nothing," said Donovan.

Pace shook his head. "I can't tell what he's up to."

Gordon was silent for a few moments. "Run the tape back to where he enters the documents area," he said, tension in his voice.

Pace went to the tape machine and ran the tape backward to the spot where Greenwood had first appeared at the control desk. They watched him approach, talk with the man at the desk, laugh at something the guard said, sign in and walk into the documents area.

"Stop," said Gordon. "That's it."

"What's it?" said Donovan.

"He never showed the files. He just signed in and went in."

"But how does he get anything out? He's taking documents back."

Gordon smiled. "He already has it out—we don't know if he's bringing it back." He turned to Pace. "Check the sign-in log. I want to know exactly what files he was returning, and I want them checked to see if everything is there."

"Will do," said Pace as he moved to the door.

Donovan made a fist and punched it into his other palm. "The guard is supposed to check the incoming files," he said.

"Familiarity breeds inattentiveness," Gordon repeated. "Greenwood's become a regular down there."

"Okay," Donovan said. "So he gets some of the files out, how does he get them back?"

"Takes the same file out and replaces the documents. Or maybe next time he goes back to the documents room he drops a file on the floor and puts the stolen one back. As long as he gets it back before someone else asks for it he's safe."

"Look," said Donovan and they watched Pace appear on the screen. He was talking to the guard at the desk. Together they went to the file area and began to pull out the files that Greenwood had replaced.

"Even if he does get papers this way, how can he get them out of the building? We have sensors at every exit. The papers are treated to set off an alarm."

Gordon was watching the screen. "We'll figure that out when the time comes." He watched Pace. "He's got something."

Pace was holding up a file and pointing to it as he faced the camera. They watched him take all three files and leave the area.

Donovan paced nervously until Pace returned, while Gordon sat quietly, lost in thought and seemingly unperturbed.

Pace burst into the room, holding out the three folders. "Something's missing from each one," he said.

"You sure?" asked Donovan.

Pace nodded, looking at Gordon. "All the enclosures are numbered consecutively. There are gaps in the numbers in each file."

"Son-of-a-bitch," said Donovan, moving to the door. "Let's grab him right now."

"Let's wait until quitting time. I want to know how he's going to get this stuff out of the building. In the meantime check every file he's touched in the past two weeks."

At 4:00 P.M., when all briefcases were turned in to Security, Jerry Greenwood's was inspected carefully. There was nothing out of the ordinary in the case.

Gordon picked up the case and examined it. "Take everything out," he said.

The case was emptied.

Gordon took the case and felt the weight of it.

The security men looked at each other skeptically.

"Take it apart."

One of the guards looked on in disbelief. "That's a real expensive briefcase, Mr. Hardwick."

Hardwick smiled. "If I'm wrong I'll buy the young man a new one."

Donovan opened the case and began ripping out the lining in the lower section of the case. He stopped. "What have we here?"

Everyone moved closer.

"Some kind of metal shield," said Donovan as he peeled back a section of what looked like aluminum foil that had lost its luster. The foil was removed and peeled apart to reveal four pages of documents marked "Classified."

"Lead," said Gordon. "A thin sheet of lead on either side of the documents to beat the sensors at the door. With this he could bring items in and out at will."

126

"Pretty interesting," said Donovan. "Where do you get something like this?"

"I've got a pretty good idea," answered Gordon. "But let's get Mr. Greenwood in here and find out who he says he's working for."

Two armed guards were dispatched to Jerry Greenwood's work section with instructions to use force if he resisted. He did not, and five minutes later he was seated across from Gordon's desk in the security office. Bill Donovan, with his hands in his pockets as if to control the urge to grab Greenwood, stood by the door.

Gordon opened the briefcase and wordlessly shoved it toward Greenwood, who looked at it once and then back at Hardwick. "You caught me," he said disdainfully.

"Yes we did," said Gordon, "and we'd like to know who you're working for."

Greenwood looked around the room. He did not speak.

"It'll go easier for you if you cooperate with us," said Gordon.

Greenwood laughed. "C'mon, who are you kidding? This is no big deal. It happens all the time."

"Oh," said Gordon, his face without expression, "does it?"

"Yeah. One company wants to know what another company is up to so they pay some underpaid flunky a few bucks to find out for them."

"Which company are we talking about?"

Jerry Greenwood's eyes clouded over. "I don't know."

"You don't know?"

"No—that's the truth. I was contacted by someone who explained the deal to me. Said there'd be a few thousand dollars in it for me if I could bring some classified documents out for them to examine."

"Any particular documents?"

"No. They just wanted classified documents. A selection from different files." Greenwood leaned forward. "If you'll look at them carefully you'll see that I picked from the lowest classified, least sensitive documents in the file. These aren't worth anything."

"Is that right?"

"Yeah. This is nickel-and-dime stuff."

"Maybe, but you've bought yourself more than a dime's worth of trouble."

"C'mon, Hardwick. Don't be such a hardass. This is no big deal. If I'd wanted to I could've gone for the really big stuff."

Gordon tried to keep the disgust from his face. "Tell me how you would do it," he said. "Get out the 'big stuff,' I mean."

"Same way. I'd take the files from the documents area and when I was scheduled to return them I'd slip one or two papers out of the folder and put them in my briefcase. I'd take them out and copy them on the outside, then bring them back the next day. The next time I went for that file I'd replace the missing papers before I delivered them." He smiled. "Simple."

"Real simple," said Gordon. He wasn't smiling. "When are you supposed to meet your contact?"

"After work. I'm supposed to make copies and meet at Coyote Point Park to make the exchange."

"And you don't know the man you're supposed to meet?"

"I only met him once. That was when he gave me the briefcase."

"He gave it to you?"

"Yes. He even told me how to beat the security system."

"He told you?"

Greenwood nodded. "He seemed to know more about the security system than I did." Greenwood looked admiringly at the leather briefcase. "Real nice case, huh?"

"Real nice," said Gordon. "Now here's what you're going to do. You're going to meet with your contact and we're going to be following you when you do."

"Why should I cooperate with you?"

"Because if you don't I'm going to see that you get ten years in prison."

"For this stuff? It's not worth ninety days."

"Espionage at a top-secret installation where high-priority government research is going on is not a ninety-day offense, Mr. Greenwood."

"But the documents are worthless."

"How do we know that this wasn't just a test run? How do we know that next time you didn't intend to walk off with some really big stuff? How do we know that *last* time you didn't walk off with a million dollars' worth of research material?"

"But—but," sputtered Greenwood, "I didn't."

"I don't know that. The government doesn't know that and the judge who sentences you won't know that. I'd say you're looking at ten to fifteen years for espionage."

"And if I help?"

"If in fact these documents are as unimportant as you say, we'll corroborate your story."

Greenwood sank back in his chair. "What do you want me to do?"

"Lead us to your contact."

Greenwood did just as he was told. Under surveillance by the FBI and the CIA, he followed the prescribed routine for meeting his contact. He sat on a bench in Coyote Point Park for over three hours. No one ever showed up.

Later, after Greenwood had been turned over to the police for arraignment, Donovan and Hardwick drove back to TMK.

"What do you think happened?" asked Donovan.

"Whoever it was was either tipped off or Greenwood somehow broke the usual routine."

"Maybe the contact was watching the plant and when Greenwood didn't come out at his regular time he figured that something was wrong."

"Maybe," said Gordon.

"Do you think Greenwood tipped him off somehow?"

"I doubt it. I think he was scared shitless."

"You know what I don't understand?" said Donovan.

"What's that?"

"Why would anyone go to such trouble to steal the kind of documents that the kid took? I mean, the computer boys said they were practically worthless. And Greenwood said his contact didn't seem to care what they were, just so long as it was a fair sampling." He shook his head, mystified.

"It's a test," said Gordon.

"What?"

"A test. Someone is testing our security system. They just wanted to see if they could do it easily and now they know they can't. Somebody's after something and they'll try again, but next time they'll be more sophisticated."

"What the hell are they after?"

Gordon shrugged, "What's the biggest project going at TMK?"

"Prometheus II?"

"If I was going to steal something, that's what I'd steal."

129

They drove the rest of the way in silence, both men disturbed by the enormity of what Gordon had said. Donovan sat brooding, staring out the window as the landscape rushed by, his thoughts filled with arrest and capture and accolades.

Gordon was just as silent—only his thoughts were filled with devastation and disaster.

Seventeen

Friday

Viktor Rozanov was the special assistant to the first secretary of the Soviet mission to the United Nations. His office, large, bright, and cheerful, was on the thirty-fifth floor of the Secretariat Building and commanded a magnificent view of midtown Manhattan. For all intents and purposes Rozanov, small and dark and constantly smiling, was the soul of Russian diplomacy. In actuality he was the KGB *rezident* at the United Nations with full responsibility for all Soviet "illegals" in the eastern part of the United States. Rozanov was a colonel in the KGB's Directorate S—the Illegals Directorate—and like most supervisory personnel in S he himself had once lived as an illegal in the United States.

Rozanov listed each of his illegals by a code name in a notebook that he kept in his office safe. He rarely contacted any of these illegals, maintaining contact with them only through coded messages that were sent to his office.

Rozanov's stable consisted of twenty-five illegals who lived in the Northeastern sector of the United States—New York, New Jersey, Pennsylvania, and New England. The duty of an illegal was to insinuate his or her way into the fabric of American society, hopefully by gaining employment in some sensitive position. Most illegals never reported anything of any real value to Rozanov. Only occasionally did any of their reports contain anything significant, but it was comforting to know that there were people out there who were part of the home team.

Most of the people who met Rozanov at diplomatic meetings or at the endless rounds of cocktail parties attended by UN personnel found him charming and gracious. His quick wit and booming laugh made him popular with the gentlemen and his dark, brooding good looks—bushy eyebrows over dark, penetrating eyes—made him extremely popular with the ladies. What most of these people did not know was that Rozanov had been personally responsible for the deaths of more than a dozen enemies of the Soviet Union—two of whom he had killed with his bare hands.

This morning Rozanov was puzzled by the latest coded communiqué from Moscow Center. After decoding the message which had been delivered by courier that morning—Center had too much experience with intercepting transmitted messages ever to attempt sending them to Rozanov or others like him by any method other than personal delivery—he found that he was instructed to make personal contact with an illegal now in his jurisdictional area. What puzzled Rozanov was the fact that he had absolutely no knowledge of the existence of this illegal.

Normally this fact would not have disturbed him. The KGB's operations were so compartmentalized that the left hand rarely knew what the right hand was doing. The fragmentation of responsibilities had obvious benefits. If the Americans were somehow—by one method or another—able to gain access to a *resident*'s files or even if a *resident* defected, the only loss would be that particular man's stable. All others would remain operative.

Rozanov was, of course, well aware that there were several other *residents* in the United States with stables as large as or even larger than his. It was rumored that the San Francisco *resident* near the strategically important Silicon Valley had more than forty illegals under his jurisdiction.

What was not normal, however, was the method of contact. Usually if an illegal moved into his jurisdictional area, even temporarily, he would be given a full background briefing of the man and his activities. With this one he had been given nothing—only a terse order to establish contact.

He thought about it and realized that there was only one other possibility. This particular illegal did not come under the jurisdiction of the Illegals Directorate and that meant Department 8.

Other than his own Directorate S, only Department 8 controlled its own illegals. Because of the very special nature of Department 8 these illegals, unlike Rozanov's quiet stable of eavesdroppers and informants, were very special. It was the illegals of Department 8 who were responsible for all assassinations, political murders, and sabotage—the activities the KGB calls *mokrie dela*, "wet affairs."

Department 8 was first organized as the Administration of Special Tasks, a subgroup of the forerunner to the KGB, the NKVD. With the reorganization of the state security services in the early 1950's, this Special Tasks group became Department 13 of Line F in the newly formed Komitet Gosudarstvennoy Bezopasnosti. Then with the further reorganization of the KGB in 1969, Department 13 became Department V of the First Chief Directorate, KGB. Finally, in the 1970's, Department V became Department 8 of Directorate S.

There were many who felt that the name "Department 13," with its mysterious and somewhat satanic implications, was considerably more appropriate to the department's activities than the current appellation.

In recent years, in order to present a better face to the world, the KGB had attempted to distance itself from such violent activities by using the security forces of its communist satellites to perform *mokrie dela*. After the near-disastrous involvement of the Bulgarians in the attempted assassination of the Pope and the implication of the KGB in the plot, however, the KGB had concluded that it was preferable to conduct such affairs as "in-house" operations.

Rozanov did not appreciate being reduced to the role of messenger but there was little he could do about it. One did not involve oneself with or protest too vigorously the operations of Department 8.

The communiqué instructed him to contact and deliver a message to this person. The directions were clear. He was to make contact by telephone between eleven and eleven-thirty P.M. on the day he received the message and establish a time and place for a meeting on the following day. Rozanov was given a telephone number, an identification code with which to establish contact, and a sealed envelope which he was instructed to pass along unopened to this illegal. He was further ordered to withdraw twenty thousand dollars from his diplomatic account—a KGB authorization was included—and give this amount to the illegal at the meeting.

Rozanov slammed his palm on his desktop. He did not like being treated as an errand boy. Furthermore, he did not like the fact that an agent was in his territory but apparently beyond his jurisdiction. He sat back in his chair, holding the sealed envelope. It was thin and could not have contained much more than a single sheet of paper and a blank which would prevent inspection of the message by holding the envelope up to a strong light. Rozanov's impulse was to pry open the envelope, read the message, and then reseal it—a practice at which he was adept—but he immediately realized the impulse would be foolish and even dangerous. KGB letters were often sent on light-sensitive or chemically treated paper so that if the envelope's seal was opened the paper inside would change color. Anyone receiving such a message would know immediately that the envelope had been tampered with.

Rozanov dabbed at his forehead with his handkerchief. It had dawned on him that this must be one very special illegal. Who is he? he wondered as he placed the sealed envelope in his desk drawer, out of the way of temptation. I don't know him. Have never heard him mentioned. I, a colonel in the KGB, am being used as a messenger to contact him.

It was all highly irregular. For the rest of the day, many of those who came in contact with Rozanov thought he seemed somewhat distracted and not his usual witty, charming self. He constantly checked his watch as if he had some important appointment that he did not want to forget, and questions directed at him by friends and colleagues had to be repeated before Rozanov responded.

At exactly 10:30 P.M. he left his apartment at the Soviet mission and had his chauffeur drive him to a midtown restaurant. He instructed the driver to return in half an hour and pass the restaurant every ten minutes until he appeared. Then he went inside, strode over to the bar and ordered a vodka martini, looked at his watch, finished his drink and ordered another. At exactly eleven P.M. he left the bar and headed for the downstairs rest rooms. At the base of the stairs, in a quiet alcove, stood a single public telephone.

Rozanov had used this restaurant—and several others like it in the midtown area—to make telephone calls when he wanted to make sure that his calls would not be monitored. America was a wonderful place, he thought wryly. There were so many public telephones where one could place calls to anyplace in the country without fear of detection. In Russia there were listeners everywhere.

He paused at the bottom of the stairs for a moment, listening for any exceptional sounds. Hearing nothing, he deposited his coins, and reading from the small piece of paper in his hand, dialed the number.

The phone rang over twenty times before it was answered with a simple, "Yes?"

"This is your cousin Georgi calling," said Rozanov. "I have a message from your uncle."

There was a long pause and Rozanov could hear a man breathing on the other end. He began to think that the man might hang up, but his instructions had given him no other identification signal so he could do nothing to prevent it.

Finally the man spoke in low, carefully controlled tones. "It has been a long time, Cousin. How is Uncle?"

"Vladimir is fine. He desires that you and I should meet and renew our old friendship."

After a pause, the man said, "When?"

"Tomorrow. As soon as possible."

"Very well."

"I think—" began Rozanov, but he was immediately interrupted.

"Are you familiar with Saint Patrick's Cathedral?"

"Yes . . . but—"

"Ten A.M. Tomorrow," said the voice. "Be on the first step."

"How will I know you?" sputtered Rozanov.

"If you are where you are supposed to be," the voice said coldly, "I will know you."

As Rozanov started to protest the line went dead. He slammed down the phone. I will let him know what I think of his impertinence when I meet him tomorrow, he thought. But as he made his way up the stairs to the bar, he knew that he would do no such thing. He was a man who was used to following orders. Doing so had brought him to his present position of prominence. It would be foolish to jeopardize such a position in a moment of pride. No, he would do what he had always done. He would do as he had been told.

He shook his head as he reached the top of the stairs. Who is this man? he thought again.

He paid for his drinks, left the second untouched on the bar and went outside to the street to wait for his car.

Eighteen

Saturday

The first two times K.C. called the number there was no answer, and the third time he almost hung up when Diane said, "Hello."

He paused, trying to remember a few of the witty lines he had rehearsed but, like his ability to speak, they seemed to have deserted him.

"Hello," she said again.

He settled for, "Hello, this is K.C. Hardwick."

"Oh," she said, sounding surprised and nothing more.

That didn't help him much. "I hope it's not too early to call," he said.

"No," she said, "I've been out running already. I just got back."

"I've been running in place since I talked to you yesterday."

"Is that right." There was a distinct chill in her voice.

"Trying to get some exercise." He hated having to explain his feeble joke. He was struggling now and realized that this was going to be even tougher than he had imagined. "You're probably wondering why I called."

"Yes."

This girl is no help at all, he thought. "About yesterday. I wanted to apologize for being . . . for whatever it was I was being. I thought maybe I could take you to dinner—you could make sure I eat something healthy."

He heard a chuckle. Perhaps the ice was melting.

"I'm sorry," she said dashing his hopes. "I have to work tonight—on a story. I'll be in San Francisco."

"Okay," he said, resigned to failure. He was about to say good-bye when Diane added, "I'm sorry about yesterday. I really don't know why I was so dumb."

"That's okay, I was pretty dumb myself."

There was a pause. "Well, have a nice trip back to New York."

"How about tomorrow?"

"Tomorrow what?"

"Dinner?"

"I thought Carol said you were going back to New York tomorrow."

"I could change my plans."

"You mean if I agree to have dinner with you, you'll change your plans?"

"About everything. I might even vote Republican."

"Let's not get carried away."

"Well? Is it a date?"

"If you're crazy enough, why not?"

"And how about later?"

"Later?"

"When you get finished with your work . . . in San Francisco. We could have coffee or something."

"You're not wasting any time, are you?"

"I don't have much time."

She thought for a minute and he held his breath as he waited. "Do you like Vivaldi?" she said finally.

"Who?"

"Vivaldi. The composer. That's where I'm going tonight. I wangled an assignment on the concert at the Opera House tonight."

"I love Vivaldi," he lied. "He's my favorite."

She was laughing now and he loved the sound of it. He wished he could watch her laugh like that.

"Well he's my favorite composer, and after tonight he just might be yours too. I'll pick you up at seven," she said. "Wear something nice."

"Should I eat dinner, or will we be going out for a salad after?"

"Don't get me started. I was just beginning to like you."

Nineteen

Saturday

At exactly ten A.M. Viktor Rozanov's limousine stopped in front of Scribner's bookstore on Fifth Avenue. Rozanov exited and walked the two blocks to St. Patrick's, where he took up his position on the bottom step.

The man across the street at Rockefeller Center watched him pace back and forth. In his black coat and hat Rozanov looked just like what he was, the man thought, a KGB agent waiting to meet a contact.

The man crossed Fifth Avenue at Fiftieth Street and approached the Russian. Without preamble, he spoke. "Good morning, Cousin. It is good to see you again."

Rozanov inspected the man carefully before responding. The illegal was surprisingly young—no older than his late thirties—with strong good looks, dark hair, and steel-gray eyes. "Good morning," Rozanov said, forcing himself to sound jovial. He extended a hand in greeting but at that moment the illegal looked away, leaving Rozanov's hand extended aimlessly. Rozanov wondered whether his gesture had been rebuffed, or if the man had not noticed his courtesy.

"I have a message for you," Rozanov said.

The man nodded. "And I may require you to provide me with certain items," he said.

"Let's walk." He turned away, heading north on Fifth Avenue. Rozanov had to hustle to catch up.

They walked in silence for a time, the man occasionally stopping to look in store windows. At one of the stops, Rozanov studied the man's face in profile as both stood in front of a jeweler's. It was a face that might have been chiseled in marble, classically handsome but incredibly cold. It was a face devoid of expression—no amazement, no wonder, no joy, no fear. The expression seemed to have been set

137

at some moment of determined reflection and never to have changed since that time.

"The message," said the man suddenly and in a quiet voice that startled Rozanov with its intensity.

"Now? Here?"

They were walking past a store that sold cameras, tape machines, video games, and other mini-wonders of the electronic age. The man had steered Rozanov into the foyer of the store where a kiosk-style display window enabled window shoppers to completely circle the merchandise without entering the store.

The man led Rozanov around the window display and when they were protected from the street he held out his hand. "The message," he said again.

Rozanov reached into his coat and gave him the two envelopes. One slim, containing the message, the other bulky, containing the money. Rozanov looked left and right. "There's a good deal of money there," he said.

Without comment the man relieved Rozanov of the envelopes. "I'll walk north," he said, leaving unspoken the suggestion that Rozanov should go in the other direction.

"Wait a minute," Rozanov said, recovering from his momentary stupor. "I want to know who you are."

The man looked at Rozanov and his eyes narrowed in what for him was an expression of puzzlement. "Nothing in my instructions leads me to believe," he said calmly, "that you have any need to know who I am."

Rozanov was amazed at such effrontery. His voice was stern as he invoked the full authority of his position. "Do you know to whom you are speaking?"

"Yes, Comrade Rozanov. I am speaking to a man who has grown fat and lazy at the expense of the people. To a man who does not know when he exceeds his authority or when he risks his somewhat tenuous position as a representative of the Soviet government. Do I make myself clear, Comrade?"

Rozanov was stunned into silence. The man gave him a long, withering look, turned on his heel, and left Rozanov, mouth agape, standing beneath a sign that advertised "Best Prices in New York."

When Rozanov looked up again the man had already blended into the throng moving north on Fifth Avenue.

Twenty

Back in his hotel room, Karpenkov opened the envelopes that Rozanov had given him. He removed the money from the first envelope and threw it casually on the bed without counting or examining it. From the second envelope he removed two typed sheets of paper. Both were partially in code.

One sheet contained the details of Belenkov's defection and several details about the man's personal life and habits.

Karpenkov read that Belenkov's only child had died in infancy thirteen years ago and that his wife had died last year. His psychological profile, obviously altered to fit the present circumstance, portrayed him as extremely depressed and distraught and not in control of his own emotions. Psychiatrists at the Serbsky Institute of Forensic Psychiatry in Moscow had found him "paranoid and potentially schizophrenic."

Karpenkov shook his head and gave a small ironic smile at this notation. The good doctors at Serbsky had apparently examined Belenkov *in absentia*.

The report went on to detail the facts. Belenkov was athletic; liked women; drank too much vodka; had a fondness for American jazz and cigarettes. His hobbies were chess and collecting phonograph records.

Karpenkov smiled again. That description fit ninety percent of Russian males.

The final paragraph stated that "Belenkov possesses information of such vital and sensitive nature that for his own benefit he must be persuaded to return home for psychiatric diagnosis and treatment." The report concluded by stating, "It is absolutely imperative that Comrade Belenkov not divulge any of what he knows to the agents of the United States who would use such information to their own devious ends.

This possible threat to the security of the Soviet Union must be removed right away."

The wording was clear. There was no possible mistaking what it meant.

The second sheet was much shorter but more interesting than the first. According to information supplied by someone in British Intelligence, Belenkov was due to arrive in Washington on Monday or Tuesday. Today was Saturday, so that gave Karpenkov a few days to prepare.

The rest of the report applied to Gordon Hardwick and to himself, Chameleon. Preliminary reports from KGB contacts in Washington made it appear likely that Gordon Hardwick had indeed been brought in to meet with Belenkov. There followed a brief description of Hardwick and his presumed capabilities, most of which Karpenkov was familiar with. Apparently the CIA had decided to sequester the two in a safe house. Unfortunately, none of the contacts had been able to offer any help in pinpointing the location. A brief list of previously used safe houses was included, but Karpenkov doubted if any of these would be used in this instance.

The report suggested that once he was sequestered, Belenkov would be virtually untouchable and that therefore the only possibility was to get to him before this happened. A list of possible "locations of opportunity" was given, but Karpenkov dismissed them one by one as he read. The Americans were not fools. Belenkov would be heavily guarded at each point of his journey. Once he and Hardwick met they would be surrounded and guarded closely while the debriefing or interrogation took place.

Karpenkov dropped both sheets of the report into a metal wastebasket where he proceeded to set it afire. He was impressed with the quality and depth of the information he had been given, but as he watched the papers burn he realized that they contained very little that could help him carry out the task he had been assigned.

It seemed almost impossible.

Karpenkov sat in a chair pondering the advantages and disadvantages of the situation. The disadvantages were many— the advantages few.

The advantages were linked to Gordon Hardwick. If indeed he was coming to meet with Belenkov, then it was possible that he could lead Karpenkov to the defector. And Karpenkov had one other advantage that was not listed in the report. He knew when and where Gordon Hardwick was arriving in Washington. It had been a simple matter to display on his computer all the commercial flights from San Francisco to Washington and to browse through the passenger lists. There, he found that a Gordon Hardwick had purchased a first-class ticket on American flight 209 leaving San Francisco at nine P.M. Saturday and arriving in Washington at five A.M. Sunday.

Belenkov would be guarded but more than likely Hardwick would not. Karpenkov also knew that Hardwick had reserved a room at the Georgetown Inn in Washington for one night, and he assumed that Hardwick would stay there until Belenkov arrived from England. Then both would be taken, probably separately, to the safe location. Karpenkov knew that his only chance of finding Belenkov was by staying as close as possible to Hardwick. He had reserved a room in the same hotel. He could only hope that Hardwick would do something foolish, something that would add to Karpenkov's slim list of advantages.

Karpenkov went to his suitcase, which lay open on the unmade bed. He removed a smaller leather case containing his makeup, a gray suit that was several sizes too big, and the strap-on padding he would use to make him appear heavier and more portly than he really was.

He opened the case and tried one of his assortment of mustaches. The first was too bushy and inappropriate for the look he required. He found one he liked and held it in place above his upper lip. Fine, he thought. Overweight, overaged businessman comes to Washington. Some lines and wrinkles and gray hair should do it.

He did not want to go overboard on the disguise. He wanted something that he could quickly remove at the proper moment. He wanted Hardwick to know who he was before he killed him.

Twenty-one

As it turned out, K.C. did like Vivaldi. But it was as much a result of how much she seemed to relish the music as it was because of his own personal enjoyment.

Afterward they went to Houlihan's, where she could have her salad and he, as she put it, "could pig-out on a hamburger."

"So," she said as they sat over coffee, "you really did enjoy the concert?"

"Yes. I really did."

She was beaming—imagining she had made another convert to the world of classical music.

He watched her and smiled. Her hair was long and curly and she wore it like a frame around her face. In heels she was almost as tall as he was, but he didn't care. At the concert he had felt that everyone had been looking at her with admiration— and at him with envy. He wanted to know everything about her.

"This is the part," he said, "where you tell me all about yourself."

She shrugged. "Not much to tell."

"Nothing?"

"Afraid not." The smile faded a little. "You know that I was married before?"

"I knew there must be a dark secret."

"It's no secret," she said sadly. "Right out of college. One good year, three miserable ones. That sound about right? Isn't that the usual percentage?"

Not knowing what else to do, K.C. said nothing.

"I worked for a small-town newspaper in Marshalltown, Iowa." She shook her head and sipped her coffee. "You don't want to hear this."

"Yes, I do . . . honest."

"My husband ran a sporting-goods store—he was a jock who didn't know what to do with himself after the cheering stopped—and he wasn't doing too well. When I landed a television job in Des Moines it didn't help the already shaky situation. My success—moderate as it was—upset him."

"What did you do in Des Moines?"

She smiled, shaking her head. He thought she was almost blushing. "I was the Channel Three weather girl."

"Weather girl? You know a lot about weather?"

"I can tell you when it's raining outside. All I did was look pretty and point to the map while I read the National Weather Service reports."

"I like to look at a pretty face while I get my weather report."

She made a stern face as if to warn him to be careful. "It was a job—demeaning—but a job nevertheless. I thought of myself as the next Diane Sawyer and here I was . . ." She fumbled to find the right comparison.

"The next Willard Scott," he said helpfully.

This time she laughed. "Not exactly, but you've got the picture. Anyway, things sort of fell apart with the marriage and I decided to seek fame and fortune in sunny California. I heard about an opening at KLSF, here in San Francisco. Unfortunately, being a weather girl doesn't carry too much credibility. I didn't get the job, but I decided to stay anyway." She shrugged. "That's about it, that's the dark secret. I was once a weather girl."

As she finished her story he was thinking how easy it would be to fall in love with her. "I'll bet you were great," he said.

She laughed as if he were only kidding, but he meant every word.

Twenty-two

On Sunday morning K.C. woke up at seven o'clock thinking about Diane. He knew he was in trouble. He paced around for an hour, sat for a while trying to read the morning paper, but even the reports of Darryl Strawberry's destruction of the Giants the day before didn't seem to interest him.

At eight he dialed her number. "I know it's early," he said when she answered, "but I just wanted to check with you about tonight."

"Tonight?"

"Y'know. Dinner."

"Yes. We are going out to dinner."

"I know. I mean where do you want to go?"

He heard her laughing. "I don't have the foggiest notion," she said.

"I didn't wake you, did I?"

"No. I was just on my way out to run."

"Had breakfast yet?"

"No. Not yet."

"How about if I get some lox, bagels, and cream cheese and come over. We can have breakfast together."

"Give me forty-five minutes. I've got to get my miles in and take a shower. Okay?"

"Okay. See you in forty-five minutes."

He couldn't find lox or bagels and had to settle for sourdough rolls and creamed herring in a jar. He tried to stall for time but when he arrived at the parking lot of her apartment building he was at least ten minutes early. He was sitting in his car, waiting for the forty-five minutes to be up, when Diane, in T-shirt, shorts, and running sneakers, appeared, running with long graceful strides.

She saw him and stopped in front of her ground-floor

apartment. Hands on her hips she gave him a look of displeasure then shook her head and smiled. She waved him forward.

K.C. got out of the car, his paper bag in his hand. "I got lost and got here early," he said incongruously.

"I think I'm going to have lots of trouble with you," she said.

She took him inside and put coffee on. He watched her moving about the small kitchen. She wore light blue nylon shorts. Her legs were long and lean with well-muscled calves.

Finding that his stock of small talk was diminishing rapidly he asked, "Do you run every day?"

She took a kitchen towel and wiped her face and then her neck. "Four—five days maybe."

Her T-shirt was damp with sweat and he could see the outline of her breasts beneath the fabric. K.C. had to force himself to look away. His glance bounded from ceiling to floor and from wall to wall.

"Okay," she said, "coffee's on. You can get your bagels ready while I take a shower."

He thought of trying some witty remark like, Need someone to scrub your back?, but better judgment prevailed and he mumbled something about sourdough bread and how hard it was to find bagels.

When she returned she was wearing a long blue robe, her hair wet and combed straight, hanging to her shoulders. She wore no makeup. "Lucky you," she said. "You get to see the real me."

K.C. wanted to say something wonderful—about how marvelous she looked. It would be something that would send her racing into his arms. Instead, his tone mock serious, he said, "Beneath the glitter and romance of the world of journalism, this, ladies and gentlemen, is the real Diane Rollins."

She laughed as she fluffed up her hair with a towel. "You're funny," she said. "From what Carol told me about you, I didn't think you'd be funny."

"What *did* you think I'd be like?"

"I don't know. Serious. Quiet."

He was off again as if he were a talk-show host. "He's all those things, ladies and gentlemen. He's serious, he's quiet, he's funny, he's romantic . . ." He stopped at midpoint, losing track of where he was heading.

Diane raised an eyebrow. "Romantic, too?"

He was having a hard time meeting her eyes. "Sometimes," he mumbled. He looked up with a smile. "Usually I'm just serious and quiet." He felt foolish, like a ninth-grader on his first date.

She touched him lightly on the back of his hand. "That's nice. I like serious and quiet."

They were silent for a moment, having run out of small talk. K.C. was determined not to continue with more foolishness.

Diane spoke first. "When are you going back to New York?"

"Tomorrow night."

"Doesn't give us much time," she said softly.

"I'll be back."

"That's what they all say, sailor." Now it was her turn to cover up her feelings with mischief.

They both laughed uncomfortably, and stopped. Then she was in his arms and they were kissing without knowing who had moved first.

After a moment she pulled herself away. When he moved toward her she took a step back. "I've got to get dressed." Her robe was partially open and he could tell she wore nothing underneath.

"I'll help you," he said.

"No you won't," she said. "You'll stay right here and pour two cups of coffee. I'll be right back."

His shoulders slumped. "OK," he said, "but would it be all right if I doused myself with some cold water first?"

Laughing, she was on her way to the bedroom. "You're being funny again." She stopped in front of her bedroom door. "You busy today?"

He grinned. "What did you have in mind?"

She ignored his lecherous look. "Let's drive down to Monterey. I know a great place on the ocean where we can have dinner before we drive back."

"Sounds great."

Her smile lit the room. "Terrific. Now pour that coffee while I get dressed."

He poured the coffee and thought about her on the other side of the door. Right now, he thought, she's slipping that robe off and is standing there naked, rummaging through a drawer looking for something incredibly sexy to put on.

146

He made a conscious effort to cut off the picture in his mind. Instead he thought about Stanford and how he would call this morning and accept their offer to be a visiting professor in the fall.

Twenty-three

From his vantage point in the tall grass Karpenkov watched the house. He had carried a high-powered starlight scope in his backpack, and by using the electronic sighting device the dim light was amplified, enabling him to penetrate the dark night. He had a perfect view of the front of the house, the driveway, and the front lawn, as well as a partial view of the backyard, which fronted the choppy waters of the Chesapeake Bay.

If Gordon Hardwick and Belenkov were to appear right now, he thought, I could pick both of them off with very little trouble.

He looked to his left and then to his right. The house sat on a quiet narrow road and was surrounded by similar summer houses. Some, like the one he was watching, were small and unobtrusive. Others had been expanded and modernized until the original shell was barely recognizable.

It was early in June and the weather was cool and blustery. None of the surrounding houses was as yet occupied.

But one will be soon, thought Karpenkov.

The windswept spur of land on which the small cluster of houses was perched was surrounded on three sides by the bay; a narrow road provided the only access. At the moment all was quiet, but in less than twenty-four hours Karpenkov predicted that this small peninsula would be swarming with security personnel. Access and egress would be restricted—if not stopped altogether—and his ability to determine his course of action would become increasingly more difficult. Hit and run would be impossible. He knew he would be apprehended within ten minutes of any attempt at Belenkov.

If he were willing to give up his life or his freedom he would be able to accomplish his task, but nothing he had been told had led him to believe that his target was more valuable than his life. Besides, it was Hardwick he was after. The other thing was only a peripheral consideration to him.

He shifted his position, the weapon under his armpit jabbing painfully into his ribs. He had told Rozanov he wanted a Stechkin and a starlight scope and had been disappointed when he had been provided instead with a Smith and Wesson. He was glad now. The Stechkin, with its long nine-inch barrel for improved accuracy and its twenty-round clip, would have been incredibly bulky. Besides, the 9mm parabellum ammunition would instantly have identified the assassination as the work of the KGB.

He had already decided that the use of the firearm was out of the question and that more subtle methods were required. With a little bit of luck he knew he could accomplish his task.

So far his luck had been excellent.

He had arrived in Washington early on Saturday afternoon, checked into his hotel, and prepared himself for Gordon Hardwick's arrival. He rented a van and a motorcycle using the false identification provided by Rozanov and bought some clothes at an Army-Navy store. Once he called American Airlines information to make sure that Hardwick's plane would arrive on time.

While he waited, he toyed with the idea of planting a listening device in Gordon Hardwick's hotel room but decided against it. It was unlikely that Hardwick would allow himself to be put into the room where he had a reservation. Any agent with Hardwick's years of experience would never allow that to happen. And even if he did he might have the room swept electronically and the discovery of the device would only serve to alert him that he was under surveillance. Karpenkov would just have to be patient and wait for Gordon Hardwick to make a mistake.

He didn't have to wait long.

When Hardwick did arrive, Karpenkov, safe beneath his disguise, managed to get behind him at the check-in desk.

"Mr. Hardwick," said the desk clerk. "We've been expecting you. Room 203 is ready and waiting."

Karpenkov stifled a grin when he heard Hardwick say, "I'd prefer something on another floor if you don't mind. Street noise keeps me awake."

The desk clerk expertly kept the welcoming smile from drifting from his face. "Certainly, sir. And how long will you be with us, Mr. Hardwick?"

"I'll be checking out Monday morning," said Gordon.

Mistake number one, thought Karpenkov, who now had verified his earlier information that Belenkov would arrive from London on Monday.

"Also," said Gordon to the clerk, "I'd like for you to arrange a rental car for me."

"Certainly, sir. Any particular car or company you'd prefer?"

Hardwick seemed uninterested. "Anyone who can get a car here this evening. I'd like to use it later. Any kind of car will do, but nothing too flashy."

The clerk nodded. "Very well, sir. I'll call right away. Here is your room key—Room 505. Your bags will be brought to your room shortly."

Hardwick pocketed the key and left. Karpenkov watched the desk clerk make a face in Hardwick's direction, then look through his list of car-rental agencies.

Mistake number two was more serious and came even earlier than Karpenkov had expected. It provided Karpenkov with the break he had been looking for, and for all intents and purposes it sealed the fate of Mikhail Belenkov.

A short time after arriving at the hotel, Hardwick appeared in the lobby and walked past Karpenkov, oblivious of his presence. After conversing briefly with the desk clerk, Hardwick left the hotel with Karpenkov following a safe distance behind. He walked two blocks and went into a liquor store. Karpenkov waited for a few minutes and went inside too.

"I want the best," Gordon was saying to the proprietor as Karpenkov browsed through the selection of wines in the aisle across from them.

"This is it," he heard the man say. "Imported from Russia. Best vodka I've got."

"I'll take two bottles and one of these."

Karpenkov smiled. A little gift, perhaps? A little something to take away the ache of homesickness for a visiting friend?

He watched Hardwick pay for the two bottles of Russian vodka and another bottle of cheaper American vodka, then head back to the hotel with his purchase inside a brown paper bag. Already Karpenkov's mind was working. The Russian vodka was obviously for Belenkov—a welcoming gift. It was a typical tactic: make sure the defector is comfortable. Obviously the CIA's information about Belenkov's drinking preferences was as good as his own.

Karpenkov had devised his plan even before he arrived back at the hotel. It was quite simple and covered perfectly the various parts of his assignment. It was obvious that Gordon Hardwick was going somewhere that evening. He had expressly requested the car for that night. It was equally obvious that he would return to the hotel that evening. Why else bother to check in at all? When Hardwick left the hotel in his car, Karpenkov would enter his room, carefully unseal the vodka, poison the contents, and reseal the bottles. It was perfect, he thought. Hardwick would personally carry the method of Belenkov's destruction to the secret location. Karpenkov smiled as he pictured the two toasting each other with drink after drink. His smile broadened as he saw the scene the next day when the two lay dead and the bewildered officers of the CIA tried to imagine what had happened.

Back at the hotel, Karpenkov gathered his material and returned to the lobby to wait. To avoid suspicion he went into the bar and positioned himself in a seat where he could see the elevators and the front desk.

After he had waited for more than two hours and was beginning to wonder if Hardwick had made a change in plans, he saw the elevator door open and Gordon Hardwick step out, approaching the desk. Karpenkov's eyes shot wide open: Hardwick was carrying the paper bag that contained the vodka.

He's taking it with him, he said to himself as he watched his carefully constructed and easily executed plan go down the drain. There was a brief moment of indecision that passed as quickly as it had come, and then he was moving quickly toward the stairs that led to the parking garage. He wanted to be there before Gordon Hardwick arrived.

He opened the back of his rented van, quickly removed his jacket and tie and placed them inside. The van was parked nose-out so that no one would notice that inside was a black Kawasaki with an electric starter and a quiet running

1,000 cc. engine. Karpenkov pulled on a black turtleneck and a black zip-front jacket and climbed into the van.

Less than five minutes later, as expected, Gordon Hardwick appeared. He still had the bag in his hands. He looked around the garage until he found his car—a dark blue four-door Ford—and drove off.

Karpenkov followed. He had no other choice.

Now, two hours after leaving Washington, Karpenkov lay in the sand and tall grass, beneath a starless sky, watching a small house on the shore of Chesapeake Bay. He had left the van on the Marlboro Pike, continuing his pursuit on the motorcycle, which was now hidden off the road about a mile back.

Lights went on and off in the house as Hardwick went from room to room inspecting the layout. Karpenkov understood that he was familiarizing himself with the interior and making a final inspection before Belenkov's arrival. He felt a rush of excitement knowing that he had found the safe house to which Belenkov would be brought for his initial debriefing. He had hoped Hardwick would make an error, but had never dared expect that when it came it would be a blunder of such magnitude.

All the lights went off and a few seconds later Hardwick appeared at the front door. Karpenkov watched closely through the scope and saw that Hardwick was empty-handed. He had left his package behind in the house. Hardwick shut the door and checked to make sure that it was secure, then headed for his car.

Karpenkov waited for ten minutes after Gordon Hardwick's car had disappeared before getting up and moving swiftly toward the house. It was a perfect night for such ventures—moonless, with a low cloud cover that blocked even the light of the stars. He went to the back and with a small penlight inspected the back door and windows. As he'd expected, there was an alarm system, metallic tape plainly visible on the windows. Karpenkov gave a silent curse. It was not that alarm systems were difficult to circumvent. At the Balashika training center just outside Moscow, part of his training had been in the elimination of such security systems. Most burglar alarms were surprisingly ineffectual and intended to thwart only the clumsiest of intruders, but the problem here was that not only must he defeat the system but he must not leave any trace that the system had ever been tampered with.

He would have to go in and out of the front door. That was the door Gordon Hardwick had used and obviously the control panel would be near that entrance. That control panel would be the problem. If it were operated by a key—even the round keys that most alarm systems used—he would have no trouble. If it were operated by a digital keypad and a number code, he would need an ohmmeter and several connectors to unscramble the code.

His options were two: hope that the alarm was key-operated or purchase an ohmmeter at any electronics store and come back tomorrow, at which time he might find the area crawling with security personnel. So far his luck had been excellent. He decided to take a chance.

He went directly to the front door, confident that there was no one around for miles. He removed his backpack, took out his key set, inspected the lock on the door, and selected the proper key and a tapered sliver of metal about four inches long. He inserted both in the lock. In less than fifteen seconds the door was open and Karpenkov stepped inside.

The clock was running and mentally he began to count off the seconds, knowing that systems such as this might have as little as a fifteen-second delay during which time the control box must be turned to the "off" position. If that were not done the police would automatically be notified of the intrusion.

He had two things in his favor, however. Most people, allowing for fumbling in pocketbooks for keys, or other such momentary postponements, had the alarm delay set for an inordinately long time—even a minute or two. The other thing was that the control box was always placed in close proximity to the entry door, so he would not have to search everywhere to find it.

He was standing, his back against the door in a small entry foyer. He swept the walls with his penlight, the slim beam casting elongated shadows across the floor. He did not see the control box.

To his left was a coat closet, the logical place to hide the control box. He opened it and swept the interior with the light. Nothing!

He pulled back the drapes on the windows and felt along

both sides—nothing. The clock was still running. If this system was on short delay, he was already in trouble.

He walked quickly into the room closest to the foyer, sweeping thin light across the walls. Directly in front of him on the opposite wall was a door. He stepped forward and opened it. A closet, and the control box inside. As soon as he saw the flashing red light he knew by its frequency that the alarm would soon sound. He smiled when he saw that the device was key-operated.

He held the penlight between his teeth, focusing on the control box. Hands steady, fingers sure, he took another of his keys—a short, stubby round one—and the same thin slice of metal and slipped both into the lock. He held the short key firm while he probed delicately with the thin blade. As the red light flashed its insistent warning, Karpenkov twisted the key but nothing happened. He knew he did not have much time left. He tried again, being careful not to exert too much force. This time he heard a distinct click and the red light switched to green.

He took a moment to calm himself and to let his eyes adjust to the darkness. The house was small—downstairs a living room, dining room, a kitchen, and a small den. The bedrooms were on the second floor. He did not go upstairs.

Before entering a room, Karpenkov would stop on the threshold and inspect the interior for motion sensors, infrared detectors or weight-activated devices placed under carpets. But other than the perimeter system there did not seem to be any other intrusion alert systems in the house.

It did not take him long to find what he was looking for. In the den, in a cabinet below a row of bookshelves, he found the liquor cabinet. Inside, sitting at the front of the cabinet next to several other bottles, he found the Russian vodka.

"Expecting someone?" he whispered to the bottles as he took them from the cabinet. "A traitor perhaps."

Moving quickly he took the bottles into the kitchen and placed them on the countertop next to the stove. He took a small kettle from the stove, put in a small amount of water, and turned the front burner on high. While he waited for the water, he removed from his backpack a razor-blade knife and a small vial of clear liquid. He placed both on the counter next to the bottles.

In just a few minutes the water was boiling and Karpenkov

held the neck of one of the bottles close to the escaping steam. After a brief moment, he slipped the knife beneath the loosened glue of the tax seal and painstakingly removed the seal from the bottle. Careful to keep the seal intact he unscrewed the cap and placed it and the now opened bottle on the counter top. He then repeated the process with the second bottle.

Next he cut through the transparent tape with which he had sealed the small container of liquid and removed the cap. He sniffed the contents and as expected he detected no odor. Then he poured half the contents of the vial—about three tablespoons of liquid—into each bottle of vodka. Smoothing down the seals to the bottle neck, he noted with satisfaction that the glue, now cooling, was once again securely holding the seals to the glass. He swirled the contents of the bottles around a little, and then inspected his work by flashlight.

Someone, he noted with confidence, would have to make a minute inspection of the seals to determine that they had been tampered with. The addition of the clear liquid had not changed the appearance of the vodka in any way and he was quite sure that the KGB's Technical Operations Directorate would not have passed along a poison that would change the taste of the vodka in any detectable way.

Karpenkov replaced everything, rearmed the alarm system, and in minutes was walking quickly down the road to where he had left his motorcycle.

The night was still dark but somewhere off beyond the horizon a dim glimmer of light held the promise of dawn. As Karpenkov made his way down the narrow road he could not help but smile. He was very pleased with himself. All the resources of the KGB had been used in an attempt to find the defector, but it had been he, Karpenkov, who had found him. Things could not have been better. He had just eliminated his target and his most dangerous adversary at the same time. It could not have been easier. "Perfect," he said to the night as he neared the spot where he had left his vehicle. "Just perfect."

Twenty-four

They left in the early afternoon, heading south on U.S. 101 with the coastal mountains to the west and a hot bright sun in their faces. At San Jose they turned west and picked up Route 1 at Santa Cruz, where again they headed south. Now the Pacific stretched out in front of them and the mountains were behind and to the east.

Diane played with the buttons on the radio, trying to find a station that played classical music. "You'll love the peninsula," she said between her fiddling. "It's my favorite place in the whole world."

"You've never been in Brooklyn," he reminded her, laughing.

"Just you wait till you see it," she said.

Even the drive down was spectacular. Lush green hills plunged down into a deep blue Pacific that crashed onto a rocky shoreline. The air was crisp and clear and the sky seemed almost purple.

They arrived in Monterey before noon and went to Fisherman's Wharf. After parking the car they walked down the pier. Seafood restaurants and gift shops lined both sides. Seagulls swirled around them, their shrill calls like the cries of lost children at a great distance. Diane was so excited she skipped several paces ahead of K.C. "Don't you just love it?" she asked. He laughed and agreed and followed her to the end of the pier, to a place called Sam's Fishing Fleet, where they bought what was advertised as "Sea-Lion Food." From the end of the pier they fed the sea lions, huge, blubbery creatures that barked like hoarse dogs and swam with the grace of ballerinas whenever a chunk of fish was tossed their way.

They had lunch in a restaurant that overlooked Monterey

Bay and the tall-masted sailing boats and brightly colored fishing boats bobbing at anchor there. K.C. had clam chowder—thick and creamy—and a monstrous Dungeness crab. Diane settled for the inevitable salad, but this time with crab chunks.

"This is great," said K.C., his mouth full of crabmeat. He was as happy at that moment as he could ever remember.

Later, because he wanted to see the golf courses, Pebble Beach, Spyglass Hill, and Cypress Point, they drove along Seventeen Mile Drive. Every time he stopped the car to admire a particularly scenic hole on one of the golf courses, Diane made sarcastic comments and refused to get out of the car.

"Look at the beautiful scenery," she said pointing at the ocean, "and the man wants to look at golf courses."

They laughed the afternoon away, but as the day went on Diane became increasingly quiet. He noticed but didn't say anything because he knew what was on her mind.

They wound up in Carmel, and after browsing through shops they found a nice place on the bay for dinner.

Diane's silence grew during the meal, while K.C. rambled on merrily, trying to avoid the inevitable question. Finally, after she had said practically nothing for almost five minutes, he felt compelled to ask, "What is it?"

Elbows on table, chin in her hands, untouched food in front of her, she said, "I've had a wonderful time today," and then, before he could respond, she asked the question that had been hanging in the air all day. "Am I going to see you again? After tomorrow I mean."

"Yes," he said immediately.

She raised her eyebrows in a question. "Three thousand miles is a long-distance romance."

He took a bite of food and said, as if it were of no consequence, "I'm taking the job at Stanford. As soon as I can clean up my business back east, I'm moving out here."

Her eyes widened and a smile played about her lips. "That's a big decision," she said. "Did you give it much thought?"

"Hardly any," he said, then reached for her hand across the table. "I want to be with you. It's that simple. If you don't want to be with me, I'll do my year as visiting professor and go home."

She almost blushed, her eyes looking down at the table

and then around the room to see if anyone was watching. "I've been thinking, too," she said.

He chuckled. "Always a sure sign of trouble."

She looked up, holding his eyes steady with hers. "Why don't we stay here tonight? There are lots of pretty places overlooking the ocean. We could leave early and still make it back in time for your flight."

He smiled, and although his head was pounding and the lump in his throat threatened to cut off his supply of air, he managed to say, "Sounds terrific to me."

Diane smiled mischievously. "I did pack a few things in my bag in the car."

He signaled the waiter. "Check, please."

Diane smiled. "But we haven't finished dinner yet."

The startled waiter was at their table, a look of bewilderment on his face. "Sir?"

"Only kidding," K.C. said to Diane. He turned to the waiter. "Another bottle of wine, please."

Twenty-five

Gordon Hardwick was starting a fire in the big brick fireplace in the living room when he heard the cars pull up outside. He put another log on and pulled the screen closed before going to the door. DDO Hanson was already halfway up the path when Hardwick opened the door.

"Everything in order?" asked Hanson, stepping inside.

"Yes," said Gordon. "The security boys went over the place with a fine-tooth comb about an hour ago."

Outside sat one limousine, motor running, and three plain four-door sedans.

"We'll have men in the house across the road and on either side."

Gordon was looking at the limousine in front of the house. "You got him with you?" he asked.

Hanson turned to look outside. He seemed annoyed. "He's in there, don't worry. I just wanted to check everything out." He looked closely at Gordon. "You all right?"

"I'm fine," said Gordon, puzzled by the question.

Hanson walked into the living room and stood by the fire warming his hands. The fire would take the chill out of the house, Gordon thought. Hanson opened his coat and stared into the flames. The house was quiet except for the crackling of the dry wood.

"Problem?" asked Gordon.

Hanson did not turn to face him. "I'll level with you, Gordon. You've always been one of my best men."

"But?"

Hanson turned to face him, his face grim. "But the accounts I've been getting from California lately haven't made me too happy."

Gordon's face fell. "I'm doing a good job out there, Tom."

"Your reports are sloppy, incomplete, and careless. Birdwell sent them on to me. You know how I feel about careless reports."

Gordon nodded. "A careless man writes careless reports."

"Are you getting careless, Gordon?"

"No," said Gordon defensively. He hadn't expected this. "I've had some problems at home."

"I don't want to hear that bullshit," Hanson said quietly and without anger. "You have two lives. The one at home and the one with the Agency. It's up to you to decide which is more important."

"I've never had a problem with that decision," said Gordon quietly.

"The truth is," said Hanson, "I would never have considered you for this assignment unless Belenkov had asked for you."

Gordon looked down at the floor. He had nothing to say in his own defense.

Hanson went on. "Don't mess this up, Gordon. This may be one of our biggest defections in years. I don't know what the hell's happened to you out there in California. Maybe it's just middle-aged craziness, maybe it's too much booze, maybe it's too many women"—Gordon started to say something but

158

Hanson held up a finger and silenced him—"but whatever it is, it stops now. You've taken a good, solid career with lots of promise and punctuated it with too many question marks." Hanson paused and looked into the fire and when he continued his tone had softened. "I want you back on track, Gordon. I'm counting on you for this one."

Gordon nodded. "What do you want me to do?"

"Just do your job, but do it right. Make this Belenkov comfortable, try to open him up, feel him out on his area of expertise. Hopefully he'll feel comfortable enough in a day or two so we can bring in a debriefing team and put him through the wringer." He reached into his pocket and produced a folded sheet of paper. "Here are some general areas you might probe. Don't get too specific, leave that for the debriefing team."

Gordon took the offered list and glanced at it briefly. He nodded. "Should I take notes?"

Hanson shrugged. "That might make him uncomfortable."

Gordon put the list in his pocket. "Are we convinced his defection is genuine?"

Hanson screwed up his face. "The British think so."

Gordon said nothing, but his expression left no doubt as to his dissatisfaction with Hanson's answer.

"I know," said Hanson. "The British evaluations aren't top quality. But they seem convinced on this one—put their top people on it." He clapped his hands together. "Let's get him in here and get this show on the road. I've got to get back to the office."

Gordon Hardwick followed Hanson back to the front door and both stepped outside. Hanson looked around, saw nothing amiss, and waved to the limousine in the driveway. All four doors popped open simultaneously and four young men in dark blue suits stepped out. From the back door they were followed by a man in a dark overcoat who looked in all directions as if unsure of himself. When he saw Gordon Hardwick a small smile registered on his face. He made a brief, almost unnoticeable bow.

Two of the four men who had been in the limousine escorted Belenkov up the path to the house. One of them carried a file folder which he gave to Gordon Hardwick.

"Mr. Belenkov," said Hanson in overly formal tones, "I believe you know Mr. Hardwick."

"How are you, Mikhail," said Gordon shaking Belenkov's hand.

Belenkov smiled. "Somehow we always knew we would share this moment. Is it not so, my friend?"

Gordon seemed to be remembering something from a long time ago, but he merely nodded and led Belenkov inside the house.

Hanson seemed edgy and unsure of what to do. "Well, I've got to be going," he said brusquely. "Everything is in order. This whole area is sealed off and we've got men all around."

"Everything will be fine, Tom," Gordon Hardwick said. "Don't worry."

Hanson nodded but he looked worried anyway. He shook hands with Belenkov and with a long, searching look at Gordon Hardwick, headed for the door. On the threshold he stopped and turned as if to say something, but at the last moment he changed his mind, shook his head, and left without a word.

The American and the defector sat in front of the fire and eyed each other with a mixture of affection and suspicion. Despite the respect each had for the other, too many years as deadly enemies made it difficult for them to lower the guards they had erected. They sat for some time in stormy silence, staring, sometimes into the fire, sometimes at each other, through eyes clouded with past visions of long-ago but not-forgotten struggles.

The first thing Gordon Hardwick had asked the Russian when they were alone was, "Why me? Why did you ask for me?"

Belenkov had smiled and said, "Remember Budapest?"

Gordon nodded but did not get the connection.

"My wife and I had just lost our son. She never forgot how kind you were."

"That was almost fifteen years ago," said Gordon, his eyes wide with amazement.

Belenkov shook his head. "Only thirteen," he said as if it were yesterday.

Belenkov was in his late forties, but his hair was white and his face drawn and pale. He could have been sixty. Perhaps it was the long trip or the harrowing events of the past few days, but he had the look of a man who needed a

160

long rest but knew that he wasn't going to get it. He had his feet up on the hassock in front of the fire, a glass of vodka in his hand and the bottle nearby on a small table. He downed the vodka and reached for the bottle. "Are you sure you won't have another?" he said, pouring himself a drink.

Gordon lifted his glass and shook the ice cubes. "No thanks. This one is still fine."

Belenkov nodded and took a sip. "I believe," he said, in remarkably unaccented English, "that it is my responsibility to prove to you that I am worthy of your trust."

Gordon Hardwick shrugged. "I also have a responsibility," he said in flawless although accented Russian, "to make you welcome and to let you know that we appreciate what you have done."

Belenkov chuckled. "Now that we have mouthed the obligatory platitudes, perhaps we can get on with this." His smile widened when he saw Gordon Hardwick responding to his honesty. "Perhaps we may once again regard each other—if not as friends—then at least as worthy adversaries."

Gordon Hardwick nodded and both raised their glasses in salute.

The Russian drained his glass and seemed disappointed when Gordon only sipped at his drink.

"Where shall we begin?" said Belenkov.

"Where else but the beginning," said Gordon, staring into Belenkov's eyes as if he might better discern the truth. "Why did you defect?"

Belenkov sighed. He had already told this story so many times, first to the British and then to the Americans who had come to claim him in London. Now he realized he must start all over again.

He spoke in a monotone as if to show how much the question bored him. "For quite some time—perhaps as long as ten years—I have had grave doubts about the Soviet system . . . not in ways you might think of, but in a more general sense. There is a lack of efficiency from top to bottom. The system has a built-in inability to deal with the consequence of change."

Gordon seemed puzzled. "Are you talking about the persecution of dissidents?"

Belenkov made a face of displeasure. "Dissidents will always be persecuted," he said. "That's what makes them dissidents. If they were not persecuted they would merely be complainers."

Gordon smiled. "You don't feel uncomfortable with the state persecution of dissidents."

Belenkov was emphatic. "No. The state exists, not for the benefit of those who disagree, but to perpetuate its own power. The state has no moral obligation to promote the views of those who oppose it."

"But you left."

"And if enough people followed my lead the state will wither and die."

"Not likely, though," said Gordon.

Belenkov agreed. "Not likely at all."

Gordon looked through Belenkov's file, which he held open in his lap. "According to this statement you worked for Directorate S of the First Chief Directorate, KGB, for more than ten years, and before that for Department A—Disinformation."

Belenkov nodded. "It is now known as Service A."

Gordon nodded, still looking at the file. "The statement says that you were part of the attempt to infiltrate Russian agents into the United States as ordinary United States citizens."

"That is correct."

"How many of these . . ."

"Illegals?" said Belenkov, interjecting the word that Gordon sought.

"Yes, illegals. How many of these illegals would you say are presently residing in the United States?"

"No more than one hundred."

"Do you think you could identify most of them?"

"If you turn the page of my file," said Belenkov, "you will note that I have listed over thirty names. Names of agents here in the U.S. who live as ordinary citizens."

"Yes. I saw the list and they are rather ordinary. Haven't any of these illegals insinuated their way into the government, into intelligence or defense or . . ." He left his question hanging.

Belenkov smiled. "I would love to tell you that the Vice-President of the United States is an illegal or perhaps the Director of the CIA. As effective as that might be, it is quite difficult to achieve. Most illegals are relatively unimportant. I have no doubt that one or two illegals may have worked their way into positions of some authority, but if they have, their names are closely guarded secrets."

"Even from you?"

"In my country we trust no one." He spread his hands, his palms to the ceiling. "And, as you can see, for good reason."

"You said there were around one hundred of these people in the U.S., but you give a list of only thirty. What about the others?"

"In the KGB, responsibility is fragmented so that no one man knows more than he has to. I was responsible for only about ten of these people. Through contacts and some overlapping of responsibilities I learned the names of some others. Over the past year or so, I committed names to memory whenever I encountered them. The rest are kept secret even from me. You will have to wait for another defector."

"Most of these names have been checked out and most of them are relatively insignificant." He looked at his file. "A machinist at Electric Boat in Groton, a maintenance superviser at Rockwell International on Long Island."

Belenkov shrugged. "It is not easy to place illegals in positions of great responsibility. One must be willing to start at the lower echelons and hope that the agent will work his way into whatever industry is targeted."

"What do you get from these people?"

"Information."

"Information? That's it?"

Belenkov smiled. "In case of deteriorating relations or a war situation, we have people who are in place as potential provocateurs and saboteurs."

Gordon eyed the list again. "These people are small potatoes. You'll forgive me if I'm not impressed with this revelation."

Belenkov smiled. "Small potatoes. What a marvelously American phrase." Then he gave a shrug. "You think that perhaps the Soviet Union is willing to sacrifice a few relatively unimportant illegals in order to infiltrate a high-ranking KGB officer into your country?"

"The thought had crossed my mind. You did say that disinformation was one of your areas of expertise."

Belenkov relaxed in his chair and slugged back his Stolichnaya. He held up his glass. "Do you mind?" he asked.

Gordon motioned to the bottle. "Help yourself."

"Will you join me?" Belenkov asked as he filled his glass.

Gordon shook his head. "No thanks," he said self-consciously, "I'm trying to give it up."

Belenkov stared silently at Gordon for a moment, wondering if this was perhaps an indication that Hardwick was trying to slight him. But after a brief moment he decided that was not the case. He gulped his vodka. "Good," he said, looking at the once again empty glass. "Better than we get in Moscow. The best stuff is always exported—unless of course you have access to the 'closed' shops."

Gordon raised an eyebrow. "And you don't?"

Belenkov laughed. "You assume that if I were as important as I claim I would have access to the closed shops, eh?"

Gordon nodded grimly.

"You are right of course. Certain items and certain shops are open only to the *nomenklatura*. As a *direktor* I have access to such shops. There are also what you would call commissaries in each KGB building, where officers can buy Western goods intended for export, at very reasonable prices." He held up his glass. "But still, the top-quality vodka goes only for export or to the old men at the top." He chuckled. "We have a saying in Russia. The tree of Russia is firmly rooted in the soil of the motherland, but it roots from the top."

Gordon Hardwick nodded. "Tell me all about yourself and your work," he said.

Belenkov sighed. "From the beginning?"

Belenkov's story lasted long into the night and he consumed almost the entire bottle of Russian vodka while he told it. He was forty-nine years old, too young to remember much about what the Russians called the Great Patriotic War. His father had been a Party member and as such had been able to get him a post with the KGB. In 1961 he was given his first post and began a rather slow and methodical climb to a position of prominence. In the 1970's he had been an assistant director with the Disinformation Department.

Gordon interrupted him for a moment. "In 1976 a KGB mayor, Alexy Kuznetsov, defected to the West with a great deal of inside information about the workings of the KGB and Soviet spy rings in the West. I have always suspected he was a KGB plant. Was he genuine?"

Belenkov smiled. "A KGB plant. We sacrificed a large

number of nonproductive agents in order to bombard you with disinformation in other areas." He seemed pleased with himself. "You Americans are always willing to believe that another Soviet devil has seen the light and has come over to your side."

Gordon raised an eyebrow. "What about now? Why should I believe you're a genuine defector?"

Belenkov threw his head back and gave a laugh that rocked the room. The vodka was obviously having an effect. "You should not. You should interrogate me to the fullest and corroborate everything I tell you."

"Corroboration of such things is sometimes quite difficult."

Belenkov nodded. "Then if you cannot be certain, you should refuse my request for asylum and ship me back to the Soviet Union."

Gordon was not sure how to take that statement.

"Then," Belenkov went on, "when you read the news of my death in *Pravda*, you will be convinced that my defection was genuine."

"What about your family?"

"The Soviet Union is a society that threatens punishment to those who remain behind when one defects. My wife died two years ago. I have no one else. I left little baggage behind to hinder my escape."

The interrogation went on. Gordon's questions were sharp and probing and the Russian knew that he was in the hands of an expert. The American's questions followed no discernible pattern. They leaped from subject to subject like a frog on a lily pond, then returned to dig deeper. The Russian was given no chance to fall into a comfortable pattern with his answers. He constantly had to change tracks. He knew that Hardwick knew the answers to many of the questions he asked, and the Russian also knew that his answers to these questions were used to verify his truthfulness. He knew enough to deny knowledge of certain subjects. He was confident enough in his own knowledge that he did not feel it was necessary to embellish answers or to fabricate things he did not know. His answers were straightforward and direct. If he knew an answer he gave it—if he did not, he said so. As the evening wore on, Gordon became more and more convinced that Belenkov's defection was genuine.

It was well after midnight when Gordon threw in a question that surprised the Russian.

"Do you know anything about the KGB acquisition of the computerized guidance system technology from the TMK Corporation in California?"

Belenkov's eyes widened as he thought about it. "Very little, as far as the acquisition was concerned, but my department was in charge of the subsequent operation that leaked back to you that we had acquired the technology."

Hardwick's eyes bulged. "You—you mean you leaked back to us that you had the guidance system?"

Belenkov nodded, pleased to have divulged something that the American thought was important. "Yes," he said.

"But why? Why would you steal vital secrets from us, then let us know that you had stolen them?"

"I don't know," said Belenkov. "I was merely doing as I was told."

"What were you told?"

"To leak the information to a British agent in such a way as to make the Americans think that they had uncovered the information through regular intelligence chanels."

"But that doesn't answer why. Why let us know?"

"There are several possible reasons," said Belenkov.

"Go on."

"The simplest is that we wanted you to know that we had the technology and were capable of using it. This tends to neutralize such technological gimmickry."

Hardwick's sneer showed what he thought of that possibility.

Belenkov smiled. "I don't think much of that either."

"What else then?"

"Cover up."

"Cover up? Cover up what?"

"I can't be sure, but once in Egypt I was in charge of an operation to surreptitiously reveal to the Egyptians that we were in possession of their diplomatic codes."

"Why?"

"It appeared that they were on the verge of discovering that fact anyway. By leaking the information ourselves we were able to lay the blame at the doorstep of a minor communist functionary and divert suspicion from the real spy, who happened to be a cabinet minister in Sadat's government. We were able to protect a valuable source by blaming an unimportant one."

"What happened to the unimportant one?"

Belenkov shrugged. "Firing squad I suppose. That's not important."

Hardwick was silent for a while. "Do you think this might have happened with the guidance system?"

"I have no idea. But if I were you, I would not rule it out."

Hardwick sat back in his chair, his notes dangling listlessly at his side. He had the feeling he was into something and that one more question—the right question—would bring all the answers into place. A few years ago, he thought, I would have had that question. Now all he had was a pounding headache and a growing sense of bewilderment. Nothing Belenkov had told him about the TMK case made any sense. After a few minutes of silence he looked up. "Let's call it a night. We can begin again in the morning."

Belenkov stood up shakily and finished his vodka. "Whatever you say, my friend. I'm sure you have much to ask me, and I have much to tell you."

Twenty-six

It was almost three A.M. when Gordon came instantly awake to a sound in the hallway. He sat up, picking up the pistol on the table beside his bed, and swung his feet out onto the floor. He knew that he and the Russian were safe from intruders. CIA operatives had the house surrounded on the land side so anyone approaching would be spotted before he got within a half mile of the place. The alarm system would warn of anyone who somehow managed to get through the guards and enter the house. The only question was the Russian who was already in the house—Belenkov.

A light went on down the hallway and then Gordon heard the sound of the Russian retching into the toilet.

"Too goddamned much booze," he muttered as he listened to the painful spasms. He flopped back down onto the bed.

Three other times that night he was awakened by the Russian's vomiting.

In the morning he made coffee, checked in with Langley, then went upstairs to awaken Belenkov. He pushed open the door and saw the ashen-faced Russian shivering under the covers of his bed. He stepped into the room. "You sick?"

Belenkov nodded. "All night," he said. "Chills, vomiting, diarrhea."

"I'll call a doctor right away."

Langley dispatched a doctor immediately, but he could find little wrong with the patient. After a thorough examination he presented some pills for the nausea and an antidiarrheal compound.

"Stay in bed, drink plenty of fluids, and call me tomorrow if the condition doesn't improve."

Throughout the day Belenkov's condition continued to worsen and that evening Hardwick found him bleeding profusely from the nose. He called for an ambulance immediately.

Deputy Director Hanson met him at the emergency room of St. Leonard's Hospital.

"What happened?" Hanson asked.

Gordon shook his head. "Don't know. He got sick last night. I thought maybe it was just the booze he consumed, but it's obviously more serious."

"Somebody got to him," said Hanson.

"How? He's been under guard constantly."

"I don't know," said Hanson, looking at Gordon with a trace of doubt in his eyes. "But I don't like this one bit."

Gordon wasn't sure what that look meant, but he didn't like it one bit either.

"As soon as we find out what's going on and we get him stabilized, we'll have him transported by copter to Walter Reed," Hanson added.

"He could have been poisoned in England or while in transport and the poison is just taking effect now." It was more a question than a statement and Gordon realized he was hoping to avoid blame.

Hanson eyed him but did not say anything.

Gordon lit a cigarette and began to puff nervously. How the hell did they do it? he asked himself as he sat brooding in a chair in the waiting room. Several times a doctor came out to talk with Hanson. They talked in hushed tones and then Hanson came over to Gordon. "His condition appears to have stabilized."

"What's wrong with him?"

"They're not sure. Obviously some kind of gastric disturbance. We'll let him rest here tonight and tomorrow airlift him to Reed."

"I'll stay with him."

"No," replied Hanson carefully. "I'll assign a couple of men to stay here. You go home and get some sleep. I'll let you know what happens."

What happened was that in the middle of the night Belenkov lapsed into a coma. The nurse who checked him hourly found his right pupil dilated and fixed and his left pupil a pinpoint. He did not respond to even the most painful stimulus and his vital signs were showing rapid deterioration.

He was helicoptered immediately to Walter Reed, where a team of physicians was standing by. A CAT scan showed intercranial hemorrhage. His platelet count was below five thousand, fifty times below normal. By this time the doctors were certain they were dealing with some kind of toxic agent but had no idea what kind.

Hanson and Gordon met with the doctors in the office of the hospital's chief of internal medicine.

"Right now," said Dr. Ryan, "we're fighting a losing battle. If we knew what agent he had ingested it might help, but"—his face was full of uncertainty—"I doubt if anything can help him now."

"What can we do?" asked Hanson.

"If we had samples of what he ate and drank, we could test for whatever the toxic agent is."

Hanson looked at Gordon, who said, "The only food we ate was the food I brought with me to the house. Everything was either canned or frozen—all commercially prepared and selected at random. There's no chance that it was poisoned in advance and I don't see how it could have been poisoned afterward. Besides, I ate and drank everything he did and nothing seems to have—" He stopped in mid-sentence.

"What is it?" asked Hanson.

"The vodka. He drank almost a quart of Russian vodka—Stolichnaya—by himself. I had less than one drink." He looked at Hanson helplessly. "But I bought that vodka myself—two bottles from a liquor store in Washington. I delivered it to the house personally last Sunday—the day before Belenkov arrived. I thought Russian vodka would be a nice touch. I don't see how it's possible that—"

Hanson shook his head disbelievingly and stood up. "Let's get those bottles."

Two operatives were dispatched by helicopter to the cottage on the shore. They returned with both bottles—one full, the other almost empty—along with the contents of the kitchen garbage pail.

A team of forensic physicians under the direction of David Sauer, a professor of toxicology from Georgetown University, began the search immediately.

"We'll start with the vodka," said Sauer. "That seems like our best bet."

The first item of interest was that the tax labels which sealed the bottles had been unglued so that it would not be evident that the seal had been broken. It was soon apparent that the vodka had been contaminated with some tasteless, odorless substance. Meanwhile Belenkov's condition continued to deteriorate. An SGOT test determined that the Russian had already suffered extensive liver damage.

Sauer was able to narrow the field of toxic agents to a list of alkalyting agents that were easily soluble in liquids. He had further narrowed the list to three of these substances— methyl methane sulfonate, dimethyl sulfate, and dimethylnitrosamine—when word arrived from intensive care that Belenkov had died.

Sauer shook his head sadly while a stunned Hanson and Gordon Hardwick could only stare blankly at the floor.

"An autopsy will let us know what killed him," said Sauer.

Hanson nodded curtly. "Send a report to my desk." He turned to Gordon. "I want to know everything that happened up to and including the autopsy report." With that he whirled and strode from the room.

Sauer eyed Gordon sympathetically. "He blames you?"

Gordon shrugged. "My job was to protect him—he's dead," he said simply. "Somebody got to the man while he was under my protection. It's my responsibility."

Sauer shook his head in disbelief. "You couldn't know that the vodka was poisoned! You couldn't have prevented that!"

"Maybe not," said Gordon, "but it'll cost me anyway."

Sauer seemed mystified by this attitude. "We still have to find out what killed him. And you drank from that bottle. You may be at risk too."

As Dr. Sauer went off to assist with the plans for the autopsy, Gordon slumped into a chair in the lounge. He felt the crushing sense of failure that accompanies the loss of any source of information along with the personal sense that he was in some way responsible for Belenkov's death. He believed that what had happened had been unavoidable—at least it had been beyond his capacity to prevent it—but at the same time he knew of Hanson's displeasure and suspected that at the Agency this would be chalked up as a mark against his career, not Hanson's. The fact was, they didn't know whom to blame for this one, so the condemnation would fall on whoever had been closest to the disaster.

Twenty-seven

K.C. Hardwick was in Gordon's apartment, packing his suitcase and nervously checking his watch. Diane was in the kitchen looking for orange juice.

"I don't want to miss this plane," K.C. said.

"Don't worry," said Diane, coming out into the living room with a juice glass in her hand. "We've got plenty of time."

He was doubtful. "We should have left Carmel earlier."

She growled at him from deep in her throat. "If you had let me get dressed, we might have been able to leave earlier."

He smiled sheepishly, remembering how she had looked. She pushed her hair away from her face and he watched the faint beginnings of a smile on her face.

"Look," he said, "I can always get a ten-o'clock flight. So what if I arrive bleary-eyed."

He pulled her to him and they kissed, their bodies

pressed hard against each other. He ran his hand inside her T-shirt and felt the long curve of her bare back . . .

The phone rang.

"Shit," he said.

"Don't answer it," she said, pulling him toward the bedroom.

He looked guilty. "I have to. It might be for Gordon. I promised I'd take messages."

She rolled her eyes and went back to her juice.

He answered the phone. It was Gordon.

K.C.'s eyes narrowed and his brow was furrowed. "Gordie," he said, "what is it? You sound awful."

"I blew it, little brother."

"What are you talking about? What's happened?"

"I just threw my career down the toilet." Gordon sounded as if he had been drinking.

"Okay, slow down and tell me what happened."

"They got to him, somehow, and finished him—finished both of us."

"Who got to whom, Gordie? What the hell are you talking about?"

"Who? Who else? The Russians, the KGB, the big bad commies. You know, those nice people who brought peace and tranquillity to Eastern Europe, joy to Afghanistan, good times to—"

"Gordie," interrupted K.C., "you sound drunk. Can you tell me what happened?"

"Sure," said Gordon, his words slurred and sounding as if he might be on the verge of tears. "We had ourselves a defector—a big cheese in the KGB. He asked for me personally to protect him and they gave me the job." He laughed, but his laughter was almost a sob. "But they got to him. I don't know how they did it, but they got to him."

"What do you mean, 'they got to him'?"

Gordon exploded angrily. "What the hell do you think? They killed him. Poisoned him right under my nose. Poisoned him with booze that I bought and gave to him. Don't you see how funny it is? They used me to give him the poison."

Gordon's voice had a near-hysterical quality to it now and for the first time K.C. had the feeling that what Carol had suggested about his brother's mental condition might be true. K.C. tried to be calm and reassuring. "Gordie, I want

172

you to listen to me. I'm on my way to the airport now. I can be in Washington tonight. I want you to meet me."

"Don't bother, K.C. I'm fine."

"Now look, I want to talk to you as soon as I get there. Where are you?"

Gordon seemed unusually passive and gave him the name of the hotel where he was staying. K.C., trying not to sound overly concerned, asked him to meet him there that evening.

K.C. hung up the phone and turned to Diane, who stood waiting for him to tell her what was wrong. "He's in trouble," he said. "I've never heard him sound like this." He shook his head. "I'm worried about him. I'd better get to the airport."

Diane gave him a sad smile. "I understand."

"I wanted to say good-bye to Carol. Would you call her for me and tell her what's happened?"

"You want me to tell her about Gordon?"

K.C. sighed. "I'm not sure if she cares anymore, but tell her anyway."

Gordon Hardwick jumped at the sound of the telephone and actually had to sit for a moment to catch his breath before answering. The sound seemed to be coming from a great distance, as if the phone were underwater.

It was DDO Hanson. "I just got the autopsy report from Dr. Sauer. His suspicions were correct. Belenkov was poisoned with dimethylnitrosamine—a small amount can be enough to kill."

"What the hell is that stuff?"

He could tell that Hanson was reading from the report. "It's an industrial solvent developed as a heavy-duty cleanser for NASA and the Space Shuttle program."

"Can we trace it?"

"It's produced in large quantities and is available to almost anyone in the aerospace industries."

"Shit."

Hanson was reading again. "The autopsy revealed acute hepatic necrosis, cerebral hemorrhage, and terminal renal failure—any one of which might have killed him."

"Pretty potent stuff."

Hanson waited before responding. "You drank it too."

"Hardly any. I didn't even finish one drink."

"Nevertheless, Dr. Sauer wants you in his office today

173

for blood tests. I think he wants to keep you in the hospital for a day or two for observation."

Now it was Gordon's turn not to say anything.

"He doesn't think you're in any danger but doesn't want to take chances."

"Okay," said Gordon. "I'll call him today and make an appointment." He thought about how to phrase his next question. "What about Belenkov?"

Hanson didn't understand. "What?"

"Will there be a funeral?"

"He's already been . . . disposed of. For obvious reasons we would prefer not to reveal that we were unable to protect a high-ranking defector. We'll put out a cover story that he is in seclusion and cannot be reached."

"Well," said Gordon, "there is a certain amount of truth to that."

Hanson wasn't sure if Gordon's remark was a rebuke or merely a sick joke. He decided to ignore it. "Call Dr. Sauer and make an appointment to see him. I'll talk with you later."

Gordon waited, hoping Hanson might make some further comment. The line went dead. Gordon sat in silence, the smell of failure heavy in the air around him. He was sure he would never be rid of it.

Gordon was awakened by a far-off sound. It was dark in his room and he realized he must have slept for hours. He was drenched in sweat and had a throbbing headache. When he sat up in bed he had to hold his head in his hands. The throbbing came and went at regular intervals. Gradually he realized that the phone was ringing, the sound driving shards of pain deep into his brain.

He answered, the ringing stopped, and the pain subsided.

"Mr. Hardwick," said a voice that for one brief moment he thought he recognized.

"Yes."

"I have some news for you about a mutual friend."

"Who is this?"

"That's not important."

"Then who is the mutual friend?"

"Mikhail Belenkov."

Gordon was instantly wide-awake. "What news?"

"Belenkov will not be returning from his long journey."

"Tell me something I don't know."

"Belenkov knew more than he told you."

"About what?"

"About many things. Some of them about the TMK Corporation. I have a list of items in my possession."

"And naturally you want to sell this list."

"Naturally."

"How do I know this list is worth anything?"

"The first look is free. If you are convinced that there is some value, then we can negotiate a price."

"When?" Gordon demanded.

"Now. Meet me at the entrance to Arlington National Cemetery."

Gordon was instantly suspicious. "We'll meet at a place of my choosing. Meet me at the Washington Monument."

"Very well, but I will bring only the first page of Belenkov's notes. If you are not alone you will never see the rest."

"Agreed. Be there in ten minutes."

Karpenkov hung up the phone and allowed himself a small congratulatory smile before heading for the below-ground parking lot of the hotel.

Gordon dressed quickly. He ran his fingers across the stubble on his chin, but looking at the rumpled appearance of his clothing, decided not to shave. His shirt was wrinkled and still untucked and his tie hung loosely about his neck. He had the sour taste of bile in his mouth. Before he put his jacket on he took the snub-nosed Smith and Wesson from his suitcase and slipped the revolver into his shoulder holster. His headache was getting worse and it was more difficult than ever to think straight.

Gordon was fully awake now, his head still throbbing. He knew he should call Hanson and get some reinforcements, but he wanted to do this by himself. This, he thought, is my chance to get off the shit list.

He took the elevator straight down to the parking garage and walked through the apparently deserted area to his car. He did not notice the man who watched him from the shadows near his car.

Karpenkov smiled as he saw Hardwick approach. Look at him, he thought, as he noticed Hardwick's disheveled and distracted appearance. See how easy it is to reduce a top-notch operative into a sloppy, bungling, careless fool.

As Gordon fumbled with his keys, Karpenkov stepped

up behind him and lightly touched him between the shoulder blades with his pistol. Gordon straightened up but did not turn around.

"Open the door and get in," Karpenkov ordered.

He did as he was told.

Gordon sat behind the wheel as Karpenkov held the pistol to his temple and reached inside his jacket, very carefully removing the Smith and Wesson. Gordon did not notice that Karpenkov wore white cotton gloves.

Karpenkov lifted the lock button on the back door and climbed into the back seat behind Hardwick. "Drive," he said.

"Where to?"

"Just drive. I'll let you know."

They drove, with Karpenkov giving occasional directions as they made their way through the traffic.

"You're the man on the phone, aren't you?" asked Gordon.

"Yes."

"Did you bring the list?"

"Yes."

"You can trust me," Gordon said. "You didn't have to go to all this bother."

"It's no bother," said Karpenkov, releasing the safety on Gordon's Smith and Wesson. "I leave nothing to chance."

They were entering a park now and all the danger alarms in Gordon's brain were howling. He fought to remain calm and despite the confusion that threatened to overwhelm him he managed to formulate the beginnings of a plan for survival. Keep talking, he thought. Let him think you suspect nothing.

"Pull over here," said Karpenkov, motioning to a parking area next to a small pond.

"Sure thing," said Gordon, trying to sound calm as he turned to the left.

He straightened the wheel and pointed to a space to the right. "Right there okay?" he asked, and with one swift motion flipped open the door and rolled out onto the pavement. He landed hard on his shoulder, but rolled over and came up running as the car, still moving, rolled past him.

The car thumped into a guardrail and jerked to a stop as Karpenkov leaped out in pursuit.

Gordon heard the footsteps behind him and knew that he was in trouble. His legs did not seem to be responding as

176

they should and several times in less than one hundred yards he stumbled and almost fell. His lungs were bursting, his legs were like lead weights. He knew he was finished. By sheer power of will he forced himself to keep moving for another fifty yards but it was no use. His body had deserted him.

He stopped and turned to face his pursuer, then doubled over in an agony of retching that brought him to his knees.

Karpenkov, close behind, stopped and cautiously approached him at a walk.

Gordon looked up. "You should have seen me in '68," he said, gasping for breath. "I woulda run your ass into the ground."

"Yes," said Karpenkov, hardly winded. "I believe you would have."

Karpenkov, gun in hand, circled his prey warily from a safe distance. "Back to the car," he said.

Gordon was still fighting for breath. "Look," he said, "I'm not going anywhere. Whatever happens, happens right here."

Karpenkov approached him from behind and stood over him. "Gordie," he said, his voice changed, "I want you to know it was me."

Gordon's eyes widened in recognition and he struggled to pull himself to his feet. As he did, Karpenkov took one step forward, held the pistol an inch behind Gordon's ear, and pulled the trigger.

Karpenkov waited only a brief moment until Gordon's lifeless body had ceased to twitch. Then he dropped the pistol next to the sprawled figure, and without looking back, he walked away.

WASHINGTON (AP)—The American Confederation of Scientists, a group closely allied with Defense Department projects, claimed today that the Soviet Union was working "at a feverish pitch" to develop its own antiballistic missile system.

In a study released today the group said that a huge, high-power radar installation at Abalakova, a small village about 130 miles north of the Siberian city of Krasnoyarsk, was clearly intended to provide tracking and targeting information for an advanced Soviet ABM system.

The group also listed the number of "violations and probable violations" where the Soviet Union has ignored the limitations imposed by the 1972 Antiballistic Missile Treaty.

Group spokesman Dr. Henry Conyers claimed that since 1972 the Soviets have embarked on one ambitious project after another to assure the invulnerability of their nuclear strike force. "The Soviet technique," Conyers claimed, "was to call for a halt to any testing or development of ABM systems, while at the same time mounting a massive research and development program to accomplish those exact goals."

Twenty-eight

Captain Gorsky was at his desk, pretending to find something of interest in the small stack of documents in front of him, when a familiar face approached him. It was Captain Sudarev of Department 13.

Sudarev was having trouble containing his smile. He leaned over Gorsky's desk and said in a near whisper, "They got him."

Gorsky looked around to see if anyone was within earshot before answering. "They got who?"

"Belenkov." His voice was a soft whisper. "I just decoded the transmission." Department 13 was charged with all communications between Moscow Center and the overseas residencies. All outgoing messages were encoded by Department 13 and all incoming messages were decoded. Sudarev was the day officer in the transmission and receiving section.

"You're sure?"

Sudarev nodded. "Absolutely. I just sent along the decoded message to Melekh. This ought to make the bastard smile."

Gorsky's jaw tightened and his back stiffened. "You'd

better get out of here," he said curtly, "before someone wonders why you're here."

Sudarev seemed puzzled at Gorsky's lack of enthusiasm. Gorsky usually relished the tidbits of information that Sudarev passed along to him from Department 13. Sudarev shrugged. "Very well. I'll talk with you later."

Gorsky said nothing and Sudarev, mystified by his old friend's coldness, walked away.

That bastard Melekh, thought Gorsky. My idea, and he will get all the credit. He looked around his tiny office with distaste. "My time will come," he muttered.

Gorsky sat for as long as he could stand it before he got up from behind his desk and called to his aide, Lieutenant Sakov. "Call the garage and tell them to have a car ready. A Zhugli will do and I won't be needing a driver."

The Zhugli was a Soviet-made Fiat, small, plain, and unobtrusive. If one did not wish to draw attention to oneself, the Zhugli was the perfect car.

Lieutenant Sakov gave a quick nod of his head and clenched his teeth to control his smile. It was common knowledge that Gorsky had a mistress whom he visited several times each week. Whenever he drove his own car it was assumed he was off to meet with this woman.

Her name was Virula Zolkin, a woman of thirty-five who, while not overly intelligent, possessed a rather quiet and dignified beauty. Three years ago Gorsky had arrested her and her husband and gathered the evidence that sent Virula's husband to prison for seditious activities. The activity was in smuggling written works by Russian authors out to the West.

The couple's property had been confiscated and the woman had been forced to vacate a relatively comfortable two-room apartment in central Moscow for a single room in the Kutuzov district on the other side of the Moscow River.

Both husband and wife could have been sentenced to lengthy prison terms even though the evidence against Virula was rather sketchy. Gorsky had personally intervened, telling the prosecutor that he was certain the woman was not personally involved in this matter. The prosecutor did not need any further encouragement, they dropped the charges immediately, and the woman went free.

Virula was bewildered but grateful to her benefactor, who told her how sorry he was about her problems and that if he could ever help her in any way she should feel free to ask.

Unbeknownst to her, her benefactor had also arranged to have her evicted from her apartment and to lose her job. Finally, in desperation, she turned to Gorsky.

Gorsky arranged for her to be reinstated at her job and for a new and better apartment near Gorky Street. Soon after she was settled he visited her, buying flowers and a gift of fresh meat. He was a perfect gentleman and made no demands upon her whatsoever, but Virula noticed, after his visit, that the other tenants in the building treated her with renewed respect. To be the woman of a captain in the KGB was a position of some respect.

Gorsky continued his occasional visits, usually bringing small gifts along with something to eat. The visits were brief; she made him coffee and offered him a piece of cake; they talked, he inquired after her health and usually told her that her husband, who was forbidden to communicate with anyone, was in good health and working well on the road to rehabilitation.

Still he made no advances, and Virula began to wonder when the inevitable moment would come and how she would react to it when it did. She spent many long and sleepless nights imagining how he would react when she rejected him. Sometimes she allowed herself to think what it would be like if she did not reject him. Lately she spent most of this sleepless time wondering about the latter.

But still he made no advances.

On his fourth or fifth visit, after the coffee and the cake and the brief conversation, during that part of the visit when he usually began to look at his watch and soon after reach for his coat, he asked Virula for a second cup of coffee. As she put the kettle back on the stove, her heart was thumping in her chest and her mouth was dry.

Today, she thought with a mixture of fear and anticipation, is the day.

She took him his coffee and sat in the chair across from his, being careful to cover her knees with her skirt when she sat.

Gorsky watched her over the lip of his cup, smiling a little at her nervousness. He was used to people being nervous in his presence; it gave him a warm feeling to know that this was true. He could tell in her eyes that she was waiting and wondering.

He took out his wallet, removed some paper money, and

placed it on the table between them. Virula's eyes widened in surprise, then narrowed in suspicion.

Gorsky pushed the money toward her. "I want you to go on a little shopping trip today," he said.

"Shopping?"

"Yes. Buy some sweetmeats at Yeliseyev's on Gorky Street and then a nice dress for yourself at Gum. I saw something there yesterday up on the second floor in the first aisle across from men's hats. . . . A very nice dress with blue flowers. I thought you would look very nice in it."

She was uncertain. "Thank you," she stammered.

He looked at his watch. "I would like you to make a pot of tea and put out the rest of the cake that I brought." He smiled at her puzzlement. "Put out two more cups . . . please."

"Of course."

They were having guests.

He looked at his watch again. "When shall I go shopping?" she asked.

He smiled. She was not unintelligent. But of course, he knew that. That was why he had picked her. Not too quick, not too slow. That and the obvious fact that she responded to authority. "As soon as the tea is ready you can go. You will be gone for one hour—not a moment less."

Virula nodded obediently.

Gorsky went on, "When you return, look for my car. If it is still there, take a walk until it is gone. Do not return to the apartment until you are certain that I have left. . . . Do you understand?"

She swallowed, then nodded. "Yes."

"Then make the tea," he said gently, "and go buy yourself that pretty dress."

"Don't you want to see me in it?" she asked, feeling foolish immediately.

"Next time," he said uninterestedly. "Next time."

This became a part of their normal routine. Gorsky would visit for a brief time, give her some money, and send her on a shopping expedition. Sometimes she was told only to buy bread, but always the instructions were explicit. "Do not come back in less than one hour." She realized then that Gorsky did not want her for her body, he merely wanted her as camouflage. He was holding meetings with someone in the apartment and had used her to disguise those meetings. No one would suspect that a KGB officer would meet someone else in his mistress's apartment.

On this day as on all the others, Virula fixed the tea and the cake and then she left. Fifteen minutes or so later Gorsky heard a sharp rap on the door. He opened it to admit a dark-haired man in his late thirties wearing a gray topcoat and a sable fur hat. He was Colonel Petrunin of the GRU.

"Marshal Ushenko sends his regards," said Petrunin as Gorsky motioned him to a seat. "He was sure you would understand why he cannot be here himself."

The GRU—Glavnoye Razredyvatelnoye Upravleniye—or Soviet Military Intelligence, was a division of the Soviet General Staff. The GRU was independent of, and in constant competition with, the KGB. It was to the Soviet Army what the KGB was to the Communist Party, and while the Army had always considered itself subservient to the Party, the GRU had never accepted a secondary role in its relationship to the KGB. The constant infighting had made the two services bitter enemies.

The Soviet military has always—or perhaps only since the great purges of the thirties, which decimated the ranks of the officer corps—viewed the machinations of the KGB with great distrust, and the recent ascendancy of several officers of the KGB to the Politburo, the Soviet pinnacle of power, had done little to dispel that distrust.

Each service ran its own operations, its own training centers, had its own spaces in Soviet embassies, and jealously guarded its own secrets. The KGB was determined to reduce the power of its rival and make it and its forces merely another arm of the Komitet Gosudarstvennoy Bezopasnosti. The GRU was equally determined not to accept any diminution of its authority.

Colonel Petrunin removed his topcoat and carefully laid it across the back of the sofa. He was a relatively short man but carried himself with great authority.

He sat down across from Gorsky, who poured him a cup of tea. "I did not expect to hear from you so soon, Comrade Gorsky."

Gorsky nodded and filled his own cup.

Petrunin went on. "Marshal Ushenko was extremely grateful for the information you passed along about the defection of Belenkov. He was also quite impressed with your powers of deduction about the whereabouts of the traitor."

"Obviously so was Director Melekh."

Petrunin was not sure he understood.

"They got Belenkov yesterday," Gorsky said.

Petrunin, obviously impressed, asked, "How?"

"I don't know, but my former charge, Chameleon, was the one who did the job." He smiled. "Just as I suggested he might."

"The marshal has of course relayed to you several times his feeling that you have not been properly rewarded for the successes of this man."

"You may tell the Comrade Marshal that I am unworthy of his praise."

Colonel Petrunin eyed Gorsky carefully, agreeing with Gorsky's self-appraisal. A career officer in the GRU, he had an inherent distrust of anyone in the KGB and felt a personal disgust of anyone who would betray his own service. Although he acknowledged the importance of working with the *stukach* Gorsky, who over the past several years had provided the GRU and Marshal Ushenko with many interesting tidbits of information that the KGB would have preferred to keep secret, he could not bring himself to enjoy it. He swallowed the words he wanted to say. "Well, Captain Gorsky," he said, forcing a smile, "if things go as scheduled you may yet become a man of great power and influence."

Gorsky's look was self-effacing. "Thank you, Colonel."

"Now," said Petrunin, drinking the last of his tea, "what has brought us here today so soon after our last meeting?"

Gorsky smiled and removed a roll of film from his pocket. "At our last meeting the marshal expressed an interest in the secret installation at Abalakova."

Petrunin's eyes widened and he took the film from Gorsky. "Is this Abalakova complex, as the KGB claims, merely a communications center for the interception and transmission of messages?"

Gorsky smiled wickedly. "If so, why would Professor Dimitri Turkin, the number-one Soviet scientist in the development of particle-beam weapons, be transferred there?"

Petrunin's back stiffened. "Then it is a weapons complex?"

"Apparently. Read the documents on the film."

The colonel stood up in obvious agitation. "Why would the KGB and the Party develop a secret weapons complex in central Russia without informing the Soviet military? It doesn't make sense."

Gorsky shrugged. "That I can't tell you. But the evidence is clear—they are building something out there."

Petrunin was in a hurry to get going. He slipped on his coat. "This may be of great significance, Captain. I'm sure the marshal will be most grateful." He paused for a moment. "The marshal is a man of his word. You can be sure he will keep his promises to you."

Gorsky nodded. "All I have ever desired is to run the KGB."

Petrunin stifled a smile. When the marshal came to power the KGB would be stripped of much of its authority and the GRU would take over most of its functions. "The marshal will keep his promise," he said, moving to the door.

"What has he promised you?" asked Gorsky.

Petrunin seemed shocked by the suddenness and perhaps by the impertinence of the question. He thought for a moment, then with a stiff smile he said, "The marshal often tells me that he will make me the military commander of the occupation forces of Western Europe." His smile broadened. "Of course, I am sure he only speaks in jest."

Gorsky was removing the teacups from the table. "I was not aware that the marshal was prone to speaking in jest."

Petrunin said nothing, but gave a quick nod in farewell and was gone.

After waiting a few minutes, Gorsky followed.

Neither Gorsky nor Petrunin saw the lead man from the KGB surveillance team that had followed Gorsky when he left headquarters two hours before. As Gorsky got into his car the man lit a cigarette. Around the corner another car started up and the driver eased the car out into the afternoon traffic on Lesnaya Street.

WASHINGTON (UPI)—The Federation of American Scientists, in a direct rebuff to Administration claims, stated today that "there is absolutely no tangible evidence that the Soviets are building an antiballistic missile system in central Russia."

The statement was in direct response to Administration and American Confederation of Scientists' claims that a Russian radar installation in Abalakova, Siberia, was "very likely in violation" of

the 1972 ABM treaty and the Stategic Arms Limita-
tion treaties.

"It is more likely," said the Federation, "that the
Abalakova complex is intended as a massive communications center to provide instant information to
the far-flung Soviet military forces."

At the Pentagon, spokesman Jim Walsh said
that the Defense Department would have no immediate comment on the report.

Twenty-nine

Several hundred people attended Gordon Hardwick's
funeral on a bright but chilly morning at a small cemetery
near Bethesda, Maryland, where Gordon and Carol had lived
when he was with the CIA. There was a Marine honor guard
at the gravesite and six of his former colleagues from the CIA
acted as pallbearers.

K.C. stood with Carol, each helping support the other.
The sky was a deep icy blue, and the bright flowers at the
gravesite seemed oddly out of place.

It wasn't until Carol was presented with the flag that had
draped Gordon's coffin that K.C. thought how odd it was that
all the CIA people were there: DDO Hanson, Robert Birdwell,
even Carey, the director, had arrived in a black limousine
just before the ceremonies began.

When the Marine sergeant handed Carol the flag and
said, "Your husband served his country well," something
clicked in K.C.'s mind like an unlocking door. Looking around
at the gathered assemblage of three-piece suits, he thought,
they're here because Gordon died in the line of duty. Despite the official pronouncement, none of them believed for a
minute that Gordon had killed himself.

K.C. himself had refused to believe it—he thought he

had known Gordon too well to believe his brother could take his own life. It had taken a great deal of persuasion from Carol, who had convinced him that Gordon was not the same person that they had known and loved, before he would even begin to consider the possibility. But the fact that Gordon had been killed with his own gun had been persuasive. The clincher, however, had been the coroner's report, which had stated that death had been caused by a "self-inflicted wound to the head." As evidence the report detailed gunpowder residue removed from the area around the wound, which included metallic fragments, unburned grains of powder, and burned grains of powder in the form of soot which travels only an inch or two from the barrel of the weapon. That indicated that the weapon had been held within inches of the dead man's head and was the most persuasive evidence of suicide.

Now that evidence, which he had accepted only reluctantly, was blown away as if by the cool cemetery breeze. Carol felt him stiffen and turned to offer him encouragement but her eyes widened when she saw his clenched jaw and the anger in his face. She squeezed his hand to remind him that she was there but saw more fury in his face than she had ever seen before.

Gordon would never kill himself, said K.C. to himself over and over again until it was ingrained into his memory.

When the ceremony was over and the mourners were walking back to their cars, K.C. watched as Hanson and CIA Director Carey conferred briefly before getting into their respective cars. K.C. led Carol to their car and asked her to wait for him.

K.C. went to Hanson's car and as he approached, the rear window glided open and Hanson leaned forward with a sad smile on his face. Birdwell was also in the back seat.

K.C. was tight-lipped. "I want to talk with you."

"Of course, K.C. Anytime you say," said Hanson.

"Today. Now."

Hanson frowned and looked to Birdwell and then back to K.C. "I'm not sure I can get the time today. I'm ver—"

K.C. interrupted. "Make the time. This can't wait."

"What is this all about?"

"What else would it be about? Gordon was murdered, wasn't he?"

Hanson's eyes roamed the cemetery. "The official coroner's report says that—"

"I don't care what the official report says, you and I know better."

Hanson sighed. "Perhaps we could meet for a drink later. Say around seven-thirty?"

K.C. paused, then nodded. "Fine."

"Where are you staying?"

K.C. gave him the name of his hotel and Hanson said, "I'll be there. We can talk about this."

As K.C. returned to his car, Hanson pushed the button and the rear window slid to a close. "Well," he said to Birdwell, seated beside him, "what do you think?"

"Seems a little more volatile than I had expected."

"Oh he'll be all right," said Hanson. "Once he calms down he'll be just fine. I think we can use him to our advantage on this, don't you?"

Birdwell nodded in agreement but doubt was written all over his face.

K.C. watched Deputy Director Hanson enter the hotel lounge and realized that Hanson was not as nervous as he was. Self-confident son-of-a-bitch, he thought, as he watched the Deputy Director walk—almost swagger—across the room.

Hanson sat next to K.C. There was no offer to shake hands, no exchange of pleasantries. "Okay," said Hanson. "I realize today that you were upset with something about your brother's death. I also realize that at times of such terrible tragedies we often don't think as clearly as we otherwise might. I hope you're not going to blame the Agency for what happened to your brother." He waited for K.C. to say something.

"It's such a good speech, Hanson, I really hate to interrupt. Was my brother murdered?"

Hanson looked down at his hands. He spread his fingers as if he were inspecting his nails. "Your brother was one of the best men I have ever had the pleasure of working with. I considered him a very dear friend."

"Was he murdered?"

"That is classified information."

"Which means yes."

"You may choose to interpret it that way if you wish."

"You're a cool son-of-a-bitch," said K.C. "My brother is

187

dead and I can't even get a straight answer out of you about how it happened."

Hanson stared into his eyes. "Are you sure you want to know?"

"I want to know."

"It's not pretty, or heroic, or anything like that."

This time K.C. was not as vehement. "I want to know."

Hanson nodded. "Very well. As you suspected, your brother was murdered—executed would be a better word for it." Hanson looked steadily into K.C.'s eyes.

K.C.'s mouth was dry.

"If our reconstruction of the . . . event is accurate, we believe that Gordon was on his knees at the time, someone approached him from behind, and with Gordon's own weapon shot him behind the ear." He touched his index finger to the spot where the bullet had struck Gordon.

Involuntarily K.C. shuddered at the description. "Must have been more than one of them to be able to do that to Gordon."

"Careful scrutiny of the site shows that there were two people present. Your brother and his killer."

K.C. looked at Hanson disbelievingly.

"I'm afraid your brother had not been as effective lately as he had been in the past."

"But you assigned him to this job anyway."

"Sometimes in this line of work, we take great risks and we lose."

"When was the last time a DD was killed in the line of duty?" said K.C. sarcastically.

Hanson smiled self-consciously and went on. "Your brother was a fine man and a fine American. He did what he did so that our country would be more secure and the world a better place to live."

"Please," said K.C. "I don't want to hear this."

"Why not?"

"You sound just like Gordon."

Hanson smiled. "Exactly. And just like Gordon, I believe every word of it."

K.C.'s face was beet red in stifled anger and Hanson's calm demeanor served only to increase his fury. "You people are all alike," he said. "Cold, calculating, dispassionate. You don't care about people. You play your little games with people's lives, then walk away, untouched, unhurt."

Hanson tapped his fingers absently on the table. "I can see that you're angry," he said, "and I don't blame you, but it is possible that you are directing your anger at the wrong people."

"Meaning?" K.C. asked sharply.

"Don't be angry with the people your brother worked for; be angry with the people who killed him."

"People? I thought you said one man killed him."

"We don't know who pulled the trigger, but we can be certain who directed the whole operation."

"The Russians?"

Hanson nodded.

K.C. gave a long sigh of exasperation. "You people are unbelievable. When you catch a cold, do you believe the Russians did it?"

"No, but if I ever get a fatal whiff of mustard gas, I'll know where it came from."

K.C. started to get up. He had heard enough of this paranoia.

Hanson raised his hand in a "stop" motion. "Shall I tell you the result of Gordon's autopsy? You might be very interested. It explains a great many things."

K.C. slumped back into his seat. "Such as?"

Hanson raised an eyebrow. "Gordon's behavior over the past year."

"Go on."

"The coroner found traces of a drug called Aminazin in Gordon's blood. There's no reason for Gordon—or anyone—to take such a thing."

"What does it do?" asked K.C., his head beginning to throb.

"It induces depression and wild mood changes—depending on the dosage."

K.C. looked down at his hands. These were the symptoms Carol had often described.

Hanson went on. "Aminazin also causes stiffness and pain in the joints, but most important, it destroys the memory and creates a sense of confusion. We sent one of our best men to California and someone destroyed his effectiveness." Although Hanson's eyes were moist and he wiped at his nose with a handkerchief, his voice did not waver. "The medical report says that it is remarkable that anyone could continue to

189

function at all—even with diminished capacity—under these conditions."

K.C. was quiet now, and neither man could look at the other.

Finally K.C. spoke. "I want to know what happened."

Hanson shook his head. "I'm afraid that's classified."

"I talked with Gordon the day he was killed. He told me he had failed somehow, that a defector had been killed."

Hanson thought for a moment, considering how much he could tell. "What happened was that someone was able to get into a well-guarded private home and plant a poisonous substance which was probably intended to kill both your brother and the man he was charged with interrogating."

"Doesn't sound as if the Agency was doing its homework."

"You are right to be dissatisfied with our performance in this matter. Apparently we were guarding the wrong man."

K.C. looked puzzled.

"We had tight security around the defector. But someone apparently followed Gordon to the house and placed the poison even before the defector arrived in Washington." He shrugged. "We've gone over every possibility—that's the only way it could have been done. . . . Unless . . ."

"Unless what?"

"Unless Gordon did it himself."

"You don't believe that?"

"No—I don't. But there are others who consider it a possibility."

"That's absurd."

Hanson nodded. "Perhaps. This is a business where the absurd is often commonplace."

"Why are you telling me all this?"

"You said you wanted to know."

"You've told me more than I wanted—more than you had to. Why?"

Hanson was direct and to the point. "I want you to help us."

"What?"

"I want you to take your brother's place."

"You're crazy."

Hanson shrugged, implying that the possibility was not so farfetched. "I told you that the absurd was commonplace. We've tried putting our own people in place and it hasn't

190

worked. With your background and experience you'd be perfect for the job."

"Forget it!"

"You could do your country a great service."

"Not interested."

"You could help vindicate your brother and help us find his murderer."

K.C. hesitated for a moment. "That's your job."

"Yes it is. And we won't rest until we find or eliminate him. But you could make it much more likely that we will succeed."

K.C., deep in thought, said nothing.

Hanson smiled. He had found, just as he had known he would, the vital cord. "You don't have to answer now. Think about it. One of my men will contact you tomorrow. Someone who will be able to answer all of your questions."

"Why me?"

Hanson smiled gently. "Because you have the necessary knowledge of the field and the objectivity of an outsider. You also have the extra added incentive of a personal motive." Hanson paused. "You want to find your brother's killer."

K.C. sat in stunned silence.

"But as I said, you don't have to answer now. Think about it and one of my men will be in touch."

Hanson rose from the table. They shook hands and K.C. was left sitting at the table, lost in thought and near bewilderment at this turn of events.

Thirty

The next morning K.C. Hardwick left his hotel near the Dulles International Airport for the thirty-minute ride to the Langley headquarters of the CIA. Ten miles from downtown Washington, the CIA building—a modern, seven-story, campuslike complex of attached buildings—sits high above the Potomac, overlooking the George Washington Parkway.

As he had been instructed, K.C. drove to the Dolley Madison entrance, one of the three gates that permitted access to the grounds. The guard at the gate took his name and checked it against a list on his clipboard before waving him through. He parked in the visitors' parking area and headed for the front entrance.

Inside the gigantic entrance foyer K.C. tried not to gawk like a tourist at the high, white marble walls and decorative columns. Etched on a far wall were the words "Ye Shall Know the Truth and the Truth Shall Make You Free." K.C. could not help but remember Nazi work camps that had carried the motto *Arbeit Macht Frei*, "Work Shall Set You Free."

A uniformed guard directed him up a flight of steps to the Badge Office, where he was again checked on a list and then given a visitor's badge to wear on his lapel.

"You will be escorted to the third floor by a security officer," he was told by a young woman in the Badge Office. "You must wear your badge and whenever you pass a checkpoint, insert your badge in the slot."

She saw the puzzled look on his face. "Helps us keep track of everyone in the building," she said smiling.

He was escorted to a blue elevator, one of four, and then taken to the third floor, where he followed his fast-walking escort down a long corridor with brightly colored doors on both sides.

Twice he used the badge checking system before he arrived in B corridor and at the office of the Technology Transfer Assessment Center.

Robert Birdwell was waiting to greet him at the door with a warm handshake. K.C. recognized him from Gordon's funeral.

"I knew your brother well," Birdwell said. "And like everyone at the Agency, I respected his work."

Birdwell was young and looked Ivy League. He wore his blond hair short and his face was open and agreeable. His choice of clothing ran to tweeds and flannels, and K.C. felt sure he had an unlit pipe in there somewhere waiting to be lit.

Birdwell's office was not large. He indicated a chair in front of his desk and K.C. sat down. Birdwell stood, his back to the window that looked out over the parking lot. "I spent last night going over your file," said Birdwell, "and I want you to know that I think you'd make an excellent choice for this operation."

K.C.'s smile was almost a snicker. "And I want you to know that there's very little chance I will work for you or the CIA."

Birdwell's face revealed nothing of what he was thinking; then he smiled. "You're here aren't you?"

"Only to hear what it is you have to tell me about my brother."

"Very well. Deputy Hanson has authorized me to answer whatever questions you ask. Your security clearance is to be regarded as 'most secret.' You need only give me your word that whatever is discussed here will remain secret—between us."

"That's it? I promise not to tell and you'll tell me everything?"

Birdwell shrugged. "Deputy Hanson has taken full responsibility for your trustworthiness. I might add, however, that your agreement with these terms brings you under compliance with Presidential Order Number G5363 which prevents you, under penalty of law, from discussing or revealing in any way with any other person any classified information that we are about to talk about."

Birdwell's smile was genuine. "Most of what we are going to discuss is common knowledge and available through the pages of your local newspaper. These precautions are taken only because our discussion might border on several classified areas that could be useful to the agents of a foreign power."

K.C. thought for a moment. "Okay, let's do it."

"Then you are agreed?"

After a moment's hesitation K.C. said, "Yes."

"Then fire away."

"What was my brother doing in California?"

"He was involved in a long-term project to protect American technological secrets from being transported to the Soviet bloc. He reported directly to this office."

"Sounds like pretty mundane stuff for someone as high up as Gordon."

"Perhaps it sounds that way. And we do have scores of people involved in this kind of thing, but your brother was involved in what may be the most important aspect of this work."

"I know that you people are paranoid about secrets," began K.C.

Birdwell cut him off. "Right now there are over 150 Soviet agents—ranging from Soviet-bloc businessmen to certified KGB agents—operating in the Silicon Valley and in and around San Francisco. Another fifty or so operate in the Los Angeles area. These people would do anything, pay any price, to get the technological information that their governments covet. Everything they buy or steal eventually winds up in Moscow and soon thereafter becomes part of their military hardware. In short, Mr. Hardwick, we are being threatened by our own technology."

"Kind of ironic, isn't it," said K.C. "Most of the information they acquire is sold to them by Americans."

Birdwell nodded glumly. "There are some who don't recognize what they're doing—and some who don't care—and some who for the right amount of money—would sell or do anything. My job is to see that they don't. Y'know, in this country everybody has a right to his opinion—we don't try to force anybody to believe what we think is right or wrong."

"Sounds like my seventh-grade civics class."

"Bear with me for a minute. We Americans pride ourselves on examining both sides of every issue. Consequently we have a fair percentage of people who doubt a lot of what the U.S. government tells them."

"So?"

"The other side has no such problems. They tell their people what to believe and ninety-nine percent of them do just that."

K.C. sighed and rolled his eyes to the ceiling. "Is there a point to this?"

Birdwell nodded. "Unfortunately for us, some of the people in our own country who don't believe what our government says believe what the *Soviets* say, which puts us in a rather untenable position. Some Americans believe that their own country is the villain in every possible situation. Some of our own citizens believe that it is in the best interests of 'world peace' to pass along our technological secrets to unfriendly powers. Some do it for money and I have nothing but contempt for them. But for those who do it for reasons of conscience, I can feel only pity for them. If they're wrong they may doom us all."

"Your problem," said K.C., "is that you believe there is only one side to every question—our side!"

Birdwell's lips made a thin line across his face. "Your brother believed that too."

"I know. That didn't make it right."

"There have to be some of us who believe that. If not, what happens to our way of life? If our military leaders and our intelligence forces don't believe in what we are, where would we be?"

"Talking to you," K.C. said, "is like listening to my brother. You're all the same."

Birdwell smiled. "You're probably right. But what I have to know is, will you help us?"

"Help you do what?"

"Find out the source of these leaks—find out who killed your brother."

"How can I help you? I'm no cloak-and-dagger man."

"You have the necessary background in computer science. We can help place you at the same company where Gordon worked. You can get work there without the burden of being attached to the CIA."

"I don't know if I can do that."

"You *can* do it. The question is *will* you?"

"Why me? You must have others who are better qualified."

"Right now we think that someone outside the Agency, known only to Hanson and myself, would do the best job."

K.C. eyed him warily. "You don't suspect someone in the CIA has been leaking information?"

Birdwell shrugged. "We don't know whom to suspect. All we know is that at every turn our next move is anticipated. You as an outsider, reporting directly to me, would not have that problem."

"What about my name? It's hardly unknown at TMK."

"I can arrange a new, temporary identity, close enough to your background particulars—same age, same college, same employers, et cetera—so that you won't have a problem with it."

"I don't know."

"You'll think about it?"

He knew he would. "Yes."

"Good enough. I'll contact you tomorrow. Talk to Carol

about it. I'm sure she'll encourage you." He stood up. "I'll tell you what. Why don't we meet at this time tomorrow. When you decide, I'll give you all the details."

"You sound pretty sure I'll say yes."

"You're a Hardwick, aren't you?"

Carol was already back in California when K.C. called her. She was adamant. "You must be crazy," she said. "Tell them to stuff it. One Hardwick dead for the cause is quite enough."

"I really don't think there would be any danger."

Carol was incredulous. "You're really thinking about it, aren't you?"

K.C. closed his eyes. "I think Gordon would want me to."

"Gordon's dead," she said harshly. "You never did anything he wanted you to do when he was alive. Why start now?"

"Maybe that's the reason. Maybe I feel I owe him one."

"That's foolish, K.C. Go on about your life. Let them get someone else." She waited for him to respond and in that wait she knew that against the better judgment of both of them he had already decided to go through with it.

Thirty-one

Birdwell seemed ecstatic when K.C. told him the news.

"Welcome aboard," he said. "I knew we could count on you."

"One thing," K.C. said. "If I'm going to do this, I'm going to do it my way. I'll work with you, but not for you. I'm more interested in finding out who killed my brother than in your precious secrets."

Birdwell's tone was not so enthusiastic. "Very well."

"And I want it clearly understood from the beginning that I won't take orders from anyone in the CIA."

Birdwell was struggling to keep the tone of his voice steady. This conversation had not gone exactly as planned. "Will we be able to make an occasional suggestion?"

"Yes."

"Thank you," said Birdwell, unable to keep the sarcasm from his voice. "There is one thing though that we must insist on."

"What's that?"

"That no one know that you are working for us. We'll have to prepare a new identity for you. If anyone knows who you are, the whole operation could collapse like a house of cards."

"But . . ." K.C. stammered.

"No buts," said Birdwell. "This operation depends upon you being able to move about freely at TMK without anyone suspecting who you are."

"Carol will know."

"That's unavoidable and controllable. You don't know many people out there so it should be relatively easy to keep your identity a secret."

K.C. thought of Diane. "I'm not sure that I can do that."

Birdwell shrugged. "Then it's no go. If you want to find out who killed Gordon, there's no other way."

K.C. shook his head helplessly, then nodded. "All right," he said reluctantly, "I agree. What now?"

Birdwell sighed. "I get you prepared for the job. We talk about what you should look for, what you should do. We prepare your new identity."

"When I apply for a job at TMK, aren't they going to check my résumé?"

"Of course they are, but they'll check it through the CIA and the FBI."

"When do we start?"

"Right away."

Over the next two weeks K.C. and Birdwell met for several hours each day going over everything K.C. would have to know in minute detail. Each day Birdwell left him with a stack of documentation prepared by the Technology Transfer Assessment Center that detailed the hemorrhaging of American technical secrets to the Soviet Union. It was a theme Birdwell never tired of propounding.

"The loss of technology is practically epidemic in Silicon Valley," he said. "We've found it practically impossible to stem the flow. It's only in the past five years or so that we've gotten together with the Commerce Department and Customs Service to even try to stop it."

He handed K.C. a typed report of the known technology acquired illegally by the Soviet Union. The report was more than thirty pages long, single-spaced, and listed by category—computers, guidance and navigation equipment, electro-optical sensors, propulsion design, manufacturing techniques—and all of the military applications of the stolen technology.

"And that's just the stuff we know about," said Birdwell. "God knows how much they've got that we haven't found out about."

K.C. shook his head in disbelief.

"Here," said Birdwell, handing him another stack of papers. "This is a list of Soviet acquisitions that are considered marginally or nonmilitary in nature."

The list was almost as long as the first.

"A lot of this stuff is available for export under licensing arrangements—they steal it anyway. That way they don't have to pay for it."

K.C. made a face. "C'mon. Are you trying to tell me they won't pay for anything?"

Birdwell shrugged. "Only if they have to." He ran his fingers through his hair. "Let me give you an example. About three years ago Kodak came up with a new film process—quicker, cheaper, better color reproduction."

"Yeah, I've seen it advertised on TV."

"It cost them millions and took maybe ten years to develop this process. They demonstrated the new technique at a trade convention in Frankfurt. After the convention they packed everything up and went to the airport but it seems the Kodak equipment and quite a few other products never made it to the plane."

"And you blame the Russians?"

"Six months later the Soviets announced a new 'revolutionary' advance in film. Developed, of course, by Russian scientists working night and day to bring better living through chemistry."

"Okay," K.C. said, "you've convinced me. But what are

they going to do, invade us with hordes of tourists snapping pictures with a new revolutionary film?"

Birdwell's face showed his exasperation. "I show you these things only to demonstrate the enormity of the problem. In an open society it's difficult to stop this kind of thing, but just because we have an open society do we have to bleed ourselves dry? The Russians must chuckle themselves to sleep at night thinking what dopes we are."

K.C. said nothing and returned to his reading.

"We don't have the manpower to put someone into every small company that deals with sensitive technology. The only thing we can do is place people where we think they are most needed and where they will be most effective."

"TMK?"

Birdwell nodded. "Your brother was remarkably effective in tightening up security there. So effective that someone wanted to eliminate him." He handed K.C. a medium-sized notebook.

"What's this?"

"It belonged to your brother. The first half is fairly straightforward and easily understood. The second half is increasingly disorganized and illegible. I thought perhaps you could . . ." he searched for the right word ". . . decipher the contents."

K.C. took it as if it were a fragile flower and leafed through the pages. It began in Gordon's neat, easily readable print and ended in an almost illegible scrawl. "I'll try," he said.

"Take it. We have copies," Birdwell said. "I thought you might want the original."

Both of them were quiet for a moment and then Birdwell added softly, "Your brother may have died for what is in that book."

One day during the second week of what K.C. Hardwick had come to think of as his "propaganda indoctrination," Birdwell came into the small office that they had appropriated for their use. He was carrying several large envelopes and he seemed in an especially jovial mood.

"Envelope number one," he said, handing K.C. a large brown envelope.

"What is it?"

"It's the response to your employment application from TMK."

K.C. went to open the envelope and then saw that it was already opened. He looked at Birdwell, who merely shrugged. "Why don't you just tell me what it says," said K.C.

"They are very pleased that someone with your credentials is interested in them. They want you to call and set up a personal interview. They'll fly you out, at their expense of course."

"Can it be this easy to get a job there?"

"You've got terrific credentials. They don't find people like you every day. Besides, high-tech companies out there in the Valley are finding it increasingly difficult to attract the kind of people they want."

"Why?"

"Most people don't want to spend two or three hundred thousand for a house or a thousand a month to rent an apartment. We're talking high-rent district, K.C. A lot of bright prospects just turn around and go home when they see what they get for their money."

K.C. shook his head in wonder. "TMK, here I come."

"We've already replaced Gordon with another of our operatives, but you'll have absolutely no contact with him. We're hoping you can find a place in the research division. We've doctored your résumé to make it seem like that's where you'd be best situated—but it's a long shot. Chances are they'll start you elsewhere, but you can still keep your eyes and ears open."

"Just exactly what am I looking and listening for?"

Birdwell pulled up a straight-backed chair and sat across from K.C. "Your brother was convinced that someone either at TMK or with contacts inside the company was responsible for previous leaks. If Gordon was right, that person is still there, and right now is in a position to do great damage to the United States."

K.C. looked skeptical.

"Right now," said Birdwell, "TMK is in the final stages of putting together the key component in a workable antiballistic missile system. The weaponry has been tested successfully, but the guidance system is so complex that it requires a whole new generation of computer technology."

"Jonathan Kincaid."

"Precisely. Kincaid has developed the machine that will

track, aim, and fire. It will even calculate the difference between decoys and the real thing. It's fantastic."

"If it works, it changes the whole balance of nuclear power."

Birdwell rolled his eyes. "Without a doubt."

"I'm not sure that's a good idea."

Birdwell's face fell. "Wake up, for Christ's sake. We need this system. We've got to have it!"

"Why? What good is it?"

Shaking his head as if he were explaining a difficult problem in math to a small child, Birdwell said, "Every year it gets tougher and tougher to push through money for spending on nuclear weapons. Look at what's happened with MX. The Democrats want to use the money to throw away on more bullshit welfare programs and the taxpayers don't want to spend money on anything more than the bare essentials. If we get a Democrat in next year or in ninety-two or ninety-six, the money could just dry up. But the Russians keep spending and building. Nobody tells them it's too expensive; nobody marches in the streets when they deploy new missiles; nobody bitches when—"

"I get the point."

Birdwell was on a roll. "The point is, right now they've got more hardware aimed at us than they know what to do with. Our deterrent capability is crumbling. One of these days they're going to think they can take us out with one quick hit. This ABM system could save our ass. At the very least it will make them think twice."

"At worst it will scare them into doing something stupid."

"That's highly unlikely," Birdwell said. "They don't take risks. What they will do is try to get their hands on this system and build one just like it. Where do you think we'd be if they deployed it first?"

"That's highly unlikely," K.C. said, trying to mimic Birdwell.

"Maybe," said Birdwell, walking to the window, "but maybe not. One area of research in which the Russians are at least our equal is particle beams and lasers. That's the first component of the system. Three months ago one of our communications satellites sent back a momentary report that it was being bombarded by an intense beam of light. A fraction of a second later we lost contact. Two weeks ago a Space Shuttle repair crew brought the satellite back to earth.

It was shot clear through and all its internal components were shredded."

Birdwell handed K.C. a satellite photograph. All K.C. could make out were several small buildings in a row, one very large one, and what might have been several vehicles at various locations. He looked up from the photo. "What's this?"

"This is a satellite photograph of a Russian ABM facility at Semipalatinsk. The large building contains the power source for what is believed to be an advanced particle-beam weapon."

"But you can't be sure. You haven't seen inside."

Birdwell gave him a second photograph, similar to but not identical to the first. "This is another site at Saryshagan. This is believed to be a testing facility."

"Once again you can't be sure."

Birdwell's voice was matter-of-fact. "We know that they've tested this weapon against satellites and that their success rate is excellent. If they wanted to they could probably knock out most of our reconnaissance satellites with this weapon." His face was grim. "But that's not the worst of it. Since 1980 the Soviets have conducted more than one hundred test firings against reentering warheads. Our best estimates are that at present their success rate is no better than sixty percent—not good enough but still a remarkable accomplishment."

K.C. swallowed hard.

"They've got the hardware," said Birdwell. "They just haven't got the guidance system yet." He threw two large brown envelopes on the table in front of K.C. "Here's the rest of your surprise. Your new identity and a history of TMK and the Ameronics Corporation." He went to the door and paused. "I'd study them both real well if I were you—a lot of people might be counting on you."

Thirty-two

After Birdwell left the room, K.C. sat for a long time staring at the photographs. He viewed them from every angle but nothing changed much. The photographs could have been of anything. He looked closely and thought he could make out the oval shape of what might have been a running track. For all I know, he thought, these pictures could be of some Russian university. For that matter they might even be an American university. He looked again. It was impossible to tell anything with the untrained eye. He had only Birdwell's word that these photographs showed what he said they did.

K.C. opened one of the other envelopes and emptied the contents out onto the table. Here he found his new identity—social security card, driver's license, four credit cards, a library card, a Red Cross blood-donor card, a college I.D., with picture, identifying him as a member of the faculty at Columbia. All the identification was issued in the name of Kevin Collins—his actual first and middle names. Easy to remember, he thought.

The background biography included in his package was also very close to his own. Kevin Collins, the biography said, had been born in Ithaca, New York, in 1956 and attended public schools there. A note at this point explained that his high school had been severely damaged in a fire in 1973 and many student records had been destroyed—including, of course, those for Kevin Collins. K.C.'s fictional counterpart had gone to Ithaca College and then completed his graduate work in computer engineering at Rensselaer. The fictional Kevin Collins was at present an associate professor at Columbia University in New York City.

At first K.C. marveled at how quickly the CIA had been able to put together this history and fake documentation, but then slowly he began to realize that such an effort required a great deal of preliminary information about his past. Had they had all of this information "on file" waiting for future use? If so, why, and for what purpose? He could feel his old animosity and suspicion toward the Agency begin to rise anew.

He stood up and walked to the window from where he could see the parking lot, and beyond, the George Washington Parkway. Nothing ever changes, he thought. It's still the same old gang at the CIA—devious, intrusive, manipulative. He shook his head sadly. He had almost bought the whole thing. They had caught him at his most vulnerable and fed him the usual line, bolstered this time with facts and figures and satellite photographs. But what did it mean? It meant what it always did—and that was whatever they wanted it to.

He was here only because he wanted to know what had happened to Gordon. Who had killed him and why. The rest of it was none of his business. Let the CIA and the KGB and whoever else might be involved play their silly games. He was not interested.

They had worked on his ego, telling him how much he was needed and how he was one of the few people who could help his country at this critical juncture. When that didn't work they went to the ace in the hole—they brought in the bait.

The bait had been the chance to find Gordon's killer. He could see that now. They had dangled that in front of him and he had taken it, as they must have known he would, hook, line, and sinker.

He was ready to change his mind, ready to call the whole thing off. He began to gather up the material he had been given and put it back into the oversized envelopes. He would get great satisfaction out of dumping everything on Birdwell's desk and telling him and the CIA to "stuff it."

As he cleared the papers and cards from the table he uncovered Gordon's notebook. K.C. stopped. He looked at the notebook for a long time and then picked it up. Without reading he flipped through the pages, imagining Gordon making entries in his usually neat and straightforward handwriting and wondering who and what had been able to make his brother scribble the illegible hieroglyphics he saw there now.

Whatever else was true or false here, K.C. knew one

thing: his brother was dead, his brother had been murdered. And he wanted to know who had done it. He wanted to know why. And for what reason.

Nothing Hanson or Birdwell had told him meant anything to him. For all he knew they might be trying to cover up their own incompetence—or even their own involvement. After all it was their "official" report that claimed that Gordon had died by his own hand, If K.C. had not challenged Hanson at the funeral, the matter, in all likelihood, would have ended there.

He sat down, elbows on the table, head in his hands. If he walked away from this now, he would never find out what had happened. He had no other choice.

K.C. pushed the other materials aside and opened the last envelope. It contained a brief history of the Ameronics Corporation and a history of its subsidiary companies. The report also listed the Ameronics people who had moved into positions of influence in the government and K.C. was amazed at the depth of their involvement. Ameronics and the U.S. government seemed to have an open-door agreement, moving people freely back and forth from one to the other. Nothing was stated, but it was obvious the situation was fraught with potential for conflicts of interest. No fewer than six formerly high-ranking officers of Ameronics presently served in some capacity or other with the U.S. government, ranging from Secretary of Defense to the ambassador to South Korea, and several former government officials now served on the executive board or as highly paid consultants to Ameronics.

The last three pages of the report gave in more detail the history of the TMK Corporation and the background information on its surviving founders, Michael Tolbert and Jonathan Kincaid. Kincaid was a certified genius who consistently developed new ideas. His developmental process did not progress in any logical or easily defined method. His ideas moved in leaps and bounds and often moved beyond the next logical development into areas only dimly perceived by others. The report claimed that his work on computers was so far ahead of others in the field that it might be ten years before anyone else caught up. It was therefore of paramount importance that his work not be delivered into the hands of any potential adversary. It was people like Jonathan Kincaid who gave the United States the technological edge it needed to stay ahead of the Soviet Union.

Michael Tolbert, on the other hand, seemed to be a man of no discernible talent. Other than his ability to bring the right people together and his obvious organizational abilities, K.C. was at a loss to discover what it was that had made this man the master of the far-flung empire of Ameronics.

Tolbert had brought together the genius of Kincaid with the financial backing of David Morton to create TMK. He had then married the daughter of Mason Whitaker, the man who owned Ameronics, and when Whitaker lost his only son, Tolbert had taken over the reins of the parent company. As far as K.C. could tell, Tolbert had reached his present position of wealth and power by a tantalizing combination of charm, persistence, and shrewdness, topped off with a rather large dollop of good fortune.

With its vast array of contacts in government, and a huge lobbying apparatus already in place, TMK, through Ameronics, was able to move aggressively in the acquisition of Defense Department contracts. Because of the vaunted genius of Kincaid and the people he had gathered around him, the company had been able to garner billions of dollars' worth of government contracts. That genius had also made TMK a target for espionage.

As K.C. continued to read, he noted that the report was reverting to the singular theme Birdwell had hammered at for the past week: espionage had been a way of life in the Silicon Valley for years. One company stealing from another, one employee selling his company's secrets to a competitor or to another government.

Even though security was exceptionally tight at TMK—thanks to the efforts of Gordon Hardwick—it was feared that the Russians would mount a massive attempt to obtain the crucial technology that was being developed there.

K.C. put the papers aside. He knew as much as he wanted to know. He would go along with Hanson and Birdwell until he could find out what had happened to Gordon. If he helped the CIA along the way, that was okay, too. If he didn't—that was their problem.

He took his identity package and began to examine it more carefully. If he were going on a job interview, he'd better have a clear idea of who he was.

When he got back to his hotel there was a message that Carol had called. He called her immediately.

"Diane was here today," she said, not wasting any time on preliminaries. "She's a little confused."

"About what?" K.C. asked, knowing immediately what it was.

"It's been almost two weeks since Gordon's death and Diane hasn't heard from you."

K.C. did not say anything.

Carol rushed to fill the silence. "She seemed to feel you two had something going and just wondered if she would see you again."

K.C. had known that this moment would come but had been unable to resolve what he would do. "I'm not sure," he said.

"Not sure," said Carol, the edge in her voice obvious. "What does that mean?"

"Look, Carol," he said, "if things go well, I'll be working at TMK under an assumed name. No one is supposed to know that I'm Gordon's brother or that I'm trying to find who killed him."

"I think you're making a mistake."

"I know how you feel about me working for the CIA—"

"I'm not talking about that. I still think you're being foolish about that, but I'm talking about Diane. You'll be making a mistake if you just walk out of her life."

"I think it would be better if we put this on the back burner for a while. Maybe after this is all over I can—"

"Don't be stupid," Carol interrupted. "If you let this go now, you may never get another chance. Women like Diane don't grow on trees."

"I know that, Carol."

"Well?"

"I think it would be better if she didn't know about any of this."

"Will you call her—talk to her?"

"What can I tell her? That I'm working undercover on a secret mission for my government? She'd think I was crazy."

"You'd rather tell her nothing? Let her think you've forgotten about her?" Carol was silent.

"I'll write her a letter telling her I've decided not to take the job at Stanford—which is true."

"Coward. I think you should call her."

"You're probably right but I don't know how else to handle it."

"Tell her what you're really doing."

"I can't."

He heard the sigh of resignation in Carol's voice. "And you can't tell her anything either, Carol," he said. "You can't say anything to anyone."

"It's your life. But I think you're throwing away a golden opportunity."

"You might be right, but I have to do this."

Carol hesitated. "Will I see you when you're out here? Or will I be off limits too?"

"I'm sure we'll be able to get together once in a while," he said, but his tone was not convincing.

"I'll look forward to it." Her tone wasn't convincing either.

He decided to take Carol's advice and call Diane. It was not one of the most pleasant conversations he had ever had.

She offered her condolences about Gordon, but he could tell she was hurt and confused by his failure to call her. After a conversation filled with empty spaces and careful maneuvering around the important places Diane finally asked the inevitable question. "When am I going to see you?"

"I don't know," he said hesitantly.

"What about the job at Stanford?"

"I'm going to have to rethink that. I'm not sure."

"Oh," she said, and K.C. thought he could detect a quaver in her voice, but when she spoke again it was strong and firm. "Well, that's it then. I guess we both have a lot of rethinking to do."

"Look," he said, "my not taking the position at Stanford has nothing to do with you. What I mean is—when I get straightened out here, I'd like to see you."

There was a long silence before she spoke. "I don't think so," she said. "I really don't like having people drift in and out of my life. I think you may have gotten the wrong impression from me and that's too bad. Maybe things went too quickly for us. I should've known better."

"I'm sorry if—"

"Don't be sorry. I'll be fine—I'm fine already. Just a little puzzled. We're both adults. No need for recriminations or sad stories."

He was feeling awful. There had to be something he

could say to her. Something that would at least make him feel better. "Let me try to explain," he began.

"That's not necessary," she said quickly, silencing his feeble attempt at excuse. "Let's just leave it as it is. I'd prefer it that way."

There was a thunderous silence during which he could think of nothing to say.

"Good-bye," Diane said pleasantly. "Take care of yourself."

He continued to hold the phone to his ear for a long time after she was no longer on the line. Usually when it was too late he could always think of the right thing to say. This time he could think of nothing.

WASHINGTON (UPI)—Joseph Cardinal Bernardin, Archbishop of Chicago, and Archbishop John J. O'Connor of New York, in testimony before Congress today urged the Congress to reject the President's call for an antiballistic defensive system and to begin "a new effort in creative diplomacy that will pull the world back from the brink of catastrophe."

The bishops called upon the President to renounce first and second use of nuclear weapons. "Even if attacked," said Bernardin, "the United States should refrain from a disastrous retaliation."

Cardinal Bernardin's testimony before the House Committee on Foreign Affairs was, he said, intended to redefine the scope and intent of the pastoral letter "The Challenge to Peace," issued by the Roman Catholic bishops some five years ago.

Archbishop O'Connor called upon the Congress to "scrupulously measure, by political and moral criteria, the consequence of this technological advance."

Both bishops, speaking for the United States Catholic Conference, called upon the President and the Congress and the American people to "reject the voices of war" and find a "common bond of brotherhood with those whom we would make our enemies."

Representative Frank Colby, Republican of Iowa, challenged the bishops' interpretation of the President's policies and portrayed the pastoral letter released by the United States Catholic Conference, the public policy agency of the Catholic bishops, as "naive, pacifistic, and seeking unilateral disarmament."

"The Catholic bishops," said Mr. Colby, "would have us destroy the deterrent value of our present nuclear arsenal and refuse us the right to deploy a defensive system to protect us against the Soviets."

Committee Chairman Walter Dugan, Democrat of Michigan, agreed with the bishops and vowed to fight the President's proposals. "This pie-in-the-sky system could potentially be the most expensive in a long list of expensive military projects proposed by this President." Pounding his fist on the table, Dugan said, "We don't need it and the American people don't want it. Let the President find better ways to spend the taxpayers' money."

Thirty-three

Getting the job at TMK proved to be as easy as Birdwell had promised. K.C. was flown out for an interview, and after a few hours with the personnel department and lunch with one of the vice-presidents, he was immediately offered a job. He was told that the offer would be contingent upon a CIA investigation of his background and the successful completion of a polygraph test to demonstrate that he did not seek employment at TMK for any other than his stated reasons.

The polygraph threw him a little bit. He hadn't expected that, but a quick call to Birdwell early that afternoon assured him that the polygraph—just like the background check—would be administered by the CIA.

"You've got nothing to worry about," Birdwell said.

Birdwell was right. K.C. went to an office in San Francisco, where, without ever taking the test, he was passed with flying colors on a security-check polygraph.

On the basis of the fake polygraph, the CIA was able to recommend to TMK that Kevin Collins be employed immediately. Until his background information was cleared by the CIA he would have no security clearance and would not be allowed entrance to any classified section of the building, but Birdwell assured him that this would be taken care of in a short time.

"Security check usually takes from two to three weeks. We don't want to tip anyone off to your presence at TMK by giving you immediate clearance. Take two weeks to get yourself acclimated. Your clearance will come along through normal channels and then maybe we can get you into the research section."

So less than one month after Gordon Hardwick's funeral and little more than three days after his first visit to TMK, K.C. Hardwick—now Kevin Collins—reported for work at his new job in California.

K.C. found an apartment in Sunnyvale in a fairly new building in a quiet section of town. The complex was one of those fake Spanish mission style buildings that dot California. It had two stories and was built in a U shape around a small, well-kept courtyard with a pool in the center. All of the entrances to the apartments opened out onto the courtyard and most of the tenants seemed to be in their twenties and early thirties.

K.C. bought some furniture and moved in immediately.

He found the atmosphere and the work at TMK stimulating, and the people who worked there seemed interesting and fun to be around. Many of the programmers, analysts, engineers, and designers who worked there were around K.C.'s age. Except for the heavy work load and the manic atmosphere of working at a dynamic company, K.C. found that it was a lot like being back in college. There was a sense of camaraderie at the company, a sense that they were all working for some common purpose. Although K.C. had never been particularly adept at making new friends, he found it relatively easy to fall into conversation with most of the people who worked there.

Outside of work he spent most of his time in his apartment and much of that time was spent working on Gordon Hardwick's notebook.

The early part of the book and of Gordon's investigation was no problem. Gordon's clear, concise style made it obvious that he was gathering as much information as he could find about TMK and its key personnel and about the serious security problem that he believed existed. It was also obvious that Gordon was convinced that someone inside TMK was responsible for the breach in security. In his typical methodical fashion he had begun a systematic evaluation of most of the people who worked at the corporation. His method seemed to aim at establishing, through a chronological listing of names and events, who at TMK was present at the time of the security violations, who had access and therefore opportunity, and finally who might possibly be linked to one or more of these security "incidents."

Gordon had listed many of the names of the people at TMK and at various times had crossed them off his list with a single stroke of a red pen. Alongside that single stroke Gordon had written some brief notation that indicated why that person's name had been removed from his "suspect list."

By this method Gordon had eliminated one suspect after another until he apparently had reduced the number to around twenty people who had what Gordon described as "reasonable opportunity."

Unfortunately, at this point Gordon's rational, methodical investigation had begun to unravel. K.C. noted that organization had been the first thing to go. Where earlier he had been able to follow his brother's line of thought from entry to entry and page to page, the notations now began to jump around in no discernible pattern. It grew worse, and soon it was like trying to decipher a personal code without any clues. Apparently at some point Gordon had started making random notations in his notebook—disassociated words and phrases were everywhere.

There were frequent references to Reid Lawson, often followed by the word "Traitor," but K.C. knew from the dates of the entries that most were around the time of Gordon's breakup with Carol and her subsequent attraction to Lawson. Later the references to Lawson came more frequently and became more vehement, often appearing with red, angry lines through the name, as if Gordon had used his pen like a knife to slash at his enemy. Lines and arrows radiated outward on the pages like explosions and names were obliterated in heavy blobs of red, as if the writer intended to bludgeon those he had rejected. Dark, angry smudges expunged the record of others.

K.C. read on, fascinated and disturbed at the same time, as the notations became even more indecipherable. Occasionally a phrase made sense: "Watch Progano—Untrustworthy—Could be him." There were several illegible notations after this and then "Suicide 5/15—guilty????" Another notation obviously referred to Birdwell—"Is Bird still with his old department?"

But always the references came back to Reid Lawson. "Must stop him!" "Can't let him get away with it." "Poisoned Carol against me."

It was obvious, thought K.C., that Gordon, in his muddled state, had confused Lawson's taking Carol away from him with someone stealing secrets from TMK.

There were several late entries in the book that intrigued K.C. because the dates placed them within days of Gordon's death. Few of them, however, made any sense. "Talk with the Birdman. He knows who it is," was one. "See Lieutenant MacDonald YYZPD," read another. And then, almost as if a cloud had lifted, Gordon had written in a fairly legible hand, "Check Lawson's business trips."

The last two pages were notes made about the visit with Belenkov. K.C. could see nothing of any import there. He put the book aside sadly. This was his brother's legacy, all he had left behind to mark the fact that he had ever been here. I owe it to him, he said to himself, to find out who did this to him—who destroyed his effectiveness and ultimately took his life. The last notation ran through his mind. "Check Lawson's business trips." That, he thought, was as good a place as any to start.

Thirty-four

Every Friday after work a large group of people from TMK gathered at a local bar—a place called the Little Byte—to celebrate the end of the work week and the beginning of the weekend. After K.C.'s first full week at TMK he was invited to join the Friday gathering.

The bar was packed—mostly with TMK employees—and K.C. noticed that most segregated themselves by job description—programmers in one section, analysts in another, noncomputer employees in yet another. The secretaries joined in with any group they desired.

K.C. worked around the fringes of the computer people, not saying much, responding only when spoken to. He was introduced in a very casual manner to a lot of people he had not yet met and knew that he would never remember all their names. He got into a conversation with one of the secretaries, a very attractive blond from the sales department, but she was quickly whisked away by a programmer from research who had tickets to a rock concert for that evening.

Mostly, K.C. sat watching, sipping a few beers, and trying to take in as much as he could. He could not keep his mind from playing "spy games"—what about that one, he would ask, is it him I'm looking for? Or what about him—he's got kind of a sneaky look to him. Maybe it could be a woman. He tried to pick out the most likely candidate as if one could tell a spy or a murderer by the turn of a nose or the curl of a lip.

Some of the Special Projects people were playing chess over in a corner. K.C. ambled over in that direction to find three boards and six obviously intense participants with several interested observers around each table. With each move some observer inevitably groaned his misgivings and the player would look up in disgust at his tormenting kibitzer.

K.C. smiled as he watched. Computer people, he thought, have an obvious fascination with chess. Perhaps it was the intricacy of the game or the logical progression of the moves.

"Do you play?" a voice said, interrupting his thought.

K.C. turned and saw a man about his age standing next to him. "A little," he said. "Not very well."

The man smiled. "Good," he said and K.C. wasn't sure if it was good that he played, or good that he didn't play well.

"You're new," said the man, extending his hand. "I'm John Cowans. I'm with systems design."

K.C. nodded. "Kevin Collins, research."

"Where from?"

"New York," said K.C., and when that elicited no response he added, "Columbia."

Cowans smiled. "Ah, another academic decides to head for the land of fame and fortune."

"Something like that."

"You'll like it here," said Cowans. "TMK is a pretty good place to work."

Cowans was tall—well over six feet—with longish, shaggy hair and a full beard. He had a plain open face and a quick smile and K.C. found him easy to talk to. They sat for a while, talking and watching the progress of the games. Occasionally someone would walk past and Cowans would grab him by the arm and introduce him to K.C.

One of those was Ted Nichols. "Ted's the project director at Special Projects," said Cowans by way of introduction.

Nichols seemed more interested in one of the chess games going on in front of them until Cowans gave K.C.'s name. Nichols turned to face him. "You're Collins," he said as if he were the only one who knew.

"Yes," said K.C., slightly puzzled by the reaction.

Nichols smiled at K.C.'s expression. "Personnel sent me your file yesterday."

K.C. raised an eyebrow. "Oh?"

"I think they're considering moving you over to us at Special Projects. I guess they wanted to know what I thought of your qualifications."

K.C. waited for Nichols to continue, but when he did not he couldn't resist saying, "And?"

215

Nichols nodded vigorously. "Excellent credentials. I think you'd be an asset to our project."

K.C. was relieved. "I'm glad to hear that."

"What do you think—would you like to move over to Special Projects?"

"I really hadn't thought about it," K.C. lied. "Sounds like it might be interesting."

"Good," said Nichols. "We'll talk some more when your security clearance is completed."

When Nichols had walked away, Cowans looked at K.C. with an expression of renewed respect. "You must be one of the heavy hitters," he said.

"Why's that?"

"That's all they have at S.P.—heavy hitters."

K.C. was pleased with himself. "Is that right?"

"Don't be too happy," said Cowans. "Things aren't as easygoing over there as they are for the rest of us." He sipped his beer. "Lots of tension, lots of stress."

The pleased smile faded from K.C.'s face.

Cowans nodded knowingly. "Some people can't take it over there. We even had a few breakdowns over there."

He kept saying "over there" as though the Special Projects division was somewhere in Europe.

"There's tension in any job, I suppose," said K.C.

Cowans thought carefully before answering. "Some people wind up dead from this kind of tension."

It was almost 7:30 when K.C. arrived back at his apartment building. He had his key in the door when a voice called to him from below.

"Hey there."

He turned and looked down into the courtyard to see a small blond girl whom he had seen several times with a man he assumed was her husband. "Hi there," he said, smiling.

"I'm Grace Kallin. Welcome to the neighborhood."

"Thanks. I'm Kevin Collins."

"New to California?"

He laughed. "Does my New York City pallor give me away?"

She laughed back. "First thing anybody notices."

He nodded, and not knowing what else to say, smiled.

Grace Kallin went on. "In a little while my husband and

I are having a small get-together with some of the others here in the apartments. Why don't you drop by and have a drink."

"Sure, thanks."

"We're in the corner apartment," she said, pointing. "Most of the party will be out here in the courtyard. Anytime after eight." She waved. "See you later."

K.C. watched her go. California, he thought, was just loaded with good-looking women.

K.C. had tried to dress in what he imagined was California casual—Izod shirt, beige slacks, and deck shoes—but everyone seemed to be more casual and infinitely more stylish than he.

Grace Kallin introduced him to her husband, Tom, and to a few of the neighbors—some of whom he had already said casual hellos to in the mornings before work—and then left him to his own devices. His own devices were particularly ill-suited to this type of situation. He was not very good at introducing small talk and after the usual quota of questions about where he was from, what he did, and where he was working, most of the guests smiled pleasantly and went back to talking with the people they had been talking with before K.C. arrived. Consequently he found himself in the rather uncomfortable position of sort of standing around listening to other people's conversations and never being part of them.

Grace rescued him once or twice and introduced him to a few people, but she obviously was trying to enjoy her party and wasn't going to invest much time in this uncommunicative stranger.

K.C. spent more than ten minutes with two people he would normally avoid like the plague and then found himself alone once again.

Grace walked up with a kind of resigned smile that said: Shape up, chump, I'm only going to try this one more time. Instead she said, "Have you met everyone?"

K.C. looked around as if he were actually searching for a face he hadn't met. "I think so," he said, wanting to add: Don't worry about me, I'm never very good at this. But Grace Kallin's face lit up and K.C. followed her gaze to the back of a young man with very broad shoulders who was holding court with two obviously impressed young women.

"Come with me," said Grace and dragged him toward the threesome. As they approached K.C. heard brief snatches of conversation. Things like—"extra protein . . . pecs . . . curls . . . muscle mass." The two women were obviously impressed.

George Stamatelos," said Grace Kallin, "I'd like you to meet Kevin Collins." George's face was a blank so Grace added, "Your new neighbor."

K.C. shook hands with George, who made the formality a test of strength, but as soon as he realized there was no contest he relaxed his grip. K.C. gamely tried not to check his hand for broken bones.

George continued his conversation with the two young women about the joys of weight lifting. He wore a sleeveless shirt and every once in a while made a small flexing motion that made his muscles ripple. Both women's eyes widened each time he did it.

All three ignored K.C., who clinked the ice in his glass a few times and nodded as if he were included in the conversation. At one point he made a valiant effort to include himself in the conversation. "How long does it take to build yourself up like that, George?" he asked.

George looked him up and down. "You don't have enough time left," he said with a smirk, and both women struggled to suppress giggles.

At that point K.C. was wishing he had taken those karate lessons he had thought about some years ago. He would have enjoyed a finger jab at George's throat. Instead he smiled pleasantly and said, "It was nice meeting you all. I think I'll go get myself another drink."

He went back to his apartment, careful not to let Grace Kallin see him sneak away, made himself another drink, and fell asleep in front of the TV.

CHICAGO (AP)—In a speech at Loyola University today, Senator Lloyd Carmichael, the top contender for the Democratic presidential nomination, said "the clock is ticking" in the nuclear-arms race and proposed a freeze on all uses of "so-called defensive systems in space or on the ground."

In a speech laced with criticism of the President and his proposals to develop and deploy defensive ABM systems, Senator Carmichael said that such weapons "would dangerously destabilize the already deteriorating relations between the United States and the Soviet Union.

In a jab at the current Vice-President, who is widely believed to be the front-runner for the Republican nomination, Carmichael said, "And what about the Vice-President, what does he say to all this? Does he raise one finger in protest? Does he say to his boss, 'Enough is enough'? No. He runs around the country like a marionette mimicking everything his boss says. One is just as dangerous to the peace and security of this country as the other."

Thirty-five

One week later, K.C. looked up from his desk to see Ted Nichols standing in front of him. Nichols didn't say anything but flashed a huge grin. He had his hands behind his back as if he were holding something.

"Ta dah," he sang and dropped an envelope on K.C.'s desk.

K.C. picked it up. "Don't tell me I've been drafted."

"That," said Nichols, "is the government security check report." His voice was mock serious in his best TV anchorman impression. "You are hereby entitled to call yourself a loyal and patriotic American."

"I'd like to thank all the little people who made this possible," said K.C., falling into the mood set by Nichols. "I suppose this means I get to keep my job?"

"Better than that," said Nichols. This time his smile was genuine and his tone serious. "It means that we can get you over to Special Projects."

"With the heavy hitters?"

Nichols's laugh had heads popping up all over the room. "I know that's what they call us." He looked around the large room and everyone went back to work. "You've got the credentials. Are you interested in joining us?"

"Sure. What would I be working on?"

"We've got some developmental work going in artificial intelligence. I read your paper on the subject and thought you'd be interested in continuing your work here."

K.C.'s eyes widened and he swallowed hard. How, he thought, could Nichols have read work that had been published under his own name? "You read my work?"

"Yes," said Nichols. "The government forwarded some of your published papers to us along with your security clearance."

K.C. breathed a sigh of relief. Birdwell thought of everything. "What did you think?" he asked.

"Fascinating. I'd love to talk to you sometime about your theories."

K.C. nodded agreeably. He was pleased to have the value of his work recognized. "What about this government project you're working on, the one everyone whispers about?"

Nichols smiled. "It's finished."

"Finished?" said K.C. in astonishment.

Nichols nodded. "There's still some testing and refining to do, but basically the work is complete. The Defense Department will probably begin testing next week."

"Wow!" was all that K.C. could think to say.

Nichols laughed softly. "Wow is right." He started to go. "We'll talk Monday about your transfer, okay?"

K.C. nodded. "Sure."

"See you at the Little Byte later?"

"I'll be there."

"Get there early, maybe we can get a chessboard." With a quick wave, he was gone.

After work K.C. had a few beers at the Little Byte, and Nichols thrashed him in three straight games of chess. It was after eight o'clock when he arrived back at his apartment building and realized with a shudder that the Kallins were having another of their Friday-night get-togethers. He tried to sneak upstairs to his apartment unnoticed but was only half-way to the second floor when he heard a familiar voice call his name.

"Hi, Kevin."

He took a deep breath and forced a smile before he turned to face her. "Hi, Grace."

"You're not going to miss the party, are you?"

"Actually I had a few drinks after work and I'm a little bleary-eyed," K.C. answered.

"Good," she said cheerfully as if he had said he was feeling wonderful, "it will loosen you up a little."

He tried again. "I think I'll just take a shower—"

"Go ahead," she interrupted. "Take your shower, and I'll talk to you when you come down." She was shaking a finger at him. "Don't be long."

He watched her go back to the party. Grace Kallin was one of those people to whom polite refusal meant nothing. He gave a short shrug and trudged upstairs. One half hour, he said to himself. I'll give it one half hour.

He was back downstairs in the courtyard in less than an hour, showered and moderately refreshed. It was a warm evening and several people were in the pool.

"Did you bring your suit?" asked Grace. "It's a great night for a swim."

K.C. took a quick look at the tanned and muscular bodies around him and knew he had made a wise decision. "No," he said simply.

He handed Grace a half-full bottle of vodka. "This is all I had in the house," he said. "My contribution."

"You didn't have to do that," she said but took the bottle anyway and placed it on a table next to the front door of her apartment.

Soon Grace was dragging K.C. around introducing him to the crowd again. He noted with embarrassment that many of them were the same people he had been introduced to before. He found it incredibly boring going through the same litany over and over—"Where are you from . . . where do you work . . . do you run . . . do you eat meat?"

He still wasn't very good at it but a few drinks made it a little easier. After a while he realized that if he didn't think about what he was going to say, if he just opened his mouth and started talking, he was okay and his conversation didn't seem any less intelligent than anyone else's.

He saw George Stamatelos on the far side of the pool talking to another couple, and decided to stay as far away as he could.

He had another drink, engaged in one or two brief, mindless conversations and even a reasonably lengthy one with a small dark-haired girl named Susan who had very large breasts. She wore running shorts and a bikini top and he was having trouble keeping his eyes from constantly drifting to her chest.

The party was breaking up and people were splitting into couples and going their separate ways. K.C. felt rather conspicuous in his singleness as he stood alone chewing on the ice from his glass. It was as if someone had rung a bell and at the signal everyone had grabbed a partner—everyone except K.C.

It was at that point that he felt he was being watched. He could feel eyes on him as if he were being touched between the shoulder blades. He turned and looked behind him but saw only George Stamatelos, whose back was turned to him, on the other side of the pool. Stamatelos was still talking with the same couple and another woman who was hidden behind his massive frame.

Just as K.C. was about to turn away, the woman behind Stamatelos shifted her position and he got his first real look at her. Their eyes met from across the pool and his heart thudded in his chest.

It was Diane.

She looked away as if she had not seen him or had not recognized him. K.C. was immobilized. He had always recognized the possibility that someday he might accidentally bump into Diane but had never allowed himself to believe that it could really happen. He was speechless, his brain suddenly a useless mass of tissue.

He started toward her, stopped, started again, and finally slumped down into a chair at poolside. He watched her from across the pool but for the most part she remained hidden. Once or twice he thought she might be looking his way, but their eyes never met, and he could not be sure.

What I ought to do, he said to himself, is walk over there and speak to her—explain to her. Explain what? Sorry, Diane, but I'm working undercover for the government. She'd laugh in his face. And rightly so.

What, then? Sit here like a fool and do nothing?

Which, of course, is exactly what he did.

As he sat looking across the pool, hoping to catch Diane's eyes, someone approached him from the other side. He turned to see a young woman standing next to his chair with two drinks in her hands.

"Hi, Kevin," she said. "Grace asked me to bring you a drink."

He sighed. Grace the matchmaker was still at work. He took the drink and nodded his thanks.

"My name is Julie," she said. "Mind if I sit?"

She began talking. K.C. saw Diane's eyes move in his direction. He opened his mouth to speak and noticed out of the corner of his eye that she had detached herself from her group and was moving. Oh shit, he thought, she's coming this way. He started to rise from his chair. Julie, puzzled, followed his gaze and saw Diane approach. "Oh, oh," she said warily. "Am I interrupting something?"

"Not at all," said Diane with forced politeness as she stopped in front of K.C.

"Hello," he said, feeling incredibly inept.

Diane did not answer. Instead she looked him up and down as if deciding whether or not he was worth speaking to. Finally, after what K.C. felt was about an hour, she spoke. "If this were a movie, I'd probably slap your face."

"I'm sorry," was all he could muster.

Julie stood up. "I think I'll go get myself a drink."

No one said anything and she quickly departed.

"How long have you been back in California?" asked Diane, her face revealing none of the anger her voice betrayed.

"Couple of weeks."

"Couple of weeks?" She shook her head in amazement.

"I've been very . . ." he didn't want to say it.

"Busy?" said Diane helpfully. "You've been very busy?"

He nodded helplessly. He was hoping the ground would open up and swallow him.

She shook her head sadly, a look of disgust on her face. "I was hoping for a better explanation . . . but I guess that's as good as any."

K.C.'s mouth opened and closed silently and his hands made small circular gestures of futility. Say something, his brain implored—speak!

"Diane," he stammered. "It's not what you think."

She laughed derisively. "Don't worry. I know what it is—what it *was*. It was just a roll in the hay with a California bimbo. Another notch in the old shootin' iron."

"It wasn't like that at all."

Diane turned to walk away but was intercepted by Grace Kallin, who appeared as if from nowhere and grabbed her arm. "Diane," she said, happily unaware of what was going on. "I see you've met Kevin."

K.C. winced noticeably.

"Kevin," said Diane, raising an eyebrow. "Kevin, is it?"

Grace was suddenly perplexed. She looked to K.C. for help.

"My friends—people I knew before—always called me K.C."

"Oh," said Grace, suddenly unsure of herself. "I see."

"Gotta go, Grace," said Diane. "Nice party." She looked at K.C. "Take care of yourself . . . Kevin."

Thirty-six

He couldn't get Diane out of his mind. If only I hadn't seen her, he thought, it might have been easy. Well, if not easy, at least easier.

But he had seen her.

His mind had played tricks on him. When he had thought of her, his mind in self-defense had made her picture less beautiful than she really was, exaggerating the small bump in her nose, emphasizing the gap between her front teeth, minimizing the near-perfection of her body. Now that he had seen her again he realized the lies he had told himself. Carol's words came rushing back: "I think you're throwing away a golden opportunity."

"Dammit!" he said aloud, the sound echoing around the bare walls of his apartment. "Why do I always do the wrong thing?"

For diversion he turned on the TV and flipped through the channels looking for a ballgame. There was nothing of interest, but the commercials reminded him that he hadn't eaten since lunch. He took a Stouffer's frozen dinner from his freezer and popped it in the toaster oven. When it was ready he sat at the kitchen counter, eating by rote, watching a CBS nighttime soap opera in which everyone seemed to be plotting to destroy everyone else. It made no sense at all to him.

With every other mouthful he would sprinkle a dash of salt on his food, taking some pleasure in the fact that no one was there to reprimand him. One of the few consolations of eating alone, he thought, was being able to indulge oneself in such ill-considered addictions without suffering the raised eyebrows or unwelcome comments of a dining partner.

After cleaning up he lay back on the couch. The sound from the TV was hypnotic, like crashing surf or rain on the roof, and he let himself drift with it, not wanting to open his eyes and face the reality of his existence.

He awoke around three A.M., the TV still mumbling softly, dragged himself from the couch, and fully clothed, dropped onto his unmade bed.

Things were going well at TMK. On Monday he was, as promised, called into Nichols's office and his transfer to Special Projects completed. That evening, when he reported the move to Birdwell, the CIA man was elated. "Everything," he said, "is right on schedule."

K.C. wished that he could be as enthusiastic. He found himself thinking about Diane all the time, trying to invent excuses to call her. He was becoming more of a recluse than ever, studying Gordon's notebook and conducting his own research into the background of some of the people at TMK. Through his desktop terminal he was able to gain access to many of the records that TMK kept on its employees. Although technical information was classified and protected from surreptitious entry by a voice print identification system at the terminals, the personnel files were protected only by password. K.C. requested the password from Birdwell, who passed it along to him the next day. From then on K.C. spent his lunch hour browsing through the background material on anyone at TMK. By this same method he was able to invade the records of expense accounts and check into the business trips made by Reid Lawson. So far he had found nothing out of the ordinary, other than the fact that Lawson was not reluctant to spend company money when he was traveling.

He also gathered information by the simple method of talking to the people he worked with. He tried to go about the business of collecting data in the most indirect way possible, trying never to ask a direct question or to engage the same person twice in similar conversations. His method was to lead the conversation in the direction he intended to pursue without raising the suspicions of those he talked with.

It was a frustrating and time-consuming process and sometimes he was unable to get the information that he was after, but he was determined to mask his purpose and equally determined not to reveal his association with the CIA. So he continued, in his own roundabout way, his fact-gathering mission. Later he would check his own notes against the material in Gordon's notebook.

Gradually K.C. began to make friends at work and a couple of attractive secretaries seemed to be expressing some interest in him but he was unable to rid Diane Rollins from his thoughts. His Friday afternoon forays to the Little Byte were his only recreational activity and he was resolved after last week's disaster to avoid the Kallins' parties at his apartment complex.

On Fridays at the Little Byte he at first sipped his beers and listened to the usual ritual list of jokes and job-related complaints. But by the second or third time he was right in the thick of the revelry.

One of the standard items of ridicule was the security system at TMK and the presence of the CIA and the FBI in the restricted areas of the complex. Although his brother was never mentioned by name, K.C. could feel his throat constrict and his palms grow moist when someone questioned or ridiculed the security setup that was part of what he considered to be his brother's legacy. But gradually he came to realize that to these men any kind of security setup was regarded as a challenge—a game to be played. They had grown up playing games with computers. Many of them, when younger, had made a habit of breaking into what were considered "secure" computers just for the excitement. Now they had graduated to more sophisticated levels of expertise and their conversation was sprinkled with the braggadocio of conquest—not of women, although there was that too—but of the security systems they had broken and the computer files they had entered surreptitiously.

As K.C. looked around the tables he could not help but wonder who—if anyone—was planning a break into the computer files at TMK.

What was comforting was the knowledge that most of

Gordon's security precautions were still in effect and K.C. often marveled at his brother's efficiency and attention to detail. It was difficult to imagine that anyone could get anything out of the classified areas of TMK. The classified computer files, unlike the personnel files, were protected against outside or unauthorized entry by a complex sign-in procedure that made unauthorized entry highly unlikely. The classified computer files were not accessible by phone, only by inside lines at the TMK complex, and any entry—authorized or not—was tracked and traced to the terminal of origin. Every authorized user had his own personal password and had to join that with the program password to gain access. It was unlikely, thought K.C., that secrets would leave TMK through computer theft by unauthorized persons. Whether or not secrets would be lost to authorized persons was another story.

If technological secrets were to be lost at TMK, K.C. was sure that it would be through the oldest manner on record—loose talk. The people at TMK talked about their work endlessly and K.C. was concerned that the Russians need only spend a few hours each week on Friday afternoons at the Little Byte to discover everything that was happening at TMK. Even the top-secret, high-speed computer guidance system for the new ballistic defense system was discussed as openly as last night's baseball scores.

Only when Project Director Nichols was around did the Special Projects people refrain from discussing the most secret aspects of Professor Kincaid's work. Several times K.C. had witnessed the conversation abruptly change course when Nichols arrived, or a loose-lipped programmer intimidated into silence by a harsh look from the project director.

Most of the time K.C. just sipped his beer, played a game or two of chess, and tried to follow the threads of conversation that were woven around him.

His chess game was improving, but so far he had found little if anything to help him in his investigation. When he complained to Birdwell he was told to maintain his cover and stay with it.

On a Friday night two weeks after he had seen Diane, K.C. managed to get back into his apartment before being discovered by Grace Kallin. He made himself a strong drink to go with the several he had had earlier and spent the next hour wondering if Diane was at the party. He finally resorted to spying on the festivities from his darkened bedroom window. He saw Stamatelos but thankfully he was with someone else—K.C.'s dreams had been filled with distressing scenes of Diane cavorting nude with his muscle-bound neighbor.

For the hundredth time he picked up his phone and dialed Diane's number, but this time he did not hang up before it rang.

"Hello," she said and his momentary bravado collapsed. He hung up.

He hated himself for his cowardice.

Another drink bolstered his courage and he dialed again. This time her hello was more cautious.

"Diane," he began but quickly faltered.

She knew it was him but refused to give him that satisfaction. "Who is this?" she said sharply. "Did you call here earlier?"

"It's me, Diane. K.C."

"Who?" She was trying to make this as difficult for him as possible.

"K.C.," he repeated, wishing he had not done this.

"You mean Kevin, don't you?"

He groaned and decided he had to risk complete and total capitulation. "Diane, I'm sorry."

"Sorry?" she said calmly. "Sorry for what?"

"For everything. You know what I'm sorry for."

"Are you drunk?" she asked. "You sound drunk."

The question sounded foolish to him. How else would he be able to call her if he were not drunk? He resisted the temptation to tell her so and continued on his path of contrition. "Yes," he said. "I'm afraid I am a little drunk."

"I don't like getting phone calls from people who are drunk," she said. Her voice was cold but he hoped he detected the beginnings of a thaw.

"May I call you sometime when I'm sober?" he said with mock formality. For some reason he felt he was playing a scene in an English comedy. Peter O'Toole, he thought, would be perfect for the part.

"God damn you!" she said almost softly. "Why are you doing this?"

"Because"—he was struggling now—"because I miss you."

"So you're drunk and you're lonely. Am I supposed to run over there and make you feel better?"

228

"No," he said, feeling very sober now. "I just hope you'll say that I can call you again and that you'll see me again."

"I don't think I want to see you again."

There was hope in that word "think." "Can I at least call you—talk to you sometime?"

She thought for a long time before answering. "Only if you're sober."

"Thank you," he said. "I'll say good-bye now." He hung up and called her back immediately. "I'm really feeling much more sober now," he said.

She hung up on him without a word. But it was a beginning.

Early on Monday morning, on the way to his office in the S.P. building, K.C. stopped to look down into the large open room where the prototype of the Prometheus II computer sat. Things were not as hectic now as they had been only a few months earlier. The work at TMK was basically completed on Prometheus and testing had already begun at the government-operated Livermore Laboratories, which were less than thirty miles away on the other side of San Francisco Bay.

Prometheus II stood in the center of the room, silent, like some ancient monolith created to defend a place of worship. To the untrained eye, Prometheus II might indeed have been a piece of outdoor sculpture created to decorate the entrance to a new office tower or to a suburban shopping mall. It had none of the blinking lights or flashing digital readouts of the Hollywood conception of the supercomputer. Instead, Prometheus II looked like a cylinder encased in a stack of oversized doughnuts.

"Beautiful, isn't it?" said Ted Nichols, who had appeared silently at K.C.'s elbow.

"Yes," K.C. said, knowing exactly what Nichols meant. "Will it do everything they say?"

"And more—it's incredibly fast. More than a billion logical inferences per second."

K.C. gave a low whistle and then both men were silent as if in the presence of a superior being.

After a moment K.C. broke the silence. "Last year I saw some literature on Kincaid's original machine—Prometheus I. It seemed very similar in design to this model except for the speed."

Nichols smiled. He recognized that K.C. was asking a question, but it was one that he did not feel at liberty to answer. Instead he framed his response in a question. "How would you increase the speed of an already incredibly fast machine?"

"I'd make it smaller—if I could—to miniaturize the circuitry and cut the travel time of the electrons, which would speed the rate of calculations."

Nichols was nodding in a noncommittal manner. "That might increase speed by a factor of three or four, but there's only so much miniaturization that is feasible."

K.C. thought for a second. "Wafer scale integration," he said. "Cram the circuitry into oversize silicon chips."

Nichols smiled. "Now we're back to the problem of size."

"Cool the chips so that they can be packed in a denser package. That eliminates heat accumulation and further reduces size."

"Yesterday's technology," said Nichols.

K.C.'s eyes widened. "Not where I come from."

Nichols smiled. "We're way ahead of you." He turned to leave. "I've got a meeting in my office. I'll see you later."

K.C.'s mind was racing. "Then it's got to be the chips," he said, and Nichols stepped and turned back to face him. "We've already reached the full capacity of silicon—it has to be some other material."

"That," said Nichols, "is what you might call the sixty-four-thousand-dollar question."

"Gallium arsenide chips would be around five times faster than silicon but that still wouldn't explain the tremendous increase in speed. Besides, gallium arsenide is incredibly expensive."

Nichols's face broke into a grin. "The cost is inconsequential and gallium arsenide was eliminated from consideration because it was not fast enough."

"So that—"

Nichols held up his hand. "That's as much as I can say. I'm impressed with your interest and your knowledge but we are already moving into classified areas of discussion and I would prefer that it stop right there." His tone was pleasant but firm.

K.C. nodded. "You're right. I just got kind of carried away for a moment."

Nichols gave a nod that signified he understood. "Gotta go," he said and quickly left.

So that's how Kincaid did it, K.C. thought. He's come up with some new material for the chips that allows the message-bearing electrons to race through the chips at an incredibly rapid rate. More likely, he thought, he's combined all of the methods: wafer scale integration, new material, miniaturization, chip packing, and some kind of cooling process.

He took one more admiring look at the Prometheus II, feeling in some strange way that he should acknowledge the presence of superior intelligence. He gave a quick nod in the direction of the machine and then quickly moved toward his office.

At lunchtime K.C. sat in the cafeteria with Nichols and a small group from Special Projects. The talk was nothing out of the ordinary—women, baseball, computers—and K.C. was half-listening as he chewed on a sandwich. He was paying so little attention that the first piece of useful information he had picked up in almost a month of casually listening to conversation almost slipped past him.

It started innocently enough with another knock at the CIA and the security procedures. By this time K.C. was so inured to this particular topic that he gave it very little attention. One of the programmers, a young man that K.C. knew only as Rick, complained that someone had been snooping around in his wastebasket. "CIA snoops," he said and looked directly at K.C., who flushed, wondering if somehow his compact with the Agency had been discovered. Until that moment he had not really felt that he was actually in association with the CIA.

"Big Brother, snooping around in my wastebasket," said Rick in disbelief. "Looking over my shoulder every time I turn around."

Everyone grumbled in unison, with K.C. feeling conspicuous in his silence.

Someone shrugged off the complaint with, "They're always digging for dirt. That's their job."

"You can say that because it wasn't your wastebasket," said Rick.

Ted Nichols laughed. "They probably found more interesting stuff in your wastebasket than they would find on your desk," he said good-naturedly.

Everyone laughed and Rick waved his napkin as if in surrender.

The situation defused, the group returned to more amiable conversation. K.C. waited awhile and then asked Nichols, who sat next to him, "Is the CIA a problem?"

Nichols seemed unconcerned. "Not really. They get underfoot once in a while."

"Pain in the ass," mumbled Rick, who had tuned in to the conversation.

Nichols shrugged. "Necessary evil. No CIA—no Prometheus project. No Prometheus project, and most of us are looking elsewhere for work." He looked at K.C. and made a face as if he had tasted a medicine that was unpleasant but necessary. "They do their job. We do ours."

K.C. nodded and turned his attention back to his sandwich.

Rick mumbled something that was almost unintelligible. "CIA didn't stop the Birdman."

K.C.'s mind had already drifted off to another place, but somewhere in the backwaters of his brain a sensing device heard, translated, and sent off the alarm. K.C.'s head snapped up as if he had been slapped, and in order to cover his sudden movements he coughed as if he had been choking.

"Birdman," someone said, raising a can of soda in mock salute. "A real American."

Remembering the words "Talk with Birdman" in Gordon's notebook, K.C. asked, "Who is this Birdman?"

"Carl Burns," said Nichols. "Used to be employed here at TMK."

"Until he walked off with half the company's secrets," added Rick.

"Sold them to the Russians," added another voice.

"Why the name Birdman?" K.C. asked.

Nichols shrugged. "Everyone called him that."

"He liked birds. Kept tropical birds or something."

"He was always kinda weird."

Everyone was homing in on the conversation now and K.C. was careful not to seem too interested.

"He was weird all right," said Rick. "He sold about five million dollars' worth of information for twenty-five thousand."

"Is that right," said K.C., casually sipping his milk.

"You must have read about it in the papers," Nichols said.

K.C. feigned indifference. "I don't think so."

Rick was heavily into the topic now. "Biggest thing to happen at TMK since Tolbert moved up to the big company. Burns got forty years for espionage. Right now he's at Lompoc" —K.C.'s face was a blank—"the federal correctional institution," added Rick as explanation.

K.C. whistled. "Forty years."

"They should have given him life," said Rick, and after a pause added, "for not having enough brains to get what the information was worth."

Almost everyone laughed but Nichols's voice stopped them cold. "He's *also* the reason we had to lay off forty percent of our employees. He's the reason we went two years without a government contract. And he's the reason the place is crawling with what you call spooks." Everyone was silent now. "Because of Burns this company almost went out of business," said Nichols.

There were nods and shrugs and grudging agreement and after a brief lull in the conversation most went back to talking about less controversial and less painful topics. K.C. looked at Nichols, who sat, his jaw clenched, his eyes unblinking and fixed on some distant spot as if he saw some threat of attack just beyond the horizon.

K.C. could barely contain himself. He felt as if he had made—however minor—a breakthrough, and he couldn't wait to talk with Birdwell. The rest of the day dragged along and he even thought of leaving early but dismissed the idea as too risky. He did not want to draw any attention to himself. He tried to lose himself in his work but Gordon's words, "Talk with Birdman," kept popping into his head.

The day was amazingly long.

As soon as he arrived home he called Birdwell on the private number he had been given. He told him about Burns.

"I want to talk with him," said K.C. "Gordon thought he knew something."

"Talking to him won't be easy," said Birdwell. "The FBI has jurisdiction in that case."

"I don't care how you do it. Get me in to talk with him. I'm sure he knows something."

Birdwell sighed. "I'll do what I can and get back to you as soon as I can." He paused. "Good work, K.C. This might be our first break."

K.C. felt a sense of exhilaration that he had not felt for a long time. He wanted to share it with someone and immediately thought of Diane. That was enough to bring him back to earth, his mood plummeting like a wounded bird.

He had called her twice since Friday and although she had talked to him she had been cool, and after a few minutes she had given him some excuse to get off the phone. His earlier hopes for reestablishing their relationship were beginning to recede like the tide.

He fixed himself a vodka and tonic and sat on the couch, his head back and his eyes staring at the ceiling. It's no good, he thought. I've lost her for good. His eyes went around the room and fell on Gordon's notebook. He raised his glass in mock salute. "Here's looking at you, Birdman," he said. "Gordon's little brother is on his way."

WASHINGTON (AP)—In an apparent break with current Administration policy, Major General John Wilson of the Joint Chiefs of Staff said today that the U.S. ABM system was "obviously an offensive weapon."

"If I can stop your offense while still maintaining my own," said the general, "I've obviously increased my offensive potential.

"There is a very narrow line between what constitutes defense and strategic offense," said General Wilson. "If the situations were reversed, I would hate to stake my survival on the Soviet assertion that this system is purely defensive."

Administration sources claimed that the general had been quoted out of context and that he would have a clarification of his statement prepared for the press tomorrow.

General Wilson was unavailable for further comment.

Thirty-seven

The Federal Correctional Institution at Lompoc sat low and ugly on the flat, fertile plains of Southern California. Situated between San Luis Obispo to the north and Santa Barbara to the south and just inland of the Vandenberg Air Force Base, the prison rose gracelessly up out of the flatlands that run from the mountains on the east to the Pacific.

K.C. left Sunnyvale early on Saturday morning, taking Highway 101 south to where it merged with Route 1 three hours later at San Luis Obispo. It was a good drive, the road mostly flat and straight with mountains on the horizon on either side. He drove mindlessly; the early morning traffic was light and the radio, blaring an innocuous collection of top-forty hits, carried him onward.

After spending the night reading the transcript of Carl Burns's trial and the newspaper accounts of the arrest, all of which had been given to him by Birdwell when they met to discuss K.C.'s cover story for his visit with Burns, K.C. had written down the questions he wanted to ask. The questions he most wanted answered had come from Gordon's notes. What did Burns know and what did Gordon mean when he wrote that Burns "knows who it is"?

At Route 1 he continued on, now nearer the coast, past Vandenberg, exited at Lompoc where road signs discreetly declared "Federal Correctional Institution" as if the maximum-security prison was a minor tourist attraction.

K.C. followed the signs to the prison and parked his car in the administration lot, careful to obey the signs that told him to lock his car and take his keys. At the registration building, which was outside the two rows of chain link fence topped with coils of razor-sharp steel that completely encircled the maximum-security facility, he registered with a uniformed guard who regarded him with the suspicion that was the staple of his trade. The fact that K.C. was using yet another fictitious name made him more uncomfortable than he would normally have felt under the guard's scrutiny.

After a cursory "pat-down search" he was led to a gate and escorted across the ten-foot-wide "dead man's land" between the chain link fences. His mouth was dry and between his shoulder blades K.C. thought he could feel rifles being aimed at him by the guards in the towers that dotted the perimeter.

At the inner gate he was turned over to another guard who seemed if anything less friendly and more suspicious than the last. K.C. was led to a small building near the fence and ushered into what he was told was the visitors' room. The room was small with a long table and several chairs in the center. Against the walls were a couch and two upholstered chairs.

The guard spoke his first words to K.C. "Have a seat. Burns will be here soon."

"Soon" turned out to be almost forty-five minutes.

When Burns finally did arrive, K.C. was surprised by his stature—the man was little more than five feet tall. He wore blue denims and a pale blue, short-sleeved prison work shirt. His dark eyes contrasted with his closely cropped blond hair.

Naturally suspicious, he eyed his visitor for a brief moment and then without comment sat in the straight-backed chair on the other side of the table. K.C. leaned forward and Burns allowed him a limp handshake.

"Kevin Johnson," said K.C. "Nice to meet you."

"I've never heard of you. They said you were a writer."

K.C. shrugged. "Magazine articles mostly—*Life, Reader's Digest.*"

"I didn't have to see you, y'know," Burns said in a surprisingly soft voice.

K.C. nodded in agreement. "I know that. Thank you for your time."

Burns chuckled. "Time is the wrong word to use around here."

K.C. gave an embarrassed smile. "Thanks anyway."

Burns watched him carefully. His expression gave away nothing of what he was thinking. "What do you want with me, anyway?"

"I just wanted to talk to you about a few things," said K.C., trying to keep the conversation light.

"They said you were writing a book or something."

That was the cover story arranged by Birdwell and the FBI. "Maybe," said K.C. with a shrug. "Right now I'm just researching a magazine article. If there's enough that's interesting here I might do a book. Maybe about you."

Burns's grin was genuine. He was obviously not immune to the lure of having his ego stroked and his story told. "There's enough here," he said, serious again. "You might not want to print it though."

"Why's that?"

"People don't want to hear about the madness of their own government. They don't want to know what's happening."

"Tell me. I'm listening."

Burns's eyes narrowed. "Don't you read the papers?" he said disgustedly. "They're ready to blow up the world."

"I don't follow you. Who's ready to blow up the world?"

Burns's look of disgust turned to one of amazement. "C'mon," he said. "You don't think this new ABM system is really intended for defensive purposes, do you?"

"What then?"

Burns laughed. "As soon as it's installed and we feel immune from attack, we will annihilate the Russians."

K.C. said nothing, but his expression was skeptical.

"You don't believe me?" asked Burns. He aimed a thumb over his shoulder. "They're testing this thing night and day at Vandenberg. I've been here for two years," he said. "Normally they test one of these missiles every month or so. For the past six weeks they've been launching three or four a day. When it's ready they'll come up with some excuse and it's bye-bye Russia."

"It's hard to believe our government would consider such a thing," said K.C.

Burns gave a sigh of exasperation. "We Americans are a warlike people. We relish confrontation. We revel in violence. Our government is ready to unleash a holocaust."

"You're not alone in that point of view, but it is difficult to prove that the U.S. government is—"

"Proof!" exploded Burns. "You want proof?"

K.C. was startled into silence.

"When I was at TMK," Burns went on, his outburst over, his voice soft again, "I spent a lot of time talking politics with the CIA people and the FBI who were assigned to work there."

"And?"

"Everyone—to the last man—was convinced that we were close to a nuclear war and every one of them felt that we should strike first and annihilate the Russians." He shook his head sadly. "And these were people who knew what was going on in the government."

K.C. knew then that Burns interpreted his world view through his own narrow and distorted field of vision. "And that's why you decided to do something."

"Somebody had to do something," Burns said simply.

"You felt that by helping the Russians, you were helping prevent a nuclear war."

Burns nodded. He seemed incredibly sad. "The only way to save the world is to make sure that one superpower doesn't have the opportunity to overwhelm the other."

"Do you think you're the only one who feels this way?"

Burns smiled. "No."

"Were there others at TMK who felt this way?"

Burns's eyes narrowed and his look was again suspicious. "There were a few."

"That was a few years ago," said K.C. "What about now? Do you think there are people there now who feel the way you do?"

Burns looked away. "Do you have any cigarettes?"

K.C. took a pack, purchased for the occasion, from his pocket and pushed it toward Burns. "These are for you."

Burns took them without comment, ripped open the pack, and lit one. "I think the CIA got them all," said Burns. He blew a cloud of smoke. "Sooner or later they get everybody." Burns looked at K.C. "When they finish with you they get rid of you"—he looked around the room—"one way or the other."

"At your trial you maintained that the documents you fed to the Russians were worthless and that they were deliberately leaked to you by the CIA."

Burns nodded, his face shrouded in a cloud of smoke.

"What did you mean by that?"

Burns hesitated before answering, as if he were tired of answering this question—or any question. He put his hands together on the table and stared at a space on the wall. "At first I was on my own. I took some relatively unimportant

238

documents to the Russians. It was all I could get my hands on, but I wanted to do something. Of course they wanted more. They said I had to prove myself."

"And?"

"I tried, but there was little else that I had access to." He nodded his head and a sly look came over his face. "Then all sorts of strange things happened."

"Like what?"

"Like I was transferred to another department. Suddenly I had clearance and access to a whole new range of material. I was given responsibilities that I had never had before. It was almost as if they wanted me to steal it."

"They?"

"The CIA—who else. They used me to funnel phony information to the Russians."

"But you said you started on your own."

"I did. I don't argue that. But they found out about it—maybe they had me under surveillance—and decided to use me for their own purposes."

"I've interviewed some people with Central Intelligence— some of them relatively high up—and no one has ever intimated that you were a plant."

Burns looked at him incredulously, his eyes growing round until the irises seemed pinpricks in a sea of white. "D'you think they'd tell you? Tell anybody? That would destroy the whole purpose of the operation."

"Which was?"

"Disinformation. Pass phony facts to the Russians. Now they have to make it look real—seem important. That's why I got forty years. That's why my appeal for clemency was denied."

K.C. was skeptical but Burns laughed maniacally, then continued. "I'm the fall guy. The CIA set me up, let me leak counterfeit secrets, and then threw the book at me to make the whole thing look good." He made a waving gesture with his hands to indicate how simple the whole idea was.

K.C. had to admit that it did make a crazy kind of sense. How else would a nobody like Burns get access to vital secrets unless somebody wanted him to? If that premise was acceptable, then everything else started to fall into place. Before he could continue that line of thought, Burns jumped in again.

"And that's why I'm talking to you. Once the Russians

find out I was used by the CIA, there'd be no reason to keep me here any longer."

"I see," said K.C., beginning to understand Burns's motivation.

Burns misunderstood K.C.'s expression. "Don't feel bad, Johnson. Everybody gets used. The CIA used me—you use me to write your book—I use you to get out of here."

At that moment K.C. felt a twinge of sadness for Burns. Everybody used everybody else. It was a hard philosophy to carry through life. He was beginning to see Burns sympathetically.

"You're not the only one who's writing a book about me, you know."

K.C. raised an eyebrow. "Oh?"

"Orville Tompkins," Burns said, as if K.C. would instantly recognize the name. When he did not, Burns went on, "You know—the guy who used to work for the CIA and wrote the book spilling the beans on how corrupt the whole operation is."

K.C. nodded. "I read about that. They tried to suppress publication."

Burns nodded enthusiastically. "Right. He knows all about the games they play and agrees with me on what happened in my case. He says it's happened before."

"So this Tompkins is writing a book about you?"

Burns's cocky smile faded. "Well . . . not just about me. It's about dirty tricks played by the CIA. My story is probably going to be one chapter."

"I see."

He looked hopefully to K.C. "But your book would be just about me—right?"

K.C. nodded, feeling guilty about playing with Burns's pipe dreams. "If I can get enough information on this case—all about you and TMK—yes."

"I'm writing down everything I know. The next time you come to see me, I'll have more for you. I've got lots of things to tell."

"That's what I want," said K.C. "I want people to hear your side of the story."

Burns looked away for a moment, staring at a wall as if it were a window and beyond lay freedom. Then he began, almost in a monotone, a long diatribe of complaints, not just against the CIA and the U.S. government, but against the

240

media, the prison system, the inability of people to live together in harmony. K.C. said nothing. He let Burns ramble on nonstop for almost ten minutes. He realized that this was a man with a grievance against the human condition who had made a wild and desperate attempt to bring some kind of outlandish order to his existence. Then, as suddenly as he had begun, Burns stopped and stared at the wall. Both were silent for a moment as K.C., nodding with what he hoped was an air of sympathy, let Burns gather his thoughts.

"When will you be back?" Burns asked, almost sad that their time was running out.

"In a few weeks," K.C. said, hating himself for lying to this pathetic creature. At that moment he had fresh insight into what lying and secrecy and duplicity could do to depress the human spirit. He wondered how Gordon could have done it all those years and now he understood at what cost. He stood up quickly, anxious to be done with this. "I'll have to do some research. Then I'll get back to you."

"Anytime," said Burns enthusiastically. "You'll find out that I'm right." He paused, still holding K.C.'s hand. "You do believe me, don't you?"

"What you say makes a lot of sense," said K.C., extricating his hand from Burns's grasp. "I'll talk with you soon."

K.C. went to the door and knocked. While he waited for the guard to answer he was unable to look back at Burns.

Thirty-eight

It was after seven o'clock when K.C., weary from a long day behind the wheel, arrived back at his apartment. He made himself a drink and called Birdwell but had to be satisfied with leaving a message on an answering machine. While he waited for Birdwell to return his call he made himself a sandwich. He was just about to sit down in front of the TV with his sandwich and a fresh drink when the phone rang. It was Birdwell.

"No way," said Birdwell emphatically when K.C. told him about Burns's claim of CIA involvement in his treason. "The guy is handing you a line of shit."

"But it's possible, isn't it?" K.C. persisted.

"No way. He'd say anything to get his ass out of prison. The guy is a head case. You've got to discount half of what he says."

K.C. was doubtful. "He sounded pretty convincing to me."

"He's been telling that story since they caught him with his hand in the till. Next week he's testifying at a federal hearing in San Francisco and I'm sure he'll tell the same old story that he was railroaded by the CIA to anyone who will listen."

"But if what he's saying is true—you wouldn't admit it to me anyway—would you?"

Birdwell exploded. "That's one of those 'When did you stop beating your wife?' questions. If I don't admit that something is true then it must be true—is that how it goes? There are people who believe the Agency assassinated President Kennedy and their only evidence is that there is no evidence."

"Is it possible that you don't know about Burns?"

Birdwell paused a moment and took a deep breath. "Let me put it this way: To the best of my knowledge and to the knowledge of anyone else I know of around here, the Agency had nothing to do with feeding Burns any information of any kind until he was under actual surveillance."

"What does that mean?"

"It means that once we were watching him we may have permitted him access to some documents so that we could nail his ass to the barn wall."

"So you did permit him to give documents to the Russians?"

"Only to trap him and his contact, and as far as I know, only on that final time. To the best of my knowledge we arrested him as soon as possible. He was working in too sensitive an area to mess around."

K.C. was aware how carefully Birdwell was framing his answers. He was reminded of the labyrinthian legalese of the Watergate hearings—"At that point in time" . . . "To the best

of my knowledge" . . . "I have no particular recollection"
—when answers were shrouded in a protective cocoon. He
was thinking again of Gordon's notebook. "Is Birdwell still
with his old department?"

"What department are you with, Bob?" asked K.C.

"Huh?"

"What department?"

Birdwell was puzzled. "You know I'm with the Technology Transfer Assessment Center."

"But before that. What department were you with before that?"

Birdwell hesitated before answering. "C'mon, K.C., you're really letting this guy get to you."

"What department, Bob?"

Birdwell sighed in defeat. "I was with Disinformation for four years." He quickly added, "But that doesn't mean—"

K.C. cut him off. "I'm sure it doesn't mean anything at all, Bob."

There was a long silence as K.C. waited for a response from Birdwell. When it did not come he said, "I'll talk to you soon. I've got lots of things to think about." Before Birdwell could respond, K.C. hung up the phone.

Thirty-nine

For a long time after his conversation with Birdwell, K.C. sat on the couch without moving. His vodka and tonic sat on the table in front of him, ice melting, bubbles dissipating, until the drink was flat and tasteless. He rubbed his knuckles into his eyes, feeling as if he were grinding them with sandpaper.

Christ, I'm tired, he thought, putting his head back and closing his eyes. The darkness felt good—quiet and comfortable—and he did not want to open his eyes. Once or twice, though he was not truly aware of it, he drifted off into a fitful sleep, but most of the time he was suspended in a drowsy wakefulness where sleep was waiting like a thief around the next corner.

His mind worked at a sluggish pace, following its own dictates and ruled by a daydream logic. Was the CIA telling him the truth? Was he being used? Had Carl Burns, as he claimed, been used as a sacrificial pawn in a game of intrigue between the CIA and the Soviet Union? How could he tell if Birdwell was telling everything he knew?

In his semidream he saw Birdwell's face, the lips curled in a sarcastic smirk, and told himself that the man from Disinformation was as likely to lead him astray, if it suited his purpose, as any Soviet agent. His doubts about the CIA—never far below the surface—almost overwhelmed him and he was unable to ward off the mistrust he felt toward the service his brother had devoted—and ultimately given—his life to.

There was a knock on the door and he sat up with a start, surprised to find the apartment in darkness. He hadn't realized how long he had sat there.

He opened the door and saw Diane Rollins and he was too dumbfounded to speak.

"Hello," Diane said.

K.C. managed to close his mouth and then was unable to open it to speak.

"Ask me in," she said quietly.

He stood back and she walked past him. "This place is a mess," she announced.

"I'm sorry," was all he could muster before he went around picking up newspapers, cushions, and assorted debris.

Diane saw his untouched sandwich on a paper plate on the coffee table. "I'm not interrupting dinner, am I?"

His eyes followed her gaze to the sandwich. "No, I . . . lost my appetite."

"Small wonder," she said, looking around as if his place was unfit for human habitation.

He started to recover from his shock at seeing her and then wondered if she had come merely to insult him. "What can I do for you?" he asked uneasily.

"I called you a couple of times today and got no answer—then a constant busy signal."

"Sorry," he said, vowing to himself to stop apologizing.

"I was out and then"—he pointed to his phone—"I took the phone off the hook when I got home. I've been working."

"On what?"

He moved his hands in small helpless circles. "Things."

She sighed and shook her head sadly. Whatever her reason for coming, she was beginning to think it had been a bad idea.

"I didn't expect to see you again," he said.

"Didn't expect to—or didn't *want* to?"

"Didn't expect to. I had no reason to hope you could forgive me."

"I don't mind admitting that I was hurt that you waited so long to call me," she began tentatively. "Then when I ran into you I was furious that you were back in California and hadn't tried to contact me—hadn't given me an explanation. Then suddenly you're calling me—talking about missing me." She shook her head in disbelief. "I didn't know what to think. So I decided to talk to Carol. She told me you had reasons for not contacting me. She said she couldn't tell me what they were but that I should ask you."

He said nothing.

"So I'm asking," she said.

He thrust his hands into his pockets. "I can't tell you."

"Are you in some kind of trouble?"

"Do you want a drink?" he asked.

"You are in trouble." She sounded relieved.

"I'm not in any kind of trouble."

"What did you do today?" she asked, feigning innocence.

He gave her a suspicious look. "Nothing out of the ordinary."

She shrugged. "It's none of my business. If you don't want to tell me, don't tell me."

"It's not that I don't want to."

There was a long, growing silence between them and K.C. began to think that if he didn't speak soon she would leave. His mind was a blank.

"Scotch," she said.

"Huh?"

"That drink you offered me. I'll take Scotch."

He hustled off to the kitchen to make her a drink.

"Can I tell you something?" she asked, calling to him from the living room.

"Go ahead," he said without conviction. He could feel some kind of lecture coming on.

"One of the reasons I came out here was to get away from my husband."

"The ex-jock with the sporting-goods store?" he said, coming back with her drink.

She nodded. "When things started going bad for him he didn't know how to adapt. He couldn't get used to being a nobody."

K.C. waited patiently for the point of the story.

She went on, "He started dealing in drugs—started getting involved with some very ugly people. We argued about it a lot." She sighed. "I got scared and ran. I never went back."

"I thought you came out here to pursue a television career."

"That too. But I could've gone back when it didn't work out. I didn't. I didn't want to."

K.C. nodded as if he understood.

"The guy I was involved with before that turned out to be an alcoholic."

K.C. shook his head, puzzled by all this.

"What I'm trying to say," Diane said, "is that I'm beginning to think that I'm a lousy judge of character."

"Don't tell me that your friend George is a muscleman for the Mafia." He was trying to be funny.

She wasn't laughing. "I'm not talking about George. I'm talking about you."

"Me?"

"Just do me a favor. Don't drag me into your life and then let me find out you're some kind of criminal or something."

"Drag you in?"

"You know what I mean."

He was beginning to see what she meant and the thought brought a smile to his face. "Tell me," he said.

She saw his smile and for the first time she, too, was smiling. "This is hard enough," she said.

He went to her and cupped her face in his hands before kissing her. "I did miss you," he said.

"I'm not sure I should get involved with you again."

He was kissing her. "I promise you I'm not involved in anything illegal."

"You're not a cop?"

"No."

"FBI?"

"No."

She shook her head, puzzled.

He tried to change the subject. "Did I tell you I couldn't stop dreaming about you?"

Diane was having none of it. "Look, I'm a reporter, which means I'm naturally inquisitive. I make it my business to keep my eyes and ears open. You're up to something and the only something anyone is up to here in the Valley is computer theft."

He raised an eyebrow. "I said it wasn't anything illegal."

"Then you're trying to stop computer theft?"

He didn't say anything.

"I'm close, aren't I?" she asked excitedly.

Her tenacity amazed him. Now that she had her teeth into something, she refused to let go.

"I could use a good story," she said. "It would really help me." She saw the dismayed look on his face and added, "I could help you."

"I don't need any help."

She got up and moved away from him as if proximity to him made it difficult to think. "Let me run what I've got by you, OK?"

He did not respond so she went ahead. "I met you here in California two months ago—you're supposed to be a college professor but now I'm not so sure. The woman who introduces us is married to the security chief at TMK. She says you're her brother-in-law and your name is K.C. Hardwick. We"—she paused a moment—"became involved."

K.C. took a good long drink from his glass.

"Less than a week later I hear that your brother has committed suicide back east. You don't call—you seem reluctant to see me. The next thing I know, you're back in California working at TMK under an assumed name—or maybe it's your real name. What do I know? You're very secretive. You don't make any attempt to see me until I run into you by accident. You don't go to see Carol—she told me that but wouldn't say anything else."

K.C. buried his face in his glass and said nothing.

"I don't know what all this means," Diane said. "But if I keep digging I'll find out what I want to know." She waited for him to say something, then continued, "Do you want me to keep digging?"

"No," he said, shaking his head slowly.

"Then tell me why not."

"I can't."

"You've got to do better than that. I don't even know who you are. I don't even know your name."

"If I asked you just to drop this, if I asked you to do that—for me—would you do it?"

"That's not fair!"

"I know it's not. But would you do it?"

She pushed her hair away from her face, then looked away from him. She was remembering how much it had hurt when she thought she had lost him. "If you really wanted me to," she said haltingly, not really believing what she was saying, "yes, I would."

"Thank you," he said, his words final, like a curtain dropping on the scene they had just played.

He moved toward her and put his arms around her. She did not resist, but when he went to kiss her she moved her face so that his kiss fell on her cheek.

"What's wrong?" he asked foolishly. He knew exactly what was wrong.

She extricated herself from his arms. "I feel like I've just been screwed—and it wasn't as much fun as it should be." Her voice was incredibly sad. "Maybe I'll just go home and take a nice long bath."

"Let's have dinner," K.C. said, hoping to salvage something.

She shook her head. "Not tonight. I'm tired." She started toward the door.

"Should I call you tomorrow?"

Her back was to him and she did not bother to turn. "If you like."

Now that she was here he could not bear to see her go. He felt himself becoming desperate; he was afraid he might never see her again. "My brother—Gordon Hardwick—worked for the CIA. He was murdered."

Diane, her eyes widening in amazement, turned to face him. Their eyes locked.

"I'm trying to find out who killed him, and why."

"Murdered?" she said in a whisper.

He nodded.

"But it happened back east. Why look out here?"

He sipped his drink.

Diane's mouth formed a circle. "You think that his death was related to his job at TMK."

"Maybe. He left a notebook that leads me to believe that that's what happened."

"And that's why you're using a fictitious name?"

"Yes."

"And that's why—"

He cut her off. "And that's as much as I can tell you."

"I can help you."

"I don't want you to. I can do the job myself."

"Have you gone to the police?"

"No police," he said quickly.

She looked at him, her eyes narrowing slightly. "You're working for the government too, aren't you?"

"No," he said hurriedly. "Not really . . . well, sort of."

"Sort of?"

"I report to the CIA, but I'm on my own. I'm only interested in finding out what happened to my brother."

She came to him and touched her fingers to his cheek. "I'm sorry I badgered you. I shouldn't have."

"I tried to avoid you when I came back to California," he said, "because you were the only person, other than Carol, who could link me with Gordon."

"I understand," she said, kissing him.

"I didn't want to stay away. I thought about you constantly."

"It's OK now." Her body was molded to his. "You don't have to tell me any more."

Now that his secret was out, it was as if the floodgates had been opened and he knew that he would tell her everything. "I want to tell you," he said. "I don't want secrets to come between us ever again."

She was unbuttoning his shirt. "You can tell me later." She was kissing his bare chest. "Right now we've got some catching up to do."

Forty

The phone rang at precisely ten o'clock on Sunday morning and Karpenkov answered on the first ring.

"Hello?"

"Is Dorothy there?"

"No. I'm afraid you have the wrong number."

"This isn't 555-2723?"

"No, it isn't."

"I'm terribly sorry."

Karpenkov hung up and jotted down the number he had been given. It was a simple code and he had only to subtract the numbers of the month and day from the last four digits that he had been given to know the number he should call.

He left immediately and drove for more than twenty minutes to a pay phone he had not used in several months. There in the parking lot of the shopping center, he dialed the number.

"Who is this?" asked a stern voice at the other end.

"This is Jack. Dorothy asked me to call."

The voice relaxed. "Hello. How are you today?"

"Fine," said Karpenkov. "Any problems?"

"The company is still waiting for your final report."

"Very soon," said Karpenkov. "Perhaps within the month."

"Time is growing short," said the voice. "Our competitors are rushing their product to the market."

"Rumors have it that certain design flaws will cause production delays. I'm sure," Karpenkov said, "that we will be able to maintain a competitive position. Perhaps in a short time we will be able to dominate the market again."

"Excellent," said the voice of the man whom Karpenkov had never seen. "The directors are looking forward to having you back with the home office again."

"So am I. Is there any other message from the company?"

"We are facing a potential problem with an employee."

"Yes? Anyone I know?"

"Do you remember Wilson in acquisitions?"

Karpenkov thought quickly. That was the code name given to Carl Burns. "Yes. Of course. What's the problem?"

"It seems that he has been talking to people outside the company."

"We thought that might happen. Does he know anything that can hurt the company?"

"People like that always have vague collections of information that can be damaging if given to the wrong people. It has also come to our attention that he is being brought to San Francisco sometime soon to meet with our competitors."

"Interesting," said Karpenkov.

"We thought you might find it so."

"Recommendation?"

"The company feels that there is no other choice but termination."

"Agreed. Any preference as to method?"

"We'll leave that up to you. You have always been resourceful in the past."

"Very well. I'll need more information on his travel plans."

"It will be sent to you at the usual place. When I call and ask for Wilson, you will know that the information is waiting."

"How much time do I have?"

"Less than a week. Probably on Wednesday or Thursday of this week."

"I'll be ready," said Karpenkov.

"We know we can always count on you," said the toneless voice and hung up.

Karpenkov scanned the parking lot for anything suspicious before leaving the phone booth. Already his mind was working on a method. He would have to go to the garage he rented and pick up a few things.

Outwardly calm, he could feel a surge of excitement pulsing through his body. He was smiling by the time he reached his car. Small diversions such as these, he thought, are what make life an interesting game.

Forty-one

Headlights slicing through the predawn darkness, the prison van rounded the sharp curve of the highway, slowing to less than thirty miles per hour as the driver kept his right foot poised above the brake.

"Hate this part of the drive," he said. His name was Jack Hamilton.

The guard who rode in the front seat with him said nothing.

The highway snaked off into the distance, disappearing beyond the reach of the headlights while on either side the road was enveloped by high, grassy hills, like humpbacked serpents lying in wait.

Jack sneaked a quick look at his companion, Sam Fullerton. They had made this trip dozens of times together, transporting prisoners to and from Lompoc or Soledad or San Quentin. Sam, he thought, was usually much more talkative.

Sam lit another cigarette and as if to belie the truth of Jack's thoughts said, "Be light soon."

The road had changed from the flat straightaway it had been when they had started the trip more than three hours ago to a winding spiral that rose into the hills as it passed from Monterey County into San Benito.

Jack Hamilton increased the pressure on the accelerator to maintain a constant speed as they rose higher into the hills. On the right side of the highway a metal guardrail separated the road from the steep drop on the other side.

"Car coming up fast from behind," said Sam, his eyes fixed on the sideview mirror.

A black sedan, tires squealing, hurtled past them doing at least twice the speed limit.

"Crazy bastard," said Jack as the taillights of the sedan

raced off into the darkness and disappeared around the next curve.

"Jerk must be drunk as a skunk," said Sam.

They drove on in silence. Jack stifled a yawn and rubbed at his eyes as he rounded another curve. The darkness of the night was giving way to the gray of early morning and the half light of the predawn tired his eyes more than driving in darkness.

"Hate these night jobs," said Jack, aware that he was forcing conversation.

Sam shrugged. He didn't care one way or the other.

"It's because of Burns—the little guy," said Jack, as if Fullerton had asked a question. "He's got to be at the courthouse by morning."

Finally Sam was dragged into the conversation. "You'd think they would know at least a day in advance when they were going to need his testimony. That way we could've driven him up yesterday afternoon."

"Lawyers and judges," said Hamilton. "What do they care?"

Sam Fullerton reached under the seat and pulled out an oversized thermos. He began unscrewing the top. "How about some coffee?" he began, then abruptly stopped when he saw the twin skidmarks on the road that led to the gaping hole in the guardrail.

"Christ," said Hamilton. "Someone's gone over the edge."

The two men looked at each other. They were not supposed to stop for any reason.

"Maybe it happened last night," said Fullerton, "and the Highway Patrol has taken care of it already." Even as he said it he knew it could not be true. The Highway Patrol wouldn't leave a gaping hole in the guardrail.

"Better take a look," said Hamilton, pulling to a halt across from the shattered barrier.

Both men got out and loped across the highway. There below, one hundred feet from the broached barrier, sat the black sedan. "It's that stupid bastard who passed us a while ago," said Jack Hamilton.

Sam only shook his head in amazement.

The car had gone through the rail at perhaps the best possible spot—fifty feet on either side and it would have been straight down to certain destruction. The car was still upright but leaning rather precariously as if it might tip over at any

253

moment and continue on down the cliff. The front door was open and both men saw the driver slumped across the front seat, his head and one arm protruding through the open door.

"Radio for help," said Fullerton. "I'll go down and see if he's still alive."

Hamilton raced back across the road while Fullerton began carefully to make his way down the steep slope. He slid on his hands and backside until he was near the small platform that held the car, then carefully, on all fours, moved closer.

The man lay face-up, sightless eyes open, on the front seat, his head toward the open door, one arm straight out, the other hidden beneath him. His face was covered in blood.

"You okay?" Fullerton called, feeling foolish, knowing that if the man were okay he would not be immobile.

He worked his way closer and just as he was about to touch the accident victim the man moved slightly and Fullerton jumped as if touched by a hot poker.

Fullerton turned to call out that the man was alive but never got the chance to say the words. As Fullerton turned, the man sat up, raised a silenced pistol, and shot Fullerton once in the back of the head.

Karpenkov jumped from the car and without pausing to look at the dead man, scrambled quickly to the top of the slope. Nearing the top he slowed his pace and peered carefully over the top at the scene on the highway. He watched as Hamilton climbed down from the van after having made his call and started back across the road to the edge. Karpenkov ducked down and waited just below the edge. He counted to five, then stood up, gun pointed at Hamilton's midsection.

Hamilton's jaw dropped and his eyes bulged at the sudden appearance of this bloody apparition. He was too startled to do anything other than gawk.

Karpenkov waved the pistol in Hamilton's face as he climbed the last few steps to the roadway. "Don't move—or try anything," he said. "I won't hesitate to kill you."

"Where's Sam?" asked Hamilton, finally able to unscramble his thoughts.

"Down there," said Karpenkov, casually jerking his left thumb back over his shoulder.

Hamilton's eyes widened again in comprehension and he swallowed hard, knowing he was close to death.

"I want the keys to your van," said Karpenkov. "And I want you to remove one of your prisoners."

"Anything you say, Mac," said Hamilton. "The keys are in the truck."

Karpenknov nodded and moved the pistol to indicate that Hamilton should start walking back to the truck.

As Hamilton turned, he sneaked a glance to the sky and Karpenkov knew that he was hoping the California Airborne Patrol would soon pass overhead.

"Let's move quickly," said Karpenkov.

At the van Karpenkov watched carefully as Hamilton removed the keys from the ignition. "Which prisoner you want?" he asked.

"Burns."

They moved to the rear of the vehicle and Hamilton opened the rear door. "Burns—out here." he called.

Eyes shaded from the first rays of sun, Carl Burns emerged slowly from the van. "What the hell's goin' on?" he demanded. His eyes widened when he saw the bloodstained face of the stranger, then when he saw the gun in Karpenkov's hand he smiled. "You've come to get me out," he said joyfully.

"Yes," said Karpenkov without mirth, then to Hamilton he said, "Climb in."

Hamilton hesitated for a moment, his eyes fixed on the gun, then wordlessly he climbed into the rear of the van. Karpenkov slammed the door shut, tested it to make sure it was locked, then turned to Burns. "Get in the truck, we're leaving."

"In this?" said Burns. "We'll never get away in this."

"Don't worry. I have transportation waiting for us a few miles down the road."

As he moved to the front of the vehicle, Karpenkov's eyes anxiously scanned the skies. If the Highway Patrol plane arrived he would have to shoot Burns on the spot and make a run for it on his own.

Inside the cab of the van, Karpenkov started the engine, threw the transmission in gear and lurched forward.

"Who sent you?" asked Burns as the van picked up speed.

"You know who sent me," said Karpenkov.

"I was beginning to wonder if . . ."

"You were told that if you kept your mouth shut, someone would be sent to get you out."

Karpenkov's eyes were on the road, but he could feel Burns's eyes on him. He turned to face his passenger. "What is it?"

"It's hard to tell with all that fake blood, but don't I know you? Have we met before?"

"That is quite unlikely," said Karpenkov. "We travel in somewhat different circles."

Burns nodded but his eyes were still on Karpenkov when the Russian pulled the van over to the side of the road and stopped. "Okay," he said, "let's go."

"Where?"

"Just follow me," said Karpenkov, jumping out and running quickly across the road. Burns followed as Karpenkov plunged into the trees at the edge of the road and down a steep, heavily wooded gully. At the bottom of the slope Karpenkov kicked aside some branches to reveal a trail bike lying on the ground. He righted the machine, climbed on, and started the engine. "Get on," he said to Burns, who climbed on behind him.

"Hold on," he said and slammed the bike into gear and raced off down the canyon toward a heavily forested area to the east.

Twenty minutes later Karpenkov stopped the bike one hundred yards from the shore of a large lake. "We walk from here," he said.

"Walk?" said Burns incredulously. "How far do you expect to get with me in these prison clothes?"

Karpenkov's face was impassive. "I have a boat a few hundred yards from here. On board I have food and clothing. In less than an hour we'll be on the other side, where another car is waiting. You will be given money and identity papers to enable you to make a new start."

With Karpenkov leading the way, they walked through the trees, following the contours of the lake until they stopped parallel to a cabin cruiser moored in shallow water.

"Wait here," said Karpenkov. "I'll see that everything is clear. When I wave, you come out casually, just as if we were going off for a day of fishing. Put this on," he said, removing his jacket and giving it to Burns.

Karpenkov emerged from the trees and walked across a rocky beach, looking left and right up the long curving shoreline. He walked across a narrow walkway and stepped down into the boat, then looked back at the shore. His eyes carefully picked out each detail along the shore. Nothing was amiss. He waved to Burns, who emerged cautiously from the trees, then walked quickly toward the boat.

"Go below," said Karpenkov, busy with starting the engine, as Burns stepped aboard. "You will find a change of clothing. Stay below until I call for you."

Burns, without comment, did as he was told. He heard the deep-throated rumble as the engines kicked to life and soon the cruiser was picking up speed heading across the lake.

Burns changed into a T-shirt with some kind of slogan imprinted across the chest, a flannel shirt, and brown corduroys. Most of the clothes were too big for him but he did not feel like complaining about the fit. He looked out from one of the cabin portholes and saw the shoreline shrink in the distance.

He found a pack of cigarettes and some matches on a table and, helping himself, lit up a cigarette and settled into one of the couches, letting the sound of the engines lull him into a pleasant state of forgetfulness.

Twenty minutes into the trip the engines changed to a lower register and the boat slowed, then, abruptly, the engines died altogether.

Burns went to the doorway and peered out. "Anything wrong?"

"No," answered Karpenkov.

"Why are we stopping? I thought we wanted to get across to the other side as quickly as possible."

"I don't think we need to be in such a rush," said Karpenkov. "I thought I might try a little fishing."

"Fishing!" Burns exploded, coming out of the cabin. "Are you crazy," he began but stopped when he saw the gun in Karpenkov's hand. After the first registration of shock, a look of puzzlement passed across his face. "I don't get it," he said. "Why get me out if you're only going to kill me?"

Karpenkov shrugged. "Simple really. To keep you quiet."

"I haven't said anything to anyone. I wouldn't."

"Wouldn't you, Mr. Burns? A man who would sell out his country for a measly twenty-five thousand dollars is not the kind of man I would trust with my life."

Karpenkov had washed away the theatrical makeup that had covered his face and now Burns was certain he had seen him before. He was wise enough, however, not to indicate that fact.

"But I wouldn't talk. Honest!" Burns said. His voice was clear and rang with sincerity.

"Really?" Karpenkov asked. "How can I be sure?"

For a brief moment Burns saw light at the end of the tunnel. "I promise," he stammered. "I'll speak to no one. Just give me the chance to disappear. No one will ever hear from me again."

"I understand you've been having visitors in prison."

Burns's eyes widened. "Yes. I was going to tell you about that."

"Tell me about it now."

"Not much to tell."

Karpenkov merely stared.

"His name is Tompkins," Burns stammered. "He's ex-CIA and he's writing a book about spies."

"What did he want with you?"

Burns shrugged. "He doesn't know anything. The guy's a jerk."

"What did he want with you?" repeated Karpenkov.

"He wanted to know how it was so easy for me to get my hands on classified documents at TMK."

Karpenkov raised an eyebrow.

"He asked me if I thought it was too easy."

"Too easy?"

"Yeah. He asked me if he thought I had been set up."

"Set up?"

"You know—if somebody made it easy for me to get to the documents."

"And what did you say?"

"Well, after he said it, it made a lot of sense. I mean, how is it possible that I could've gotten my hands on such valuable stuff so easily? It was just lying around *asking* to be stolen."

Karpenkov sighed and Burns was sure he could talk his way out of this. "It makes sense, doesn't it?"

Karpenkov said nothing.

"If I just stick to that story, sooner or later some judge is going to blame the CIA for entrapment or something and let me out. Right?"

Karpenkov nodded. "You might be right."

Burns smiled and gave a soft sigh. He was almost home free.

"Anyone else you've talked to?" asked Karpenkov.

Burns thought quickly. There was no sense in keeping anything from this one. If he were caught in a lie, he would be as good as dead. He would tell everything. "Someone—another writer—came to see me last week."

"Who?"

"Said his name was Kevin Johnson. Writes for *Life* and *Reader's Digest*."

"Never heard of him."

"That's what I said."

"What did he want?"

Burns shrugged. "Same thing as the other one. Said he's writing a book about my case. Wanted to know all about the people at TMK."

Karpenkov's eyes narrowed as he listened. "Describe him," he said.

Burns thought for a moment. "Late twenties, early thirties . . . dark hair . . . close to six feet tall." He shrugged as if his reservoir of recollection was dried up.

"Anything else? Eyes—ears—teeth—scars?"

Burns's eyes lit up. "Yeah—he had a V-shaped scar under his left eye." He placed his finger under his own left eye to indicate the spot.

Karpenkov nodded, but Burns noted that for the first time his attention seemed elsewhere. He was silent for a moment and then asked, "Anything else? Did you talk to anyone else?"

"That's it," said Burns. "I think I've done a good job of keeping my mouth shut. Don't you?"

Karpenkov nodded his affirmation and shot Burns in the forehead.

Burns's eyes widened in surprise and then he toppled backward in a heap.

Karpenkov quickly knelt next to him and placed a plastic bag around Burns's head to contain the blood. There was only a slight amount on the teak deck, which he quickly wiped away with a sponge dipped in the lake. When he was satisfied he slipped the sponge inside the plastic bag and tied a cord around Burns's neck, sealing the bag.

He scanned the lake and the sky to make sure there would be no intrusion, then took a nylon rope and tied it several times around Burns's waist. He dragged the body to the rear of the cabin cruiser, where he uncovered two concrete blocks that had been hidden beneath another plastic bag. He looped the other end of the rope through the openings in the concrete blocks and knotted the end several times. After checking to make sure that both man and blocks were securely fastened, he lifted Burns's body and pushed it over the side. The rope grew taut until Karpenkov picked up the concrete blocks and dropped them overboard. Burns's body disappeared immediately.

SAN FRANCISCO (AP)—Rumors are running rampant today about the escape of convicted spy Carl Burns from a California prison van en route to the federal courthouse in San Francisco from the Federal Correctional Institution at Lompoc, California.

One prison guard was killed and the other locked inside the prison van that was being used to transport the prisoner in what federal authorities claimed was a "well-planned and ruthlessly executed" escape plan.

The guard and driver were apparently enticed to stop at the scene of a staged accident. While trying to help the "victim," the guard, Sam Fullerton, 32, of Orcutt, California, was shot in the head at close range.

The prisoner and the unidentified male who killed the guard and locked up the driver made their escape into a heavily wooded area of San Benito County.

Federal authorities refused comment on the escape or on the reason for Burns's transfer to San Francisco, other than to say he was being questioned in a continuing investigation.

Forty-two

From a phone booth in San Bruno near the San Francisco International Airport, Karpenkov called a private room number in San Francisco. The phone rang in the basement room of the Soviet consulate at 2790 Green Street and was answered before the first ring had ended.

"Yes?"

"This is Chameleon," said Karpenkov.

"Yes, Chameleon. Is there a problem?"

"Perhaps. I need some information that you might be able to provide."

"We will do what we can, Chameleon."

"I have left a package for you to pick up. A message inside explains my requirements."

"A man will be dispatched immediately. Where?"

"Do you have my personnel sheet in front of you?"

The voice hesitated and Karpenkov could hear a drawer opening. "Got it."

What Karpenkov called his personnel sheet was actually his personal code book, which was used by no other agent and used only infrequently by him.

"Page seven," he said, although there was no page seven.

The man at the other end of the line looked at the list in front of him and counted down seven places. "Got it," he said, his finger resting on a line which read, "San Francisco International Airport." "What time?" he asked.

"Twelve-fifteen."

"Got it," said the man. He knew that at 12:15 in San Francisco it was 1:15 in Moscow and that the package was at locker number 115 in the San Francisco Airport. He was about to give some farewell message to Chameleon when the line went dead. He smiled. Chameleon was the most careful agent. He had no time for pleasantries.

What Chameleon had left in what was called a "dead drop" or a "dead letter box" was a request for any information on Kevin Collins. He had included a photograph taken with a telephoto lens—somewhat grainy but still clear enough that Collins' features were clearly recognizable—and a brief background biography lifted from the personnel files at TMK.

The "dead drop" technique in which information is left to be picked up by an associate was a common method of exchanging information. As Karpenkov knew, it was also one of the weak links in the espionage chain. More agents were identified and arrested through FBI surveillance of dead drops than through any other method. The method was simple— follow the agent until he led them to a dead drop location. Once the FBI discovered a drop location the usual technique was to place the location under surveillance and then photograph and follow anyone who either picked up or dropped off material of any kind.

Karpenkov never used drops that had been selected or used by anyone else. He selected his own—always different— and then informed the Illegals Support Officer at the Soviet mission where to pick up the material. Using this method for years, Karpenkov had safely transmitted hundreds of classified documents to the Soviet Union. His preferred course of action was to avoid using this technique and to have someone else convey stolen secrets, but occasionally he had no other option. This was one of those times.

He had full confidence in the ability of the KGB to find the information he needed. Was Kevin Collins, as he suspected, the man whom Carl Burns had described? If so— who was he, why did he use a false name, and what did he want with Burns? He expected to have the information within a few days.

He knew that the investigating powers of the KGB— even in a foreign country—were second to none. Besides, in America information was given as freely as a casual hello. In America secrecy was considered to be sinister and harmful to the public welfare. It was almost laughable. How could a nation survive without secrets? It was not unknown for Soviet officials to visit government offices in Washington and request classified documents as if they had every right to receive them.

Such things, he told himself, would not be possible in civilized societies. In a society where the rights of many were protected against the desires of the few, such activities would be severely punished. What the Americans considered freedom was in reality not freedom at all. It was license—license to avoid one's obligations to the majority. And that license would one day—and that day would be soon—contribute to the ultimate destruction of what was known at Moscow Center as the *Glavni Protivnik*—the Main Enemy, the United States of America.

WASHINGTON—Last night in a nationally televised address, the President declared that the vaunted and much-debated American antiballistic missile system "has been thoroughly tested and proved to be one hundred percent effective."

For the past month, the President said, the U.S. has been conducting extensive tests from Vandenberg Air Force Base, where ICBM's of the type used by the Soviet Union have been fired out across the Pacific at simulated targets more than 6,000 miles to the west. "Without exception," the President said and then repeated his words for emphasis, "without exception, the missiles' multiple warhead packages were destroyed."

According to the President, the next step is to have the Congress fund the deployment of a series of these ABM systems at various strategic locations across the U.S. "For the first time in almost forty years," the President said, "the U.S. is invulnerable to the threats of destruction from those who would rule by terror."

In a pointed reference to the Soviet Union, the President declared that "the days of communist expansion are over," and in another reference which some observers saw as a veiled threat but White House spokesmen later claimed was not intended as such, the President declared that those who would rule the world by force had better "fall back or face the consequences."

Forty-three

A silence fell across the room as the General Party Secretary was brought into the room in a wheelchair. This was the first time in more than a month that Chernetsov had attended a Politburo meeting and the first time in several weeks that the other members of the governing body of the Soviet Union had seen their designated leader. Only the gravity of the situation had brought him from his sickbed to this meeting.

The General Secretary looked old and worn and incredibly feeble. His skin seemed transparent, but most in the room chose not to stare.

He was wheeled to his customary place at the head of the table, where his aide poured him a glass of water and placed a small container of pills in front of him. Chernetsov picked up the glass, his hand trembling so much that water spilled on the desk. He looked sharply at his aide as if to say, I told you not to fill the glass. The aide, a sober-faced, middle-aged Party functionary, quickly wiped up the spill. Chernetsov maneuvered the glass to his lips and took a small sip, then slumped back in his chair as if exhausted by the effort.

Most of the men in the room averted their eyes from the spectacle. It was embarrassing to see the leader of the most powerful nation on earth too feeble to hold a glass of water.

One who did not look away was Defense Minister Marshal Ushenko. Ushenko had replaced the aging Ustinov as Defense Minister and was the Army's choice as General Secretary after the death of Andropov. Chernetsov had been the compromise candidate between the two warring factions of Soviet politics—the KGB and the Army—and Ushenko was now a brooding and antagonistic thorn in the side of the men who had bested him in the intricacies of Soviet politics. If Chernetsov could have removed Ushenko as Defense Minister he would have done so but the marshal had the firm support of the military and to remove him would have been a dangerous step that could have untold repercussions.

Ushenko was biding his time, gathering his strength. He watched Chernetsov's struggles with a look of disdain on his face. The General Secretary was obviously terminally ill, an empty shell waiting only for the facade to collapse and reveal the emptiness within.

Chernetsov raised a quivering hand and began to speak in a soft, thin voice punctuated by a rasping wheeze. "Gentlemen," he said, "we have been called here to discuss this latest threat from the West. This so-called 'defensive system' is the gravest crisis that has faced our motherland since the Nazi invasion."

Ushenko interrupted rudely. "How do we know it works?"

Chernetsov's eyes, eyes that had burned holes in men of lesser arrogance, fixed on Ushenko. Ushenko did not flinch.

"You can be sure, Comrade Marshal, that our intelligence reports and the independent verification offered by .invited observers to the testing of the weapons system are certain of one thing—the system does work. We cannot be certain that the American claim of one hundred percent accuracy is reliable but we can be certain that it does work." Chernetsov paused and coughed gently into his handkerchief, inspecting the linen before returning it to his pocket. "The question that is to be discussed at this meeting is—what, if anything, can be done about it?"

Ushenko was the first to grab the opportunity to speak. "The situation is intolerable," he said. "If the system works as well as the Americans claim, then we may just as well relinquish any claims to our status as a leader of nations. The Americans could bring us to our knees."

"Perhaps," ventured Grigori Romanov quietly, "the Americans are sincere in their declaration that this system is merely defensive."

Foreign Minister Gromyko, himself pale and ill, snorted in derision. "There is nothing defensive about a system that threatens our destruction."

The gathering fell silent.

"Suggestions?" asked Chernetsov, knowing what Ushenko's answer would be.

"Preemptive strike," said the Defense Minister. "Now, before the system is in place."

There was a breathless silence in the room as the men waited for a response.

Chernetsov smiled. "A nuclear exchange, Comrade Marshal? To assure the complete and total destruction of our two societies? I did not become General Secretary of the Party to preside over the ashes of a charred motherland."

"If we strike now," said Ushenko, "there is a chance of survival. If we wait—"

Chernetsov interrupted. "The Americans know that we must consider a preemptive strike. Our sources inform us that all U.S. military units are on alert and standing at constant readiness. All we could hope for is the destruction of both countries. That is totally unacceptable."

"But . . ." Ushenko stammered.

This time Chernetsov's glare silenced him.

"If you, Comrade Marshal—or anyone here—could show me how we could strike a blow at this system while we remain invulnerable to a retaliatory strike, I would give the order now. But I will not preside over the annihilation of one hundred million Russians."

Chernetsov turned away, trying to direct the discussion to other areas, but Marshal Ushenko was, although subdued, still relentless. "Excuse me, Comrade General Secretary, but if I may be permitted one last question."

Chernetsov's expressionless face hid his anger. "Proceed, Marshal Ushenko."

"Am I to understand that the policy of the Soviet Union in regard to this American defensive system is to do nothing? Are we just to sit back and wait for the Americans to throw their weight around? I can only repeat what we all know to be already true—the Americans, emboldened by their technological surprise, are already beginning to provoke us. Our military attaché in Washington was told informally at a dinner party by a member of the U.S. Joint Chiefs of Staff that three months after this system is in place there would not be a single Russian in the western hemisphere. He specifically spoke of our presence in Cuba as being a thing of the past.

"What is next?" he went on, his passion growing, the room hushed. "Will it be a thrust in East Berlin, or perhaps the People's Republic of Germany? Offers of help to dissidents in Hungary, Czechoslovakia? Where will it end?"

266

Ushenko sat, his arms folded across his chest, his posture belligerent. The room was silent as everyone considered the frightening possibilities. Was it possible that the expansionist days were over? That they were to preside over the decline of the Soviet Empire?

Premier Nikolai Tikhonov spoke first. He was seventy-eight and had served on the Politburo longer than any other man here. His head shook and his voice quavered, the result of a stroke a year ago, but he still commanded respect in this group. "We must act," he said, "and we must act soon. We cannot allow the Americans to dominate us. Their natural aggressiveness—particularly with this cowboy in office—would be a danger, not only to us, but also to the community of nations. We as the protectors of the have-nots who constitute three-fourths of the people of this globe cannot allow this to happen."

Chernetsov's eyes bulged in surprise for just a moment. He had not expected Ushenko to gather support from that quarter. For the first time he began to realize that during his illness-enforced absence new alliances had been formed. He had not wanted to believe, but should have known, that the jackals would begin dividing the spoils long before the carcass was cold.

Ushenko, his eyes on Chernetsov, smiled when he saw the look of shock on the General Secretary's face. There are a few other surprises for you, Comrade General Secretary, he thought.

Chernetsov saw the consensus running away from him and knew that he must act quickly to reposition himself in the lead. "We all agree, Comrade," he said, beginning carefully, forming his words only split seconds after the thoughts occurred to him, "that something must be done. To do nothing would be suicidal. But"—he paused and gave his doleful stare to every man in the room—"to act precipitately and without thought would be equally suicidal. It will be no victory if we destroy the U.S., only to be destroyed ourselves. Which of you wishes to be responsible for the deaths of one hundred million of his own people?"

Ushenko saw that Chernetsov had quickly recaptured the momentum and moved just as quickly to cut him off. "No one here would ever consider such a disaster, Comrade General Secretary. You yourself said that we would only consider a preemptive strike if the possibility of retaliation were eliminated." He paused for a response and Chernetsov, his eyes narrowed in suspicion, gave a careful nod of agreement. "I think then," continued Ushenko, "that that should be our policy. To find a method to eliminate their retaliatory capacity and then strike a blow at this defensive system."

The General Secretary blinked several times as if trying to stay awake. He was woefully tired and knew that he was physically unable to participate in this discussion for much longer. But he was unwilling to leave with the matter unresolved because he was sure that Marshal Ushenko would dominate the proceedings once he had gone. He attempted a sip of water but gave up the glass halfway to his lips. He turned to Tikhonov, hoping to isolate him from Ushenko. "This action that you call for, Comrade Premier, I assume that we are talking about nonmilitary means."

"Absolutely," said Tikhonov. He nodded in Chebrikov's direction. "We turn loose the antiwar and antinuclear people in Europe and America. We step up the campaign of opposing deployment of Prometheus. Just as we stopped deployment of the neutron bomb in Europe and the full MX deployment in the U.S., we can perhaps prevent deployment of this so-called defensive system. If enough voices are raised against this deployment, we may once again prevail."

Chebrikov, the KGB chief, sat up as if his competence had been questioned. "I can assure the Premier that our people have already begun a massive campaign aimed at forcing the Americans to reconsider deployment. Only yesterday there were demonstrations in Bonn, London, Paris, and Amsterdam."

"I'm afraid," said Ushenko with a slick smile, "that words or demonstrations won't stop the Americans."

Chernetsov nodded. "We're hoping for a delay of at least several months to enable us to deploy our own defensive system."

Ushenko's eyes narrowed. "My understanding is that our system is at least several years behind the Americans'."

Chernetsov raised a bushy eyebrow and smiled. "There is always the possibility of an unexpected breakthrough." He looked to KGB Chief Chebrikov for encouragement but Chebrikov remained stonily silent.

"We know what unexpected breakthroughs have meant in the past, Comrade," Ushenko said. "But this time the Americans have thrown up a blanket of secrecy around this project that will be impossible to penetrate."

Chernetsov shrugged. "That is of course very possible, but with their perverted sense of freedom it has always been very difficult for the Americans to keep secrets."

"And let's say that six months from now we are able to deploy our own system—what then?"

Chernetsov seemed puzzled by the question. "Why then . . . we return to the present situation that has been operative for the past fifteen years."

"Exactly," said Ushenko. "But in that interim period the Americans will have expanded their areas of influence in Africa and quite possibly threatened us into falling back in Europe. Then, of course, when the map of the world is completely revised, we will return to a period of normalcy with neither power able to dominate the other. The only difference is that we will have forfeited the gains of twenty-five years."

Chernetsov interrupted. "It is very unlikely that the Americans would be so reckless."

"Reckless!" screamed Ushenko in an explosion of spittle. "What is the risk? The risk in opposing them is all ours. 'Fall back or face the consequences' is what I think their cowboy President said."

"Sheer bluster," said Chernetsov.

"Perhaps," said a suddenly calm Ushenko. "But you yourself said that you would only order a preemptive strike at the U.S. if there was no possibility of retaliation, and that is exactly the position in which the American President finds himself now. Why should he not seize the same opportunity that you yourself would?"

Chernetsov sighed, seeing how well Ushenko had laid the trap for him. He hadn't really meant to imply that he *would* attack if it were safe to do so, only that he would attack if it were safe to do so and he had no other option. If he had not been so damned tired he would have seen it coming and been able to to parry Ushenko's deft thrust. He had not scrambled his way up through the ranks without being adept at this game of cutthroat politics. His experience helped him now. When in doubt or in danger of losing control, remand the problem to a committee. "I think, gentlemen," he began, "that we need further study on this matter before we decide to precipitate action. Comrade Premier Tikhonov will chair the committee to be composed of Comrades Ushenko, Chebrikov, Aliyev, and Gromyko." He was deathly tired now and prayed for no more dissent. "Are we agreed?"

Almost as an act of mercy there was no dissent. Marshal Ushenko tried to conceal his smile. This committee of five, which Chernetsov had thought was stacked three to two in his own favor, was actually split evenly, two against two, with one wavering. The alignments on the Politburo, never very firm, had begun to shift.

"Then if we are agreed," said Chernetsov, "the committee will report to me in three days and we will once agan convene this same body and decide what course we are to take." This would give him breathing room, he thought. In that time he hoped to pressure the other members to take a more conciliatory stance. He was convinced that the Soviet Union could survive this crisis, just as it had many others, without the threat of self-destruction. He paused to gather strength; his whole body was slumped in his chair, and those at the table were amazed that he was able to continue. "May I remind you, Comrades—all of you—that what we decide in the next few days may decide not only the fate of the Russian people but of the entire world."

Chernetsov signaled to his aide and was immediately wheeled away from the table, a weary figure who seemed to have shrunk in size since entering the room.

He would die two days later, leaving effective control of the Soviet Empire in the hands of the Committee of Five.

MOSCOW—The Communist Party daily newspaper *Pravda* released today the text of what was reported to be an interview with Communist Party General Secretary Nikolai Chernetsov. Although Mr. Chernetsov has not been seen in public for over a month and is reported by informed observers to be seriously ill, the *Pravda* article claimed that a "serious but obviously healthy" Mr. Chernetsov had submitted to a grueling series of interviews with journalists from *Pravda*.

In the interview, Mr. Chernetsov denounced the American President's "mad search for nuclear superiority" and called for the people and the Congress of the U.S. to reject "this President's lust for power."

270

"The people of the world reject the idea that American security can be bolstered by threats to the survival of the Soviet Union," said Mr. Chernetsov, "and the American President must be told this by all who are concerned with peace.

"It would be a sign of political maturity," Mr. Chernetsov is reported to have said, "if the American people would once and for all renounce this death-dealing ABM system that the President alone desires.

"This ABM so disturbs the doctrine of parity that all peace-loving men and women can only stand in horror at the thought of its deployment," Mr. Chernetsov is reported to have said.

"The fuse is lit and time is short," said the leader of the Soviet Union. "Only the outraged voices of peacemakers can save the world from destruction."

Forty-four

On Friday the seventeenth of July, the TMK Corporation threw a party to celebrate the successful completion of the government's testing program for the Prometheus II. Work stopped at noon and all employees gathered in the company cafeteria for a round of self-congratulatory speeches by the company president, several of his top executives, and by a General Winslow, who represented the Department of Defense.

After their brief remarks Reid Lawson gave a toast to the continuing good fortunes of the company and to the continued success of the project. With a glass of champagne in hand, everyone sat down to lunch and the festivities continued well into the early evening.

Afterward, Reid Lawson hosted a more private party for

the top executives and some of the key personnel who had participated in the project. Carol Hardwick had wangled an invitation for K.C., but at first he had been reluctant to attend.

"What reason do I have to be there?" he had asked Carol when she called with the invitation. "I wasn't even with the company when this project was completed."

"It'll give us a chance to see each other," Carol said. "We've hardly talked since you came out here."

"People might wonder what I'm doing there—why you wanted me there. It could give me away."

Carol laughed. "C'mon, Mr. Cloak-and-Dagger. Nobody'll suspect anything."

"Didn't Lawson ask why you wanted me on your invitation list?"

"You're not on my list," Carol said. "I asked him if I could invite Diane. He knows Diane through me and I told him she was dating someone at TMK. He didn't even ask who, he just said it was no problem."

K.C. was still reluctant to attend but Diane's enthusiasm for the event proved persuasive.

"We can ask all kinds of questions," she said. "Probably get more information in one night then we could in a week of interviews."

K.C. seemed doubtful. "Don't you think it might be just a little suspicious to go around asking questions?"

"For you maybe—but not me. I'm a reporter, remember? I can do a story about TMK, the Prometheus project, and the people who made it happen. It's a natural." She laughed. "My editor would love it."

K.C. grumbled a little but had to admit that Diane was probably right. Besides, the prospect of finally getting to meet Carol's new boyfriend was enticing.

Reid Lawson lived in a rented house overlooking the Pacific on Half Moon Bay. The location was ideal, almost halfway between the corporate offices in San Francisco and the TMK Corporation in Mountain View, and the house, perched high above the Pacific, was perfect for entertaining.

"I'm impressed," was all that K.C. could think to say when he and Diane pulled into the circular driveway that led up to the house.

Inside the party was already in full swing. Thirty or forty couples, drinks in hand, were engaged in conversation either in the main room or outside on the large patio that surrounded the pool and overlooked the ocean. Carol rushed to greet K.C. and Diane as soon as they entered. She hugged Diane and gave K.C. a quick peck on the cheek while whispering, "I want to give you such a hug."

She stood back, looking at them as if she were admiring a work of art. "I'm so glad you guys got together again," she said. "You look good."

Diane laughed and held K.C.'s arm. "I won't let go," she said happily. "I promise."

"He's the one who shouldn't let go," said Carol seriously.

K.C. looked at Diane. She was tanned and gorgeous in a white skirt and matching loose-fitting jacket over a blue blouse. He decided Carol was right.

Carol led them to the bar where a red-jacketed bartender was fixing drinks. "Everything going okay with . . . uh . . . your little adventure?" Carol asked, keeping her voice low and a smile on her face.

K.C. looked around, noting that no one seemed particularly interested in his conversation. He nodded. "So far no problems."

Carol scanned the room. "You probably know everyone here," she said. Then, haltingly, as if she was trying to practice the sound of his new name, she added, "Kevin, I want you to meet Reid—he's around here someplace." Her eyes found K.C.'s and for a moment she held him in a stare. "This isn't going to be tough for you, is it?" she asked. "You know what I mean?"

He knew exactly what she meant. She was his sister-in-law and to him she would always be his brother's wife. He shook his head. "No problem," he lied.

Carol knew him too well. She touched his arm gently. "You sure?"

He nodded. "It's fine," he said, but without as much conviction as before.

Carol led them across the main room and out through long sliding glass doors to the patio. There, on the far side of the swimming pool, his back to the blue Pacific, Reid Lawson was holding court in the center of a group of TMK executives who looked out of place in casual dress. Not Lawson. He wore a blue and red Hawaiian shirt and white pleated slacks. He looked tan and fit and completely in charge.

K.C. recognized most of the faces of the men who were

listening to Lawson—Kincaid and Nichols from Special Projects, and a collection of others from various departments.

"And this is only the beginning," Lawson was saying as Carol, K.C., and Diane approached. "Tolbert is determined to make TMK the top company of its kind in the country."

Carol interrupted him. "Forget all that business talk, Reid. I want you to say hello to someone."

If Lawson was annoyed by the intrusion he did not show it. He put an arm around Carol, and K.C. had to bite his lower lip to keep his expression from revealing his thoughts.

"Hello, again," said Lawson pleasantly to Diane.

"You remember my friend, Diane," said Carol.

Both nodded and smiled.

"This is her friend Kevin Collins, who just happens to work at TMK."

Lawson shook hands with K.C. "How long have you been with us, Kevin?" he asked.

"Just about a month."

"Where were you before that?"

"Teaching college—Columbia, in New York."

Lawson's eyes widened and his smile broadened. "I see. The god of wealth makes another convert, eh?" Then without pause he added, "You've made the right choice. And you've come to the right company." He looked at Diane and then back to K.C. "And you've obviously found the right woman."

K.C. said nothing but Carol interrupted with, "That's just about what I'd expect from a chauvinist like you." She punched him playfully on the arm.

"I only say that," said Lawson, laughing, "as someone who has also been fortunate enough to find the right woman." He pulled Carol closer and gave her a peck on the forehead. They were the picture of the perfect couple—happy, handsome, wealthy.

Carol saw K.C.'s face begin to crumble and quickly moved to remove him from the scene of his distress. Carol disengaged herself from Lawson's grasp and took hold of K.C. by an elbow. "Let's get away from here," she said, forcing a small laugh. "I want to show you the rest of the place." She turned over her shoulder and said to Lawson, "You can talk to him later."

She dragged them back inside. "My God, K.C.," she said, "if you want to give yourself away I can't think of a better place to do it than in houseful of TMK executives."

"I'm sorry," said K.C. "I didn't think it would be so hard to see you with . . . with someone else."

Carol touched him lightly on the cheek. "Don't worry," she said, "it wasn't easy for me either."

There was a long silence until Diane chimed in, "Hey, is this a party, or what?" She kissed K.C. on the cheek. "Let's get another drink and mingle a little. I've got some questions I want to ask."

"Good idea," said Carol, then looked at K.C., her expression serious. "Are you going to be okay?"

"I'm fine," he said.

"It's all right to be upset," Carol said, "but for a minute I thought you were going to cry."

"I'm all right now," K.C. reassured her.

Carol seemed satisfied. "Then I'll leave you on your own. If you need me, just holler."

Diane, as it turned out, was a very good "mingler." It was easy for her to get the attention of any man in the room and even easier still to get them talking about their jobs at TMK. She made no secret of the fact that she worked for a newspaper or that she might write a story about the Prometheus project at TMK and the people who had made it possible.

After a while K.C. let her go off on her own while he found a suitable stool by the bar and settled in for some baseball conversation with a small group of men who had gathered there. He swiveled on the stool so his back was to the bar and he could watch Diane as she moved from one group to another.

He was happy to note that in a roomful of very good-looking women, Diane managed to stand out above the rest. He also noted slightly uneasily that when she moved from one group to the next she was invariably followed by the stares of the men she had just left.

"Lotta horny execs at this party," said a voice, and K.C. turned to find John Cowans standing next to him. K.C. had not seen much of Cowans since his transfer to Special Projects. "If you're going to bring the best-looking woman to a party," Cowans went on, "you'd better get used to having her stared at."

"I guess you're right," said K.C.

"She writing a story or something?"

K.C. shrugged innocently. "Don't know. Said she'd like to if she could get some interviews with the right people."

Diane was talking with Ted Nichols now and K.C. could hear her laughter from across the room. Diane turned and both she and Nichols waved in K.C.'s direction before going back to their conversation. Nichols was obviously saying something very funny and K.C. felt a strong desire to go over there and find out what it was. Instead he stayed at the bar and talked to Cowans and a few of the others. Every once in a while he would look around the room to see how Diane was doing. She was engrossed, and had been for quite some time, in an apparently serious conversation with Ted Nichols.

Out of the corner of his eye, K.C. picked up another group standing near Diane and Ted Nichols, and he momentarily shifted his attention to them. Reid Lawson was part of a small circle of men and women engaged in conversation, only this time, K.C. noticed, Lawson was silent—others were doing the talking. As he watched the group K.C. realized that not only was Lawson not doing any talking, but he didn't appear to be listening either. Instead his gaze and his attention seemed to be fixed on Diane and Nichols, about ten feet away. Lawson's jaw was set, his teeth clenched, and his expression was one of dismay. He seemed distressed by something and K.C. could only believe it had something to do with Diane's conversation with Nichols.

Abruptly Lawson turned on his heel and left his group looking at each other in a kind of mild surprise. K.C. watched Lawson as he went to Carol and pulled her outside the sliding glass doors. He talked with her in subdued tones but his hands were moving in short angry thrusts. With every few sentences he turned and looked in Diane's direction, as she, oblivious of the fact that she was the focus of attention, continued her talk with Nichols.

As K.C. continued to watch this confrontation in pantomime, Carol gave an open-armed gesture, her palms facing up as if to suggest that Lawson was in some way overreacting. But Lawson would have none of it, his index finger was jabbing at the air with apparently increasing anger. Although he seemed to be speaking in low, controlled tones, it was obvious that something had upset him.

Just as K.C. was about to go to Carol's rescue Carol saw him at the bar, and placing a hand on Lawson's arm as if to calm him, she quickly approached K.C.

"Problem?" asked K.C. before Carol could say a word.

Carol seemed embarrassed. "I think Diane is overdoing the investigative reporter bit. She's asking everybody about security problems at TMK." One eye narrowed and Carol gave K.C. a suspicious look. "I think you've got her doing your dirty work."

"Dirty work?"

"You know what I mean."

"Reid doesn't like all the questions?"

Carol shrugged. "He thinks it's inappropriate for a guest to grill the other guests at a party. If Diane wants interviews she can call the P.R. man at TMK."

K.C. smiled. "Maybe you're right. I'll get her out of here."

"You don't have to go," Carol said quickly. "Just get her to cool it a little."

"I think it would be better if we left."

Carol made a mild protest but K.C. could tell she was glad to be spared a potentially embarrassing incident.

"Will I see you soon?" she asked.

"I'll be in touch," K.C. said and when Carol gave him her best sisterly look of concern he added, "Honest."

Diane seemed genuinely bewildered when K.C. dragged her away from Nichols. "We have to be leaving now," he said as she stuttered a baffled protest.

"I'm just starting to get somewhere," she whispered as he led her by the arm to the door.

"The host is getting upset with the Nosey Parker routine," said K.C. "It's time to beat a hasty retreat."

Suddenly Reid Lawson was in front of them, barring their way to the door, and K.C. prepared himself for a difficult moment.

"Leaving so soon?" Lawson said, a pleasant smile across his face.

K.C. stammered an apology. "We've got plans for this evening that we couldn't change."

"That's too bad," said Lawson with apparent sincerity. "I hope we'll see the two of you again soon. I know Carol would love for us to get together sometime."

"That would be just fine," said Diane. "We've had a lovely time."

Still smiling, Lawson shook hands with them both. "Drive

safely," he said, and with a quick wave he went back to his guests.

At the door K.C. turned and saw Lawson talking to Nichols in a far corner, the amiable host persona suddenly absent. Lawson had Nichols pinned against the wall, and was wagging a finger in his face. Nichols kept shrugging his shoulders and showing his palms in an apparent protestation of innocence but Lawson was having none of it. Finally, after a brief period of mild objection, Nichols surrendered. Shoulders slumped, head down and nodding, he was the perfect picture of humbled subservience.

Diane covered her eyes, not wanting to watch. "He's catching hell," she said. "I should go and tell Lawson that we hardly talked about TMK at all."

"Let's just go," K.C. said. "I think we've stirred up enough trouble for one day."

In the car they rode in silence for a while, disturbed by what they had left behind.

K.C. attempted to break the somber mood. "I guess we won't be invited to the company picnic."

Diane shot him a dirty look. "I feel terrible that Ted is in trouble because of me—*us*," she added with a withering look.

"Don't worry," K.C. said with more optimism than he felt, "everything is probably back to normal already."

"I'm not so sure."

He struggled to change the subject. "So what did you two talk about if you didn't talk about TMK?"

Diane shrugged. "Lots of things. Classical music mostly."

Oh?" said K.C., trying to hide the jealous tone that had crept into his voice. He was largely unsuccessful.

"Jealousy is such an ugly emotion, don't you think?" Diane said with just a hint of sarcasm.

"Sorry. I just noticed what a good time you two seemed to be having."

Diane patted his knee like a mother reassuring a hurt child. "Not to worry," she said soothingly. "The man is nice but not really my type." She paused. "Although it is nice to meet someone who shares my interest in classical music."

"You should hear my Buddy Holly collection sometime."

Diane chuckled. "Nichols has an absolutely marvelous record collection—lots of Vivaldi."

278

"No doubt he invited you up to his place so that the two of you could listen together."

Diane was smiling broadly now. "As a matter of fact he did. I thought it was kinda cute. A variation of the 'how'd you like to come up and see my etchings' theme."

They were both laughing now.

"I'll bet," said K.C., "that he gets lots of girls who are just dying to go to his place and listen to Vivaldi."

They drove for a while in good spirits, the dismal part of the return trip forgotten.

"So, what did you find out—other than about Nichols's great record collection?" K.C. finally asked.

"Not much. Everyone is very willing to talk about the success of the project but as soon as you mention security problems or suggest some kind of connection between the people who have been arrested while at TMK, everyone just stares vacantly at you or changes the subject."

"Understandable I guess."

"Nichols was a little more informative than the others."

"I'll bet," said K.C., quickly regretting his reversion to type.

"C'mon," said Diane. "Be nice. He said some nice things about you."

"He did?"

"Yes. And he was complimentary about Gordon too."

"What did he say about Gordon?" said K.C., his voice doubtful.

Diane thought for a moment. "Well, when I asked about the security situation, he admitted that they had had some problems but that their last security officer—and he mentioned Gordon by name—had done a good job of turning things around."

"What else?"

"That's it. I didn't want to be obvious by asking any more about Gordon."

K.C. nodded his agreement. "So, did you get anything out of this?"

"Not much. Now that he has escaped, everyone mentions Burns of course, but no one thinks there is any connection between him and Greenwood. Several people were certain that the two didn't even know each other. They were only with the company at the same time for a very short period."

K.C. sighed.

Diane, sensing his disappointment, said, "I know. I thought I could come up with more."

"That's not it."

"What then?"

"I was just thinking that I'm probably going to have to have a visit with Jerry Greenwood in person."

She knew how much he had hated going to talk with Burns. He was not good at deceit—it showed in his face. She sighed also. "You're probably right."

They drove the rest of the way making light conversation but the gloom that had left them for a while was back, and Diane had a strange feeling it would be with them for some time to come.

WASHINGTON (AP)—All four potential Democratic presidential candidates joined today in demanding that the United States share its antiballistic technology with the Soviet Union as "the only possible way to maintain the strategic balance of power." Reminding the President of earlier promises to share technology, the candidates said, "Now that the technology is apparently a reality, the President has been noticeably silent on his earlier assurances."

The joint statement, released by the Democratic National Committee, calls upon the present Administration and the Republican candidate for the office of President to "pledge to the American people and to the people of the world that the technology developed in the United States is designed solely for defensive purposes.

"The only way to demonstrate this to a waiting world is to share the technology. The people of the Soviet Union must be made aware that the U.S. poses no threat to their security. When all nations are free from the possibility of nuclear attack then the world will once again be a safe place in which to live."

Forty-five

The phone rang. It was two A.M.

Diane sat up in bed, startled by the sudden, insistent noise. She was disoriented, her heart pounding, and it took her a brief moment to realize where she was.

She shook K.C. awake. The phone was on his side of the bed.

He reached for it in the dark and knocked it to the floor. Then, muttering curses, he fumbled around on the carpet, trying to find the suddenly silent phone.

He grabbed it. "Yes," he said sharply.

"Is this Mr. Hardwick?" asked a voice that he did not recognize.

K.C. was about to answer when a small alarm began jangling in his brain. "Who is this?" he asked cautiously.

"If this is Mr. Hardwick, I have some important information for him."

K.C. hesitated only for a moment. "I'm sorry," he said, "I'm afraid you've got the wrong number."

"I'm sorry to have bothered you," said the voice and the line went dead.

"Who was that?" asked Diane.

"Someone who wanted to know if my name was Hardwick."

"But how—?" she began, and let her voice trail off to a whisper.

"Good question," he said.

K.C. was wide-awake now, his mind racing. He sat up and swung his legs out onto the floor. "I'd better contact Birdwell," he said. "Maybe this is some kind of test."

"Wait till morning," Diane said, touching his back.

The phone rang again.

K.C. picked it up and held the phone to his ear but said nothing.

"You're probably wondering how I knew how to find you," said the voice.

"Listen you—" K.C. began, but the speaker went on as if he had not heard.

"I have information about the death of your brother."

"Who are you?"

"Gordon and I were associates. We were in the same line of work." The voice paused. "Shall I go on?"

"What do you know about Gordon's death?"

"I know that he was murdered."

"Tell me something I don't know."

"I might know who was responsible."

K.C. swallowed hard. He knew he was probably making a mistake. He should hang up now and call Birdwell in the morning. Somehow his cover was blown and Birdwell had said if that happened they would pull him out immediately. But was that what he wanted? Right now what he wanted was to find out what had happened to Gordon. "So, tell me," he said.

"I'm afraid the information must be given to you personally."

"How did you get this information?"

"I can't reveal that, but I do want you to have it."

"Then bring it to me—or let's meet somewhere."

"I can't do that either, Mr. Hardwick. There are people who would kill me if they knew I had talked to you. I can not be seen with you."

K.C. shook his head to clear the cobwebs. "What then?" He wasn't thinking too clearly. The lack of sleep had him disoriented.

"I could leave the information in a place where you could pick it up."

"Fine. Where?"

"Do you know the Japanese Tea Garden in San Francisco's Golden Gate Park?"

K.C. had to think for a moment. "Yes. I know where it is, but couldn't we do this someplace closer?"

"I'm afraid not."

"This sounds crazy to me. If you know something about my brother's death, tell me now."

The man went on as if he had not heard. "Tomorrow at

ten be at the Japanese teahouse. Stay there for fifteen minutes. When I am certain you are there and that you are alone, I will leave a package for you on the grounds."

"Where?"

"A waitress in the teahouse will deliver a note to you, telling you where to look. Do you understand?"

"Yes, but . . ."

"If you do not arrive I will assume that you are not interested."

The line went dead. K.C. stared at the phone for a full minute before gently replacing it on the cradle and flopping back down onto the bed.

"What is it?" Diane asked, unable to contain herself any longer.

"Someone with information about Gordon's death. He wants me to go to Golden Gate Park tomorrow morning."

"I don't like this—I don't like it one bit."

K.C., eyes wide open, stared into the darkness. "I don't like it either, but I don't have much choice."

"You could call Birdwell."

K.C. sighed. "He'd pull me out of it."

"And rightly so."

He turned to face her, seeing only the dimmest outline of her features in the dark. "I'm here to find out what happened to Gordon," he said. "I don't want to quit now."

She moved toward him, curving her body to fit his. "I'm afraid for you," she whispered.

"Don't be afraid," he said because it seemed like the thing to say. "Everything will be fine." He held her close, hoping she could not hear his heart pounding against his rib cage.

Diane had been awake most of the night, lying quietly so as not to disturb K.C. He had tossed and turned restlessly for hours but to Diane's amazement he had been able to sleep. It was obvious to her that someone knew who K.C. was and what he was doing, and equally obvious that he should tell Birdwell what had happened. Now that K.C. had been discovered his plan of anonymous investigation was no longer workable. Someone else—anonymous and perhaps deadly—was watching K.C. She carried that thought with her through a long and fearful night.

They were up early, and while he showered, Diane made sausage and eggs and coffee.

He sat down at the table, hair still wet, and without tasting his food he laced it with salt.

"Those sausages are salty enough," she said disapprovingly.

He shrugged. "That's why I buy them."

He finished his breakfast and at 8:15 they left the apartment and walked to the car. The streets were quiet and very few people were out at that hour. Neither noticed the man in the car parked across the street from the apartment building. As soon as K.C.'s car pulled away the man got out of his car and crossed the street. He climbed the stairs and paused outside K.C.'s door for a quick look around. Unobserved, he inserted a pick in the lock and quickly slipped inside the apartment, closing the door behind him.

The Japanese Tea Garden in Golden Gate Park was a marvel of the Japanese concept of simple complexity. In a relatively small area the garden provided the impression of a much larger space. Well-tended shrubbery provided a background for a reduced-scale, tiered temple, helping to give the illusion of size. A visitor could wander across private paths that seemed secluded from the rest of the garden, watch giant carp swim lazily in pools crossed by stepping-stone bridges, and gaze in wonder at a gateway, a swept-winged torii that sat above a waterfall which cascaded gently down an intricately landscaped hillside.

The impression given was one of serenity, and visitors spoke in hushed tones, as if subdued by the beauty of their surroundings. Dotted throughout the gardens were stone benches where one could escape the hustle and bustle over the garden walls and sit quietly, contemplating the beauty of nature.

K.C. entered through the West Gate and immediately made for the teahouse. It was almost ten A.M. He found a seat at one of the small tables and waited. A kimono-clad waitress approached with a pot of tea, a cup, and a small plate of rice cookies. K.C. paid her, wondering if she had the message for him, but she did not meet his eyes.

He poured his tea, a dark brew with leaves floating in it, and sipped as he looked around. There was nothing out of the ordinary. The open-air patio was crowded with families and tourists, none of whom seemed the slightest bit interested in him. He nursed his tea, waiting for something to happen.

Finally, after about ten minutes, he was approached by a different waitress. "Are you Mr. Hardwick?" she asked.

"Yes," he said.

She handed him a postcard. "Gentleman said to give this to you."

"What gentleman? What did he look like?"

She seemed puzzled, as if she did not understand the question. K.C. asked her again.

She smiled pleasantly. "He left a few moments ago."

"How did you know it was me?"

"You are the only man alone here."

K.C. looked around. It was true. He thanked the woman and then looked at the postcard. It pictured the multitiered Japanese temple that he had passed on the way to the teahouse. He turned over the postcard and saw a single word. "Here!"

There was nothing else.

He left immediately and walked toward the temple, which seemed to tower over the other structures in the garden. The path he chose meandered through rock formations, across footbridges, and past various ornamental shrubs. At every turn there were tourists posing for or taking photographs.

Close up, K.C. realized the temple was smaller than it had seemed from a distance. It was a tall, wooden, brightly painted structure with multiple roofs in the typical swooping style of Japanese architecture. At the base it was open and large enough for several people to gather beneath its roofs. K.C. entered and looked around.

At the moment it was empty, most people preferring to photograph the structure from the outside, where it was flanked by a torii and a huge stone lantern.

K.C. looked out from the rear, down the steep slope to the waterfall that cascaded gently into the carp-filled pond below. This seemed to be the most photographed area in the garden, K.C. thought, noticing several parties with cameras below him on the far side of the pond.

K.C. looked around on the dirt floor. There was nothing. He reached up and felt behind the wooden beams that supported the structure. His fingers touched something and he pulled down a large clasp envelope. He looked inside and found a single photograph.

"I don't know what to make of it," said K.C., his voice showing traces of exasperation.

"Let me look again," Diane said. "There must be something."

K.C. slapped the photograph down on the table irritably. "A long drive for nothing," he said. He had stopped at Diane's apartment on the way back from San Francisco.

Diane picked up the photograph. It showed a group shot of TMK employees posed outside the front entrance to the main building. The group, about sixty in number, stood on the front steps in three rows. K.C. recognized Gordon, standing in the second row, and many of the others in the photograph. But in the back row, just to Gordon's left, an unfamiliar face was circled in red ink. It was the face of a young man and he seemed to be looking directly at Gordon.

"Any idea who this guy is?" asked Diane.

K.C. shook his head. "None."

"So what have we got?" Diane asked.

K.C. shrugged helplessly. He searched the envelope again in vain, as if there might be a secret compartment. "We've got a picture of someone who looks as if he might be staring at Gordon."

Diane was looking closely at the picture. "Do you think someone is trying to tell us that this is the man who killed Gordon?"

"Then why not just say so?"

Diane nodded in agreement, then, squinting a little at the photograph, said, "This face seems familiar somehow. I get the feeling I should know him."

"I don't," said K.C. "I don't think he works at TMK now."

"Ask your friend Birdwell."

K.C. shook his head vigorously. "I don't want him to know about this. If he finds out, I'm finished with this case."

"Show the picture around at work."

He was shaking his head again. "That might give me away."

"Then let me take it to the office now. I'll go through the picture files or ask around. I'll bet somebody knows this face."

K.C. shrugged. "Why not. It's worth a try." He took one last look at the photograph before Diane sealed it in the envelope. The image was grainy and indistinct but to K.C. there was something ominous about the man's watchful stare.

"Will you be at home?" Diane asked.

"Yes." K.C. nodded but his eyes and mind were on the malevolent stare of the man who lurked behind Gordon.

"Less than an hour later Diane called.

"Any luck?" K.C. asked.

"Instant jackpot," she said. "I told you I thought I recognized him."

"Who is he?"

"That is the famous Jerry Greenwood. The man your brother arrested just days before he was killed."

K.C. released his breath in a slow exhalation. "Very interesting."

"One problem," said Diane. "He was in federal custody when Gordon was killed, so that lets him off the hook on that one."

K.C. let that sink in and cursed silently. Nothing was ever that easy, he thought. "I think I'd like to talk with Mr. Greenwood anyway. He's up to his neck in this mess."

Forty-six

"Where'd you get this photograph?" Birdwell asked. He was looking at the group photo of the TMK employees in which Jerry Greenwood's face was circled. K.C. had called him almost immediately after talking with Diane and Birdwell had agreed to meet him right away. They were sitting in K.C.'s car in a shopping mall parking lot near the Central Expressway.

"I found it with some things of Gordon's that I was going

through. I just wondered if you knew who it was and why Gordon had singled him out." He watched Birdwell's face carefully, looking for some telltale sign—a change in expression, a raised eyebrow—anything that would indicate whether or not Birdwell had accepted his fabrication.

Birdwell shrugged. "This is Jerry Greenwood and I guess your brother singled him out because he was about to have him arrested for stealing company secrets." He handed back the photograph. "Why the interest?"

"I'd like to see Jerry Greenwood—if that's possible."

"I doubt it," said Birdwell. "He's being held in San Francisco, awaiting trial. His lawyer won't let him see anybody."

"Try it," said K.C. "Tell them I want to hear their side of the story."

Birdwell shrugged. "If it comes through me or any of my people, your request will wind up in the litter basket."

"What then?"

"We've got some—not many—sympathetic newspaper editors who might be willing to provide you with a cover. I'll see what I can do."

"Good enough. Let me know as soon as you can."

He turned to face K.C. "Now, you said you had other things to talk about. Things that couldn't wait."

K.C. shrugged. "I just wanted to tell you about Lawson's party last night."

Birdwell's eyes lit up at the mention of Lawson's name. "Anything happen?"

"Only that he got very upset when Diane started asking some of the guests about security problems at TMK."

"That's interesting—anything else?"

K.C. gave him a brief rundown on what had happened, including Lawson's angry confrontation with Ted Nichols after Nichols had talked with Diane.

"Nichols, eh?" said Birdwell. "He was also very helpful to us in the Burns case."

"How?"

Birdwell thought for a minute. "He was one of several people who were first suspicious of Burns and what he was up to. Gordon trusted him also."

K.C. remembered what Diane had said about Nichols speaking well of Gordon. He filed that thought away for future reference.

"Anything else?" asked Birdwell.

"Just don't forget my meeting with Greenwood."

"Will do," said Birdwell, his hand on the door, ready to exit. He seemed anxious to be on his way.

Birdwell did not call for several days. When he did he seemed unusually enthusiastic. "You're all set," he said. "Greenwood has agreed to see you. You're a free-lance writer doing a piece for the *Examiner*. Apparently he wants to have his say before he gets his day in court."

"That's great. When?"

"Tomorrow—that okay?"

"That's fine."

There was a silence.

"Birdwell?" K.C. asked, feeling his way cautiously.

"Yes?"

Another momentary silence.

"Is there something I should know? Something you're not telling me?"

"Look," said Birdwell, a trace of irritation creeping into his voice. "You probably think I just sit around the office, waiting for you to call, but I assure you that I do have other things to occupy my time. I've got someone working this, and when he gets back to me, I'll get back to you."

"That's fair enough," said K.C. "I'll get back to you after I talk with Greenwood."

They both gave perfunctory farewells and hung up. K.C. wondered if Birdwell were merely having a bad day or if his questions had struck an exposed nerve.

Jerry Greenwood was led into the room by a uniformed guard. He looked around warily and K.C. thought how strange it was that prison garb made all men look the same.

Greenwood looked directly at K.C. "I don't have to talk to you if I don't want to," he said belligerently.

K.C. nodded. "I understand that."

"My lawyer said I was foolish to talk with anybody."

"Then why do it?"

"Because I want people to know my side of the story."

"That's what I want to hear. That's why I'm here."

Greenwood eyed K.C. suspiciously, then began a long uninterrupted monologue in which he told about his childhood and how his upper-middle-class father had virtually ignored him. He had been a brilliant boy and always a loner. In college he had drifted toward radical politics and for the first time felt the comfort of belonging to a group or a movement. There had been little that was outwardly anti-American in his background, he was mostly concerned with poverty and worldwide hunger, he wanted to save the whales, save the seals, save the trees, but somewhere along the way these sentiments had led him to believe that the U.S. was the prime cause of much of the world's distress.

After almost forty-five minutes of speaking, he paused and K.C. took the opportunity to prod him with a question. "What do you think is America's greatest crime?"

Greenwood spoke without hesitation. "That this country is preparing to commit genocide against the world."

K.C. watched the wild look in Greenwood's eyes. "How?" he asked.

"You've heard, no doubt, about the great defensive system that has been developed at TMK? This so-called 'defensive system' is probably the greatest threat to peace since the discovery of the bomb itself."

K.C. was silent, waiting for Greenwood to finish. What struck him was how similar to Burns's were Greenwood's words.

"This system will make the U.S. virtually impregnable to attack."

"That isn't good?"

Greenwood laughed. "Don't you understand? Don't you read the papers? The President is flexing his nuclear muscles already. Telling the Russians to get out of Afghanistan, stay out of Central America, butt out of the Middle East. This system has made it 'safe' for us to throw our weight around everywhere."

"Is that why you wanted the Russians to have it too?"

Greenwood stopped and a sly smile came over his face but he remained silent.

K.C. went on, "It makes sense, doesn't it? If we both have the system no one has to worry about nuclear attack."

Greenwood nodded but said nothing.

"And you alone, Mr. Greenwood, would make that decision? You alone would decide the fate of the world?"

The sly smile slipped from Greenwood's face. "I'm not alone," he said almost in a whisper.

K.C.'s throat was constricted. "There are others?" he asked carefully.

"Oh yes. There were more of us but the secret police have been picking us off one by one. Killing us, driving some of us insane," he smiled, "imprisoning others."

"Do you know who the others are?"

"No. But I know there are others."

"How can you be sure? I mean, if you don't know who they are, how do you know they have been killed or imprisoned?"

Greenwood looked around the windowless room and raised his hands, palms up, to shoulder level. "Here I am."

"But you're not dead. You said some had been killed."

"Jim Progano is dead. They killed him."

K.C. looked puzzled. "I heard he killed himself."

Greenwood chuckled. "They made it look that way."

"They?"

"The secret police. The FBI, the CIA, whatever you want to call them."

"Why would they want to kill him?"

"He knew what they wanted to do with this system."

"But he helped design it. Helped build it."

"That was when he believed it was going to be used to bring about peace. He was a scientist, he built the brain, someone else made the weapon. When he found out it was a war machine just like all the other war machines, he tried to stop them. He protested to Kincaid but his head was in the clouds. His wife told the police that the last person he talked with was Gordon Hardwick, the CIA security coordinator at TMK. The next thing you know, Progano is dead. They killed him."

K.C. tried to appear noncommittal but couldn't prevent the look of doubt that ran across his face. This man, he thought, thinks that Gordon had something to do with Progano's death.

"You don't believe me?"

"Well . . . Of course I *want* to believe you."

"Burns is dead too."

"Carl Burns?" said K.C. incredulously. "He escaped just a few days ago."

Greenwood shook his head sadly. "That's what they want you to think. You'll never see him again. They've killed him. To shut him up."

"Do you have any evidence to—"

"Evidence!" Greenwood screamed. "Evidence! He disappeared, didn't he? Do you think that someone could get out of their clutches unless they wanted him to? You wait. Someday soon you'll be reading that I escaped too. You'll never see me again either. It's the oldest trick in the book. Shot while trying to escape." He shot a vicious glance at K.C. "Evidence," he mumbled. "I have all the evidence I need. That's the only reason I'm talking to the press. I'll be dead soon. I want my story told. Tompkins will tell my story."

"Tompkins. The writer? You've talked with him too?"

After that outburst, Greenwood sat in silence, responding with grunts and shrugs to K.C.'s questions. It was evident that the interview was over.

K.C. got up from his chair. "Can I come back and talk to you sometime?"

Greenwood looked up at him with disgust. "You haven't heard a word I've said, have you?" He looked away and stared at some imaginary window. "I'll be dead soon. The secret police have driven me mad—now they'll kill me." He lapsed into silence and finally, after a long wait, K.C. moved away. He knocked quietly on the door until a guard opened it from the other side. He took one last look at Greenwood as he left, but the man had not moved. He slipped quietly through the door.

Outside the visitors' room he took a few deep breaths to clear his head of the image of Greenwood.

The guard spoke. "Dr. Littler would like to see you for a few minutes."

Puzzled, K.C. nodded.

"Follow me," said the guard, who proceeded to escort him to an office down the corridor from the visitors' area.

Dr. Frank Littler stood up as K.C. entered the office. He was a small man in his late fifties with bright eyes and a shock of almost white hair.

"Mr. Collins," he began as they shook hands, "Robert Birdwell—a mutual friend—called me this morning and asked that I speak with you." He indicated that K.C. should sit in a chair in front of the desk. "Forgive the mess," he said, looking around the room. "It's not my office. I only come here once a week or so and there are some obviously untidy people sharing this space."

K.C. sat down. "What did Birdwell say we should talk about?"

Littler's eyes narrowed a little. "Jerry Greenwood, of course."

K.C. nodded. "What's your part in all this, doctor?"

Littler sighed. "I'm with the Psychology Department at Cal State—here in the city," he added. "I'm presently working on a government grant. Apparently we are working for the same employer."

K.C. nodded but made no other acknowledgment of his status.

Littler went on. "My study is an attempt to identify potential security risks—before it's too late."

"Which brings us to Greenwood."

"Exactly."

"What's his problem?"

Littler smiled. "I'm not sure."

"Government doesn't seem to be getting its money's worth, doctor."

The smile faded from Littler's face. "Greenwood's is one of the most intriguing and disturbing cases I've ever encountered." The doctor shook his head slowly from side to side. "He displays most of the symptoms of paranoid schizophrenia . . . but . . ."

"But what?"

"But in most ways he is not typical of that group. Most schizophrenics limp along the borderline of psychotic behavior for many years before they are finally recognized as suffering from a genuine mental disorder. In Greenwood's case there is no hint of mental illness or even depression. Before a few months ago he seemed quite normal."

"And it's unusual for someone to go from normal to schizophrenic in such a short time?"

"It's not unheard of—but it is unusual. People don't just wake up one day and find themselves mentally ill"—he paused for effect—"unless . . ."

"Unless what?"

"Unless the transition is precipitated by some severe psychotic break or traumatic incident. A severe emotional shock, for instance—a death in the family, a serious illness, a serious financial reversal. Drug abuse is another possibility."

K.C. was thinking about Gordon and what had happened to him.

293

"As far as we can determine, however, none of those possibilities fit in Greenwood's case."

"Not even drug abuse?"

"People who know him claim he occasionally smoked marijuana." He shrugged. "Not enough to account for his behavior."

"Maybe he's normal and we're crazy," K.C. said.

Littler chuckled. "Maybe. You know we are all a bit paranoid. That's what makes it so difficult to identify genuine paranoid behavior. It's really quite healthy to be on the lookout for potential threats to our well-being—as long as it's not overdone. It's not abnormal behavior to avoid dark alleys in bad neighborhoods."

K.C. nodded in agreement. He knew that Littler had more to tell him.

"Sometimes it is not difficult to take that normal caution and redirect it toward what we would consider abnormal behavior."

"I'm not sure I follow you."

"As I said, we're all a little paranoid. Republicans think Democrats are bleeding hearts. Democrats think Republicans are totally without compassion. Conservatives think that liberals are spineless, liberals think conservatives are trying to blow up the world." He shrugged. "We all carry around our predispositions like unnecessary baggage."

"Go on."

"Take someone like Greenwood. He's mildly antiestablishment, antimilitary, wants to save the whales, rescue the environment. Give him a little push and he just might begin to think that his own country is a danger to world peace."

K.C. coughed nervously. "He's not alone in that conception."

Littler nodded. "True. But most of them try to change things on election day. How many are willing to sell out their country to a foreign power?"

K.C. thought about that for a while. "You said give him a little push. What did you mean?"

Littler coughed into his clenched fist and his eyes could not meet K.C.'s. He seemed embarrassed at what he was about to say. "At the Serbsky Institute in Moscow they have become quite adept at inducing schizophrenic behavior."

K.C.'s eyes widened in disbelief. "The Russians? Who sounds paranoid now?"

294

Littler smiled but he seemed genuinely discomfited. "I know how that sounds but I only meant to suggest—"

K.C. cut him off. "I think there are enough Americans who are concerned with what is happening in this country. The Russians don't have to drug people make them concerned."

"Perhaps not," said Littler, "but consider this. As the government gets more and more adroit at recognizing potential security risks, it becomes increasingly difficult for these people to move into positions where they can do anything about their concerns."

"So?"

"Wouldn't it be easier to find people who are already in those positions, people whose concerns are only mildly unsympathetic with their own government—the kind of people who would have no problems passing a security check—and then, once they are established, give them that little push we talked about?"

K.C. stood up, thrust his hands deep in his pockets, and walked to the door. This, he thought, is what happened to Gordon. Only in Gordon's case it had made his natural anti-Soviet predilection into something of an obsession. He paced nervously and then returned to his chair.

"The interesting thing about this," said Littler, "is that the person who is affected by this would be the last one to recognize the signs of abnormal behavior."

"You think this might have happened to Greenwood?"

"I don't know," said Littler honestly.

"Can't you test him or something?"

Littler tapped a pencil on the desk. "Trouble with these things is that most of the drugs used are quickly excreted from the body within a few days of ingestion. They don't show up in liver samples. It's even difficult to trace in an autopsy."

"Autopsy?" said K.C., recoiling from the word.

"Most of the drugs used to stimulate a schizophrenic state can kill if administered in improper dosages. Small quantities can cause the kind of symptoms exhibited by Greenwood and others."

"Others?"

"James Progano for one. I understand he went through some drastic mood changes before his suicide."

"Burns?"

"I'm not sure about him. He seems to have displayed a

fairly consistent pattern of behavior for a number of years."
He shook his head sadly. "What I'm trying to tell you is that
this is mostly guesswork. It is very difficult to determine when
one's natural tendencies have been tampered with. We're not
talking about a reversal of behavior pattern here, we're talking about an enhancement of an existing condition. Take a
married man who likes to chase after women. Give him one
of these drugs and you don't make him stay at home—you
make him chase after more women."

K.C. swallowed hard. He wondered if Littler was talking
about Gordon. "Are we talking about an epidemic here?"

Littler chuckled without mirth. "No. We're talking about
several men, who happened to be engaged in the same line of
work, who all seem to exhibit similar symptoms of mental
breakdown."

"Maybe it's just the stress of the job and some don't
stand up to the strain."

"Maybe," said Littler but K.C. could tell that he didn't
believe it for a minute.

"So you think that someone deliberately poisoned these
men."

Littler shrugged. "It's only a theory."

His face hardened. "But let me tell you something . . .
when I started this project, it was just that—another govern-
ment-funded project. But now I'm convinced that we are
dealing with a potentially catastrophic situation."

K.C. raised an eyebrow. "Catastrophic?"

Littler nodded. "If what I'm suggesting is true, any
project can be sabotaged by eliminating one or more of the
key people involved. It doesn't take much."

"Does your theory say who might have done it?"

"That's not my province," said Littler, his eyebrows
arching. "You government types will have to figure that out."

K.C. was already out in the parking lot before he realized he didn't like being called a "government type." He
didn't care much for Dr. Littler's theory either. Gordon may
have been deliberately disoriented by some toxic substance,
but it was impossible to determine how it was done and who
was responsible. K.C. was damned if he was going to believe
that everybody who opposed the ABM system had been
poisoned by the Russians. That's just what Birdwell and the
rest of his cronies at the CIA would like everyone to believe.

Heading home on the 101 he passed Candlestick Park,

allowing himself for just a moment to think of something other than theft, suicide, and murder. But as Candlestick receded in the rearview mirror, once again his thoughts picked up the trail he had been following. He had talked with Burns and learned little more than that Burns felt there were others involved and that he might have been set up by the CIA. He had talked with Greenwood and heard a similar tale—there were others, but the "secret police" had eliminated them. It was time, he thought, to begin asking questions of people who were still with TMK. Birdwell would object because too many questions might arouse suspicions, but Birdwell didn't have to know.

From his apartment he called Diane at work.

"How'd it go?" she asked.

"Okay, I guess. Not much new. Although Greenwood also mentioned this Tompkins who is doing a book. Apparently he's covering the same ground I am."

"Maybe you should have a talk with him."

"That's just what I was thinking. I was also thinking it's time for me to start talking to people at TMK. Eavesdropping is okay, but it doesn't get the job done."

"Why don't you let me interview Nichols?" Diane said. "He was willing to talk to me. That way you don't risk giving yourself away."

"After the party, I doubt he'll be giving interviews."

"It's worth a try."

He thought about it for a moment. "I guess you're right. . . . Maybe I could go with you?"

Diane laughed. "To protect me?"

"You know how you get when you listen to Vivaldi."

"I think I can resist." She paused. "Will I see you later?"

He looked at his watch. "I hope so. I'm going to call Birdwell and see if I can get a line on this Tompkins guy. I'd like to speak to him. Find out what he knows."

"Okay," she said. "I'll call Nichols. Call me later."

He hung up the phone. K.C. had a deep sense of misgiving that he could not shake. Was it something that Diane had said? Maybe it was her quick—too quick—offer to talk to Nichols. Maybe it was Birdwell's suddenly suspicious attitude.

There was something there, he knew. But he didn't yet have all the pieces. Something was lurking in the background but he was unable to put it together.

He was giving himself a headache and tried to put his

suspicions aside for the moment. But somewhere deep where demons lie in wait a small nagging doubt began whispering in his ear.

WASHINGTON, D.C.—In a nationally televised address before a special session of the Congress last night, the President stunned the nation by announcing the first deployment of the new antiballistic missile system. "The system," said the President, "has already been installed to protect the nation's MX missile sites in Wyoming and Utah, insuring the invulnerability of these weapons from Soviet missile attack."

Within six months the U.S. intends to protect at least five other key strategic naval and military bases in the U.S. and several major population centers. By the end of the decade it is expected that the entire continental U.S. will be invulnerable to any kind of missile attack from any foreign power.

This defense system, said the President, has been tested fully and has demonstrated an accuracy rate at "above" 98 percent. In what was seen as a clear warning to the Soviet Union the President said, "If any adversary sends one hundred missiles in our direction he must realize that his chances of penetrating our defensive shield with more than one missile are practically nil. That adversary must also realize that the full retaliatory power of the U.S. sits ready and able to reply to any such attack."

The President in an ebullient mood offered several options to potential adversaries of the U.S. "Now is the time," he said, "to put aside the weapons and the devices of war. We must all join in a serious attempt to convince the Soviet Union that the time to stop the madness is here."

In answer to a question about the U.S.-Soviet treaty on antiballistic missiles which forbids antimissile systems in space, the President smiled broadly and stated that "no part of this system is in space. It is completely land-based and at present deployment levels represents no possible violation of the treaty."

When asked about future deployment the President merely shrugged and said, "No comment."

Forty-seven

It was another spectacular sunset over Pescadero Point on the northern tip of Carmel Bay and the beach below the rocks was still crowded with strollers who had come to admire one of nature's most beautiful vistas.

One, however, was not here for the view.

Karpenkov wore navy blue nylon shorts and a black T-shirt with the name of some awful-sounding heavy metal rock band emblazoned across the front. He despised the satanic implications of the logo but it was, he felt, typical of what American youth found themselves attracted to.

He wore Nike running sneakers and carried a backpack. He looked tanned and fit as he walked along the beach leaving waffle-dotted footprints in the wet sand. He had parked his car a few miles down the road and set out across the beach as if he were bent on an early evening walk across the sand and rocks. The Pacific was wild tonight, surf pounding the rocks with a steady malevolent beat. He loved the ocean when it was like this. More than once he had had to beat a hasty retreat as the waves rushed up to seek a higher waterline. Every once in a while he would stop, take his binoculars out of his backpack, put them to his eyes, and sweep the horizon. To any casual observer he was just one of many who enjoyed an evening stroll along the beach, thrilling to the sights and sounds of the magnificent Pacific. That was what had brought everyone here to the Monterey Peninsula in the first place, wasn't it? What few would notice was that the panoramic sweep of the binoculars always ended with the glasses fixed on the same house that sat high above the beach. It was a modern house of contemporary design—much glass and rough-sawn cedar—with a spectacular view of the Pacific. What would also go unnoticed was the fact the binoculars were fitted with a starlight nightscope that permitted him to see clearly in the dark.

As dusk approached Karpenkov made his way to the rocks below the house. There was a wooden stairway that led from beach to house but that did not suit his purpose. There was always the possibility, however unlikely, that the stairs would be wired with some kind of warning device. He walked past the stairs, his eyes selecting the most suitable path up the rocks, and continued past the house, on up the beach.

After dark, when the beach was almost deserted, he returned and stood near the steps, looking left and right, listening for any approaching footsteps. There was nothing. He started up the rocks, moving quickly and expertly to a spot less than one hundred feet from the house. There he nestled down to wait.

From his perch he could look directly into the rear of the house where sliding glass doors opened the inside of the house to a panoramic view of the ocean. Only one light was on but gradually as the darkness deepened other rooms were lit and he watched the man, Orville Tompkins, move from room to room.

A television set was on in what appeared to be the darkened living room, but Tompkins was in another part of the house. Karpenkov peered through the scope of the nightsight, trying to pick out another figure in the room who might be watching TV, but all of the chairs in the room were empty. He watched Tompkins prepare dinner and make himself several drinks as he did. Karpenkov took some dried fruit from his backpack and chewed it while he watched Tompkins at dinner.

After dinner Tompkins moved to a room in the front of the house where Karpenkov could not see him and after waiting for a few minutes Karpenkov moved quickly to the side of the house. He found the phone box and snipped the wires, then went to the front of the house. At the front door he rang the bell and waited.

Tompkins opened the door and Karpenkov could have killed him right then and there but there were things he needed. "Yes," said Tompkins with only the slightest touch of wariness in his voice.

"Carl Burns asked me to speak with you," said Karpenkov.

Tompkins's eyes narrowed and his face immediately mirrored his suspicions. "Why didn't he call me?"

Karpenkov shrugged. "He thought your line might be bugged."

Tompkins wasn't sure. "How do I know you are from him? How do I know you're not a cop?"

Karpenkov removed his backpack, opened it, and withdrew Burns's prison jacket. "Then where would I get this?"

Tompkins took it and looked at the jacket carefully. It was indeed the same type of jacket he had last seen Carl Burns wearing when he talked with him at Lompoc.

"Come in," he said.

Orville Tompkins was a tall, muscularly built man in his late forties. For almost fifteen years he had been a staff officer with the CIA, rising to the rank of GS14, which was the equivalent of an Army colonel. Tompkins had done two tours of duty in the Middle East, one at headquarters in Langley and one in Tay Ninh province in Vietnam.

Somewhere along the way, Tompkins had become disillusioned with the Agency and the country he had once served so well. When questioned, he could never quite identify the incident or the moment of his disenchantment. It had been something that had happened gradually, like termites eating away a wood foundation. One day he woke up and knew that he had to leave. For a time he worked at an advertising agency in San Francisco but the tedium and triviality of the work drove him to something else. He tried newspaper work and for a while seemed satisfied but soon the lust for adventure that had brought him to the CIA in the first place began scratching at his toes. To expurgate his wanderlust he wrote a book—a spy thriller—a thinly disguised chronicle of some of the most unsavory events in his CIA past. The book was well-reviewed—the liberal press delighting in his insider's tales of the nefarious goings-on at the CIA—and to Tompkins's surprise quickly moved onto the best-seller lists.

Tompkins had found a new career and newfound wealth but he had also drawn the lifelong enmity of his former colleagues.

In his next book, Tompkins tried to outdo himself with his insider's revelations about the Agency. Although advertised as a work of fiction, the plot of the book was extremely close to actual events. The CIA moved in, bringing legal action against Tompkins in an attempt to block publication.

The case had gone all the way to the Supreme Court,

where Tompkins had finally won his battle to publish his book. Now, embittered by his court battle, Orville Tompkins was determined to get even with the CIA and with the government that had hounded him. He would find a story that would show them up for what they were—one they could not stop him from writing.

Tompkins had been intrigued by the news reports about Carl Burns's arrest and conviction. Something in his gut told him there was a story there, and he had gone after it. After talking to Burns and then to Greenwood, he had begun his own investigation. Now he was certain that he was sitting on top of a huge story.

He led Karpenkov down a hallway into the living room and turned on the lights. "Does Burns know that I'm going to have to rewrite my chapter on him now that he's escaped?" he said good-naturedly.

Karpenkov smiled. "I don't think he gave that much thought one way or the other." Karpenkov looked around the room. "Nice place," he said admiringly.

"Thanks," said Tompkins curtly. He didn't feel it was necessary to mention that the house was borrowed from his San Francisco publisher, who used it only on occasional summer weekends. He thought for a moment. "Who are you?" he asked.

"Just a friend of Carl's."

"Did you help him escape?"

Karpenkov smiled but said nothing.

"What's your name?" asked Tompkins.

Karpenkov thought for a moment. "You can call me Max."

Tompkins nodded in resignation. "Can I get you a drink or something, Max?"

"Thank you," said Karpenkov. "Some vodka over ice would be nice."

Tompkins went into the kitchen and Karpenkov dropped onto a stuffed chair in front of the TV. The news was on and he thought that tomorrow's news would probably show pictures of this house—perhaps even this room.

Tompkins returned and gave him his drink. "Now what can I do for you?" he asked.

Karpenkov took a long drink from his glass before responding. "Carl wanted me to act as a messenger between you and him."

"Can't we arrange a meeting somewhere?"

Karpenkov shook his head slowly. "That would be impossible. He's afraid of betrayal."

"Doesn't he trust me?" Tompkins looked wounded.

"Oh yes, of course he trusts you, but he is just afraid that you might be followed or someone will spot the two of you together."

"Can't we talk by phone? I'd really like to talk with him in person."

"I understand," said Karpenkov, "and perhaps that can be arranged—at some later date." Tompkins, he thought, was an unusually careful man.

Tompkins shrugged in resignation. He could see he was not going to get anywhere with this one. "What did you come to tell me?"

"Well I have some information for you from Burns that he thinks will be most helpful in your investigation. But first I must tell you that he is very much afraid that anything he says to you will somehow lead the authorities back to him."

Tompkins seemed puzzled. "How?"

"Well, he trusts you implicitly, but is afraid that if anyone reads your manuscript or has access to another copy, they might feel compelled to go to the authorities with the information."

"I don't see how that could lead back to him. He knows I'll protect him to the best of my ability."

Karpenkov seemed doubtful.

"Look," said Tompkins testily. "No one else sees my manuscript until it's finished. I have only an original and one copy, both of which are here in the house."

Karpenkov smiled but resisted the temptation to ask where.

"If he can't trust me," said Tompkins, "then I don't know what else I can do. He knows I'm more interested in this story than I am in anything else."

Karpenkov nodded as if satisfied with Tompkins's explanation. "All right," he said. "Burns wants you to know that he is having reservations about the idea that the CIA masterminded this whole thing."

Tompkins chuckled and shook his head sadly. "Burns doesn't have any idea what to think. I first proposed to him the idea of CIA involvement and he grabbed at it like a drowning man clutching at a lifeline. Now that I've investigated, I've changed my mind so he's changing his." Tompkins laughed softly. "But he still wants me to think that the ideas are his own. He is a young man who is very susceptible to suggestion."

Karpenkov smiled, nodding in agreement. "I think you are right." He paused a moment. "Do you have any specific ideas as to who it might be that you are looking for?"

For a brief moment a cloud of suspicion passed across Tompkins's eyes but it was nothing more than the novelist's reluctance to discuss an unfinished story. "I think the problem lies within the company itself. TMK has not had a good history of protecting its secrets. I'm becoming convinced that its problems are internal."

Karpenkov's eyes narrowed. "What makes you say that?"

Tompkins smiled. "I'm not sure. I just feel that the people who've been involved have been moved around from position to position. I think that they've been manipulated by someone. Somebody has to be able to see that they get into positions where they can get their hands on the right information."

"And your book shows that?"

"It's not all worked out yet, but it'll come together pretty soon. You can tell Carl that sooner or later I'll figure it out," Tompkins replied.

Karpenkov nodded. "Carl's dead," he said.

Tompkins continued smiling; Karpenkov's words did not register. "How's that?" he asked.

"Carl's dead," Karpenkov said in a monotone.

The smile slipped from Tompkins's face. "I don't understand."

Karpenkov took the pistol from his pack. "Do you understand now?"

Tompkins went white. "What do you want?" he asked, surprise mingling with fear in his face.

"Your manuscript."

"You're not going to kill me, are you?" said Tompkins, his voice cracking a little.

Karpenkov noted that Tompkins was maintining control of himself. "Only if I have to," said Karpenkov. "Where is the manuscript?"

"In my office."

Karpenkov got up, still pointing the pistol at Tompkins. "Let's get it—and the copy."

Tompkins got up and Karpenkov followed him down a hallway. As he went he fitted a silencer onto the pistol. Tompkins led him to a small room that had been converted into a work area. There on the desk, next to a typewriter and some reference books, lay a stack of typed pages.

"There," said Tompkins, motioning toward the desk.

Karpenkov leafed through the pages. "Put them in my pack," said Karpenkov and Tompkins did so.

He picked up some other papers on the desk. "This?"

"My notes."

Karpenkov put them in his backpack also. "Now the copy. Where is it?"

Tompkins hesitated. He had noticed the silencer and was beginning to feel the oppressive certainty of death. His mind raced desperately from one alternative to the next. He knew the copy was the only thing keeping him alive. "I'll trade you," he ventured.

Karpenkov smiled. "You've nothing to trade. I could kill you and search the house."

"You'd never find it."

"Then," said Karpenkov with a sigh. "I'll have no other option than to force you to tell me where it is."

Tompkins mustered a small show of bravado. "I won't tell."

"I'm an expert at inflicting pain, Mr. Tompkins. I don't think you want to test your threshold of pain against my abilities in this area."

Tompkins's mouth was very dry. His thoughts ran to flight and his mind watched like a ferret for the first moment of opportunity.

Karpenkov recognized the thought behind the darting eyes and without warning shot him once in the right kneecap.

The blow was so sudden, so unexpected, that for a brief moment Tompkins did not realize his right leg had been shot out from under him. Then came the blinding flash of pain and he crumpled in a heap on the floor.

"I have no time for games or heroics," said Karpenkov, standing over Tompkins. "Tell me where the copy is."

Tompkins opened his mouth to scream but Karpenkov bent over and muffled his cry with his left palm pressed across the man's mouth.

"Enough of this," he said, holding the gun to Tompkins's forehead.

The pain had instantly robbed Tompkins of his resolve. Tompkins, eyes rolling wildly in fear, nodded and Karpenkov released the pressure of his hand.

"File cabinet," gasped Tompkins. "Downstairs. Middle drawer."

Karpenkov got up. "That's the only copy?"

Tompkins gasped, "Yes, I swear it."

Karpenkov left, leaving Tompkins writhing on the floor. Alone, some of the fear, but none of the pain, left him. The will to survive forced him into action. He pulled himself to a sitting position, gasping against the shrieking pain of the effort, and dragged himself backward toward his desk. He pulled open a bottom drawer and fumbled inside for a moment, then withdrew an old Army .45 he kept there for security.

"Blow that fucker's head off," he mumbled. He reached for the phone and pulled it down to him. It was dead. Shit, he thought. I'll have to do it myself.

He opened the middle drawer and fumbled inside before pulling out a small notebook. This book contained most of his important notes for the manuscript he had written; he had used it to interview Burns and Greenwood. Used it to jot down questions to himself and the answers when he had found them. Much of the material was dated and no longer significant but some of the later entries were what had caused him to redo his book. Next to the manuscript and the copy, this was the most important thing he owned. It couldn't fall into enemy hands. He had to hide it where "Max" would never think to look but where it would be found later, if he didn't get out of this alive. He dragged himself over to the bookshelves against the far wall, wincing with the effort, and there on the second shelf from the bottom, next to the book of Tennyson's poems where he kept his spare cash, he slipped the notebook into position with the other books.

He was already light-headed from the loss of blood. He had to do something quickly or he would pass out. He removed his leather belt and cinched it around his thigh, just above the knee, hoping to stem the flow of blood. It seemed to work and he felt, above the pain, a surge of hope that he might survive. He dragged himself backward into a corner where he could sit up without supporting himself. His right leg lay in front of him, twisted at an insane angle. He held back the vomit, the taste rough and raw in his throat like incredibly cheap whiskey.

He waited.

Karpenkov found the copy and placed it beside the original in his backpack, then searched the files but found no other copies. He looked around the room carefully, taking his time, methodically opening drawers, inspecting boxes, but found nothing else of interest.

With one final look around he started back up the stairs. The first thing he noticed was the silence. He smiled. Tompkins was waiting for him. The bastard was tougher than he had thought. He had been sure the writer would lie whimpering, waiting for him to come back and put him out of his misery, but at the top of the stairs he heard nothing. The excitement of the hunt coursed through his veins.

Karpenkov listened carefully, weapon at the ready. His training told him that Tompkins would still be in the room waiting for him to come back, but his training also told him to beware of the unexpected. Quietly he removed his shoes, then padded softly down the hallway to where he had left Tompkins, making certain that his own shadow didn't give him away. Outside the small office he stopped, listening for any telltale sounds. After a moment he heard Tompkins's careful breathing and an occasional soft grunt of pain as the man shifted to a more comfortable position.

Karpenkov backed away from the room and back out into the living room. He went to the sliding glass door and pushed it open just enough for him to get out, then inched his way to the window of the small office. There he peered inside and immediately saw Tompkins propped in the far corner, the .45 in his lap.

Karpenkov could have taken him right there with a straight shot to the head, but there was still unfinished business. He had to be sure that nothing remained which could eventually point to him. He came back inside, closed the sliding door. He took a long poker from the living room fireplace and went to the front door.

"I'm leaving now," Karpenkov called out. "You had better get medical help soon." It was ridiculous, he knew. The man must know that he would have to kill him or else all this had been for nothing. But he also knew from his training that a man who has felt himself on the threshold of death will believe almost anything that promises survival.

Tompkins heard the door close, his eyes registering amazement that his ordeal was over. It couldn't be. The man would not just leave him like this. Or would he? What if he was still there waiting?

In any event he knew he had to get help soon or he would bleed to death. He moved forward onto his elbows, gasping from the pain that attacked him like a series of waves that thundered ashore, then receded, only to thunder into his consciousness once more.

Karpenkov heard the moaning sound and knew Tompkins was coming.

Slowly, methodically—hands out first, weight on his elbows—Tompkins dragged himself to the door. At the door his dilemma was whether to stick his head out first and look down the hallway, or to continue the way he had been and put his hands out first. Neither option thrilled him but the former was too dangerous for him to consider. The second gained him nothing. He paused, momentarily unable to will himself on.

Dammit! he whispered to himself. Let's not bleed to death, here in an empty house.

He pulled himself forward.

Karpenkov saw the hands emerge first. He brought the poker down sharply across Tompkins's right wrist and stepped on the .45.

Tompkins screamed but Karpenkov kicked him savagely in the midsection, forcing the air from his lungs and stifling the sound in mid-scream.

Karpenkov stood over him. "What about the rest of your notes?" he said. "I want everything you've got."

Through his pain Tompkins realized that he was a dead man. All he had left were the notes he had made and the hope that someone would find them and use them. "I have nothing," he sobbed. "Nothing."

Karpenkov hit his shattered leg with the poker. "Where are they?"

Tompkins screamed in pain. "There's nothing. You have everything."

Karpenkov ground the poker into Tompkins's shattered knee. "Don't lie to me," he said. "I can do this for hours."

Tompkins bit through his lip. Compared to his knee, the pain was inconsequential. "There's nothing else. I swear." He was whimpering now and uncertain as to how long he could last.

Karpenkov stepped back and threw the poker aside.

308

"Last chance," he said, raising the pistol and aiming directly between Tompkins's eyes.

Tompkins flinched, his eyes squeezed shut, then he opened them. "There's nothing," he said almost calmly. "You have everything."

Karpenkov shrugged. "Then this is good-bye." He sighted down the barrel.

"Tell me," said Tompkins hurriedly. "Was I close?"

Karpenkov hesitated. "Close?"

"Close to figuring out what was happening?"

Perverse to the end, Karpenkov said, "No you were not close," and squeezed the trigger.

Forty-eight

They saw the police cars outside the house and the yellow ribbons proclaiming "Crime Search Area" that surrounded the property. K.C. shot a worried glance at Diane and braked the car to a halt in front of the driveway. A uniformed policeman approached the car. He walked around to the driver's side, leaned over, and looked into K.C.'s face. "Can I help you, sir?" he said with forced politeness.

"I'm supposed to see Orville Tompkins," K.C. said, his eyes on the house. "I talked with him yesterday. Has something happened?"

"Are you friends of his?"

"No. I . . . we were supposed to talk to him."

"I'm afraid you won't be talking to Mr. Tompkins, Mr. . . ." He left the invitation to identify oneself hanging in the air.

"Collins," said K.C. "And this is Diane Rollins. Miss Rollins is a reporter and I do free-lance work. We were supposed to talk with Mr. Tompkins this morning. What happened?"

"Mr. Tompkins has been killed. Last night sometime."

K.C. looked at Diane. Her eyes were round and her mouth open in amazement.

The policeman noted their expressions. "Let me see if the detective in charge wants to speak to you." He smiled pleasantly but his voice was a command. "Wait here please."

They waited while the officer went to the front door, where they could see him talking with another policeman. The second man went inside and returned a few minutes later. He spoke briefly with the first officer, who then returned to the car.

"The lieutenant would like to speak with you for just a minute. You can go inside."

Diane coughed. "I don't want to go in there."

"The body was removed over an hour ago. There's nothing in there now, ma'am."

K.C. got out of the car and reluctantly, Diane followed. They went up the path to the house, where they were met by the patrolman at the door.

"I was told the lieutenant wants to see us," K.C. said. The patrolman pointed down the hall. He did not speak.

Diane took K.C.'s arm as they went down the indicated hall. They stopped outside the door to what looked like an office. Several men were inside. Dark stains smeared the rug in several places and the same stains were splattered across the rear wall. It was not difficult to imagine the carnage that had taken place.

"Lieutenant?" said K.C.

One of the men turned. His face grim, he looked K.C. up and down as if making an instant verdict. "You the guy who talked to Tompkins yesterday?" He was not as polite as the officer in the driveway.

"Yes."

The lieutenant stepped out into the hall. "I'm Lieutenant Josephson. I'd like to know what time that was."

"About four o'clock in the afternoon."

"Did he sound okay? Like he was under any stress or anything?"

K.C. shrugged. "Not that I noticed."

The lieutenant turned to Diane. "And you, miss?"

"I was going to do a story on Tompkins. I'm a reporter."

The cop shook his head. "Well you've got some story now."

"What happened here?" K.C. asked.

Josephson turned back to the room. "Sometime last night, someone shot Tompkins in the leg. Apparently they were looking for something, perhaps the leg was to make him tell."

"Robbery?"

Josephson made a face. "I don't think so. None of the usual places were searched—bedroom, closets, dressers, that sort of thing. Wherever the guy was he spent most of his time searching in file cabinets and desk drawers. That indicates to me that he was looking for something besides money or jewelry." He looked at K.C. and then let his eyes slide to Diane. "Either of you have any idea what that might be?"

"Is his manuscript here?" Diane blurted out.

Josephson's eyes narrowed. "His manuscript?"

"Tompkins was working on a potentially explosive book about the CIA," Diane said.

"I didn't see anything like that," said Josephson, "but I don't think anybody would kill him over a book."

Just then another detective approached from the living room. "Lieutenant, I think you'd better take a look at this." He handed Josephson a denim shirt. "This was lying on a chair in the living room. Look at the laundry mark."

Josephson held up the shirt. His eyes narrowed as he saw the State of California Correctional Institute mark on the shirttail. "Lompoc," he said softly.

K.C. could not help the swift exhalation of air and Josephson looked sharply at him. "This mean something to you?"

"Carl Burns," said K.C. helplessly. "He escaped from Lompoc last week. He's the one who told me about Tompkins's book. Tompkins had interviewed him."

Josephson gave the shirt back to the other detective. "Check this out. I'm sure we can match it to this Burns character. If so maybe we've got our killer. And maybe our motive." He smiled for the first time, as if perhaps he could finally see some clear details out of a murky picture. "I'd like you both to leave your names and addresses with one of my men at the door just in case we have any more questions you might be able to help us with."

They shook hands, and as K.C. and Diane turned to go, Diane saw through the sliding glass door in the living room a woman, sitting on a bench on the rear patio. "Who's that?" she asked.

Josephson sighed. "That's Tompkins's wife. We called her soon after we got here. Turns out that they've been separated for three years, but she came down anyway."

"Can we talk to her?"

Josephson shrugged. "Go ahead. But make sure you leave the names and addresses."

They did so, then went outside to see Mrs. Tompkins.

Below them the surf was pounding on the beach, drowning the sound of their approach. They were standing over her when Muriel Tompkins, an attractive woman in her early forties, finally realized that someone was there. She turned and looked up at them questioningly. "Yes?"

K.C. began. "Mrs. Tompkins, we are very sorry to hear about your husband."

Her laugh was soft and low, a laugh that had no mirth in it. "He wasn't my husband anymore. We've been divorced for almost three years."

"I understand," said K.C.

"I was just wondering how I'm going to tell our children. He's still their father even if . . ." Her voice trailed off into a soft murmur that was covered by the pounding surf. "He loved this place," she said, her eyes looking out across the Pacific, her thoughts somewhere in an earlier time.

"Mrs. Tompkins," said Diane, interrupting her reverie. "Would you mind if we talked with you for just a few minutes?"

The woman nodded her head. "It's all right," she said, still watching the ocean.

"We came down from Sunnyvale to speak to Mr. Tompkins about the book he was writing. Do you have any idea where it is?"

"No."

"Could he have sent it to his publisher already?"

"No."

"Why are you so sure?"

"I had a talk with him last week, and when I asked him how the book was going he told me that he had started all over again. He had found something that made him completely change the focus of the book and was redoing the entire manuscript."

"Did he tell you what it was he had found?"

Mrs. Tompkins smiled. "No. Only that he thought it was going to be an important book."

"Did he ever tell you what the book was about?"

She shook her head. "No, but our daughter—she's in high school—said he'd told her it was about industrial espionage. He also said that he felt better about the work he had done while he was with the CIA." She shook her head as if perplexed by that. "I know he talked with some of the people who are in prison for stealing defense-related secrets. You might try them."

K.C. nodded. "I've met some of them already."

Muriel Tompkins sighed. "I don't really know enough about any of this to help you," she said.

"It might be very important for us to find his manuscript."

Muriel was shaking her head. "You don't think somebody killed him because of his book, do you?"

"It's possible," said K.C.

"They wouldn't—they couldn't," said Muriel, her eyes wide, a look of disbelief on her face.

"They? Who are they, Mrs. Tompkins?" Diane asked.

"He was warned after the CIA book that he was taking a big chance by writing another exposé of the Agency."

"You think the CIA killed him?"

"Who else? Who else would gain by Orville's death? They considered him a turncoat, a traitor." She was shaking her head rapidly now from side to side as if she might erase some terrible thought. "You have no idea what a closed society the CIA is. It's hard to get in and almost impossible to get out. Anyone who does what Orville has done—did—is a marked man."

"That may be true, Mrs. Tompkins," said K.C. almost apologetically, "but it seems that your husband was killed by an escaped convict—someone who was to appear in the book."

Muriel Tompkins seemed doubtful.

"They found prison clothes in the house," said Diane.

"You don't seem to understand," said Muriel Tompkins, smiling sadly. "The CIA can do what it pleases. If they want to leave prison clothes here to make it look like someone else did their dirty work, that's exactly what they'll do."

K.C.'s face was blank. He was remembering Hanson's comment about people blaming the CIA for involvement in the death of JFK. The proof was that there was no proof. But he was also remembering Greenwood's remarks that Burns was dead—killed by the CIA. That was a scenario that, while farfetched, fit all the pieces of the puzzle. The CIA—nervous about Burns's court testimony—breaks Burns out of prison,

313

kills him, kills Tompkins, and leaves Burns's clothing to implicate the escaped convict. That method eliminated two birds—two stool pigeons—with one stone.

"What is it?" Diane asked, noticing K.C.'s expression.

"Nothing," he said, startled by her interruption. "I was just thinking." He turned back to Muriel Tompkins. "I'm sorry for the intrusion, Mrs. Tompkins, and I thank you for talking to us."

He turned to leave, but Diane was fumbling in her purse. "This is my card," she said to Mrs. Tompkins. "If you think of anything that might be important, I'd appreciate it if you'd give me a call." She scribbled on the card. "That's my number at the paper on the front, and I've written my home number on the back."

Muriel Tompkins took the card, looked at it absently, and nodded to Diane without much enthusiasm. "Good-bye," she whispered, but K.C. and Diane were already heading across the patio and on their way to the door.

Muriel Tompkins sat for a long time, listening to the sound of the ocean below and to the cries of the seabirds circling overhead. The police had gone, their gruesome work done, their endless questions finished, and now she was alone sitting in the same spot where K.C. and Diane had left her.

Muriel Tompkins did not want to admit it but she was afraid to go into the house—afraid of what she might be reminded of. Finally she stood up and made her way across the patio and stepped in front of the open glass doors. She looked inside. All was still and quiet. If she listened she could almost imagine she could hear the sound of Orville's typewriter clacking down the hall.

She hesitated, but she knew why she had come, why she had waited for the police to leave. It was almost laughable, she thought, the way the police had treated her so respectfully, impressed by her devotion to a man who had abandoned her. Where were his chippy girlfriends now? she wondered. The ones he had squandered his money on while she struggled to make ends meet. She assumed that everything he had—if he had anything—would go to the children, but she wasn't about to sit around and wait for that.

She took a deep breath and stepped inside. Deciding to do this, she moved quickly through the living room, down the hall, and stopped in front of the door to the room where Orville had been killed. Here, her resolve almost wilted but she forced herself to go inside, trying not to look at the dark stains on the rug. She went directly to the bookcase and scanned the shelves looking for Tennyson. She knew Orville better than anyone else—this was where he had always kept his money. She found it on a lower shelf and pulled it out. It was wedged firmly in place and a small spiral ring notebook tumbled out onto the floor. Muriel opened the Tennyson and smiled. There must have been six or seven hundred dollars there. She removed the money, put it in her purse—she'd be damned if this money would go to some snooping policeman or one of Orville's girlfriends—and replaced the book on the shelf. Then she picked up the notebook, which lay open on the floor. At first she did not bother to look at it but when she realized the notes were in Orville's hand she flipped through the pages. Most of it made little sense to her but knowing how Orville worked made her realize that he had thought this was important. Some of the notations had stars or exclamations after them, which she recognized as a sure sign that Orville considered these parts crucial to his work. She read quickly through the notebook, noting how the viewpoint had changed somewhere in the last third. She had already forgotten how afraid she had been to enter this room as she became more absorbed in her reading.

Muriel knew that she should turn the notebook over to the police. There might be something in it that would lead to Orville's killer—hadn't someone said it was important to find his manuscript? This notebook might be just as important. She thought for a moment. If it were important it might be worth money to someone—perhaps to Orville's publisher, or maybe to the two reporters who had been here earlier. Nothing in it could help Orville now, one way or the other. Maybe she could use this to her own financial benefit. It was certainly something to think about.

She opened her pocketbook and placed the notebook inside. As she did she noticed the card given to her by Diane. She picked it up and flipped it over to read Diane's home phone number.

She decided at that moment what she would do with the notebook.

WASHINGTON (UPI)—Speaker Thomas Carrigan said today that opponents of the President's "Star Wars" defense had enough votes in the House of Representatives to block any planned deployment.

"It is time," said the Speaker, "to put brakes on this insane arms race. This weapons system only adds to the madness and is viewed as a potential provocation by the Soviet Union."

Two sites have already been deployed and the President has requested additional funds to deploy at least six more before the end of the year. "Enough is enough," said Carrigan.

Mr. Carrigan, a Massachusetts Democrat, made the comment in a speech prepared for commencement exercises at Tufts University in Medford, Mass.

This week the House is scheduled to consider a bill sponsored by the Democratic leadership which would cut off funding for what the Speaker called "this dangerously provocative weapons system."

Forty-nine

Diane called K.C. the minute her phone conversation with Muriel Tompkins had ended.

"She says we should talk to Jim Progano's widow, Celia," Diane said, relating the details of her brief conversation with Muriel Tompkins.

"What else did she say?"

"Only that Tompkins thought Progano was murdered and that his widow knows why."

"Did she find Tompkins's manuscript?"

"No. I asked her that myself. She wouldn't tell me what she'd found. She just kept saying, 'Talk to Celia Progano.' She also said she might have more information for us."

"I'd better get on this right away. Celia Progano still lives in this area."

"Want some help?" Diane asked hopefully.

"Better let me handle this myself," K.C. said.

He did not notice the hurt tone in Diane's voice when she said good-bye.

Celia Progano seemed confused and even a little bit frightened when she opened the door and found a man standing on her threshold.

"What do you want?" she asked.

"I want to talk to you about your husband," said K.C.

"Please leave me alone," she said. "Haven't all of you done enough already?"

"Mrs. Progano," he said, "you don't understand. I have reason to believe that your husband was murdered. I want to find who did it."

"I know who did it," said Celia Progano.

"You do? Who?"

"People like you," she said. "People who wouldn't leave him alone."

She started to close the door but K.C. put out his hand and held it open. "Mrs. Progano, it's very important—"

Just then another figure appeared at the door. A woman in her early thirties with short black hair and thick glasses peered over Celia Progano's shoulder at K.C. "What do you want?" she asked. Her voice was cold and he could tell she was not afraid of him.

"I just want to talk to Mrs. Progano."

"She doesn't want to talk to you or anyone else," said the woman.

"She talked to Orville Tompkins," said K.C.

Both women looked at each other. "So—what's that to you?" asked the woman behind Celia Progano.

"He's dead. Murdered last night."

Celia Progano slapped a hand over her mouth as if to prevent some exclamation, then moved back and the other woman put a hand around her shoulders in a gesture of protection. "Oh, my God," muttered Celia.

"Go away—now," commanded the other woman. "You've got the smell of the government around you. We don't want you snooping around here."

"I can assure you," K.C. said, "I'm not in any way

connected with the government." When he said it he actually believed that it was true. "I'm only trying—"

She slammed the door shut in his face, closing the debate.

"Forget her," he said to Diane. "There's no way we can get anything out of her."

He had gone directly to Diane's apartment, feeling confused and agitated by the unexpected confrontation. Diane had been comforting, taking some of the sting out of his failure.

"Want me to give her a try?" she asked, smiling conspiratorially.

"You! Why would she talk with you?"

"Let's just say experience in this sort of thing. I've been interviewing people like her for years."

K.C. nodded reluctantly. Diane had offered to go with him to Celia Progano's house but he had refused on the grounds that he didn't want to involve her. His real reason had been that he had felt a growing discontent and perhaps a twinge of jealousy in her contributions to what he saw as "his job."

"I don't see what you can do," he said. "It's not so much interviewing skill as being able to get in the door."

She licked her lips as if being offered a choice delicacy. "Let me give it a try." She watched his face for signs of assent. "What've you got to lose?"

"Okay," he said and abruptly got up and went to make himself a drink.

Celia Progano had gone into hiding. Diane called her house several times but there was no response. Finally, on the fourth or fifth try, a woman answered the phone.

"Yes?"

"Celia Progano?" asked Diane.

"Mrs. Progano is not here," said the voice, "and I cannot tell you when she will be back."

"Will she be back today?"

"No."

"Tomorrow?"

"No."

"My name is Diane Rollins, and I'm a reporter for the San Jose *News*. I would like to interview Mrs. Progano for—"

"That would be quite impossible," interrupted the voice.

"I'd like to ask Mrs. Progano herself. Can you tell me when she will be back?"

"Mrs. Progano is staying with friends. She will be gone as long as her life is in danger."

"Danger. She's in danger?"

"We're all in danger," said the voice matter-of-factly.

"Look," said Diane, "if I give you a message—a written message—would you pass it along to her? If she doesn't want to see me I'll never bother her again."

There was a long pause, then, "Put your message in her mailbox this evening. Someone will pick it up and deliver it to Celia. If you do not hear from her—or anyone else—you can assume your request has been denied."

"Thank you," said Diane. "It'll be there."

Diane wrote a brief note to Mrs. Progano and included in the envelope clippings of several of what she thought were her best interviews. Two of the three were sympathetic interviews with women. She also included a story she had done on an antiwar demonstration held outside TMK six months earlier.

The next afternoon Diane received a phone call from a woman who identified herself only as "a friend of Mrs. Progano's."

"She has received your letter and your request for an interview."

"Does that mean we have an okay?"

"Not yet."

Diane held back a sigh of frustration. "What do I have to do?"

"You realize that Celia—Mrs. Progano—has been hounded by reporters lately. Ever since the announcement about the missile defense system that her husband helped design, her life has been a living hell."

"I understand that."

"Reporters are very persistent people, Miss Rollins." There was a slight hint of recrimination in the voice.

"That's true," said Diane. "And I apologize for my persistence. But what I want to tell Mrs. Progano is that I sympathize with her predicament and I will be entirely sympathetic to her views."

"Everyone says that. But what appears in print is something else. Mrs. Progano would like people to stop hounding her."

"Perhaps an interview would put an end to that."

The voice was uncertain. "Perhaps. The problem is that Mrs. Progano would like to give you an interview but she's afraid that because you only work for a small local paper the national reporters will still keep hounding her."

"My interview would be picked up by the national news services. It would go into papers all across the country."

There was a long pause. "Can you meet with us tomorrow?"

"Anytime you say."

"Mrs. Progano has moved out of her house. I will contact you tomorrow morning and tell you where to meet us. You will come alone and the meeting is over whenever Mrs. Progano decides. In no event will it last more than one hour. Is that acceptable?"

"Absolutely. I'll be waiting for your call."

As soon as she hung up, Diane went to see K.C. He was not overly enthused by her good news.

"What's the matter?" she asked.

"Nothing."

"You're jealous, aren't you?"

"Don't be ridiculous."

She was laughing. "You are. You're upset that I got to see her when you couldn't."

Her laughter was infectious. "No I'm not. I'm just . . . just . . . You're right. You're dealing with a man with a bruised ego here."

"Don't feel bad, I've got a lot more experience than you do at this sort of thing."

"Just make sure you ask her what she told Tompkins that he thought was so important."

"Sure thing. Anything else?"

"We want to know if her husband was a part of any group at TMK that opposed the development and deployment of Prometheus II. Or if he was aware of the existence of such a group."

"Okay, I'll ask, but first I'm going to do *my* interview. This could be a big break for me. This story will probably be picked up all across the country and I've got an exclusive."

His expression was wary. "I'm glad, but don't forget what's more important."

"Don't worry," she said, touching him on the cheek. "I know what's more important." She read the uncertainty in his eyes. "You are," she added softly, kissing him.

"That not what I meant," he said, grinning self-consciously.

She looked up at him, her face serious, her eyes holding his. "I know what you meant," she said. "I just want you to know that you are more important to me than any story."

She saw the relief in his eyes and felt the need to hold him. He was, she thought, like a little boy, afraid that her interest in this story would somehow take precedence over her interest in him. Somewhere beneath conscious thought she was also aware that her increasing involvement in this story might somehow drive a wedge between her and the first man that she had cared about in a long time.

She was determined to go on anyway.

Fifty

The next morning the expected phone call came and Diane was instructed by the same woman to wait in front of a particular bus stop on Route 82. She was there in less than a half hour. She waited for another half hour, several busses stopping, doors opening, and drivers giving her strange looks when she waved them away.

Finally a blue Ford wagon stopped in front of her and a dark-haired woman leaned over and spoke to her through the passenger window. "You Rollins?"

"Yes."

"Get in. I'm Martha Bowers. I'm here to take you to Celia Progano."

Martha Bowers was young with short dark hair and thick dark glasses. Her face was serious, as if it had forgotten how to smile, and her eyes, dark and suspicious, had a hint of terrible sadness.

Diane got into the wagon and Martha Bowers drove off. The woman's demeanor seemed to preclude any kind of greeting.

"I'm sorry for all the secrecy," said Martha Bowers, "but

the press has been driving Celia crazy." She took her eyes off the road for a moment and looked at Diane, her features softening slightly. "When we heard about Tompkins's death, she was almost hysterical." She sighed and her eyes went back to the road. "Sooner or later they get everybody."

Diane couldn't resist. "They?"

Martha Bowers gave her a look filled with import, but said nothing.

Diane did not pursue the point.

"I want to tell you that I think Celia is very close to a breakdown. The pressure of Jim's death was a lot for her to bear and now the news about Tompkins has made her terribly afraid."

"Just what is it she's afraid of?"

This time Bowers kept her eyes on the road, but again she said nothing.

They drove in silence for a while until Bowers said, "I'm asking you to be gentle with her. I read the articles that you sent. There was a kindness in them—a kind of compassion that I don't see very often from the press. We also read the article you did on the demonstrations at TMK. There was a feeling—although nicely understated—of sympathy with the goals of the demonstrators."

Diane shrugged. "I've always been against nuclear war," she said, feeling instantly foolish, as if claiming some moral high ground with a meaningless statement.

Bowers gave no indication that Diane's statement was meaningless. "That's not enough," she said. "We must act. This quote 'defensive' unquote system will lead to a confrontation between the superpowers. We must do something before it is too late."

Diane saw the fervor burning in Martha Bowers's eyes and for the briefest of moments she was slightly afraid. But the moment passed. "Did you know Jim Progano?" Diane asked.

Bowers's hands clenched at the wheel. "Yes."

"What was he like?"

"He was a peace-loving gentle man." She smiled. "Perhaps too gentle."

"Too gentle?"

"Yes. His work on the Prometheus project was too much for him to bear. He thought he was working on a device that would bring an end to war and the threat of war. In the end he came to realize that he had helped to make war more likely, perhaps inevitable." She shook her head sadly. "You need only read the papers to see that he was correct."

They rode the rest of the way in silence.

Bowers pulled off the road and into the entrance to a mobile home park just off the highway.

"This is where Celia has been staying for the past few days. After the interview she will move to another location."

Diane looked away, as if wounded that she was not trusted.

Bowers shrugged an explanation. "We can't take any chances. She's been through too much already."

She parked the car and they went inside one of the mobile homes and Diane was surprised at the roominess of the interior.

A small, thin woman with straight brown hair approached Diane and shook her hand. "I'm Celia Progano."

Celia Progano had large brown eyes and the blank expression of someone who has suffered a great emotional trauma.

Bowers went to the kitchen. "I'll make some coffee and let you two get started," she said.

The kitchen was open to the living room and Diane noticed that Martha Bowers seemed to be keeping one ear aimed toward her and Celia Progano.

Celia Progano and Diane sat on a couch and Diane took out her note pad. "I want to thank you for letting me come here, Mrs. Progano," she began conversationally and then immediately adopted a more formal tone. "Mrs. Progano, if your husband were here today what do you think he would say about the possible confrontation between the U.S. and the Soviet Union?"

Celia Progano clasped her hands together and placed them in her lap. "I think he would say that his worst fears had been realized. He was convinced that this quote 'defensive' unquote system would lead to confrontation between the superpowers." Diane sneaked a look at Martha Bowers, but the woman seemed oblivious of the fact that Celia Progano was repeating her words. "And now," Celia went on, "it looks as if it's happening." She began to wring her hands. "If Jim were alive today none of this could happen."

Diane scribbled furiously in her personal shorthand, trying to keep up. She soon found that Celia Progano tended to ramble on, each question elicited a longer response than the last. It was not that she did not answer the questions but rather that she answered too well. She would answer and then before Diane could continue, begin a long repetitious diatribe about how her husband knew that this would happen, how upset he had been. She usually ended with the statement that if her husband were alive none of this would happen. Diane politely refrained from reminding her that her husband had been one of those responsible for making it happen.

"Why didn't he leave the project sooner?" she asked.

Celia looked around the room as if seeking help. "He didn't realize until the project was almost finished what it really meant—how dangerous it was."

"But he stayed until it was completed. Why—if he believed it to be so dangerous—did he help complete the work?"

Celia hesitated for a second and looked to Martha Bowers, who gave an almost imperceptible shake of her head, but it was enough for Diane to notice.

Celia shrugged. "He thought he could influence the project. So he stayed on."

Diane checked her watch. Her hour was almost up. "Do you think your husband's suicide—as some are trying to suggest—was a political statement against the Prometheus project?"

Celia Progano's face was blank and then her eyes blinked rapidly several times and her cheek twitched. "My husband did not commit suicide, Miss Rollins."

"But the reports all stated—"

"He was murdered."

Martha Bowers was approaching rapidly.

"Murdered?"

"Yes." Tears started to flow.

"By whom?"

"The government—the CIA."

"But why?"

"Because of what he knew. He knew too much. He knew how to stop them—to destroy their precious project."

"I don't understand."

Bowers sat next to Celia Progano, her arm on her shoulder, "Now Celia," she said. "Let's not get into that again."

"But wait," said Diane. "I don't recall any doubt that Jim Progano killed himself. If what you say is true—"

"That's enough for now," Bowers said, cutting Diane off with an angry look. "I'm going to have to ask you to leave."

"They killed him and they're trying to kill me too," wailed Celia Progano.

Diane's eyes were wide open, like spotlights flashing from one face to the other. Celia Progano was near hysteria now and Martha Bowers was trying to lead her away toward the bedrooms.

"Wait for me outside," she ordered Diane.

Diane stood up and watched them go. As Celia Progano was led down the narrow hallway Diane called to her, "Mrs. Progano."

Celia Progano struggled to pull herself away from Martha Bowers's clutches. She succeeded and turned to face Diane, who said, "Was your husband involved with any group at TMK that was opposed to the development of this project?"

Martha Bowers tried to pull her away but Celia Progano resisted. A smile broke across her face. "Yes," she said proudly.

"Are there others?"

The smile quickly faded and as she stood there hesitant, Martha Bowers finally managed to pull her away and they disappeared into a bedroom.

Diane waited outside and when Bowers appeared she was cool and distant. They got into the car before either spoke. "You pushed her much too hard," Bowers said, trying to control her anger.

"I don't think so," said Diane. "She just blurted out that bit about her husband being murdered. I couldn't just ignore it."

Bowers nodded. "I suppose you're right."

"Do you think it's true?"

"About Jim being murdered?"

"Yes."

"I didn't when she told me at first, but I believe it now."

"Why?"

"Because someone has tried to kill her."

"Are you sure?"

Bowers smiled a thin smile that hardly moved her lips. "I was in the car with her when the brakes failed. Someone had severed the brake line. We were lucky. I ran the car off the road into a pile of dirt at a construction site."

"Are you sure the brakes had been tampered with?"

Bowers shrugged. "The man at the service station said that a connector of some kind had come loose."

"It could have been an accident then?"

"Perhaps."

"There's more," said Diane, "isn't there?"

"Two nights ago Celia parked her car in the garage and went to bed. Someone started the car and left it running. The bedroom is directly above the garage. If I hadn't stopped by to check on her, she would have been dead by morning." She looked directly into Diane's eyes. "And what do you think the police would have called it?"

"Suicide."

Bowers nodded. "Of course. Bereaved widow can't stand the thought of losing her husband, so she decides to end it all. That's it. Case closed."

Diane gave a low whistle. "And you think it was the government?"

"Who else?"

"But why?"

"They think that she knows whatever it was that Jim knew."

"And does she?"

Bowers's answer was a little too quick. "No."

Diane thought for a moment. "And that's what you'd like me to say in my article?"

"You can say what you like as long as you get across the point, to whoever is interested, that she doesn't know anything."

"But you're not sure if she does or she doesn't?"

Bowers drew her a sharp look. "She knows nothing. If you say anything other than that, she's as good as dead."

"I think you should go to the police."

"The police—the CIA, the FBI, the government. It's all the same thing. If one of them wants you the others all pitch in to help."

"Okay," said Diane, nodding. "I'll say she knows nothing. But I'll want to talk with her again."

Bowers wasn't sure. "I don't know."

"I have to clarify some of these things. My editor will chop me into little pieces if I leave things hanging. How can I get in touch with you and Celia again?"

"I'll be at my house. Celia will be moving on. Someone else will be taking care of her for a while. We'll keep moving her until it's safe. The Movement is dedicated to keeping her alive. Even though we may all be incinerated by tomorrow. This case is a perfect example of how everything is prostituted in this country to the nuclear god. We have to keep Celia Progano alive because she is a symbol of everything that is wrong with this country. If something isn't done soon we're going to be responsible for blowing the whole world to hell. We are dedicated to a nuclear-free world."

"We?"

Bowers's eyes were on fire. "Stop Madness is the name of our group. We work independently of other antinuclear groups. But our members are growing."

Diane had never heard of the group.

"Right now," said Bowers, "saving Celia Progano is our number-one priority so that she can tell the truth about this Prometheus project. How it is just another weapon—just another nail in the coffin."

"How will you keep her safe?"

"By keeping her on the move. She will stay with various group members. Moving from location to location. Never staying very long in any one place."

Diane framed her next question as casually as she could. "What can you tell me about those at TMK who are opposed to this project?"

There was a long silence before Bowers spoke. "Not much."

"You must know something."

"Only that the government would like to see all of them dead."

"Why?"

"They're insiders. People who know what the government is up to and want to stop them. People who feel that the only way to make the world safe again is for us to share our knowledge with the Soviet Union."

"People like Jim Progano?"

Bowers smiled. "Yes. And he died for the cause."

"Who else?"

Bowers turned to face Diane. Her eyes were dangerous. "You ask too many questions."

They were back at the bus stop and Diane got out of the car. She leaned forward to speak with Bowers. "How can I get in touch with you?"

"You can't. I'll get in touch with you, if necessary."

Diane shrugged. "Take care of Celia," she said.

"Don't worry. We intend to."

She drove off, leaving Diane at the side of the road. Diane watched the blue wagon disappear down the highway, then, shaking her head in disbelief, she began the short walk to her car.

BRUSSELS (KNIGHT-RIDDER NEWS SERVICE)—With one notable exception the leaders of the NATO alliance called upon the American President today to share the secrets of the increasingly controversial ABM system recently deployed by the American military around two of its ICBM sites in the western United States.

The one dissenting leader, Prime Minister Margaret Thatcher of Great Britain, said that she would exact a long list of concessions from the Soviet Union, including military, economic, and human rights, before she would ask the United States to "even consider sharing the ABM technology with the Communist dictatorship in Moscow."

BONN—A West German spokesman maintained today that despite Soviet pressure to cancel the visit, East German leader Erich Honecker is still expected to meet with Chancellor Helmut Kohl in the West German capital today.

The Soviet press has accused the West Germans of seeking to undermine the friendship between East Germany and the Soviet Union. Recent rumors of reunification between the two Germanys have sent the Soviet and Eastern European press into a flurry of accusations and denunciations of Western plots to divide and conquer the socialist states of Eastern Europe by promises of increased trade with the West and bank credits which Eastern European nations desperately need to buy goods in Western markets.

Observers claim that the unusually vitriolic comments from the Soviet press were precipitated by the news that Hungary had also entered into negotiations with several Common Market nations and with the United States for an improved trade status.

European experts on East-West relations noted that the new mood of cooperation between Eastern Europe and the West is evidently related to the deployment of the American ABM system. The American technological achievement has apparently lessened the authority of the Soviet Union in its relations with its neighbors. Experts further note that, for the first time, Soviet-bloc nations seem willing to chart a more moderate and independent course in international affairs.

Fifty-one

K.C. had been trying to get in touch with Diane for hours. He had called her as soon as he got home from work but she didn't answer and at the paper he was told she had been in and out all day. He was becoming increasingly frustrated by his inability to contact her and at one point decided that something must have happened to her. As the evening wore on he was even thinking about calling the police, when his phone rang. It was Diane.

K.C. was relieved to hear her voice but the only thing he could think of to say was, "Where the hell've you been?"

"Hey," Diane said, surprised at his tone, although he had been increasingly irritable lately, "I'm a working girl, remember. I had to go into San Jose to cover a City Council meeting. This is the first chance I've had to call."

"I was worried about you," he said by way of apology.

"It's nice," said Diane, her voice softening to a purr, "to have someone worry about me."

"What happened today? How'd it go?"

"I can't talk now," she said. "I've got to get back in there."

"Wait a minute," he said irritably. "I want to know what happened with Celia Progano."

"I'll stop by your place on my way home—in about an hour. I'll give you all the details."

He had no choice but to accept. "Okay—in an hour. . . . Did you eat yet?"

"Yes, I caught a bite earlier. Fix yourself something at home and I'll see you soon. Love." She was gone.

"Damn!" he said into the silent phone and slammed it down. He was surprised by his own vehemence.

When Diane arrived K.C. had just taken his frozen lasagna dinner out of the toaster oven and was preparing to sit at the kitchen counter.

"Go ahead," said Diane. "Eat. It looks so scrumptious."

He was not amused by her sarcasm.

She made herself a drink—tonic, a twist of lime, no booze—and pulled up a kitchen stool and sat across from him on the other side of the counter.

"So let's hear it," he said. "All the details." He was shaking an overdose of salt onto the almost tasteless lump of lasagna.

Diane shook her head disapprovingly but said nothing. She sipped her drink and placed her open notepad on the counter in front of her, then rubbed her hands together as if preparing for a sumptuous feast. "I think we're starting to get somewhere with this story."

While he ate, she told him everything about her meeting with Celia Progano. He was impassive, almost mechanical, shoveling food into his mouth, dabbing at his face with a napkin, sipping milk. He said nothing but every once in a while he sprinkled more salt on his meal.

"Bad for you," said Diane. She could refrain no longer.

"What?" he said, not understanding what she meant.

"All that salt. It's bad for you."

He looked at the salt shaker in his left hand as if seeing it for the first time.

Diane nodded, resigned to this minor vice, and went on with her story. Every once in a while she referred to her notes, but mostly she related the chronology of her interview from memory. Finally she slapped the book closed. "That's about it." She smiled, waiting for his approval.

He drained his milk glass and said nothing.

330

"What do you think?" she asked.

"I don't know. What do you think?"

"It seems fairly obvious to me that there has been a group—probably only a very few people—working on the Prometheus project who were not what one could call sympathetic to the program and felt that the project had put world peace in jeopardy. They therefore resolved to do something about it."

"Like what?" asked K.C.

"Like scuttle the project—somehow render it useless. Celia Progano kept saying, 'If Jim were alive this wouldn't be happening.'"

"Obviously they didn't succeed."

Diane nodded. "Apparently not, but I think the next step would be sharing the technology with the Russians."

K.C.'s eyes lit up. "Share with the Russians?"

"Yes."

"That would defeat the whole purpose of the project."

"Exactly."

K.C. gave a low whistle. "Imagine—we expend billions of dollars on this project, then the Russians get it for free." He shook his head. "More important, we wind up in exactly the same standoff where we started."

"A lot of people feel that that's exactly where we should be—back where we started."

"Neither Greenwood nor Burns could accomplish that," said K.C. "Neither has the technical expertise or knowledge of the system."

Diane nodded. "That leaves Progano."

"Which is why he was killed."

Diane shook her head. She did not want to believe. "You think the CIA killed him?"

"If he *was* killed. Maybe it really *was* a suicide. In any event it's obvious that the Russians would have nothing to gain by his death."

"His wife is convinced he was murdered—and by the same people who are out to get her."

"Dammit!" K.C. exploded so vehemently that spittle went flying. His face red with sudden anger, he slammed his palm against the kitchen countertop.

Diane recoiled and moved back as if to distance herself from his rage. She had never seen him like this. "Take it easy," she said.

He stopped short, his face muscles relaxing slowly. "I'm sorry," he said. "It's just that every scenario I put together on this comes up smelling like CIA."

"You can't be sure," Diane said, but her voice lacked conviction.

"Look at it logically," he said. "Progano is a security risk and he is dead. Tompkins writes an exposé of the CIA and he is dead. Burns claims he was set up by the CIA and he disappears—who knows if he's alive or dead." He shook his head rapidly as if trying to shake away his doubts. "If all that is true it means that Gordon was eliminated also."

"But why?" Diane protested. "Why would they kill Gordon?"

K.C. buried his face in his hands. "Maybe he found out too much. Maybe . . . I don't know. I just don't know." He was close to tears.

Diane touched him, running her fingers through his hair. "Don't torture yourself," she said softly. "It didn't happen that way. It couldn't have."

He looked up and took her hand. "I need you," he said.

She came to him and wrapped herself around him, rocking him to comfort him. "Do you want me to stay over tonight?"

"Yes," he said, kissing her, hoping to forget everything that was troubling him. "I love you," he said.

She unbuttoned his shirt from the top, kissing his chest. "I love you too," she said.

Diane was up early the next morning. Dressed in only his robe, she made breakfast, playing the radio softly as she worked. Every few minutes she looked in on K.C., who was curled up in the fetal position, sleeping the sleep of the innocent.

She smiled watching him. Last night he had tossed and turned, moaning and groaning, and once she had had to shake him from a nightmare. He had sat straight up, eyes wide open, and then flopped back down into a restless sleep.

She buttered toast, thinking she was more comfortable with this man than she had been with any man in a long time. Maybe this time she had gotten lucky—maybe they had both gotten lucky.

"Hey," she called. "You going to work today? Time to get up."

She had to call him several times before he responded. Finally he rolled out of bed and came into the kitchen and sat heavily at the table. "I feel like I've got a hangover," he said, holding his head.

"Too much lovin' for you?" she said playfully.

He ventured a weak smile. "Too much something."

"Maybe you should stay home today."

He shook his head, then stopped, as if the motion had pained him. "No, I've taken too many days off already. Someone might get suspicious."

Diane put his breakfast in front of him and he eyed his plate suspiciously.

"Poached eggs?"

"Good for you—if you must eat eggs."

He reached for the salt but she had hidden it in a kitchen cabinet. He gave her a withering look.

"I've been thinking," she said quickly to distract him, "and I'm starting to put things together on this story."

He noted that she always referred to his investigation as a "story." Perhaps, he thought, she considers it a hot news item or a scoop that would advance her career. He ate his toast and said nothing.

She went on. "You've got a lot of information that I haven't seen yet—Gordon's notebook, the personnel information from the TMK computers. Why don't you let me go over all of your notes today? Then we can sit down together and figure this out." She sensed, rather than felt, his body stiffen. "I'll bet between us we can figure out what's going on." She paused, her voice losing confidence. "If you think it's a good idea."

His face was immobile but she could see the cloud that passed across his eyes. He pushed his plate aside and stood up. "I don't think so," he said.

"Why not?" she said. "Together we could—"

"Forget it!" he said, interrupting her. "This is my case, and I'll do it my way. And I'll do it alone."

"Alone? I thought I was helping you."

He shook his head. "I shouldn't have let you get involved." He was searching for a reason. "It's too dangerous," he said. "Look what's happened already."

Diane looked down at the table. "That's not it at all, is it? It's not any more dangerous today than it was yesterday. You just don't want me in the way."

He thought for a minute. The last thing he wanted was to lose her. "You're right," he said. "There's no reason why you can't . . . help out. I'll give you the personnel data from TMK and you can go over everything."

She noticed he had said nothing about Gordon's notebook.

"Okay?" he said smiling, trying to lighten the moment.

She nodded. "Okay," she said, but the rest of the breakfast was consumed in silence.

WASHINGTON, D.C.—At a press conference last night the President announced a major shift in American strategic military policy. The President, in apparent reaction to the Democratic Party's demands that the U.S. share its new ballistic missile defense system with the Russians, stated that the U.S. policy in any nuclear confrontation would be to absorb any Russian nuclear attack without responding in kind. This "no second use" policy goes beyond anything demanded by congressional critics and is seen as an attempt by the President to silence growing demands that the new ABM technology be shared with the Soviet Union.

Said the President, "With the capability of our defensive system, we need no longer threaten mutual destruction. We need only deflect our adversary's missiles and then untouched and fully armed and prepared for continued conflict invite him to sit down and negotiate."

Democratic response that this amounted to an ultimatum to surrender was waved aside by the President with a smile and a shake of the head. "Some might play politics with this development," he said. "But I have only the safety of every man, woman, and child in America to concern myself with."

In answer to a question about NATO nations clamoring that the defensive system be employed in Europe, the President said that several American bases in Europe closest to major European cities will be considered as possible sites for the ABM system. The defensive system would only be deployed on American bases and operated by American military personnel. It is entirely possible, said the President, that European cities and bases will be protected by a growing umbrella of particle-beam stations across Europe.

This was the first time the President had ever used the phrase "particle-beam" in reference to the defensive system. Experts had long surmised that the U.S. system was a series of particle-beam weapons capable of destroying incoming ICBM's.

The President's new policy is expected to blunt the growing clamor, both at home and abroad, that the defensive capabilities be shared with the Soviets.

One analyst said that the President was "in essence telling the world that his intentions were strictly defensive." At the same time, said the same analyst, "he was also telling the Europeans that the U.S. was willing to protect them from the danger of a Soviet nuclear strike."

By refusing to retaliate, the President said, he hopes to prove to the world that the U.S. "is interested not in world domination but in the peaceful resolution of international differences."

Fifty-two

Marshal Dimitri Ushenko's snores shattered the quiet of the early morning. He lay spread-eagled on his bed, mouth open, sending his discordant notes soaring to the ceiling.

It was just past four A.M. and the marshal had only been asleep for a little more than an hour when the phone rang.

The night before had been one of great revelry. Ushenko had invited several of his closest comrades in the military to spend the weekend at his country dacha in Peredelkino, a half hour south of Moscow. Peredelkino was a small village surrounded by birch forests and in the winter was a popular for cross-country skiing. Boris Pasternak was buried nearby but it was not recorded that Marshal Ushenko had ever visited the grave.

Ushenko and his military cronies had spent the evening eating and drinking and swapping stories of past military glory. They all had stories to tell.

The list of those present was a Who's Who of the Russian Armed Forces. Chief of the General Staff Akhromeyev and Commander in Chief of the Warsaw Pact Forces Kulikov were there. Next to Ushenko, these two were the most powerful and influential military men in the Soviet Union. In addition, three Deputy Ministers of Defense were also present: Vladimir Tolubko, Commander of Strategic Rocket Forces; Vasli Petrov, Commander of Soviet Ground Forces; and Sergei Gorshkov, Commander in Chief of the Soviet Navy.

As the evening wore on the conversation became more serious and inevitably turned to the present intolerable military and political situation. These men were not revolutionaries—the thought of seizing power to alter the present situation was a topic beyond comprehension, not to mention discussion—but they were resolved that when ill health or death brought the inevitable change at the top of the Soviet hierarchy, they would not stand by idly and let other forces dictate leadership choices.

And so it was perhaps a stroke of good fortune that brought this powerful collection of military men together on a cool morning in July when the phone rang at 4:10 A.M.

Colonel Petrunin, Ushenko's aide, answered the phone by the third ring. No one else had stirred. His expression changed little, perhaps a softening around the eyes and slight upturning of the lips, and his voice revealed none of the excitement that he felt.

"Thank you for calling, Comrade General," he said. "Of course you did exactly the right thing and I will be sure to mention to the marshal that the call came from you."

Petrunin went quickly to Ushenko's room and pulled back the curtain. The soft, diffuse light of early morning flooded the room and Ushenko groaned as if prodded by the light.

Petrunin shook the Defense Minister gently and said in a low voice, "It is time, Comrade Marshal."

Ushenko was almost instantly wide-awake. He sat up. He had never lost the military commander's ability to pull himself from a deep sleep at the slightest disturbance. He looked around and gauged the earliness of the hour by the light and then looked at Petrunin. "What's happened?"

Petrunin drew himself to attention. "Word from Moscow. The General Party Secretary died in his sleep."

Ushenko stood up and began fumbling for his clothes. "When was the death discovered?"

"Less than an hour ago—General Turkin of the Moscow Garrison called as soon as he heard."

"Wake the others, Colonel. We must act quickly."

Petrunin left and Ushenko sat on the bed to pull on his boots. He was remembering the words of his mother when he had returned from the Great Patriotic War bedecked in ribbons to prove his valor. "Dimitri," she had said, "you were born to save your country."

He strode into the living room and surveyed the sleepy-eyed assembly of half-dressed generals and their aides. He walked past them to the door. "Get your drivers ready, I want to be in Moscow in half an hour."

Even before the death of the General Party Secretary the stage had been set to turn over the leadership of the Communist Party to a new generation. It had become increasingly obvious that if the reins of power were not handed to a younger, more vigorous leadership, the Soviet state would continue to drift aimlessly through a succession of caretaker governments led by old men who could not possibly survive long enough to bring the stability that the Russian people so desperately desired.

In a ruling body where the average age was over seventy it was to be expected that such a group would plot a plodding course that avoided any path that might be considered radical or progressive. The Politburo was composed of old men who had reached the top of their profession by slowly, methodically working their way up the bureaucratic ladder. There were no overnight successes here—no fair-haired favorites of the people. Decisions were made after much deliberation and consideration of the political consequences. The wheels of the Soviet government ground exceedingly slowly.

Age had taken its inevitable toll of the Politburo. Death and illness had removed several key members who had been part of what was known as the "conservative" branch of the Communist Party. Defense Minister Dimitri Ushenko, the former Soviet Chief of the General Staff, was one of the new breed of Soviet leaders. A member of the Central Committee at fifty-five and appointed at fifty-nine to the Politburo to replace the aging Marshal Ustinov, he was the second youngest member of the ruling body.

Ushenko, unlike his predecessor Ustinov, was a true military man. He had served in the Red Army for three years during the war against Germany and taken part in some of the Soviet Union's greatest victories. He had then served as a troop commander in East Germany in the late fifties and as a district commander in the Ukraine. His final post before his promotion to the General Staff was as the commander of the Moscow Garrison. His former aide, General Turkin, was now in command of the Moscow Garrison and it was whispered in some circles that the garrison was more loyal to Ushenko than it was to the Party Secretary.

As First Deputy Chief of Staff, Ushenko's area of responsibility had been to oversee the development and deployment of weapons programs. During this period the Soviet Union had embarked upon an unparalleled growth in military spending. He had also been a member of the Soviet delegation that negotiated the first strategic arms agreement, and according to some observers had been embittered by the experience. Ushenko protested to all who would listen that the Americans were interested only in one thing—nuclear superiority. The marshal, it was said, was almost fanatical in his belief that the Americans intended to launch a first strike at the Soviet Union as soon as overwhelming superiority was theirs.

As Chief of Staff he had been vociferous in his opposition to any arms control agreement that would allow the Americans to keep their nuclear missiles in Europe. "Anything less than complete withdrawal is totally unacceptable," he had often said.

Consequently, it was with some trepidation that the Central Committee nominated Ushenko as a Politburo replacement for the ailing Ustinov. The Army, however, would have it no other way. Alarmed by the increasing influence of the KGB on the Politburo and throughout the sprawling Soviet bureaucracy, the military had insisted on making its own choice as Defense Minister.

With the death of Andropov and the extended illness of his successor, the Politburo did not have the will to protest too vigorously. Ushenko was approved along with two other candidates whose allegiance to the military was well-documented.

Marshal Ushenko was a small man, rather stockily built and with the personality of a bulldozer. His method of attack was always straight ahead. In the Army his stubbornness was legendary, his anger a thing to be feared and avoided. After the downing of the South Korean airliner by Soviet Air Forces it was Chief of the General Staff Ushenko who, while others were clamoring for a scapegoat, personally visited the commander who had ordered the attack and pinned a medal on his chest. In one fell swoop Ushenko had cut off any possible apology or recrimination.

With the death of Brezhnev in 1982 and the emergence of former KGB head Yuri Andropov as the new Party Secretary, it had become obvious to the Army that the KGB was rapidly expanding its already enormous influence in Soviet life. The Party and the Army had always been the foundation upon which Soviet life was based. Both had their secret organizations, KGB and GRU, to protect the nation and themselves. The two organizations had always had a working—even if somewhat strained—relationship, but now it seemed to many that the KGB was making a mockery of that rivalry. Even though the military had supported Andropov's claim to the leadership role, the military had been slighted at every turn. Andropov's first appointment to the Politburo had been Geidar Aliyev, a former Azerbaijan KGB chief who was appointed Deputy Premier within weeks of Brezhnev's death. Vitali Fedorchuk, Andropov's crony who had replaced him as KGB chief, was shifted to the equally important position of Minister of Internal Affairs. Fedorchuk in effect was now the chief of all police matters in the Soviet Union, while another Andropov protégé, Viktor Chebrikov, was elevated to the position of Chairman of the KGB. Before the year was out, Chebrikov was also elevated to a position on the all-important Politburo.

The grumblings in the military, which had been consistent but muted, grew to dangerous proportions. The KGB, through former officials, now controlled not only the organization itself, but also, with its 700,000 agents, operatives, soldiers, and militia, the Party and the police forces.

Defense Minister Ustinov, ostensibly the Army's man on the Politburo, seemed powerless to do anything. Always looked upon with some derision by the Army because he had been merely a defense contractor and had never commanded troops in the field, nearing eighty and in faltering health, Ustinov was encouraged by the Army to step down. The logical successor as Defense Minister and Politburo member was Marshal Ushenko.

The KGB group fought the appointment, even suggesting that the position should go to Fedorchuk or Kozlin, the KGB chief in the Ukraine. Howls of protest from the Army quickly ended that discussion and with rumors of an Army revolt running rampant in Moscow the Central Committee quickly voted to promote the Chief of the General Staff to full voting membership in the nation's most important body.

Marshal Dimitri Vladimir Ushenko, Defense Minister, Politburo member, was now truly one of the most powerful men in the Soviet Union. Having had the foresight to place friends, confidants, and protégés in almost every major military position, Ushenko was assured of the complete and total loyalty of the armed forces of the Soviet Union.

His expressed desire was to thwart the power grabbers of the KGB at home and apply constant pressure to the Americans abroad. His was a voice for ever more support of revolutionary factions in the western hemisphere, suggesting that the best way to keep the Americans out of Europe was to keep them busy in their own backyard.

Once, as a military attaché to the embassy in Washington, Ushenko had lived for a time in the U.S. He had been apalled by the contrasts of poverty and wealth, righteousness and decadence. He returned convinced that America was a schizophrenic society talking about peace and freedom on one hand, but ready to strike at a moment's notice with the other.

Like the other members of the Politburo, Ushenko was convinced that the U.S. had had its day and that its collapse was inevitable. Unlike the other members, however, Ushenko was not content to wait for this inevitability to come to pass. "A snake," he said, "is most dangerous when wounded and cornered. What I fear most is that just before their collapse the madmen in Washington will decide to take us all with them."

Even though he himself was over sixty, Ushenko protested long and loudly about the Russian propensity to promote rule by an aging hierarchy. Compared to some of the doting septuagenarians on the Politburo, Ushenko was a lusty and youthful sixty-two. Andropov's long illness which had paralyzed the nation for almost two years had been a source of constant irritation to Ushenko. "Replace him and let's get on with it!" he had often proclaimed. But the KGB crowd had rallied around their choice to protect his and their own positions.

After Andropov's death, neither the military nor the KGB was ready to advance a strong candidate for General Party Secretary and so neither objected to the choice of Nikolai Chernetsov, who at seventy-two and in ill health seemed little more than a temporary selection. But Chernetsov had fooled them. He had proved stronger and more able than anyone could have anticipated and had already been in power longer than expected. In the last year, however, particularly in the last six months, his health had shown a drastic decline.

Now that the end had come, Marshal Ushenko and the Army were determined not to be denied. The KGB, they knew, was equally determined but Ushenko was well aware that as in most things the race goes not only to the swift but also to the strong.

In an attempt to revitalize the Soviet nation, Defense Minister Ushenko was willing to offer himself to the Soviet people and to the Central Committee as an able replacement for years of decrepit and impotent leadership. In case his plea was not sufficiently strong, he had almost three million troops in uniform to back him up.

Fifty-three

In the Soviet Union, rumor had the power of truth. Lacking any other source of information, the Soviet people had developed an uncanny special sense that enabled them to differentiate between unverifiable gossip and whispered reports that would sooner or later be verified as fact.

The rumors of the General Secretary's death began to spread—slowly at first and then, as more whispers were added to the flames, like wildfire—through the Soviet hierarchy. Whispers raced through office buildings, pausing momentarily to leap across streets, and then on into the next building, where they fanned out from office to office and desk to desk, even finding their way into every nook and cranny where the bureaucrats went to avoid work.

The Russian people were told nothing. Their only clues were that the regularly scheduled morning radio and television channels both showed stock footage of crowds in Red Square lined up to view Lenin's Tomb while Tchaikovsky's mournful *Pathétique Symphony* droned in the background.

Everyone who tuned in to radio or television that morning knew that something had happened, and with an ailing leader who had not been seen in public for almost two months, it was not difficult to guess.

Unfortunately for Captain Vladimir Gorsky, he had never acquired the habit of turning on the radio in the morning before work, and the small Moskvitch sedan, which he had requisitioned from the KGB garage, did not have a radio. Consequently he managed to reach his third-floor office in the First Chief Directorate Building just off the twelve-lane ring highway that circled Moscow without hearing any of the clues that would have instantly alerted him to the coming danger.

At a few minutes past eight, Captain Gorsky's aide, Lieutenant Sakov, burst into his office. "Have you heard?" he blurted before noticing the shocked look on Gorsky's face. "Excuse me, Captain," he stammered. "I should have knocked."

Gorsky said nothing. His expression was unforgiving.

"It's just," Sakov went on, "that the whole place is buzzing with the news."

Gorsky's eyes widened. "News?"

"Chernetsov is dead."

"Is it official?"

"No. But all the radio and television programming has been preempted and—"

"Any news from the boss?" said Gorsky, interrupting his aide.

"The Comrade Director?"

"Yes."

Lieutenant Sakov looked puzzled. "Not yet."

"Let me know the minute you hear anything."

"Of course, Comrade Captain," Sakov, puzzled, turned and left.

Gorsky sat for a moment without moving, but his mind raced through a list of probabilities. He shook his head and with a sad sigh opened the middle desk drawer and reached well into the back where he kept his pistol, a 7.62 Tokarev automatic. The pistol was old—a relic of the Great Patriotic War that Gorsky had acquired in the black market—but well oiled and maintained. He removed the eight-round magazine from the butt, inspected it, replaced it, then pulled back the slide and heard the first cartridge click into the chamber. He felt the weight of the weapon in his hand. It felt good. With a simple flip of his thumb he moved the safety to the on position, then placed the Tokarev at the front of the drawer and carefully slid it closed.

He waited. It did not take long.

The door burst open again, this time startling him out of his chair and onto his feet.

It was Lieutenant Sakov. This time he did not bother to apologize. "There are troops in the building, Captain."

Gorsky said nothing. It had been expected. He sat down.

Sakov went on. "I just got a call from Pogin on the first floor. He said that troops of the Dzerzhinsky Motorized Division are in the building."

The First Dzerzhinsky Motorized Division was the KGB's private military unit used to protect officers during times of disorder. The division was the KGB's protection against Army intervention or any possible coup attempt against the government.

"I assume," said Gorsky, his voice calm, "that they are making arrests." His hand moved closer to the drawer.

"Yes. There must be a hundred soldiers with armed personnel carriers outside."

Gorsky let his hand drop into his lap. What good would it do? "Return to your desk, Lieutenant, and attend to your duties."

Puzzled, Sakov turned to leave.

Gorsky called out to him. "You may leave the door open."

As soon as his aide left, Gorsky went to the window and looked out into the parking lot. There was lots of activity below, soldiers everywhere, and several armored cars.

Overkill, he thought with a sad smile of resignation.

He looked at his watch. If they had not come for him yet that meant that they were picking up others. There was still a chance he might not be on their list.

He called Sudarev at Department 13 but the phone rang unanswered. That was not a good sign. If Sudarev was in trouble, then Gorsky's problems would not be far behind.

No sooner had the thought entered his mind than the outer door of his office burst open and two soldiers in steel helmets brandishing AK-47 assault rifles rushed in. We Russians, he thought wryly, certainly have a flair for the dramatic. Sakov jumped up in surprise but as soon as the rifles were trained on him he wisely raised his hands over his head.

An officer strode in behind them and walked past Sakov, without a glance, into Gorsky's office, where Gorsky stood behind his desk.

"Captain Vladimir Gorsky?" he asked in a tone that denoted no particular animosity.

Gorsky was tempted to try a joke—something like, "He just stepped out. I'll tell him you are looking for him." Wisely, however, he said, "That is correct, Captain."

The captain wore a khaki uniform with blue flashes on the lapels and a soft peaked cap with red piping. He wore his pistol in a holster at his side. "Come with me, Captain," he said and turned toward the door.

"Can you tell me where I am being taken?" asked Gorsky.

The captain turned, his face for the first time showing any trace of displeasure. "Come with me, Captain," he repeated.

"Of course," said Gorsky and walked to the door. His question had been foolish and only served to betray his nervousness. He knew where he was going, as did the others who had been picked up that morning.

Although the name Lubyanka still conjured images of dungeonlike cells and midnight executions, it has been years since the prison in the old wing of the KGB headquarters at Dzerzhinsky Square has been used for such dark purposes. Most of the tiny cells had been transformed into small offices and much of the basement space converted to storage for the ever-growing files maintained by the KGB.

Almost all of the administrative and punitive functions of the Lubyanka had been taken over by Lefortovo Prison in central Moscow and it was here that arrested dissidents and other political criminals were likely to be taken. The KGB, however, still maintained special places for its own. In the subbasement of the Lubyanka, in cells too damp ever to be of any use for storage, and in rooms where the echoes of human screams were too recent to have faded into total silence, the KGB brought those from its own ranks who had, in some way, committed serious offenses against the organization.

Lubyanka Prison was part of KGB headquarters at 2 Dzerzhinsky Square. The headquarters itself was two distinct buildings—one a prerevolutionary remnant once owned by an insurance company, the other built by German prisoners of war. Those two mismatched, earth-toned granite structures were somewhat incongruously joined together like an old car repaired with the wrong parts.

Within the older part of the building lay a courtyard and on one side of this opening was the Lubyanka. It was through this courtyard that political prisoners made their first stop on their way to internal exile or to the forced labor camps. For some the first step was the last.

Gorsky, his hands handcuffed behind him, stepped out of the car into the courtyard. He looked around at the forbidding gray building that surrounded him on all four sides. There was little time for reflection as he was quickly moved to a gate on the far side of the courtyard, and with soldiers holding his elbows, he was escorted down two flights of damp, slippery stone steps that led into the bowels of the building.

Gorsky tried to remain calm as he was ushered into a brightly lit room in the subbasement. Seated behind a small table was a KGB major wearing the collar emblem of the Dzerzhinsky Motorized Division. The major lit a cigarette and looked up at Gorsky, who stood wordlessly before him. Gorsky recognized him as Major Visko, a notorious ass-kisser.

"Well, Comrade Captain," he said, blowing a ring of smoke in Gorsky's direction, "what do you have to say for yourself?"

Gorsky's voice was calmer than he felt. "I know of no reason why I should be brought here, Major."

The major raised an eyebrow and opened one of several file folders which were stacked in front of him. As he did, shots rang out from somewhere down the corridor and Gorsky, startled, jumped involuntarily.

The major seemed unperturbed. He looked again at

Gorsky, this time with a malevolent smile. "That was our response to someone else who did not know why he had been brought here."

Gorsky swallowed hard.

Major Visko turned his attention to the file. "According to our information, Captain, you have met on several occasions with a Colonel Petrunin of the GRU. Colonel Petrunin is a personal aide to Marshal Ushenko."

Gorsky remained silent. So far nothing said could positively incriminate him. Obviously they were hoping he would incriminate himself.

"Again according to our information, you have been relaying top-secret information from KGB files to Marshal Ushenko through this intermediary."

Gorsky's mind was working at a rapid pace. They knew about the meetings, that much was obvious, but it was equally obvious that they did not know what had been discussed. He regularly "swept" the apartment for electronic surveillance and knew that the conversations had not been recorded. The only other way they could know was if Colonel Petrunin had told them. That was possible but highly unlikely. Knowing how these interrogations worked was a great help. If they had positive proof they would show it to him, record his confession, then take him out and shoot him.

As if on cue, shots rang out again and Gorsky, nerves frazzled, jumped again.

"Well, Captain?" said Visko.

Gorsky tried to hold himself together. The strongest possibility was that they were fishing, hoping for a quick confession. "I'm sorry, Major," he said, "but your information is incorrect."

The major's eyes darkened. He had hoped that this would be a quick one. "You deny," he said, his voice growing angry, "that you met with Colonel Petrunin of the GRU at apartment 2f at 116 Khoroshevskoe Road?" He looked at the file. "I can read the dates of your meetings if you like."

"No, Major, I do not deny the meetings, but I deny that the purpose of the meetings was to pass secret information to the colonel."

Major Visko sighed in frustration. "What then?"

Gorsky looked down at the floor. "It is . . . of a personal nature."

Visko stormed to his feet. "Captain Gorsky, you are five

minutes from a firing squad. I have the authority to be your judge, jury, and executioner. If you know of anything that will save your life, speak now or carry it with you to the grave."

The game was getting more interesting now and Gorsky's confidence was growing. If only those damned shots didn't scare the shit out of him again. He knew that some of what Major Visko said to him was true—the part about the executioner—but he also knew that he had already been judged. All that remained now was to record his confession and be done with it. He was relying on the Russian obsession with confession and absolution to—if not save his life—at least let him hang on for a while longer. In volatile times like these, he knew, surviving for another ten minutes sometimes meant the difference between life and death. Those who had already been shot had quickly confessed whatever crime they had committed in hopes, perhaps, of finding leniency.

"Speak!" screamed Major Visko.

Gorsky began with a near sob, his words coming in a rush as if he had held them back for so long and was glad to be free of them. "The colonel and I are homosexuals," he whispered. "We have been lovers for several years. I keep the woman at Khoroshevskoe Road as a cover. My staff thinks she is my mistress, Colonel Petrunin's staff thinks that he also goes to visit her. I go there first, send her away for an hour, and wait for Colonel Petrunin to arrive so we can be alone together." He hung his head in shame.

Major Visko's jaw hung open, his eyes were wide with disbelief. "You disgust me," he said.

Gorsky thought that Visko would strike him. He tried not to smile.

The major wasn't finished yet. "It will go easier for you if you tell the truth."

"Do you think I would lie about such a thing?" said Gorsky. "My life—my career—is ruined."

The major sat down, somewhat bewildered by this turn of events. He carelessly flipped over the pages in the file and Gorsky's heart sank as he caught a brief look at the last sheet. It was the blue KGB internment sheet which listed the charges against him. At the bottom of the sheet were two spaces for signatures. The one on the left meant imprisonment, even torture until the internee confessed his crime. The space on the right was the authorization for execution. Gorsky's knees almost buckled when he saw that his death warrant had already been signed.

His shoulders sagged. He was finished. They would prefer his confession to satisfy their perverted sense of legality, but confession or not, he would be shot within the hour.

There was a knock on the door and one of the guards opened it. Major Visko leaned to the right to see around Gorsky, who blocked his view of the door. Gorsky did not move but heard a voice behind him say, "Others are waiting, Major."

Gorsky turned to see who his impatient persecutor could be but the figure had already gone.

Major Visko sighed and closed the file. "I hope you are guilty, Captain, because in any event you will pay the price." He made a motion with his head and Gorsky felt the guards grab at him by the elbows. "Be quick," said Major Visko. "I'll have another for you in just a few minutes."

As Gorsky was pulled to the door the phone rang and everyone stopped. Gorsky closed his eyes as close to prayer as he had ever been

"Yes," said Major Visko. There was a long silence, then he said, "I see . . . thank you."

The silence was deafening, the wait a hundred years. Finally Visko spoke. "Captain Gorsky, it seems that the Central Committee has just agreed upon the man who will be our new leader."

Gorsky swallowed.

"You'll be glad to know that your friend Marshal Ushenko is now the new General Secretary of the Party. Apparently attempts have already been made to discover your whereabouts." He paused, watching the wave of relief wash across Gorsky's face. "Unfortunately for all of us, the phone call which I just received came too late to save your life. Your death certificate will state that you were executed five minutes ago in front of a firing squad."

"Under whose orders?" said Gorsky, his voice barely audible.

"Director Chebrikov. Who else? I'm sure he will convey his sincerest apologies to the new Party Secretary."

"Bastards," said Gorsky.

Major Visko nodded in agreement, then with a wave of his hand motioned the guards to take Gorsky away. The guards yanked him roughly toward the door and out into the narrow corridor.

In a hurry to be done with it, thought Gorsky. There would be none of the usual subterfuge, he thought, none of the usual softening of the blow. It was normal in such cases to inform a prisoner that he had been found guilty and sentenced to death. As a last resort, however, he would be permitted to make one final appeal for clemency in a personal note to the General Secretary or the President of the Secretariat. Filled with hope, the condemned would be escorted back to his cell to begin his final appeal, but somewhere along the way someone would fall in step behind him, place a pistol at the base of his neck, and dispatch him with a single shot. As a member of the KGB, however, Gorsky was familiar with all the techniques. The subterfuge would serve no purpose.

He steeled himself for the sound of footsteps behind him and the gentle touch of the executioner's pistol at the base of his neck. That was how, in this very corridor, he thought, that Lavrenti Beria, Chief of State Security under Stalin, had been eliminated after Stalin's death.

They moved him swiftly along the narrow corridor. The lower half of the walls were a bright, sickly green selected by the Psychiatric Section as being the most offensive color in the color wheel. The upper half of the walls and the ceiling were a pasty reddish pink and the combination was intended to provoke a sense of unease among the prisoners who had been kept in the tiny cells that lined the corridor. It was not the color scheme, though, that had Gorsky on the verge of vomiting. They were approaching the doorway that led to the furnace room where once, many years ago, Gorsky and a large group of KGB officers had been assembled to witness the execution of the traitor Nikolayev. Sergei Nikolayev was a colonel in the KGB's Disinformation Department who had been caught red-handed passing secrets to the Americans. As an example to his colleagues, Nikolayev had been strapped, face-up, to a wide board and then slowly pushed, feet-first, into the roaring furnace. Nikolayev had been still alive and screaming when his entire body had disappeared inside the furnace.

Gorsky breathed a sigh of relief when the guards dragged him past the furnace room and turned him to the left into a dead-end corridor that had been piled with sandbags against the far wall. He was marched to the wall, turned roughly, and pushed so that his back was against the sandbags. His guards walked back a few paces and began to draw their pistols. Gorsky looked at their faces for some sign of compassion or sympathy. There was none. These were simple peasants from Kazakhstan who had joined the Dzerzhinsky Division to find the pleasures of Moscow. Their disillusionment had, as expected, turned them cold.

Gorsky looked down at the floor but the blood there made him gag. He closed his eyes, squeezing them shut as if he could shut out the noise. He wondered for a moment if he would in fact hear the shots before the bullets snuffed out his life. He looked once and saw the buffoons from Kazakhstan fumbling with their pistols and then the weapons were free of the holsters and the two guards aimed carefully. Gorsky closed his eyes and waited for the thunder.

The noise, magnified a hundred times by the close quarters, slammed Gorsky back against the wall. Eyes clenched shut, body twitching in anticipation of expected pain, he welcomed the darkness.

There were voices yelling, feet moving.

Gorsky tentatively, disbelievingly, opened his eyes. His guards had their hands over their heads; and behind them, assault weapons aimed and ready, stood four soldiers of the Moscow Garrison. Regular Army!

Striding toward him, pistol in hand, his face expressionless, was Colonel Petrunin. "Marshal Ushenko," he said simply, "does not forget his friends."

Gorsky tried to step forward, but his knees buckled beneath him and he toppled forward, landing heavily at Petrunin's feet.

Fifty-four

Gorsky was still trembling an hour later, sitting in a large mahogany-paneled waiting room on the second floor of the Defense Ministry Building on Frunze Street in central Moscow. In front of him, on a low table, was a pot of coffee and a half-full bottle of vodka.

The door opened and Colonel Petrunin entered. Gorsky stood up almost at attention, his gaze on the open door.

"Not yet," said Petrunin. "The new Party Secretary is still quite busy. But he has promised to see you before he leaves with the Central Committee for the Hall of Columns, where Chernetsov lies in state." His smile was almost a chuckle. "We must pay our respects to the dear departed."

Gorsky slumped back into his seat. "If it were not for you—and the Comrade Marshal—I would have been departed with him."

Petrunin smiled. "Yes, you were the *nearly* departed." He thought Gorsky would laugh, or at least smile, at his little joke, but Gorsky was too traumatized to see anything as being remotely humorous.

"How many did they kill?" Gorsky asked.

Petrunin made a gesture of dismissal. "Not many. Only three or four, I think. Fortunately for you, you were one of the last. We managed to rescue three others before they could finish."

"Why?" asked Gorsky, mystified. "Why did they want us dead?"

"Several of the group had had clandestine contact with us about KGB activities. The others apparently had knowledge their masters considered too dangerous."

Gorsky shook his head in disbelief, "It's incredible."

Colonel Petrunin slapped him on the shoulder. "Come

now, Captain, when there is a changing of the guard, sacrifices must be made. If this were twenty years ago, the dead would number in the hundreds; thirty years ago in the thousands."

Gorsky nodded. "Fifty years ago it might have been in the millions."

Petrunin smiled agreeably. "Yes. So you see, it's not so bad really."

Gorsky wondered, but declined to inquire, if the families of the three or four who had not been rescued would think it "not so bad." "So you think they wanted me eliminated because of my contact with the GRU?" he asked.

Petrunin poured himself some coffee. "No, not exactly. We have literally hundreds of informants . . ." He paused, and with an apologetic shrug said, "If I may be permitted to use such a distasteful word." He thought for a moment, then rephrased his words. "Hundreds of KGB agents have seen the wisdom in providing us with information about the activities of their organization. Only a handful were picked up, even though we are certain that the KGB knew about most of them."

"Why me?"

"You must know something they don't want us to know."

At that moment the door burst open, and Marshal Ushenko, the new General Secretary of the Communist Party, strode into the room. "Sit, sit," he said, as Gorsky began to rise. "Time is short and I must be on my way. I just wanted to see you and let you know that I am a man who does not forget his friends."

"You have my undying gratitude, Comrade General Secretary."

Ushenko shot a quick glance at Colonel Petrunin, who shook his head. "And your loyalty too, I hope?" Ushenko said, turning back to Gorsky.

Gorsky bowed his head. "Forever and without question," he said sincerely.

Colonel Petrunin interrupted. "Captain Gorsky was just about to tell me why the KGB wanted him eliminated."

Ushenko watched Gorsky carefully.

Gorsky grew flustered under the intensity of Ushenko's stare. "I don't know," he said. "I can't imagine what information I have that would merit my elimination."

"Are you certain, Captain?" said Ushenko.

Gorsky shook his head helplessly. "Perhaps," he replied, "some of the others who were arrested might know something."

"Nothing," said Petrunin.

"Who are the others?"

Petrunin reached into his breast pocket and pulled out a slip of paper. He read, "Mitkov, Demin, Sudarev—"

"Sudarev? Captain Georgi Sudarev of Department 13?"

Petrunin nodded. "Yes."

"Sudarev is in communications and coding. He might know something."

Petrunin smiled. "Sudarev is not telling what he knows."

"Of course he will," said Gorsky. "He and I are good friends. He has told me many of the things that go on at Department 13. He will . . ." His voice trailed off as he realized what Petrunin meant. "Sudarev is dead?"

Petrunin nodded. "One of the unlucky ones."

Gorsky's eyes narrowed. "Then whatever they are trying to hide lies in coded communications from Department 13."

"Something you too are involved with?" said Ushenko.

It hit Gorsky like a thunderbolt. "Chameleon," he said. "It could only be Chameleon. That is all Sudarev and I had in common."

Ushenko turned to Petrunin. "Take our friend Captain Gorsky and a contingent of armed troops back over to the First Directorate Building. I want him to have access to all recent coded communications in Department 13—and anything else we can get our hands on." He turned back to Gorsky. "Do you think you can find whatever the KGB thinks is so important?"

Gorsky was standing at attention. "Yes, Comrade General Secretary."

Ushenko looked at his watch. "I am leaving now with the Central Committee members and the rest of the Politburo to pay our last respects to Comrade Chernetsov. I have called an emergency Politburo meeting for four o'clock this afternoon. If I could have the information by that time, I would be most generous in my gratitude."

"I will do everything in my power not to disappoint the Comrade General Secretary," Gorsky said.

Ushenko shook his head. "I'm depending on you, Comrade," he said, and then motioned with his head for Petrunin to get moving.

"You," said Petrunin, as he rushed down the stairs with

Gorsky a step behind, "have a rare opportunity to advance your career and to serve your country at the same time."

Gorsky was too breathless to respond as he hurried to keep pace with the swiftly moving Colonel Petrunin.

The communications wing of Department 13 at the First Directorate Building was in a rare state of disorder. Files were open and papers were strewn about the code room.

"Lots of stuff is missing," said Gorsky over his shoulder to Petrunin. "Somebody has removed a great deal of material, all of it from San Francisco and all—I am sure—dealing with Chameleon."

Petrunin turned to the four men who manned the coded communications section. "Where is it?" he asked. All four stood in a row, backs to the wall opposite the door.

There was no response.

"It's probably been shredded," Gorsky said, still rifling through the files.

"Well," said Petrunin to the code clerks, "has it been destroyed?"

The four men looked at each other, but none was willing to speak.

Petrunin removed his pistol. "I don't have time for this," he said. He pointed his pistol at the man on the left. The man's eyes widened in terror and disbelief. "I will shoot the first man and proceed from left to right until someone talks. My experience in these matters is that the second man usually tells me what I want to know. Unfortunately, the first died for nothing." He raised the pistol.

"I'll talk," said the man, staring down the barrel of Petrunin's pistol.

The other three looked relieved that they would not have to make such a decision.

Two large cardboard file boxes were brought into the room. Gorsky opened the top and immediately began flipping through the pages. Every once in a while he paused to remove a page or two which he would leave on the desk. In a short time he had a small stack of papers in front of him. "I'll need a code book," he said. "Most of this is in code."

Petrunin looked at the code clerks, and one opened a desk drawer revealing a large five-ring binder.

"That's it," said Gorsky. He looked at Petrunin. "It'll

take forever to decode all this material." He held up the stack of papers he had separated from the rest.

Petrunin said, "I'm sure our friends here"—he pointed to the frightened clerks—"will be glad to help us."

If the four men had any objections to Petrunin's request they did not allow them to show.

When they were finished, Gorsky collected all of the decoded documents and took them into an inner office to read them. It was almost three o'clock.

Petrunin motioned to the two armed guards he had posted at the door. "I want these men taken into protective custody."

The guards stepped forward, and the code clerks fell back and began a howl of protest.

"Silence," barked Petrunin. "No harm will come to you if you do as you are told." He turned once again to the guards. "They must not see or speak to anyone. I want them sequestered at garrison headquarters for twenty-four hours. No one is to know where they are or for how long they are to be held." He gave a quick wave of his hand and the guards escorted the four hapless code clerks to the door.

Petrunin marched into the inner office, where Gorsky sat at the desk hunched over his documents. "Well?" he said, a note of urgency in his voice.

Gorsky put a finger to his lips to silence the colonel. Normally Petrunin would have been infuriated by this insolence, but for the moment protocol was forgotten—he remained silent.

Gorsky read quickly through the papers in front of him, putting some in a stack to his left and some in another stack to his right. Petrunin noted that very few documents went to the right.

"We must hurry," Petrunin said, looking at his watch, "if we are to see the marshal before his emergency meeting."

A look of annoyance on his face, Gorsky looked up from his task. The look was enough to restore Petrunin to silence. He took a seat by the door and waited.

Once Petrunin sat up when he saw Gorsky's eyes light up over a particular document. "What is it?" he whispered hopefully, but Gorsky ignored him and went back to his reading.

Finally, Gorsky was done. He stood up and picked up

the smaller of the two piles. "Do we still have time to meet with the Comrade Marshal?"

"It may be too late."

"Then let's hurry," said Gorsky. "I will explain everything to you in the car."

The car, a Zim limousine painted Army khaki and emblazoned with five red stars on the door, raced across Moscow using the center lanes that were reserved for official transport.

"Tell me what you've found," said Petrunin. He was almost pleading.

"As you know," said Gorsky, "some time ago, I was removed as the controlling officer of Chameleon, the agent whom I had found, recruited, and trained."

"Yes, we understand that this rebuff was the source of your disaffection with the KGB."

"Even though I was no longer involved with Chameleon, I managed to stay fairly current with his activities."

"How?" asked Petrunin.

"Others would make inquiries of me as to his methods and techniques. Sometimes a rumor would come my way, or a friend in the right place would let me know what was happening." Gorsky paused for a moment, thinking of Sudarev. "I was able to put together what he was up to." He smiled. "I knew too much about him not to know what was going on."

Petrunin was growing impatient. "Very good, Captain. So tell me what you have found out."

"As I have told you, Chameleon infiltrated the scientific operation responsible for putting together the computer technology that is the heart of the American ABM system."

"Yes."

"Also, as I have reported, with the enhanced security prodecures, it proved impossible to get any information to us about the details of the system. Chameleon reported that it might take years to gather the information needed to duplicate the American system."

"Yes, Captain," said Petrunin impatiently, "I know all that."

"Apparently," said Gorsky, unperturbed by Petrunin's impatience, "Chameleon decided that if we could not steal or duplicate the American antiballistic missile system, we would have to take other appropriate measures to preserve the security of the Soviet Union."

Petrunin was almost bursting with excitement. "Such as?"

Gorsky smiled. "Here," he said, handing Petrunin a single sheet of paper. "Read for yourself."

Petrunin snatched the paper from Gorsky's hands and began to read. Frequently he stopped to ask a quick question. Usually it was for clarification of a word that was still in code.

"What is Zebra?" he asked.

"That's the code name for TMK Corporation, where the system was developed."

"What is Tiger?"

"That is the system itself—Prometheus II."

Gorsky watched Colonel Petrunin carefully as he continued to read. He saw the eyes widen, the jaw drop, the look of amazement spread across his face.

Petrunin turned to him. "I don't believe it," he said.

Gorsky nodded once. "Soon you *will* believe it," he said.

Petrunin pounded on the glass that separated them from the driver. "Hurry," he yelled, forgetting for the moment that he could easily communicate through the intercom system. He pounded on the glass until Gorsky was sure it would shatter.

"Faster—faster," he yelled, as the driver pushed the accelerator to the floor and the car hurtled at breakneck speed through the center of the city.

Fifty-five

The members of the Politburo were sitting in an emergency session at the headquarters of the Soviet Communist Party Central Committee. The meeting had been called for four o'clock so all the members had come directly from the ceremonies honoring the deceased Party leader. The new

Party leader, General Secretary Dimitri Ushenko, however, had been inexplicably delayed. Several members were certain he was in the building but had not as yet made an appearance, and had neglected to send anyone to explain his absence.

The other members waited, trying not to let their impatience show.

Finally, at twelve minutes past the appointed hour, the door to his office opened and Ushenko ambled into the room. Although he seemed to be in no particular hurry, there was an electricity in the air as he took his seat at the head of the long table. The others watched him carefully, some with ill-concealed displeasure, for his selection had not been unanimously acclaimed.

Immediately to the left of Ushenko sat the newest member of the Politburo, former Chief of the General Staff Akhromeyev, who that morning had been elevated to the dual position of Defense Minister and Politburo member. The old guard and the KGB were well aware that the balance of power was shifting dramatically.

What made the shift in power still more obvious was the presence in the room of the rest of the Soviet military hierarchy. Seated in straight-backed chairs placed against a far wall were the six commanders in chief of all Soviet forces: Petrov, ground forces; Koldunov, air defense; Kutakhov, air offense; Tolubko, rocket forces; Gorshkov, naval forces; and Kulikov, Warsaw Pact forces.

Several Politburo members shifted uncomfortably in their seats, watching the military men who sat looking straight ahead, with no discernible expressions on their hard implacable faces.

"Comrades," Ushenko began, "we are gathered here at a time of grave crisis for our nation. The Americans, as you know, are preparing to force us to surrender the gains— military, political, and economic—that we have made in the past seventy years." He looked around the table, meeting every eye. "I say that this must not happen. I say that we must not *allow* this to happen."

Twelve heads nodded in unison—some more enthusiastically than others.

Ushenko went on. "We all know the Americans are merely waiting for the right opportunity to strike. Already they rattle their sabers in Europe and threaten to impose their will upon the world. We must be prepared to act decisively or go down in history as cowards and fools."

Several Politburo members coughed uncomfortably. Only one raised his hand in question.

Ushenko squinted at the questioner. "Comrade Chebrikov," he said. "A question perhaps." Chebrikov was the acknowledged leader of the KGB faction, fostered by former General Secretary Andropov, and was the man most frequently mentioned as a future leader of the Soviet Union.

"Not so much a question, Comrade General Secretary, as a clarification in terminology." He paused to let his words sink in. "When you speak of decisive action, are you talking about an offensive thrust by Soviet forces?"

Ushenko's eyes were dark pinpoints. "If such preemptive action is required to preserve the Soviet state, I would not hesitate for a moment."

A hush fell across the room. For the first time it was generally recognized what was being discussed.

"Do you wish to voice an objection, Comrade?" Ushenko asked. Chebrikov looked involuntarily to the impassive faces of the military men against the wall. "Not at this time," he said softly.

Ushenko nodded and forced a smile. "Very well," he said. "If I may proceed." Again he sought out every eye and made contact. Few at the table could hold his gaze for very long. "I have asked you here today," he said, "so that we might hear the contingency plans prepared by our armed forces to deal with the expected American thrust into Europe. Our military leaders are here to outline, for all of us, what steps can be taken to negate the American retaliatory capacity. What steps are available to us to minimize our losses in any general outbreak of hostilities."

Ushenko turned first to Koldunov, the man in charge of air defense, and with a brief wave of his hand, invited him to begin.

Koldunov coughed nervously into a closed fist and then spread out some papers in front of him. "I assume, Comrade General Secretary," he said, smiling, "that I have been invited to speak first because my task is somewhat easier than any of the others'."

Ushenko nodded but did not return the smile.

Koldunov went on. "The responsibility of the Soviet Air Defense Forces would be to prevent penetration of Soviet air space by American long-range bombers. The B-52 bomber is still the backbone of the air arm of the so-called Triad, and quite frankly the aircraft is not up to the task. Most of the aircraft are older than the pilots who fly them." He smiled.

"What about medium-range bombers based in West Germany?" asked Ushenko.

"Those would present a greater threat," said Koldunov.

"If I may be permitted to interrupt, Comrade Marshal," said General Kutakhov of the Soviet Air Forces.

Ushenko nodded and Kutakhov continued. "Our planning for this expected conflict has always assumed that the West would strike first, but am I to assume that we are now discussing a scenario in which we would make an all-out preremptive strike on the enemy?"

All eyes were on Ushenko. He nodded only once.

"In that case," said Kutakhov, "the tactical strike aircraft of our Frontal Aviation forces based in Poland, East Germany, and Czechoslovakia could eliminate eighty-five percent of the enemy's air force while it was still on the ground." Kutakhov paused as a murmur of conversation swept the room.

"General Kulikov," said Ushenko, "would you give us your estimate of the capabilities of the NATO ground forces as compared to our Warsaw Pact forces?"

Kulikov moved to and uncovered a large chart mounted on a far wall. It showed the relative strengths of the Warsaw Pact and NATO forces. "As you can see," Kulikov began, touching various points on the chart with a pointer, "we outnumber the Western forces by almost two to one in personnel and by almost five to two in tanks."

In a monotone, Kulikov went on to explain the Soviet advantages in a projected conventional conflict in Europe.

It was this type of conflict that the Soviet Union would prefer over any other. One in which they could swarm into Western Europe, overwhelming the disorganized NATO forces with their numerically superior ground and air forces. Kulikov reminded the members of the Politburo that as recently as 1984 a survey of American military readiness conducted by the United States Congress had concluded that the American forces could not sustain combat against the Soviet Union, and that the military readiness of the United States was declining every day.

A conventional conflict would be perfectly suited to the

Russian temperament, Kulikov declared. None of the hostilities would be contested in Soviet soil. Casualties would be heavy, but in view of the results achieved, acceptable.

As all Europe fell, the Americans and the British would have no choice but to fall back and ultimately vacate the continent. The British would go home and rattle their sabers, but the unions and the Labor Party would keep the government in line, which would guarantee that nothing but noise could come from the rattle. The Americans would either go home or sit in England and make speeches about the rebirth of freedom, while the Soviet Union did what Napoleon and Hitler could not do—create a unified Europe.

"Pardon me, Comrade General," said Mikhail Gorbachev, interrupting Kulikov's scenario for victory. "Can we really expect that if all this comes to pass, the Americans and NATO will go along with their declared intention not to be first to use nuclear weapons?" Gorbachev was the Minister of Agriculture and one of the youngest and most influential members of the Politburo.

Kulikov looked to Ushenko, who smiled and nodded. "We, due to the excellent work done by Comrade Chebrikov and his KGB, have highly placed agents within NATO headquarters. Perhaps the Comrade Chairman would like to answer that question for us."

All eyes turned to Chebrikov, who seemed to squirm uncomfortably in his seat. His eyes darted around the room, as if searching for sympathy or perhaps escape.

"Come, come, Comrade," Ushenko said pleasantly but with a trace of sarcasm. "Don't be so modest. Tell us of your great achievements."

Chebrikov's hands were fists beneath the table. "Our sources within the NATO command structure," he began, "inform us that despite ambiguous public pronouncements, NATO policy precludes any first use of nuclear weapons in Europe."

"Thank you, Comrade," Ushenko said, beaming. "The Europeans have no intention of allowing the Americans to turn Europe into a nuclear wasteland."

"The Americans," said Gorbachev, interrupting again, "may not have unilateral control over the nuclear forces in Europe, but what about their nuclear submarines? Would they not take action against us?"

Ushenko turned to the sour-faced admiral, who sat with

the other military men. "Admiral Gorshkov," he said. "Do you have a response?"

Gorshkov rose from his chair. "If I may be permitted," he said, "I have taken the liberty of inviting the naval officer who is responsible for our antisubmarine defense forces." Without waiting for any response, he nodded to Ushenko, who pushed a buzzer next to his right hand. Almost immediately the door opened, and a naval officer in his late thirties came into the room carrying a briefcase and a stack of papers. He went to a small podium next to a large map on the west wall and placed all that he carried on a table in front of him.

Captain Vitaly Ribidov looked around the room and took a deep breath. Staring at him from seats around the green-felt-topped table and from a row of chairs along a back wall was a collection of the most important men he had ever laid eyes on.

Admiral Sergei Gorshkov, Ribidov's mentor, nodded, and the captain began. Ribidov coughed, and with a nod to the Party Chairman, he turned to the large map of the Soviet Union and began to speak in a strong voice that belied his nervousness.

"Gentlemen," he said, pointing to the map, "each blue star that you see surrounding the territory of the Soviet Union represents an American ballistic missile submarine." He moved his pointer to each of nineteen blue stars in the waters to the north of the Soviet Union. "These positions are accurate as of nine-fifteen this morning. The positions are constantly monitored, their positions registered every thirty minutes." He held up a stack of computer printouts. "This information tracks the location of a certain Ohio-class submarine—which we are quite certain is the *Robert E. Lee*—since leaving New London, Connecticut, on April 17 of this year. She arrived in Scotland on April 22, remained for two weeks, then headed for her present position in the Barents Sea. This leaves her and her twenty-four Trident II nuclear missiles nine hundred miles north of Leningrad and twelve hundred miles from Moscow."

There was a barely perceptible shifting of positions at the table as the reality of the proximity of obliteration sank in. Ushenko did not move or blink.

"These positions are absolutely verified?" Ushenko asked.

"Absolutely, Comrade General Secretary," said Ribidov. "Ilyushin 38 reconnaissance planes of the Soviet Naval Air

Arm fly over these positions every day, verifying by sonobuoy their presence." Ribidov smiled for the first time. He was growing more comfortable. He patted his stack of printouts. "And we have listings for each American submarine on station in European or Soviet waters."

Ushkeno turned and nodded his head to Admiral Gorshkov, who fought to keep from smiling. "Remarkable," said Ushenko. "Perhaps you could give us some details of this remarkable achievement, Captain."

Ribidov returned to his map. "The submarines are photographed and identified by satellite as they leave their bases, and tracked across the Atlantic by heat sensors and laser detection. The data is processed, augmented, and detailed by the most modern computers."

Ushenko, beaming, turned to Chebrikov. "These are the new computers developed at the KGB labs outside of Moscow."

Chebrikov nodded, a vague smile across his lips. Everyone—with the exception of Ribidov—knew that this reference was a humorous allusion to the KGB's ability to acquire the most modern Western technology.

Ribidov wasn't sure why everyone was smiling. He took it as a good sign and went on. "When the submarines arrive at what are called 'choke points' "—here he pointed to the various narrow sea-lane passages between Greenland and Iceland, Iceland and Scotland, and the entrance to the Baltic and the Barents seas—"sensitive hydrophonic equipment detects their passage and relays the information to the command center in Archangel. Once it arrives 'on station' and rests on the ocean floor—where it often sits for months at a time—heat-sensitive satellites pinpoint its position."

Ushenko's face was serious again. "In case of conflict, and you were directed to eliminate the threat of these submarines, what would happen?"

General Tolubko, the commander in chief of the Soviet Strategic Rocket Forces, took his cue. The general was short and spoke in a surprisingly soft voice. "Each sub 'on station' is constantly targeted by an SS-21 IRBM mirved with three atomic warheads of 150 kilotons. These missiles dropped in a triangular pattern within ten kilometers of the submarine's position would eliminate any possibility of retaliation. We could, if given one hour's notice, eradicate the entire on-station fleet of American missile submarines in less than twelve minutes."

"Degree of reliability?" asked Ushenko.

Tolubko looked directly into the eye of his leader and then to every man at the table. "One hundred percent."

Ushenko allowed a reed-thin smile to split his face. He nodded in appreciation. "Thank you for your time, Comrades," he said gently. "Your lecture has been most informative." He motioned to the door with a slight movement of his head.

"And now, if you would not mind, the gentlemen of the Politburo and I have some hard decisions to make."

Wordlessly, the military leaders of the Soviet Union, followed by Captain Ribidov, who was struggling to gather his papers and stuff them into his briefcase, filed quickly out of the room.

When the door had closed behind them, the room was silent. Several members of the Politburo coughed nervously, trying not to look directly at Ushenko.

Chebrikov broke the silence. "We must remember, Comrades," he said, "that we and the Americans have identical capabilities in antisubmarine warfare. The system that allows us to track and destroy their boats is the system that we"—he searched for the right word—"acquired from them."

Ushenko nodded. "We are well aware of their capabilities, Comrade Chebrikov," he said. "What we are concerned with are numbers."

Chebrikov raised a bushy eyebrow. "Numbers?"

"Yes, Comrade. Numbers. How many have we got, how many have they got? How many can they put down on target, how many can we put down on target?" Ushenko smiled, his pale, jowly face eerily resembling a wax dummy at Madame Tussaud's. "Numbers," he reaffirmed. "That's what it is all about."

Numbers, numbers, thought Ushenko. It is all a matter of numbers. The new ASW system had effectively neutralized the seaborne arm of the American Triad, and for years Soviet planners had known that the airborne wing of the Triad was a sham and had been for almost twenty years. Until a supersonic bomber force was in place, the airborne wing of the Triad was a myth—a paper tiger, which in actual conflict would contribute next to nothing.

That left the third wing of the Triad—the intercontinental ballistic missile force. Before the development and installation of the Prometheus ABM system, the American ICBM's had been extremely vulnerable to a Soviet first strike. But that had all changed now. With Prometheus the American ICBM force was protected and immune to attack. The American strategic missile force, however, was not nearly as potent as the Soviet counterpart.

Numbers, numbers, thought Ushenko, it was all a part of the psychology of terror. The Americans might drop 150 kilotons of payload on a specified target. The Russians would drop 500,

Ushenko sat, thinking, letting the others talk. Involuntarily he reached inside his jacket to touch the sheet of paper he had folded carefully and placed there for safekeeping, when Petrunin and Gorsky had stopped him on his way to the meeting. He touched the paper and waited for the inevitable question.

The question was not long in coming.

Grigori Romanov was the first. "It is all well and good to talk about our numerical superiority to the NATO forces, and I am quite sure that NATO would provide little resistance to our military forces. But what if the Americans decide to make the conflict a nuclear one? They would sit safe and sound behind their defensive system, able to shower us with nuclear bombs."

Ushenko turned to Chebrikov.

Chebrikov was wary. He had already been burned on the "no first use" question and had remained strangely silent, as if wary of disaster, throughout the proceedings. "Romanov has an excellent point," he said.

"Does he?" Ushenko asked, smiling. Chebrikov, seeing that smile, was instantly uneasy.

"You remember," Ushenko went on, "at our last meeting, our dear departed Comrade Chernetsov said that if we could find a way to attack the Americans without bringing disaster to ourselves, we would be fools to wait for them to strike first."

The room was silent. All remembered the former Party General Secretary's comment.

"Here then," said Ushenko, reaching into his pocket and removing the precious sheet of paper. He passed it to Chebrikov, who unfolded it as though it might explode in his face. As soon as he saw the KGB file number across the top, he knew what it was.

"Perhaps the Chairman of the KGB would like to tell us what this communication says."

Chebrikov gulped. "It—is in code," he stammered.

"I have the decoded version in my pocket, Comrade. Shall I read it to you?"

Chebrikov closed his eyes and swallowed hard. "That won't be necessary," he said softly, his throat constricting.

"Well," said Ushenko relentlessly. "What does it say? What does the message tell us about the American antiballistic missile system?"

Chebrikov had no choice but to respond. "It tells us," he began, his voice faltering, and he wished he could be somewhere else, "that the American ABM system does not work."

The men around the table were silent in amazement.

"Pardon me," said Ushenko. "I'm not sure I heard you."

"It does not work," said Chebrikov, and crushed the sheet of paper in his hands.

Fifty-six

Chebrikov fidgeted nervously while Ushenko paced back and forth like a caged lion. They had adjourned to Ushenko's private office in the Central Committee Building. The KGB Chairman looked quickly to the faces of the others in the room—Petrunin, Gorsky, Melekh—as if they might offer sympathy or assistance. But the others, even Melekh, quickly looked away. Chebrikov was on his own.

Ushenko stopped his pacing and stood next to the empty fireplace, his back to Chebrikov. "Then it's true?" he inquired calmly.

Chebrikov, his eyes on the thick rug at his feet, nodded and mumbled a response.

"What?" said Ushenko twirling to face the accused, his voice rising in pitch.

Chebrikov looked up. "Yes, Comrade General Secretary. It's true."

Ushenko was in full uniform, in front of the empty fireplace, wielding a poker in his hand like a weapon. He seemed composed, his words carefully chosen, but his face was almost beet red, as if his collar were strangling him. "Explain it to me," he said. "How was this accomplished?"

"Our agent within the Prometheus program was able to recruit the man responsible for programming the computer system."

"Chameleon?" asked Ushenko.

Chebrikov nodded. His eyes, burning hatred, found Gorsky and gave him a withering look. "Yes. Chameleon," he said. "As I understand it, and it has been verified through Professor Aleksinsky of the Computer Technology Department of Moscow University, any computer can be programmed to become inoperative at a particular signal. The new program can be hidden among the maze of other programming. It will lie dormant—like a secret agent in place, only revealing itself at the designated moment when the correct signal is given." Chebrikov sighed. He was not enjoying himself. "It is called, I believe, a clandestine program."

Ushenko shook his head in bewilderment. "I know nothing of this business. Just tell me how it works."

"The key," said Chebrikov "is the American Defense Condition system. With our clandestine program in place, the ABM system will work perfectly under test conditions, and under the first three Defense Condition stages, Defcon 4, 3 and 2. But as soon as the military goes to what they call 'Defcon 1'—full war status alert with attack imminent—the Prometheus system will shut down."

Ushenko licked his lips. "Shut down?"

Chebrikov nodded. The others were silent.

"For how long?" asked Ushenko.

"According to Professor Aleksinsky, once the program reveals itself it would be relatively simple to reprogram and bring the system back on line."

"How long?"

"A minimum of thirty minutes or perhaps as long as several hours."

Ushenko turned and placed his hands on the mantelpiece

and stared into the fireplace. "This information is only useful if we wish to make a surprise first strike," he said.

"Yes," said Chebrikov. "Anything else—a slow buildup of forces, a logical progression of alert conditions—and the clandestine program will reveal itself."

"Why," said Ushenko, turning to face Chebrikov, "was I not told?"

Chebrikov inspected his fingernails. "It was felt, Comrade General Secretary, that the fewer people who were aware of the situation, the better." Chebrikov flashed a look of hatred in Gorsky's direction, but then returned to his fingernails.

"But why exclude the Politburo from such important information?"

Chebrikov sighed. It was no use dancing around it. They would just sit here for hours until he said something. "Because, Comrade General Secretary, it was felt that some hotheaded members of the Politburo might use the information to provoke an attack by the U.S., then strike at a moment of weakness."

Ushenko nodded. It did not occur to him that Chebrikov might be referring to him as "hotheaded."

Chebrikov went on. "That would be madness. Better to wait until our own system is in place to restore the status quo."

"Status quo?" said Ushenko, his voice dangerously low.

Chebrikov looked uncomfortable.

"Status quo! With the Americans shoving us around for a few years? A little shove here—a little push there." Ushenko pantomimed his actions, his face contorted in anger. He raised the poker. "And all the while threatening us with nuclear annihilation if we do not retreat. At what point would you have told us that we were dealing with a toothless tiger, Comrade?"

"As we know, Comrade General Secretary, in the fifties and sixties, when the Americans had overwhelming military and nuclear strength, we were still able to accomplish our objectives. The Americans are psychologically incapable of pressing their nuclear advantage."

"You think so?" exploded Ushenko, leaving the fireplace to stand only inches from Chebrikov and the others. "Then what is this shit in Germany? For the first time that I can remember the East Germans are seriously talking about reunification. The damned Poles are getting more militant every day. They look at us and think we're powerless. Powerless!" he screamed, his words exploding spittle across their faces.

No one dared wipe.

Chebrikov shrugged. "What do you suggest, Comrade General Secretary?"

"Attack while we can. Before it is too late."

Chebrikov blanched. "Comrade General Secretary. Even without the defensive system operating, the retaliatory powers of the Americans are almost equal to our own. We would merely slaughter each other."

"What about the American statement that they will not retaliate against a first strike?"

"That was predicated upon their system being able to stop any incoming strike. As soon as they realize the system is inoperative, they would have to retaliate."

"What if there is nothing to retaliate with?"

Chebrikov started to speak, then, his eyes narrowing, he kept silent.

"Our first strike need only be surgical. Take out the MX and Minuteman sites and perhaps the San Diego Naval Base. By the time they realize Prometheus doesn't work they would be *unable* to respond."

"The submarines?" Chebrikov asked quietly, already sure of the answer.

"A coordinated strike will take out the submarine moments before our submarines launch any missiles. It will be over in an hour. The Americans would be disarmed. We could force whatever terms we wished on them. If they wanted to survive, they would accept them."

"World opinion?" Chebrikov said hopefully.

Ushenko shrugged. "A surgical strike for purely defensive purposes. Minimal casualties—perhaps less than one million. Oh, the Europeans will quake and quaver, but what can they do? I think our friends around the world will rejoice when we clip the eagle's wings and render the bullies of the world impotent. World opinion would be mostly on our side."

Chebrikov nodded. "A brilliant plan, Comrade General Secretary," he said with some obvious sarcasm. "If only the Politburo would approve we could have tea in Washington tomorrow."

Ushenko's smile was false. "Marshal Akhromeyev, as you know, has been named to fill the seat so recently vacated by our dear departed leader. Marshal Kulikov and Admiral Gorshkov will be named to fill the other vacant positions."

"What vacant positions?" asked Chebrikov warily.

"Premier Tikhonov has already agreed to step down." Ushenko smiled. "For reasons of health, of course."

Chebrikov's eyes widened. That would give the military four positions on the Politburo, and there were enough other votes among the remaining nine members to give Ushenko his majority. Chebrikov lit a cigarette, carefully blowing out the match. "You will need another opening for one of your appointments, Comrade General Secretary."

"Yes," Ushenko said, smiling gleefully. "I understand your health has taken a turn for the worse. Something potentially fatal." He shook his head. "Smoking is so bad for your health."

Chebrikov put out his cigarette. "And if I refuse to step down?"

"You will be arrested as a traitor to the Soviet people. As a man who withheld vital information from the ruling body of the Soviet government. As a man who misused his authority as the Director of the KGB."

"And if I accept?"

"I have a nice quiet post picked out for you in Kazakhstan. Winters are so much warmer there. In a way I envy you. If I were a cruel man I would have found something more appropriate."

"I thank you, Comrade General Secretary."

"You will of course be placed in protective custody for the time being. You will not leave your home until you are given permission. Nor will you attempt to contact anyone."

Chebrikov nodded. "And what of Director Melekh?"

Melekh licked his lips nervously.

Ushenko's face showed his disgust. "You may take the weasel with you to Kazakhstan. Do with him as you wish. Comrade Major Gorsky will take over his post as Director of Department 8." He clapped his hands to signal that the meeting was concluded.

Ushenko stomped from the room and Petrunin went to the door to call in the guards. Chebrikov took the opportunity to hiss at Gorsky, his eyes narrowed in hatred, "You may just have started a nuclear war and incinerated one hundred million people."

Gorsky's face showed his dismay. "But I didn't realize . . ." he stammered.

"You didn't realize," Chebrikov repeated. "The hundred million can use that on their headstones—Gorsky didn't realize."

Petrunin was back with two armed guards, who escorted Chebrikov and Melekh to the door. Gorsky sat, immobilized in his chair. His expression was blank, as the enormity of what he had just heard began to sink in.

"*Major* Gorsky," said Petrunin, emphasizing the new rank, "perhaps you will join me in a drink?"

Gorsky looked up, startled by Petrunin's interruption. He fought to compose himself. "You will have to forgive me, Colonel, but I think I should go straight to my new post. There is much confusion and much to be done."

Petrunin eyed him carefully. "As you wish, Major," he said. "As you wish."

NEW YORK (AP)—Dr. Alan Calder, a member of Concerned Physicians, said today, in a speech to the members of the United Peace Council in New York City, that the deployment of the "so-called defensive missile system" by the U.S. would be perhaps the most dangerous move that any superpower had made in the last twenty-five years.

"How are the Soviets supposed to react to such provocation?" said Dr. Calder. "Should they just lay down their arms and surrender to the apparently invulnerable and increasingly belligerent U.S.?" In what was perhaps the most provocative remark of his speech, Dr. Calder said he would not be surprised, nor would he blame the Soviet Union, if "a preemptive nuclear strike were aimed at the defensive installations before they were fully operational."

Fifty-seven

Diane Rollins was sitting up in bed, going over the personnel sheets from TMK that K.C. had given her. She puzzled over him again, wondering about his strange behavior and why he would not let her see Gordon's notebook. Things had been strained between them since the morning she had asked him to fill her in on everything he knew. Although they had managed to patch it over, K.C. still remained a little distant and somewhat cool. She could see it in his eyes: somehow something had changed.

She turned her attention back to the listing on the sheets. The trouble with computers, she thought, is that they give too much information. She looked at line after line of data, which went on for sheet after sheet. For some reason K.C. had gathered information about all of Reid Lawson's business trips, but the only thing Diane could tell from the information in front of her was that Reid Lawson certainly did a great deal of traveling.

The list was voluminous, detailing when Lawson traveled and where he stayed. Each individual business trip, charges he made to room service, restaurants, bar bills, customer entertainment, and various other charges. After a while, the letters began to swim together into an unintelligible jumble.

Someone—K.C., she had assumed—had put a check mark next to several of the trips, and Diane checked those dates with the information she had. Sure enough, K.C. had been trying to match Lawson's business trips to such events as Progano's death, Burns's escape from prison, and even Gordon's death.

Lawson had indeed been traveling at those times, but that would seem to confirm his innocence. She noted that

Lawson had been at the Westgate Hotel in San Diego the week when Gordon Hardwick had been killed in Washington. She let her eye run down the list of charges he had incurred on that trip, saw what he paid for lunch and dinner, then estimated how many clients he must have had with him. She was about to flip the page and move on when her eye fell on something that made her stop. She looked at it again, double-checking to make sure.

There it was! In the middle of his trip the charges simply stopped—no breakfasts, no lunches, no dinners, nothing. For someone who spent the company's money as freely as did Reid Lawson, the lack of charges was certainly an unusual note. For two days he had not charged a thing. On the third day the charges were back again.

Diane flipped through the pages until she found the trip Lawson had been on when Burns escaped from prison. He had been in Seattle for five days, and sure enough, on the third and fourth days, he had not charged anything to the company. She looked at the list carefully. From the information on the sheet one could easily deduce that Reid Lawson had not been in Seattle on those days.

She hesitated for a moment, then picked up the phone. When K.C. answered she said, "You asleep?"

"No," he said, not sounding glad to hear from her.

I'm losing him, she thought, and then said, "I think I've found something in those printouts you gave me."

"What?" he said, sounding more enthusiastic.

She told him about the hotel stays in San Diego and Seattle. "Maybe in some of the others, too," she said. "I haven't checked yet."

"Let me know what you find," he said.

She bit her lower lip and figured it was worth a try. "Why don't you come over and help me?"

He didn't hesitate. "I'll be there in ten minutes."

"It's right here," she said, pointing at the list of charges. "He was registered in San Diego from the seventh to the fourteenth."

K.C. nodded as he followed her finger on the page.

They were sitting on her bed, where she had spread out all the sheets they needed to look at. She wore only her blue robe and had fixed up her hair before he arrived.

"Look at all these charges," she said. "Every day from

the seventh to the tenth he had breakfast sent to his room at seven-fifteen in the morning. He ate dinner twice in the Fontainebleau Room at the Westgate and once at the Bayview. He ate lunch at a different restaurant every day, and every night he ordered something from room service—a drink or a snack or something."

"But then," said K.C., pointing at the list, "on the eleventh and twelfth—nothing. No breakfast, no lunch, no dinner."

"It's almost as if he wasn't there."

K.C.'s throat constricted as he saw the logic of what she was saying.

"And then," Diane went on, "he's back in time for dinner on the thirteenth. On the fourteenth he reverts to the original pattern."

K.C. let it sink in.

Diane smiled, knowing her logic was impeccable.

K.C.'s hands were clenched into fists. "That would give Lawson plenty of time to go to Washington and eliminate Gordon, then get back to San Diego in time to conclude his business."

Diane lay back, resting on an elbow. "And it's the same thing in Seattle. During the week Burns escaped, Reid Lawson is away on business, but he conveniently drops off the face of the earth for two days, then reappears later." She touched K.C.'s clenched fist and brought it to her lips until he was able to relax. "If it's him," she said, "we'll get him. This is just the first step."

"Yes," he said, her touch making him feel better than he had in days. He had missed her. He touched her leg, running his hand up the inside of her thigh, beneath her robe.

Diane shivered as K.C. tugged at the belt around her waist and opened the robe. She lay back, and he was ripping his clothes off and pushing the printout sheets onto the floor. They lay side by side, touching each other, exploring each other's bodies as if for the first time. She wrapped a leg around him and he entered her easily, moving with her in an easy rhythm.

"I missed you," she whispered, but he was quiet, hearing only the rhythm of their movements and the beating of her heart.

*   *   *

Diane looked at the clock. It was almost six A.M. She kissed K.C. and untangled herself from his arms, pulling herself to a sitting position.

K.C.'s eyes popped open and he was instantly awake. He looked at her and then at his surroundings as if unsure of where he was.

Diane kissed him. "I'm sorry," she said. "I didn't mean to wake you."

"I haven't been sleeping well lately," he said. "Never seem to sleep right through the night."

"You want to talk?" she asked.

"Sure," he said, propping a pillow behind his head.

"I went to see Nichols yesterday."

He smiled. "How's the record collection?" He touched her leg.

She returned the smile. "Fine."

"Did he tell you anything interesting?"

She seemed noncommittal. "He did seem surprised when I mentioned the growing unrest in the company."

"Surprised?"

"He thought Greenwood and Burns were just two disgruntled employees who got caught and were now trying to blame the CIA for problems of their own."

"And Progano?"

She shook her head. "He was upset about him. Apparently they had been good friends. He thought Progano had suffered some sort of mental breakdown that accounted for his actions."

K.C. made a face but said nothing.

Diane seemed reluctant to go on. "We also talked about Gordon," she said cautiously.

K.C.'s face fell. "You what?" She felt his body stiffen.

"I just thought that—"

He sat up and swung his legs out onto the floor. "I wish you hadn't done that," he said. He was sitting on the edge of the bed, his back to her.

"Look," she said. "If I'm going to work with you on this, you have to trust me. You haven't even let me see Gordon's notebook."

He was silent.

"I think you should," she said.

He stood up. "I don't think so," he said, fumbling on the floor for his clothes.

"But why not? Together we could—"

"Forget it!" he snapped, whirling around to face her. "I've told you already, I'll do this alone."

His sudden anger made her aware of her nakedness. "But I've already talked to several people. I thought you needed my help."

"That was a mistake—I can see that now. It won't happen again."

"But . . ." she stammered in bewilderment, searching for a clue to his strange fluctuations in attitude. How could this be possible? "I don't understand you," she said. "One minute everything is fine, the next—!"

"You don't have to understand me," he snarled, "just stay out of my business!"

He was pulling on his clothes, tucking his shirt into his trousers. Feeling naked and defensive, she held the sheets close to her body.

His clothing disheveled, K.C. started for the door, then turned to face her. He shook his head as if trying to clear his thoughts, then shrugged as if in apology for his behavior. "I'll call you later," he said. "I've got some thinking to do."

Diane wasn't going to say anything, but could not resist a parting rejoinder. "Yes," she said, "we both do."

He watched her for a moment, his eyes uncertain, searching for some sympathy, but her hostile gaze never faltered. He turned and left. She heard the front door close behind him.

Damn! she thought. What the hell is going on here? I offer to help and I'm treated as if I want to steal something. Sure, she wanted a story, one that would turn her career around, but she didn't want it enough to jeopardize what he was doing. She went into the shower and let the hot water soak the tension from her shoulders. As soon as it was late enough, she thought, she would talk to Carol Hardwick.

At a little past 8:30, Diane drove over to Carol's apartment. She had called her on the phone and Carol had invited her to come over for coffee.

Carol was relaxed and eager to help. She looked devastatingly attractive, Diane thought, in jeans and a bulky fisherman's knit sweater.

"That doesn't sound like K.C.," she said when Diane described her situation. "Sounds more like Gordon."

"That's what I wanted to get at. I remembered you telling me that after you moved out here Gordon seemed to change. You argued more—he seemed suspicious."

"That's true, but with Gordon that kind of behavior wasn't really out of character. He was always somewhat tense, quick to anger." She smiled. "And suspicion was—I suppose—the name of his business. But K.C. has never been like that. He's always been quiet and gentle. He is perhaps the most even-tempered man I've ever known."

"So how do I explain this? Is it me?"

Carol shook her head. "I don't know. I'm sure it's not you."

"I'm not exaggerating this, Carol. His mood shifts are kind of scary. He makes me afraid."

Carol's eyes narrowed. "Afraid. I can't believe that! K.C. would never hurt anyone. I know him."

"You've never been in love with him."

Carol touched Diane's cheek gently with her hand. "K.C. and I have always been close. Maybe he's just so distraught over Gordon's death that he can't cope with any of this." She looked away for a moment. "I didn't want him to come out here, you know. I advised him to let it all go. Just accept what had happened and get on with his life." She gave a small, sad chuckle. "Of course, that was easy for me to say. I didn't love Gordon anymore. His death was a terrible thing, but it didn't touch me the way it might have two or three years ago. It crushed K.C. I never realized just how bad it was for him."

They sat for a long time sipping coffee. Diane couldn't think of anything to add, though she was still not satisfied.

"I've got to get going," Carol said finally. "I've got to shower and get ready."

"Okay," said Diane, getting up. "Just one more thing. You said that Gordon was always kind of moody and angry. How did you stay with him for so long if he was like that?"

Carol shrugged. "His job kept us apart a lot, and the reunions were always nice." She looked up at the ceiling. "He wasn't always as bad as he was here in California."

"So he did shift more violently when he got here?"

Carol nodded. "He was worse here, there's no doubt about that. I don't know if that was just because it was the first time in years we had been exposed to each other for a consistently long period." She grinned. "When you're married to someone like Gordon, it's not like being married to a nine-to-fiver. He was gone for months at a time. It was only in the last few years that he was Stateside, and we began to really live together." She made a face, as if tasting something sour. "That's when we found out how much fun it was to be together."

Diane nodded. "Thanks, Carol. I appreciate your time. Tell Reid I said hello." Then she added, "How are you two doing? I hope he's not angry about the party."

"He's away a lot." Then she realized what she was saying and laughed. "Maybe that's how I get along best with my men." She hung her head, suddenly sad.

Diane touched her on the arm and then impulsively hugged her. "It'll be all right, Carol. I'm sure it will."

Carol nodded. "I know," she said, her eyes brimming with tears. "But if you want to know the truth, I miss Gordon— the old Gordon, I mean—before he went California crazy."

"I guess that's a good way to describe what happens to everybody out here," said Diane, "California crazy."

Fifty-eight

While Diane was with Carol, K.C. had gone back to his apartment, still filled with suspicion about Diane's motives. His head was spinning with conflicting emotions about this woman in his life. On one side he saw her as beautiful and loving, as someone with whom he would want to spend the rest of his life. She was gentle and kind and he cared for her more deeply than he had cared for anyone before. But he also saw her dangerous side. The side that wanted a "story" more than anything else, wanted the big break to move her up into another echelon in the world of journalism. Right now she was playing in the Little League and, if he read her properly, she would not be satisfied until she was up there in the majors. He wondered if she wanted the story more than she wanted him. Sometimes, in fact, he wondered if she wanted only the story, and he was merely a stepping-stone to that end. Sometimes . . . sometimes he was confused about the whole thing.

He tried to untrack his thoughts by adding the information Diane had gathered from Celia Progano to the notes he had been accumulating on the case. He kept everything in a loose-leaf three-ring notebook similar to those in which he had taken notes as a student. He jotted Celia Progano's comments on a separate page, wrote down the new information on Reid Lawson, adding it to what he already had, and then opened the rings and extracted the other pages. He spread them out on the coffee table, each page headlined with the name of the person or situation whose facts it contained.

On the left-hand side of the table, he placed the page headed "Gordon," and then in a neat row, left to right, he laid out the other pages—Progano, Burns, Greenwood, Tompkins, Lawson, and then the new sheet with Celia Progano's name across the top. In between these pages he placed the others—Birdwell/CIA, TMK, Ameronics, Michael Tolbert.

Some of the pages were filled with information—times, places, events—some were relatively empty. But the information represented almost everything he knew about what had happened.

He sat, elbows on knees, chin in hands, staring at his layout for a long time, trying to make some sense of the chronology of events. Something in his orderly, logical mind told him there was a pattern to be discovered here, a pattern that once disclosed would reveal all he was looking for.

He stared at the pages until the lines of print began to swim in front of his eyes. He could find nothing.

He moved the sheets around as if he were rearranging a jigsaw puzzle and the correct placement would bring everything into proper focus.

He stared. Still he found nothing.

It was like a game show, he thought. *Concentration!* Part of the message was revealed, but blanks had to be filled in before the whole message was obvious. Too many blanks—not enough clues—not enough information.

He moved the pages back into their original chronological order. Nothing!

He began focusing on his own involvement in the events.

He put the page on Jim Progano aside for the moment. Progano had killed himself, or was murdered, before K.C. had become involved. He picked up the others, one at a time.

I come out here to see Gordon, he thought, and a week later he's dead. I interview Carl Burns, and a few days later someone helps him to escape from prison. I talk with Greenwood—and as far as I know he's still safely locked up—but he tells me about Tompkins, who is murdered the day before I'm scheduled to meet him. I try to see Celia Progano. She claims someone is trying to kill her. Now she's in hiding and refuses to see me. He shook his head sadly. I don't blame her, he thought. Maybe my reputation has preceded me. It seems that someone is always a step ahead of me.

His head was starting to ache, so he closed his eyes and sat back, resting his neck on the back of the chair. "What have I got?" he said aloud to himself. "What is the common denominator?" He answered his own question. Someone is anticipating my every move.

Something leaped into his mind that he tried to push into the background. It went slithering into some hidden recess where he willed it to remain. He looked at his "possible suspects" list. Reid Lawson had moved out into the forefront and was in fact the only TMK employee who seemed to have ample opportunity to do everything that was required. But how did he know about Tompkins? Birdwell knew. Birdwell knew his every move in advance. But Birdwell had known nothing about the visit to Celia Progano, or about the late-night phone call that led him to the Japanese Garden.

Who else? Who else knows what I'm doing?

The slithering, slimy thing was back and he could not make it go away.

"Diane," he whispered. "She knows everything I've done, every person I've talked to. She knew, and then something happened to all of them." He pulled at his hair. What's wrong with me? How could I even think such a thing? he thought. But a voice he recognized as his own whispered in his ear: She knew. She knew about everything.

She couldn't kill anyone, he protested.

Of course not, said his voice. She only passes along the information to someone else. Between Diane and Birdwell, they know everything.

Reluctantly, acting as if powerless not to comply, he wrote her name at the top of a fresh sheet of paper and began to jot down what she knew and when she had learned it. When he finished, the list was longer than any other. He placed it on the table next to the other pages. Things were beginning to come into focus now. Things were becoming much clearer.

Fifty-nine

K.C. did not go to work or leave his apartment for two days. He spent his time working on his brother's notebook and adding information to the lists he had compiled. He cross-referenced material with long sweeping slashes of a red pen, but later when he went back to look at his work he was often unable to decipher the meaning of the marks he had made.

He ate frequently, but with little regard to the time of day. He had breakfast in the afternoon and dinner at three A.M. He slept late and stayed up until the early hours of the morning. Every waking moment was consumed by his search for that single breakthrough he was sure would bring the whole picture into sharp focus.

When the phone rang he was never certain whether or not he should answer. He would let it ring for a long time, then decide he had better answer it. But before he did it had stopped ringing. He had bought a new cordless phone for the bedroom and he brought it out into the living room so he could answer it the next time it rang without going through the agony of the decision, but when it rang he could only stare at it, as if it were some alien creature. So he covered it with a pillow to mute the insistent clamor.

For long periods—hours it seemed—he stared, mesmerized by the sheets of paper he had left spread out on his coffee table. Some of them were now splattered with coffee stains and food stains from the frozen dinners he consumed at regular intervals.

For hours he had methodically charted his progress from one name to the other—Progano, Gordon, Burns, Tompkins, Greenwood. He had asked himself the same question, over and over. Who knew what, and when did they know it?

At first he had tried to reject the malignant thoughts that exploded like flashbulbs in the recesses of his brain, but as he scanned the pages, the terrible thought reappeared at the forefront of his conscious thought.

Once, as if to reject the idea, he swept the papers from the table and flung them to the floor. But as he sat there, trying to make his mind a blank, trying to start the thought process all over again with a different angle of attack, perhaps some new perspective that would lead him to other suspects, the thought was back again, clinging like a leech to that part of his brain he could not control.

He picked up the papers and sat staring, organizing, calculating. No matter which way he put it together or framed the question, the answer was always the same. It had to be the CIA. The CIA, with the help of Diane. The CIA had more to gain than anyone else by the deaths of Progano and Tompkins and the disappearance of Burns. Birdwell was in this up to his eyeballs, sending K.C. to find information for him and then eliminating those who seemed most threatening.

"Dammit!" he yelled aloud. "I'm being used."

And what about Diane? She was the only one who knew each of his steps and could use that knowledge to thwart his every move. She had even started her own investigation—interviewing Nichols at the TMK party, then seeing him again later. He remembered how they had been at the party, looking back at him from across the room and laughing together as if at some private joke that he was not a part of. Was Nichols a part of it too? As project director he had as much inside information about Prometheus as anyone.

What about me? he thought. Am I next on the list? At the moment that thought crossed his mind, there was a sharp rap on the door. He recoiled as if from the sound of a gunshot.

Cautiously he went to the door. "Who is it?"

"It's me, Diane."

He backed away from the door, his mind racing.

"Hey," she called, "you gonna let me in?"

He peeked through the drawn blinds to see if she was alone, then took several deep breaths to calm himself before opening the door.

Her face fell when she saw him. He was disheveled and unshaven. "You sick?" she asked as she entered.

He shook his head. "I was taking a nap."

She looked at him closely. "You been drinking?"

"No," he said, then, as her eyes found the vodka bottle on the table he quickly added, "Just a few to steady my nerves."

"You look awful," she said, coming forward to touch his forehead.

He shrank back and she stopped. "What is it? What's wrong?"

He laughed a shrill childish giggle. "Nothing. What are you talking about? What could be wrong?"

Her eyes never left his face. Her brow was furrowed in a frown. "You," she said softly. "That's what's wrong. Look at you. You look like something the cat dragged in. And you've been acting very strange lately."

He was calmer now, more in control. "Don't be silly. I'm fine. I'm just tired, that's all." He smiled and motioned to the couch. "Sit down," he said before remembering the pages on the coffee table. His heart skipped a beat, but he resisted the impulse to rush over and scoop them up. Instead, with what he imagined was infinite calm, he moved slowly to the table, shuffled the pages into a single pile, and picked them up. He was really in control again.

She saw him. "More notes?"

"No. Nothing important."

"Can I see them?"

"It's nothing," he said, then repeated himself. "Nothing."

Her gaze slipped from his face to the floor, and her shoulders slumped. "I think we should talk," she said.

"About what?" he said, trying to keep it light.

"You know about what," she said from the couch. "The way you act. The way you keep things from me."

"What are you talking about?"

She pointed to the pages in his hands. "Things," she said.

He looked away and said nothing.

"You can't shut me out. At first I thought that after a

while you'd trust me—you'd see that I was on your side—but you've gotten more secretive every day. The more I want to help, the more you hold back. Can't you tell I want to help you? Can't you see that this is as important to me as it is to you?"

He smiled knowingly. "But for different reasons."

She nodded, thinking that he meant it was only as a journalist that she was interested. "That's true," she said, "but it's more important to me to help you now." She shook her head sadly. "I can see what this is doing to you. I want to help you end it. But I can't help you unless you trust me."

He was silent.

"Do you trust me?" she asked.

"Of course," he said without conviction.

"Then let me see your brother's notebook. Let me see the papers you have in your hand."

He considered for a moment, his eyes searching for the door as if he might flee. Then, with a shrug, he handed her the papers. "There's nothing new here," he said. "You know all this."

He watched her carefully as she leafed through each page, her eyebrows raising as she got to the page with her name on it. He waited for the look of guilt, the acceptance of defeat, but instead her expression changed to puzzlement as she followed the red pen marks that encircled her name and the lines that led to each other name on the list.

She held out the page. "What does this mean?" She acted genuinely puzzled.

K.C. wasn't fooled for a moment. His face was frozen, his voice cold. "I think you know what it means."

Her eyes narrowed. "I don't understand what—" She caught herself in mid-sentence and then began to speak very deliberately. "You don't think I had anything to do with this?"

He sat, stonily silent.

Her voice was a choked cry. "K.C., what's gotten into you? You're acting like"—she stopped herself and the thought came to her in a flash—"like your brother."

He jumped up, roaring at her. "Don't you mention my brother." He backed away, knocking the bottle off the table.

She thought he was close to hysteria. "You need help," she said gently. "Let me help you."

He laughed. "Sure, like you helped the others. Is that

what you meant when you said you wanted to help me **end** it?"

She sighed. "I'm leaving now, but I want you to promise me you won't drink anymore. Get some sleep. You look very tired. I'll call you tomorrow and maybe you'll feel better. We can talk."

"We have nothing to talk about. By this time tomorrow I'll be out of this place. Someplace where no one will find me."

Diane nodded. "That's what I think you should do," she said, moving to the door. "But get some sleep. You look exhausted. Things will look different after you've had some rest." She opened the door and stepped outside.

As she turned to leave he felt a rising sense of panic. He wanted to say something. He tried to tell her to stay, but something stopped him and he said nothing.

After she closed the door K.C. slumped back onto the couch in exhaustion. He felt grimy and sweaty and had the taste of bile in his mouth. He felt as if he had not slept for days, but he knew he still could not sleep. If I could only rest, he thought, putting his head back and closing his eyes. In seconds he was asleep, a sleep in which he dreamed that someone was chasing him. He was running, but ever so slowly, and he could feel hot breath on the back of his neck.

He heard a noise. A distinct click and he was instantly awake. It was dark. He must have slept for several hours. With no lights on and the shades drawn, the apartment was in complete darkness. He sat up and heard the noise again. It was metal against metal. A key in the door! He jumped up, his heart pounding. Someone was using a key on his door. He moved forward to turn the deadbolt before the intruder could enter, but before he could he heard the key turn and the door slowly began to open. A shaft of light slashed across the room, just missing him. He jumped back and tripped over the coffee table and landed heavily on his back.

K.C. raised himself up onto his elbows and squinted at the figures silhouetted in the doorway. There were at least four of them. He recognized instantly the massive bulk of George Stamatelos. Next to him was a man K.C. had never seen before, and in front of both men, the key still in her hand, was Diane Rollins. He knew they had come to kill him, but it wasn't the knowledge of his own death that made him scream. Next to Diane Rollins stood Carol Hardwick.

385

The lights went on, hurting his eyes, and the door closed. K.C., eyes wide as saucers, his gaze fixed on Carol, tried to worm his way backward, away from the intruders.

"Not you," he said over and over to Carol. "Not you."

"Don't be afraid," Carol said. "We're here to help you."

K.C. wondered how she had been able to fool him for all those years and why she was crying now.

He tried to scramble to his feet but Stamatelos was on him in a flash, pinning his arms to his sides and holding him down on the floor. K.C. struggled to move, his legs thrashing about wildly, but Stamatelos held him as easily as he might an infant.

"These are friends of mine," Diane said reassuringly. "You must let us help you."

The other man stepped forward, a hypodermic syringe in his hand. "This will relax you," he said, and as K.C. opened his mouth to scream, Stamatelos clamped a beefy palm across his face and stifled the attempt.

Struggling desperately, K.C. felt the sharp prick of the needle. His eyes bulged wildly as he saw the solution injected into his arm. He thrashed about for a few more minutes while Stamatelos held him and the others stood back and watched.

Carol cried softly into a handkerchief, but Diane had a look of grim determination about her. When K.C.'s struggles had ceased and he lay quietly on the floor she said simply, "Take him. I'll follow in my car."

Stamatelos lifted K.C. easily and he and the other men moved to the door. Diane turned to Carol, who seemed hesitant of what to do next, and said, "I'll need your help to search this place. I want Gordon's notebook."

Carol nodded numbly and the two began to go through drawers and look in closets.

Diane found it in K.C.'s bedside table drawer and Carol recognized it immediately. Carol nodded when Diane held it up with a look of triumph. They leafed through the pages together. "I'll need your help with this," Diane said.

Carol nodded. "But not here," she said. "I don't want to be here anymore."

Sixty

The later entries in the notebook made little sense to Diane or to Carol. It was like trying to decipher a secret code without clues of any kind. The early entries were reasonably clear and they had no trouble determining that Gordon had begun a systematic check of one of those he had suspected at TMK. The method was, for Gordon, typically systematic. He had listed each person with an opportunity for espionage, and then, by listing limiting factors, he had gradually eliminated one suspect after another.

Reid Lawson's name was mentioned frequently. Carol sighed and shook her head. "Poor Gordon," she said, "he despised Reid so much that he even saw him as a suspect in this."

Diane kept her thoughts to herself.

They were able to trace the path of Gordon Hardwick's continuing mental deterioration as the notes went from clear, to jumbled, to indecipherable. Carol winced at the pages where Gordon had slashed at Reid Lawson's name with a red pen, sensing the violence Gordon had brought to the task.

"Look at these," Diane said and read aloud. " 'Talk with Birdman.' " She looked at Carol. "Who do you think he meant?"

Carol shrugged. "Birdwell maybe."

"What about this? 'Lieutenant MacDonald, YYZPD.' "

Carol shook her head. "I don't know any Lieutenant MacDonald."

"YYZPD? Does that mean anything to you?"

"Nothing."

"Must be some kind of code or shorthand or something," said Diane.

"Wait a minute," Carol said. "Gordon used some kind of

personal shorthand. One of the things he did was to use airline abbreviations for cities."

"Huh?"

"YYZ is the abbreviation for Toronto."

Diane still wasn't sure. "What about PD?"

"Police Department. See Lieutenant MacDonald of the Toronto Police Department."

Diane was at the phone in a flash, and in minutes had the number of the Toronto Police Department from the information operator. She looked at Carol as she began dialing. "It's worth a try."

The ring was answered almost immediately. "Toronto Police Department, this is Officer Tilton. May I help you."

"Yes, please. I'm trying to locate a Lieutenant MacDonald of your department. I'm calling from California."

The policeman on the other end did not seemed impressed. "In reference to what, ma'am?"

"I'm a reporter. I would like to talk to him about an article I'm doing for the San Jose *News*. It's about an old case of his."

"One moment, please," said the voice and there was a long pause as she was put on hold. The voice was back. "Sorry, we have no Lieutenant MacDonald with the department."

"Oh," Diane said, her disappointment obvious, and the cool voice at the other end seemed to melt a little.

"Is it possible that this Lieutenant MacDonald might no longer be with the Toronto Police Department?"

"I'm not sure," Diane said. "It's possible."

"In that case you might try the Retirement and Pension Department." He gave her the number.

"Thanks," said Diane. "I'll give that a try."

She hit paydirt immediately. There was a Lieutenant Frank MacDonald, who had worked for the Toronto Police Department for twenty-five years and had retired in 1982. In minutes she had his number and was placing a call to MacDonald, who now lived in Montreal.

Frank MacDonald answered the phone on the second ring. "Hello."

"Frank MacDonald?"

He did not recognize the voice and was immediately wary. Cops—even former cops—do not like calls from strangers. "Who is this?"

Diane explained that she was an American newspaper reporter working on a story about the Ameronics Corporation and its executives.

"I'm not sure what that has to do with me."

"I'm not sure either, Mr. MacDonald, but your name was given to me by someone who thought you might know something that I can use in my story."

"And who might that be?"

"Who?"

"The 'someone' who gave you my name."

"Oh . . ." Diane stalled for a minute, then decided to be truthful. "He's dead."

"Dead men have names," MacDonald said warily.

Diane looked apologetically at Carol and said, "Hardwick. Gordon Hardwick."

MacDonald was silent for what seemed to be a long time. "Hardwick is dead?"

"Yes."

"How?"

"Possibly murdered."

"Possibly?"

"It was reported as a suicide."

She heard MacDonald let loose a slow exhalation of air like a slowly leaking balloon.

"Mr. MacDonald," said Diane, "Gordon Hardwick thought you knew something, didn't he?"

MacDonald made a clucking noise with his tongue. "I don't like talking on the phone, young lady. I can't see your face. I don't know who you are."

"Gordon Hardwick's wife is here with me now," she said.

She could almost see his shrug of indifference. "That means nothing to me. I must say good-bye now."

"Wait," said Diane, thinking quickly. "If I fly out to Montreal tonight, will you see me—talk to me?"

He was thinking. "I suppose I could meet with you tomorrow."

"I'll call you as soon as I arrive," said Diane. "We'll arrange where we can meet."

"Very well," said MacDonald, "I'll wait for your call."

Diane hung up and turned to Carol with triumph in her eyes. "He knows something," she said.

Carol shook her head, her voice filled with uncertainty. "You're going all the way to Montreal to talk with him?"

"Yes. Check on K.C. for me. I've got to get ready to leave as soon as I can get a flight." She saw the worried look on Carol's face. "I'll be back tomorrow," she said. "And I've got a feeling that I'll have all the answers."

After Carol left, Diane flopped down on the bed. She was alone—completely alone. She could not rid herself of the image of K.C. sprawled on the floor screaming at her. K.C. was useless and would be for some time. She couldn't confide in Carol that Reid Lawson was her top suspect. Carol would laugh in her face.

She had never felt so alone in all her life.

She sat up. Nichols! He had said he would be glad to help in any way that he could. Would he still be willing if he knew she was after Reid Lawson? Nichols would be the perfect person to help her. He could check out Lawson's activities without arousing suspicion. But would he?

It was worth a try.

She called but had to leave a message on his answering machine. She then called and made a reservation on a flight to Montreal for that evening and started to pack some things in a small travel bag.

The phone rang. It was Nichols returning her call.

"It was nice to hear your voice on my machine," he said.

She knew he was flirting. That was good, she thought. She could use that. "I need your help, Ted."

"You name it," he said breezily.

"When I name it you might not be so anxious to get involved."

"Try me," he said.

"It involves Reid Lawson."

"So far I'm still anxious," he said.

"I'm trying to get some information on him that—if true—could be very damaging."

He hesitated. "Look," he said. "Lawson is not my favorite guy in the whole world, but I don't want to dig up dirt and ruin somebody's career just for a newspaper article."

"I understand that," said Diane. "But this isn't about a newspaper article. This is about theft of high technology. And it may be about murder."

She heard him whistle. "What can I do?"

"I'm on my way to the airport," she said. "I'd like to stop by and talk with you. I'd like you to double-check some information for me."

"Okay."

"I can be there in about an hour."

"I'll be waiting."

She handed him the printout sheets that listed Reid Lawson's business expenses. His eyes narrowed when he saw what it was.

"Where did you get these?" he asked; then before she could answer, it came to him. He said, "Collins. He tapped into the files and got this didn't he?"

"That's not important. What is important is that you take a look at Lawson's expenses in San Diego on June thirteenth through twentieth and in Seattle two weeks ago."

He leafed through the pages, stopping briefly at each one.

"Notice the blanks?" Diane asked.

He looked again and nodded.

"Those blanks represent gaps in time. Gaps when we don't know where he was."

Nichols was looking carefully at the list. "I see that," he said.

"Did you notice the dates?" she asked and then went on before he could answer. "He was 'missing' on the day that Gordon Hardwick was killed and on the day that Carl Burns escaped from prison."

"And you think he murdered Hardwick? Helped Burns escape?"

Diane shrugged. "That's why I want your help."

"Why not Collins? He got these for you."

"I'm afraid he can't help. He's in the hospital right now under doctor's care."

"What's wrong with him?"

"He seems to have suffered some sort of nervous breakdown."

"And that's why you need me."

She was honest. "Yes."

He smiled. "And I was hoping it was my charm."

"Will you help me?"

He was shaking his head. "But the whole thing doesn't make any sense. Why would he do it? What's his motivation?"

"I have Gordon Hardwick's notebook," said Diane. "He felt that the Russians had infiltrated the U.S. computer industry by getting people inside while the industry was still in its infancy. Have you ever heard of a 'sleeper,' or an 'illegal'? Those are agents who are infiltrated into a country years in advance of any conflict. When the conflict comes, the agents are well-entrenched and often in a position to do great harm."

Nichols seemed surprised at her knowledge. "Where do you get such ideas?" he said.

Diane grinned. "Research," she said, but then the grin was gone. "The point is that Gordon Hardwick thought someone—and he suspected Reid Lawson—had infiltrated TMK."

"Reid Lawson a Russian agent? C'mon," he said with disbelief. "I know Lawson. I can believe lots of things about him. Maybe he'd sell his grandmother for a buck—make that a million bucks. Maybe he'd sell secrets to the Russians if the price was right. But I doubt that he's a Russian agent. And I won't believe that he's a murderer."

"You could help prove that he is—or he isn't," said Diane.

"I'm listening."

Diane checked her watch. She still had a plane to catch. "For some time now," she said, "there has been a series of unusual incidents happening to people who work at TMK. No one ever put them together before—other than as a series of bizarre coincidences caused perhaps by the high incidence of stress in the high-tech life-style."

"But that's changed now?"

"Gordon Hardwick's idea was to put the whole sequence of events into one chronological pattern and determine which if any of the events was linked to any of the others and who might possibly have had the opportunity to be involved in some or all of the incidents."

Nichols looked doubtful. "Sounds rather circumstantial to me."

"Yes, it is, but it begins to point to certain people."

"And Lawson is one of the people it points to?"

"Yes. Kevin and I have added to Gordon Hardwick's list the other incidents—including Hardwick's death—that have occurred since then."

Nichols nodded. "It's logical, I suppose. Find the man with the opportunity and then find the motivation later."

"Exactly."

"What do you want me to do?"

Diane's face brightened. "I'd like you to check out Lawson's other trips during these times." She gave him a short list. "I want to know if there is any logical reason for the gaps that appear in those expense records."

Nichols took the list and looked at it carefully. "Okay," he said. "I'll do it, but I want you to know that I think you're wrong about Lawson."

"Then prove I'm wrong," Diane said. "I can link him circumstantially to most of the items on that list. You can either find something that tells us he's completely innocent, or find something that implicates him even more."

"You think I'll find something to incriminate him?"

"I don't know, but I'll tell you what I think. I think he took those business trips to set up alibis for what happened while he was away." She smiled. "But it's those alibis that are going to trip him up."

"I'll do what I can," said Nichols.

"That's great," said Diane, smiling in relief. With K.C. out of commission she had felt a great burden on her shoulders. Now she had someone to share that burden, someone to help her, someone, at least, to talk to. "I'll check with you when I get back from Montreal."

"What are you looking for in Montreal?"

She thought for a minute. "I haven't the slightest idea," she said. "I hope I'll have something to tell you when I get back."

Sixty-one

"It was a long time ago," said Frank MacDonald.

Diane looked up from her salad. "But," she said with a quick smile, "you remember all of the details."

Her smile was contagious. "Yes," said MacDonald. "I remember all the details."

She was curious. "What makes you remember so much about this particular case?"

"It's not just this particular case." He glanced away with a sheepish smile. "When I retired from the police force"—he thought for a moment, his eyes raised to the ceiling—"five years ago—I thought that I could write a book about some of the more interesting cases and live happily ever after on my royalties."

"And?"

"Turns out I was the only one who seemed to think my cases were so interesting." He shook his head a little and spooned absently at his soup.

They were sitting in a restaurant atop one of the highest buildings in Montreal. To the left, the view encompassed the old city, which stretched out below them and all the way to the St. Lawrence River. On the other side of the restaurant the diners could look out on Mont Royal Park where the ski lifts swung idly in the summer breeze.

Frank MacDonald was in his late fifties, rough-hewn, with a red face and clear blue eyes that rarely blinked. He had been a detective with the Toronto Police Department and now worked as a security coordinator for a large shopping complex in the heart of Montreal.

Diane watched him pick at his food. Even after all these years he still seemed troubled by what he was remembering.

As if he had read her thoughts, he looked at her and,

explaining his mood, said, "No one likes to be reminded of failure.'

"No one is accusing you of failure," she said.

He laughed without warmth. I'm accusing myself."

"Tell me about this case you and Gordon Hardwick talked about. Tell me why it still bothers you so much."

"Loose ends, loose ends."

She waited, letting him prepare himself.

"Gordon Hardwick contacted me several months ago," he said. "He was interested in a case that I investigated about fifteen years ago. It involved a boy—a young American—who came to Canada to evade the draft." He looked out the windows to Mont Royal only a few miles away. "The boy's name was Tolbert—Robert Tolbert—and he was found hanging in his apartment one night in 1972."

"Tolbert?" asked Diane. "Michael Tolbert's son?"

MacDonald nodded. "Of the Ameronics Corporation."

"But why was Gordon Hardwick interested in this case?"

MacDonald raised his eyebrows. "I'm not sure. I can only tell you what I would have told him."

Diane nodded and waited for MacDonald to proceed.

Finally he did. "The official line is that the boy killed himself. Hanged himself from a water pipe in his basement apartment. Supposedly driven to distraction by constant harassment by the FBI or the CIA."

"But you don't believe that?"

MacDonald smiled. "At the height of the Vietnam war we had several thousand American kids living in Canada to avoid the draft. We had several hundred living in Toronto. They were a ragtag bunch. Mostly rich kids whose parents could afford to support them while they waited out the war. We never had one single documented case of actual harassment by any agency of the U.S. government. Sure we had kids who thought their phones were tapped or that they were being followed, but we never found any of that to be true. Why would they pick out this one kid to harass? It doesn't make sense."

"Did he leave a suicide note?"

MacDonald nodded. "What we found was a letter to his father which claimed he was being harassed and stating that he could no longer stand the pressure." He paused. "Some said it was a suicide note. Others that it was a plea for help."

"What did you think?"

"It's hard to say what a person will do in that frame of mind, but in my experience most suicide notes are more specific as to intent." He shook his head and moved his hands in small circles. "You know, 'I can't take this anymore so I've decided to end it all.' Tolbert's note had the first part but not the last."

"So that's why you doubt that it was a suicide?"

"That's part of it. But only part."

Diane nodded. "Tell me," she said.

"Most people who try to kill themselves—at least those who try hanging—change their mind at some point. They discover—for whatever reason—that this is not exactly what they had in mind—it hurts too much. They start to struggle—to fight to stay alive."

"And there was no sign of a struggle?"

"On the contrary. The medical examiner's report was consistent with the fact that he did struggle." He put his fingers to his neck. "Wide pattern burns around the neck rather than the narrow rope-width pattern consistent with lack of struggle. Bruises and contusions on the neck consistent with violent motion. He thrashed around a lot before he died."

"Okay," said Diane. "So he changed his mind—he struggled—that doesn't prove it wasn't suicide."

"You're right," said MacDonald, "but there are several things about this death that have always troubled me."

He paused, watching her reactions to his story, and Diane waited for him to begin again.

"What do you do, Miss Rollins, if you find yourself hanging by the neck from a rope, several inches above the ground, and you decide you'd really rather die in bed of old age?"

Diane thought for a moment. "I don't know. I guess maybe I'd grab at the rope."

MacDonald beamed. "Exactly. You'd reach up and pull at that rope, trying to relieve the suffocating weight that was choking you. Maybe you'd succeed for a moment, then your own weight would pull you down again. Desperately—because you are getting weaker now—you'd raise yourself up again. You'd try to reach up with one hand for the pipe over your head, but when you let go of the rope with one hand you'd drop down again, choking." MacDonald was acting out the scene now. "You might even begin to claw at your throat, desperately trying to pry the rope from your windpipe."

Diane pushed her lunch away. "Why are you telling me this?"

"Because it didn't happen. There were no rope burns or rope fibers on his hands, no scratch marks on his neck, no skin or blood in his fingernails."

"Maybe he didn't struggle."

"The rope burns on his neck tell us he did."

"Maybe he didn't use his hands."

"Picture it," said MacDonald. "He is dangling there, thrashing furiously, only moments to live—with his hands by his sides? Never doing the one thing—the only thing—that could save him. How do you account for that?"

Diane swallowed. "His hands were tied?" Her eyes narrowed. "Any rope marks on the wrists?"

"Good point. I checked around the apartment for something to tie someone with that wouldn't leave burns."

"And?"

"One of his sheets had been torn. A three- or four-inch strip had been torn from one end. Certainly long enough to tie his hands together behind his back."

"But how could somebody do all this and no one hear any struggle—any noise?"

"There were also traces of a gum resin around his mouth."

"Gum resin?"

"As if someone had stuck adhesive tape of some kind over his mouth."

Diane looked doubtful. "I don't know. It seems very involved—kind of farfetched."

"There's more," said MacDonald.

Diane swallowed and rubbed her neck. Her throat was constricted, as if she could feel the rope. "Go ahead," she said.

MacDonald smiled. "Okay, Miss Rollins. You've decided to hang yourself. You put a rope around your neck, throw it over a pipe, get up on a chair, and step off. What happens?"

Diane looked puzzled. "What?"

"You land on the floor. The rope has to be tied to something solid. In this case it was tied around the leg of a heavy dresser. The back of that leg was worn away by the rope." He paused to indicate that there was some significance to that fact.

"I'm not following you," Diane said.

"Two days after Tolbert's death, I went back to that apartment with 150 pounds of weights, a canvas sack, and the same type of rope used in the hanging. I tied a knot around the other leg of the dresser—the same knot used in the suicide—threw the rope over the same pipe, filled the bag with the weights—Tolbert weighed around 150 pounds—attached the bag to the rope, and sat it on a chair." He paused, waiting for Diane to comment.

She did. "And?"

"I pulled the chair away and let the bag drop to within inches of the floor." He grinned at her discomfort. "There were no comparable marks on the leg of the dresser. The rope barely left any trace."

"The struggle," said Diane quickly. "Perhaps—"

MacDonald anticipated her question. "I pushed the bag around. Let it swing in a wide arc. Picked it up and dropped it several times. I did this for at least five minutes."

"And there were no marks?"

"Nothing of significance. Certainly nothing like the original marks on the other leg."

"That's interesting, but I'm not sure what it proves."

"I'm not finished yet," said MacDonald. He was enjoying this. It was a story that no one had wanted to hear almost fifteen years ago and he was glad to be able to tell it now. "I untied the knot and let the sack lie on the floor, then I wrapped the rope around the back of the leg of the dresser, then pulled on the rope and hoisted the bag into the air. Guess what?"

"The markings were the same."

"Bingo."

"You think that someone lifted him—hoisted him—into the air?"

"The physical evidence was consistent with that fact."

"Then why was it written off as a suicide?"

"Loose ends," said MacDonald. "There was nothing else to go on, no motive, no suspect, no other rationalization for his death. It looked like a suicide, so it was easier to call it that and close the case."

"What do you think happened?"

MacDonald reflected a moment. "Someone got him drunk or stoned—there were high levels of alcohol and drugs in his system. Or maybe they found him passed out—I don't know.

They tied his hands behind his back with cloth torn from a sheet—maybe bound his ankles together too. They covered his mouth with adhesive tape in case he woke up before they were finished, then put the rope around his neck and hoisted him up. At some point during all of this he woke up and started thrashing around." MacDonald rapped the table with his knuckles. "But by then it was too late. He was helpless. Afterward this person or persons untied the hands and feet and removed the tape, then left him hanging."

"This person—any ideas?"

MacDonald shook his head and looked away. "No one," he said in a soft voice.

There was something about his attitude that led Diane not to believe him. "No one?" she asked.

"When you're a cop and you don't have any suspects, you grasp at straws. At the top of a short list you put the name of the person who finds the body."

Diane gave him a doubtful look.

MacDonald shrugged. "It happens. Someone kills someone, then waits for someone else to discover the body. When it is still undiscovered he gets nervous and goes back to find out what's what."

"Do you remember who found the body?"

MacDonald gave her a worried look. "You wouldn't print the name?"

"No. I just wondered."

"Former roommate of Tolbert's. Name was Lawson."

"Reid Lawson?"

MacDonald smiled. "Now you know why Gordon Hardwick wanted to talk to me."

Diane felt light-headed, as if she were not getting enough air. She struggled to maintain her composure.

"Other than the fact that he found the body," she asked, "was there anything else that made you suspect Lawson?"

MacDonald thought for a moment and then made a gesture of dismissal. "Not really. Nothing you could pin your hat on. He said he had called Tolbert for a couple of days and got no answer so he went over to the apartment and got the landlord to let him in. They found Tolbert."

"But you were never able to substantiate your suspicions?"

He shook his head. "Never. I could never establish a convincing motive."

"But?" asked Diane. There had been an unspoken "but" in MacDonald's tone.

"I asked why they didn't room together anymore and Lawson said they had quarreled over the fact that Tolbert kept wanting to move all the time to stay ahead of the FBI. Their landlord said that they'd had a real brawl before Tolbert moved out. He'd threatened to call the cops on them. Lawson, by the way, was the only one who could corroborate Tolbert's claim that he was being harassed by the FBI. He said Tolbert would get calls at all hours of the night. Someone would tell him they were going to catch up with him. He also said that Tolbert had grown increasingly paranoid and was impossible to live with."

Somewhere in the back of Diane's brain a small alarm went off. "Paranoid?" she asked.

MacDonald went on as if he had not heard or did not think it important. "I thought that maybe it was a drug-related falling-out but couldn't prove anything. There was a small amount of marijuana in Tolbert's apartment, but not more than you'd call a personal supply. We did believe, however, that Tolbert at least was into heavier drugs than booze and pot."

"Why do you say that? Did anyone check the body for any specific drug content? Anything other than alcohol or marijuana?"

"Well, as I said, the M.E. said there was enough alcohol and marijuana in him to tranquilize an elephant. If I recall, there were minute traces of some other unspecified drugs in his system. Compared to the levels of the others it wasn't considered a contributing factor, but merely indicative of prior usage."

Diane shook her head, trying to put it all together. MacDonald smiled. He had done the same thing many times over the past fifteen years.

"Anything else?" Diane asked.

"Only that none of his friends admitted to visiting him at his new apartment. They mostly verified Lawson's story about his strange behavior. The landlord, however, claimed to have seen at least one of his friends leaving the apartment several times—once perhaps on the night he died—but then it might have been the night before he died."

"Any description?"

"Yes. Army fatigue jacket, long hair, and a beard." Mac-

Donald laughed. "That description fit half the Americans in Canada at the time."

"So that's it then," said Diane. "Case closed."

"Not to me," said MacDonald. "I still dabble. One of these days maybe"—his voice trailed off and he smiled—"but I doubt it."

Sixty-two

It was like coming to the surface after being submerged without air for a long time. K.C. felt himself struggling, trying to hold his breath for just one more second—then another. Desperately trying to hold on until his head broke the surface. Above him, the eerily diffused light of the sun on the surface was tantalizingly close, devastatingly far. He couldn't make it. It was too far. His lungs were bursting. He gave up—surrendered—and took in a deep breath, feeling the acrid taste of salt water bite at his nostrils and his lungs.

He sat up, gasping for air. It was dark. He looked around. He was in a bed in what appeared to be a hospital room. He moved and felt a tugging at his right arm, and found that he was attached to an intravenous tube.

Memories came rushing back—Diane standing over him, the light behind her casting an eerie halo around her head; Stamatelos's arms around his chest, crushing the breath from him; a stranger, silent and menacing, holding what in his recollection was a gigantic needle; and Carol, watching as all this happened to him.

He had to get away before they came back for him.

He ripped the intravenous needle from his arm, almost whining in pain as he stripped away the adhesive tape that held the needle in place. The rails were up on both sides of the bed and he had to lift himself up and climb over the side. As he did, the room began to spin a little—just enough to make him lose his balance—and he tumbled over the side to land heavily on the floor. He thumped against a metal cabinet next to the bed and a water pitcher and ice bucket came crashing down beside him.

Dazed, K.C. struggled to all fours just as the door opened and two nurses entered.

"Are you all right, Mr. Hardwick?" asked one.

He mumbled a reply.

They helped him to his feet and one lowered the side rail as the other maneuvered him back into bed.

"I'll get an orderly to clean up the mess," said one and disappeared.

K.C. lay back heavily, gasping for air.

The remaining nurse tut-tutted as she reinserted his intravenous needle. "If you need anything you should buzz us," she said. "You're not ready to be up and around yet."

"Why am I here?" he asked.

She smiled. "You'll have to speak to the doctor about that. Our instructions are to keep you in bed and keep you comfortable."

"When do I see the doctor?"

She wiped the perspiration from his face. "The doctor will be here at seven-thirty." She gave him a wry look. "It's only four A.M. You should be sleeping."

K.C. looked at the needle in his arm. "What's this?"

"Just some dextrose. You haven't eaten for two days."

He tried to sit up but could only make it halfway. "Two days? I've been here for two days?"

The nurse pushed him back down. "Don't worry, you'll be just fine." She turned to leave.

"Where am I?" he asked. "Where is this place?"

"You're in Sunnyvale. This is a private clinic for drug and alcohol abuse. You were brought here by friends who care about you." She was gone.

"Friends who care," said K.C. in a whisper, but he was not sure of anything anymore.

He was asleep when the doctor entered the room at a little past eight. K.C. felt someone checking his pulse and opened his eyes to see the man who had administered the hypodermic in his apartment. K.C. pulled his arm away.

The doctor smiled. "I understand you've been up and around a little bit this morning."

402

"Why am I here?" said K.C., ignoring the doctor's conversational banter.

"I'm Dr. Quist. I'm a friend of Diane Rollins."

"That doesn't answer my question."

"Diane was worried about you. She and your sister-in-law were afraid that you might do harm to yourself. She explained the circumstances to me—about your brother's death and your subsequent depression—and I agreed with her that you might be in need of the kind of help that we can provide here."

"Here? Where is here?"

"This is the Sunnyvale Private Clinic. We treat primarily teenagers and adults with drug or alcohol dependency problems." He smiled sadly. "Business is booming."

"I don't have any drug or alcohol problems."

"That's what most of those who come here say. We're trying to help you."

"By kidnapping me? By holding me here against my will?"

"Mr. Hardwick, we have no desire to keep you here against your will. You were brought here under what were considered to be emergency conditions. Even though your sister-in-law signed the admission papers you are not 'committed' to this institution. While I would recommend that you stay, you are free to leave at any time."

K.C.'s eyes narrowed. "I can leave at any time?"

Dr. Quist nodded, pointing to a closet door near the bed. "Your clothes are in there. I'll be glad to drop you back at your apartment when I leave."

"Do I have to leave with you?"

Quist smiled and shook his head. "I'll have a nurse bring in a telephone and you can call a taxi."

While K.C. tried to take all of this in, Quist picked up his things and prepared to leave.

"Where is Diane?" asked K.C.

Quist stopped at the door. "I think she's in Montreal."

K.C. was absolutely bewildered. "Montreal," he whispered.

"She said she would explain everything to you when she got back."

K.C. struggled to sit up. "I've got to get out of here," he said, but again the room was moving beneath him.

"If you do leave," said Quist, "you should stay in bed fo a few days at least and someone should stay with you."

K.C. flopped back on his pillow. "What's wrong wit me?"

"I told you," said Dr. Quist with a nod of his head. "Th is a drug treatment center."

"I don't do drugs," said K.C. emphatically.

"Denial is fairly common."

"I'm telling you the truth."

Quist came back to the bed, looking at his clipboard "Ever do LSD?"

"Never!"

"Not even in college?"

"Never. Never touched the stuff."

Quist was tracing his finger across a page on the clip board. "We found a minuscule quantity in your blood sam ple. Maybe not enough to produce hallucinations but enoug certainly to produce a certain amount of mental confusion My opinion is that it is attributable to prior usage, but . . ."

"But what?"

"Diane told me she thought you were being poisoned."

"Poisoned?"

Quist nodded. "I didn't believe her. I thought you wer covering up some substance abuse and she was trying t rationalize your personality changes."

"But now?"

Quist seemed unsure. "There are some other thing here," he said, looking at the clipboard. "I'd like you to sta for at least today so that we can do some other tests."

K.C. started to protest.

"Your sister-in-law is coming to see you this afternoon," Quist said quickly. "If you feel up to it she can take yo home. How's that?"

K.C. was too weak to argue.

Carol was there when he woke up later. She was sittin in a chair next to his bed, reading a magazine, and at first sh didn't realize that he was awake. He was able to watch her fo a while before she noticed that his eyes were open.

"Hi," she said, her smile growing. "How are you feeling?"

"Like somebody's been using my head to hammer nails."

She squeezed his hand. "I was here earlier, but yo were sleeping, so I did some errands and came back."

"Thanks," he said. He did not return the squeeze.

She found it difficult to meet his eyes. "I'm sorry about" —she looked around the room—"about this."

"Me too."

"I don't know if you can understand. When Diane came and told me what was happening, it was like it was Gordon all over again."

"She thinks I'm being poisoned."

Carol nodded and covered her face with her hands. "And I keep thinking—what if this is what happened to Gordon?" Her eyes were wet. "If someone did this to him, then it wasn't his fault." Her face was tortured. "He needed me, K.C., needed me more than ever, and I wasn't there for him. I turned my back on him."

K.C. took her hands and pulled them away from her face. The tears were rolling down her cheeks. "It wasn't your fault, Carol. You couldn't have known."

"I know," she said. "But that doesn't help now."

He was silent. There was nothing he could say.

"I couldn't let that happen to you," she said. "That's why I agreed to go along with Diane."

"It's all right," he said, squeezing her hands in his. "I understand."

"She really loves you, you lucky stiff," said Carol.

He nodded.

"I'm not sure you deserve her," she said and then she was hugging him, getting big wet tears on his face.

The door opened and Dr. Quist entered. Carol looked up, embarrassed because of her tears. She wiped her eyes and blew her nose with a handkerchief.

"Is he okay?" she asked.

Quist sat at the foot of the bed. "We did some more testing this afternoon," he said to K.C. "Again we verified the minute traces of LSD that I reported to you before. We also found a very small amount of something else."

K.C. pulled himself to a sitting position. "What?"

"It appears to be atropine. Large amounts can be quite lethal. Small amounts can cause acute confusion, or hallucinations, or even a mental state similar to paranoid schizophrenia."

K.C. and Carol looked at each other.

"Atropine?" asked K.C. "What the hell is atropine?"

"It's an alkaloid derivative of the nightshade plants. It

has several medicinal uses, but unless used with caution it's a very potent poison."

K.C. shook his head in amazement. "But how does some one poison you without your knowing that it's being done?"

"Atropine is granular. It could be put in a sugar bowl or a salt shaker, or even a—"

K.C. closed his eyes. "Salt shaker," he moaned.

"However it was done," said Quist, "you've been taking fairly small doses on a regular basis—perhaps from some contamination at home. Now that you're here, you are returning to normal and there are other things we can do to speed up the process of eliminating these substances from your body."

"It's unbelievable," said Carol.

K.C. was shaking his head. "I should have known," he said. "I should have been able to realize what was happening."

"If this had continued," said Quist, "there's no telling what might have happened."

K.C. thought of Gordon and Progano. "I know," he said. "There would have been another suicide and everyone would have said I had been acting strangely for weeks. The police would have written it off as stress-related, and that would have been it."

"Who's doing this?" asked Carol.

K.C. couldn't look at her. "I don't know," he said, but he thought he did.

"Maybe you should call the police," said Dr. Quist.

"And say what? Somebody's been tampering with my salt shaker?"

Quist shrugged. "Anyway, you'd better be careful. Somebody is apparently trying to do you great harm. If it's true—as I suspect—that someone has been giving you small daily doses of something, then obviously you have to be careful of what you consume at home. It's probably already there—in your sugar bowl or salt shaker."

"But how—?" He cut himself off and was silent. Who had access to his apartment? Mentally he ran down the list: Diane had a key, so did Carol. He did not suspect them anymore, but if Carol had access, didn't that mean that Reid Lawson could easily use her key? He looked at Carol, but her open innocent face indicated that she suspected nothing.

K.C. nodded to Quist. "I'll get rid of everything." He shook his head in amazement. "Am I okay now?"

Quist made a face. He didn't seem sure. "There is no question you're improved. You may still suffer from an occasional bout with confusion or even residual paranoia for a while, and until your body manages to recuperate and rid itself of all contaminants, you're probably going to feel weak. I'd like to keep you here for a few more days . . ." Quist let his last remark hang like a question.

"I've got to get out of here, doc. I've got things to do."

Quist nodded, resigned to the inevitable. "I don't think you're going to be able to do as much as you think you are. Your body is in a weakened state and you'll need lots of rest." He looked at his clipboard. "I want you to call me every day for the next week or so."

K.C. pulled back the covers and swung his legs out. "Will do, doc," he said and stood up. He sat back down on the bed as his legs wobbled beneath him.

Carol saw the look on his face and rushed to assist him.

"I'm okay," he said, shrugging her hand away.

"Don't push yourself," Quist said. "You need rest." With a shake of his head, the doctor left the room, leaving K.C. sitting on the bed.

K.C. looked around. "I'll be fine in just a minute," he said.

Carol nodded encouragingly, but her face was flooded with doubt. She reached into her pocketbook. "Diane wanted you to have this," she said.

It was Gordon's notebook.

K.C. looked at it in puzzlement.

"After we . . . had you brought here, Diane and I searched your apartment looking for this."

She could tell by his expression that he wasn't pleased. He didn't say anything.

"She wants to help," said Carol. "You need someone to help."

He looked at the notebook and then at Carol.

"I could have helped you too," she said. "I know more about Gordon's notes than anybody." Her tone was accusatory. "But you never asked for my help."

He nodded and then slowly got to his feet. "You can help me now," he said, putting his arm around her shoulders.

"Okay," she said, holding him. "Let's get you dressed and out of here."

407

Sixty-three

K.C. slept for almost six hours when he got back to his apartment. Carol deposited him there, fussed over him a little bit, and made him promise to call her when he awoke.

"I'll bring you dinner," she said.

At ten P.M. he awoke with a start to the strange electronic ring of his new portable phone. At first he didn't even know what it was. Gradually it dawned on him that the phone was ringing, so he jumped up and keeled over as his legs buckled beneath him.

He managed to get to it before it stopped ringing. "Hello?"

It was Diane. "Why aren't you at the hospital?" she said, a trace of anger in her voice. "I called there and I couldn't believe they had let you out."

"I'm fine," he said.

"Fine! You were acting like a crazy man."

"I'm OK now," he said defensively.

Her tone turned soothing. "I'm worried about you. I thought you were safely tucked away at the clinic. I wish you had stayed there for a few more days."

"I'm fine, really."

Diane's voice was filled with uncertainty. "I'm not sure that you should be alone."

"So get over here and keep me company."

"I'm still in Montreal. I can't get a flight out until tomorrow."

"Montreal," he said. "What the hell are you doing in Montreal?"

"Gordon's notebook," she said. "Remember it said, see Lieutenant MacDonald, YYZPD?"

"Yes."

"YYZ is Toronto."

He was getting more confused by the minute. "I'll explain everything when I see you," she said.

"Did you find anything?" he insisted.

"Did I?" she said, laughing. "Hang onto your hat."

K.C. could almost see her grinning—feel her excitement. "Tell me," he said.

She told him about the meeting with MacDonald and the former policeman's description of the death of Robert Tolbert. K.C. listened without comment until she got to the part about Reid Lawson.

"Lawson?" he said.

"He was there," said Diane. "That's why Gordon was so interested." She had a note of triumph in her voice. "Everywhere we look, Lawson turns up."

K.C. was puzzled. "I still don't get the connection."

"Don't you see, Lawson was Robert Tolbert's friend. That's his in with Michael Tolbert and Ameronics. With Robert out of the way Reid Lawson has become the heir apparent. Tolbert trusts him like a son." Her excitement was contagious.

"And MacDonald thinks that Robert Tolbert was murdered?"

"He can't prove it but, yes, he's positive that Robert Tolbert was murdered. And," she said, emphasizing the word, "he suspects that Lawson was somehow involved."

"Murder," said K.C. in a whisper.

"Lawson and Tolbert were good friends. They went to Canada to beat the draft. For some reason they had a falling-out—their former landlord reported that they were constantly arguing. Before Tolbert left they'd had a fight. Tolbert moved out to another place—two weeks later he was dead."

K.C. whistled.

"And get this," Diane went on. "The reports say that in the few months before his supposed suicide, Robert Tolbert seemed to undergo a personality change. He became argumentative, nervous and quarrelsome, and"—she paused for effect—"he apparently exhibited paranoid behavior. He felt that the FBI and the CIA were after him as a draft evader, although there's no evidence to back that up. Why him, and not his roommate? It all starts to sound kind of familiar, doesn't it?"

"Yes," said K.C. "So Lawson kills Robert Tolbert and for

all intents and purposes takes his place with Robert's father and eventually with the company."

"Exactly."

"Which puts Lawson in a perfect position to deal technology to the Russians."

"With his position," said Diane, "he was perfectly capable of doing anything that had to be done."

Her voice lowered dramatically. "He's dangerous, K.C. If he is our man, he's capable of anything. Remember, someone knows who you are, someone's watching you, someone tried to poison you. I'm afraid for you."

"Don't worry, Lawson doesn't know we're on to him."

"Someone does," Diane said quietly.

He did not seem to grasp the import of what she said.

"Where do we go from here?" he asked.

Diane smiled, accepting the implicit acknowledgment of her involvement. "I want you to sit tight until I get there. Don't do anything. Don't talk to anyone." Her voice was filled with understanding. "You're not one hundred percent yet. Promise me you won't budge till I get there. We can fill in the missing pieces together."

"Why don't we just confront Lawson?"

"C'mon," she said. "This guy has been eluding suspicion for fifteen years. Everything we have is still only circumstantial. We want to have him nailed to the wall before we confront him."

He let that sink in. "I guess I'm still not thinking too well."

"You'll be fine soon." But he could detect the lack of conviction in her voice. "Just stay put and I'll call you as soon as I get in."

"I'll pick you up."

"No," she said, her impatience showing.

"I've got my car at the airport. Besides, on the way back I want to talk with Ted Nichols. I told him about the gaps in Lawson's hotel stays and he promised to check into it for me . . . for us."

He started to object, but fought the suspicious thoughts that leaped into his brain. Diane went right on as if he hadn't said anything. "I'll call you when I get to the airport, and then I'll come to your place. I want you to stay in bed . . . waiting for me."

"Okay," he said, then stammered a little. "I'm sorry about all that other stuff."

"It wasn't your fault," she said. "No more than it was Gordon's or Progano's or Robert Tolbert's."

He felt better. "I'll see you tomorrow."

"I love you," she said, and made kissing noises into the phone before she hung up.

He called Carol and told her he was fine and that Diane had called.

"I'll come over and bring you something to eat," she said.

"No," he insisted. "I'm not hungry. All I want to do is sleep."

"I'll come over tomorrow."

"Not too early."

"I'll bring lunch. How's that?"

"Fine." He paused for a minute so that she knew he wanted to ask something.

"What is it?"

"Is Reid there?"

She laughed. "No. Not tonight. Why?"

"Just wondered."

She was sympathetic. "I'll see him tomorrow. We're having dinner at his place." She had a bright idea. "Why don't you join us?"

The thought shocked him. "No thanks," he said quickly. "Diane will be back. We want to spend some time together."

Carol laughed. "Rest up," she said.

He hung up the phone. For a long time he could think of nothing else but Carol and Reid Lawson. He tried to purge his mind of such thoughts, knowing it could only upset him. Despite his effort, the picture of Carol in Lawson's arms would not fade.

Sixty-four

The next day was a long one for K.C. He was up early and although he was hungry he would not touch anything in the apartment that had already been opened. He settled for some orange juice from frozen concentrate. He took some cardboard boxes from his closet in the bedroom and threw in everything else from the refrigerator and kitchen cabinets that was not sealed or unopened. He carried it all down to the dumpster in the parking lot and threw it in. Tomorrow he would restock his supplies.

The small effort had exhausted him and he sat in front of the television for a while, too tired to get up and change the channel. He was tired, but he felt better. The strange doubts and suspicions that had gripped him had passed. He was amazed at some of the crazy things that he had imagined.

How could I have suspected Diane? he thought. Or Carol, or Nichols, or Birdwell? Birdwell! I should have called him. I should let him know we're closing in on Lawson.

He brought the portable phone from the bedroom and dialed Birdwell's office in San Francisco.

"Robert Birdwell, please," he said when a woman answered.

"Mr. Birdwell is not in the office right now. Can I take a message?"

"This is K.C. Hardwick. Do you expect him back soon?"

"I'm not sure," said the woman, "but I'm sure he'll call in soon. Why don't I have him get back to you."

"That's fine. He has my number."

K.C. hung up the phone. Where is he? he wondered. I need to talk to him.

Shortly after noon Carol arrived. She had brought a huge chef's salad and they had lunch together. All through the meal Carol chatted away aimlessly, as if afraid that the lunch-time conversation would turn serious. K.C. listened to her inane chatter, but most of the time he was thinking about his sister-in-law and Reid Lawson. What did she see in him? It was obvious—at least to K.C.—that Lawson had used Carol. Used her to get to Gordon. It came to him in a flash that Lawson had probably used her to get to *him*, too. He felt his anger rising as he realized that Carol was the reason Lawson had been one step ahead of him all along. It was very simple. Carol knew everything K.C. was up to. Wasn't it logical that whatever she knew, Lawson knew also?

He struggled to keep the anger from his face. Carol no doubt had been foolish to tell Lawson everything, but hadn't she been the one who had tried to discourage K.C. in the first place? It had never been important to her.

That bastard Lawson. He had taken Gordon's wife and then his life, and just as he had probably known at every step what Gordon was up to, so too did he know what K.C. was doing. He fought back the small flicker of doubt about Carol that threatened to burst into flame. What was it Dr. Quist had called it? Residual paranoia? If he were going to be at all effective he would have to guard against any kind of relapse. Carol, he was certain, was an innocent party. Lawson had used her, probably used her key to K.C.'s apartment to get in and poison him, but Carol herself was completely innocent. He wanted to warn her about Lawson, but was afraid she would think he was acting crazy. And what if she told Lawson that K.C. and Diane suspected him?

Carol found him strangely uncommunicative, and soon after lunch she left, reminding him to get plenty of rest. K.C. tried to be pleasant and upbeat but the thought of Carol with Lawson would not leave him. He saw them naked together, rolling around in bed—Gordon's bed! It was all he could do to force himself to smile and say good-bye.

"If you need me tonight," Carol said, "I'll be home until seven. Then I'll be at Reid's."

He fought back the urge to leer and say, All night? Instead he said, "Thanks, Carol. I'll be all right."

She gave him a worried look and a quick kiss on the cheek and raced off as if anxious to be away from him.

He called Birdwell again but he had not reported in to the office. What the hell was keeping him? Take it easy, he told himself. Residual paranoia. Birdwell would call him as soon as he got his message.

He began watching the clock, wondering why he hadn't heard from Diane. When he started thinking about plane crashes he knew he wasn't doing too well. He took one of the pills Quist had given him, even though he was sure they made him drowsy. Sure enough, less than half an hour later he was fast asleep on the couch.

Again, it was the phone that woke him.

"Got your message," said Birdwell. "Sorry I took so long getting back to you."

K.C. was groggy with sleep. "What time is it?"

"Almost eight."

"Eight!" He hadn't heard from Diane yet.

"What's up?" said Birdwell cheerfully. "I haven't heard from you in a while."

K.C. told him, starting with the paranoia and the hospital stay and Diane's revelation about Lawson.

"Lawson?" said Birdwell. "That makes sense. A lot of TMK and Ameronics equipment winds up in the Soviet bloc."

"What should I do?"

"Do? You should do nothing. Sit back and let me verify what you've told me. We can put him away for a lot of years for selling high-tech secrets to the Soviets."

"I think he killed Gordon," said K.C.

Birdwell paused. "That won't be easy to prove."

"But that's what I want to get him on. That's what this is all about."

"Look," Birdwell said. "I want you to sit back and let me handle this. Don't do anything until you hear from me. Okay?"

"Okay," K.C. said reluctantly. "I'll wait to hear from you."

"If you need me," said Birdwell, "leave a message on my recorder at home."

"Okay," K.C. said, feeling sorry he had bothered to call Birdwell.

A few minutes later Diane called.

"I'm at the airport," she said. "Just got in."

"I was starting to worry about you."

She sounded happy. "I've got to pick up my car, then I'll start for home. I can't wait to see you."

He was beginning to feel better. Just the sound of her voice made him happy. "How long?" he asked, not trying to keep the anxious tone from his voice.

"Well," she said, "I've got to stop off at Nichols's place to talk with him, and then—"

"Can't you skip that for now?"

"But it's on the way," she said. "I won't be long. You don't mind, do you? Let me give you Nichols's number. You can call me there if you need me."

He tried not to sound sullen. "Okay. What do you want me to do in the meantime?"

"Nothing," she said. "Just sit tight until I get there. I can handle this part by myself. See you soon," she said, and hung up.

He gave an exasperated sigh. Everyone was running around doing something, while he sat doing nothing. Dammit! It was *his* case. He resented being told to "sit tight" while others finished what he had come to see as his job.

He had to do something. He sat down with Gordon's notebook, and for the umpteenth time he leafed through the pages. The later entries, those K.C. thought had been written by a man filled with jealous rage, took on a new significance. What if the references to Reid Lawson didn't refer to Carol at all? What if they referred to the theft of technological secrets? If so, then phrases like "Must stop him," "Can't let him get away with it," and "Can't be trusted," which Gordon had used in his fragmented, convoluted later entries when referring to Reid Lawson, took on an entirely new meaning.

K.C. could feel the anger surge through his veins. He turned to Gordon's final entries in his notebook, the parts that had to do with Belenkov, the Russian defector. It was clear now that Belenkov believed the Russians had penetrated the U.S. computer industry with a highly placed agent. Could it be Lawson? It was clear to him now that Lawson had the means, the motive, and the opportunity.

Now the disjointed notes that had once seemed indecipherable began to make sense. Lawson was the key that solved the puzzle. If Lawson was indeed a Soviet agent, then all the murders and disappearances had been to prevent disclosure of that fact. Except for the murder of Robert Tolbert. Why had he been killed? Had he somehow found out about Lawson's real intentions? Or was his death merely an instrument to radicalize Michael Tolbert? It was common knowledge that Michael Tolbert and consequently Ameronics Corporation had been nudged to the left by the fact that his son had been hounded to death by agents of the U.S. government. Had Reid Lawson been the one who had brought about that change?

If all this were true, then Reid Lawson had murdered Gordon! It was all circumstantial, but every gap in the scenario could be filled in by including Lawson's name.

But how could he prove it?

Not by sitting here in his apartment, that was certain. Not by letting Diane and Birdwell do all the work while he "sat tight." If he was going to prove that Lawson had killed his brother, he would have to do it himself.

How?

That's easy too, he thought. Now that I'm thinking clearly again, it all seems so simple. The idea had come to him in a flash, like a dark path briefly illuminated by lightning and was just as quickly obscured in darkness. He struggled to bring the idea back into focus before it was gone forever. His head throbbed mercilessly from the effort, and for a moment he had trouble remembering exactly what it was that he wanted to do. Then he smiled. There it was! Clear as day and perfectly obvious, he thought, to anyone with any degree of common sense.

He would use the same method that had given Lawson all the information he needed to stay ahead of him. Carol! It was obvious to him now that that was how Lawson had done it. If K.C. revealed to Carol his suspicions about Lawson, she was sure to let Lawson know—especially if he could make her think he was still paranoid.

He smiled, taking pleasure in the apparent simplicity and effectiveness of his plan. He would call Carol—she was with Lawson right now—and tell her he had enough evidence to prove that Reid Lawson was the man everyone was after. Carol would tell Lawson and Lawson would have to do something to stop K.C. from talking. K.C. would call Birdwell at home and tell him to be at his apartment to apprehend Lawson. He would do this by himself to show Diane and Birdwell that even though he had been down and almost out, he was still in the game and that he could finish it off by himself. It was all so simple! It would be over before Diane got back from her visit with Nichols.

He was almost chuckling as he dialed Lawson's number, and when Lawson answered, K.C. surprised himself by remaining remarkably cool. "Hello," he said, "this is Kevin Collins, I'd like to speak with Carol Hardwick, please."

Lawson was distant. He hesitated for a moment before saying, "Just a moment, please."

K.C. was sure he could detect a wariness in Lawson's voice.

Carol was on the phone quickly, sounding breathless and worried. "K.C.," she whispered, "is everything okay? Are you all right?"

"I know who did it, Carol," he said, his voice low and mysterious.

"Did what?"

"Everything. I know who Gordon was looking for. Who the CIA is after." He let his voice rise in pitch until it almost cracked. He was doing this beautifully, he thought. "Ask him where he was when he was supposed to be in San Diego."

Carol sounded worried. "Take it easy," she said. "What are you talking about?"

"Reid Lawson," he said, letting his voice drop dramatically. "It's Lawson. He's the one."

"Oh no," she said in a voice that was almost a wail, "you're not thinking clearly. You need help. Please let me help you."

"Goddammit!" he screamed. "It's Lawson and I can prove he's been peddling secrets to the Russians. I've got the proof, Carol. I've got the proof."

She tried to calm him. "You know what the doctor said. That you'd have moments of confusion and paranoia. Please listen to me. You must get help."

"It's your goddamn boyfriend who needs help. And I'm going to see that he gets it. You can kiss his ass good-bye, Carol." He could hear Lawson in the background, asking what was wrong.

"Please—" Carol began, but he slammed down the receiver and cut her off.

Carol stared into the phone as if she could picture K.C.'s crazed image through the wire.

Reid Lawson had been watching her. "What is it?" he asked.

Carol hung up the phone and turned to face him. "He's just out of the hospital," she said. "He sounds very upset."

Lawson's eyes narrowed as he watched her. "Why would he call you?"

Carol looked down at the floor, unable to meet Lawson's stare. "He's my brother-in-law," she said softly. "The CIA put him out here to find out what happened to Gordon."

Lawson's eyes darkened but he gave no indication that he was surprised by the revelation.

"I'm afraid for him," Carol said. "I'm afraid for both of you."

"Both of us?" Lawson bit his lip. "I don't get it."

"He said that you're the one everyone's been looking for."

"That's crazy," said Lawson.

"I know, but that's the problem. He's not acting normally. I'm afraid he's going to try to hurt you—and himself."

Lawson put his hands in his pockets. He was very casual. "What did he say?"

"He said he had evidence—that he could prove you did it."

"Did what?" said Lawson calmly. "What am I supposed to have done?"

She giggled embarrassedly, as if it was all too foolish to mention. "That you've been selling secrets to the Russians."

"That's ridiculous. Why would I do that?"

"I know that. But he needs help. He said I should ask you where you were when you were supposed to be in San Diego."

Lawson's eyes widened as if he had been slapped, but his voice remained calm. "I'll go talk with him."

Carol was alarmed. "Don't be foolish. There's no telling what he could do. I think we should call his doctor. He should be back in that hospital."

Lawson shook his head. "Let me go talk to him. I can answer any questions he has about my activities. Maybe that would calm him down." He moved in the direction of the door.

Carol stepped in front of him. "I don't want you to do that. Please don't do that."

Lawson's eyes were hard. Behind them was something she had never seen before. "Don't worry," he said gently, but his eyes were anything but gentle. "I'll talk with him and

ake care of this whole thing. I'll be back in no time." He
moved past her without another word, brushing aside her
efforts to stop him.

"This is crazy," Carol said, her hands moving in helpless
circles.

Lawson took his jacket from the rack by the door and
turned to face her. "I'll be back in an hour," he said calmly
but his eyes were unable to meet with hers.

He went to the garage and lifted the door. Inside, he
turned on the light and went to the tool bench. He moved
aside some tools on the lower shelf and pulled out a metal
box, which he opened and then removed a small cloth bag
secured at the top with a drawstring. He reached inside and
removed a pistol, checked that it was loaded and that the
safety was on, then stuck the pistol in his coat pocket and got
into the car.

Sixty-five

Diane arrived at Ted Nichols's house in Palo Alto almost
an hour after talking to K.C. on the phone. It had taken her
longer than she'd expected to get her car and escape the
airport traffic. It was after nine P.M. when she finally arrived
on his doorstep and pushed the buzzer.

Ted Nichols opened the door, his eyes lighting up with
pleasure when he saw her. K.C. is right, Diane thought, this
guy is after my body.

Nichols was in a relaxed and gregarious mood. "I was
just about to make myself a Bloody Mary," he said. "Would
you like one?"

"Would I?" she said, laughing. "Make it a good one."

He laughed. "Coming up." He went to the bar at the
end of the living room and while Diane sat on the couch, he

started mixing. "You sounded a little upset on the phone," he said. "I hope Kevin isn't any worse."

She shook her head distractedly. "No. I talked with him just before I called you. He sounds fine."

"Still in the hospital?"

She made a face. "No. They let him out. I think he should have stayed for a few more days but apparently he talked his way out."

Nichols held up the Tabasco. "A little or a lot?"

"Just a dash."

He splashed a single drop into her drink and several into his own. He stirred and brought Diane's drink to her. "This'll make you feel better," he said.

Diane nodded her thanks.

"Let me put on some music," Nichols said.

Diane sipped her drink and waved her hand to indicate that the music was unnecessary. This was beginning to look like a seduction scene, when all she wanted was to ask him if he had found anything on Lawson and get out of here. She knew K.C. was waiting.

Nichols ignored her signal. "It'll relax you," he said. "You like classical, don't you? Vivaldi, if I remember correctly."

She smiled. "That'll be fine."

As the music filled the room he came back. "You shouldn't worry. I'm sure Kevin will be fine."

She explained, "Some sort of chemical imbalance, the doctor said."

Nichols looked puzzled. "Chemical imbalance?"

"Yes," Diane said. "He's not crazy. He's somehow ingested some substance that has made him very confused. He'll be fine." She was anxious to change the subject. "You said on the phone that you had checked into Lawson's business trips."

Nichols hedged, "But first tell me what you found in Montreal."

Diane sighed. She was tired, and she wanted to get going, but she couldn't really refuse to tell him. She began in a tired monotone, telling him about her trip to Montreal and her discussion with MacDonald. By the time she got to the part concerning MacDonald's suspicions about Reid Lawson, the fatigue was gone from her voice and she was as excited as ever by the revelation.

"Being in the same city isn't exactly proof of guilt," said Nichols. "You'll need more than that."

"Lieutenant MacDonald thinks Robert Tolbert was murdered, and he suspects Reid Lawson was involved in some way."

"But this is all circumstantial—like your other evidence."

Diane stopped short. "The other evidence? What about it?"

Nichols took a sip of his drink, then gave Diane a sad, almost apologetic smile. "Well, you did ask me to look into Reid Lawson's business trips."

Diane nodded. "And you told me on the phone that you had found some interesting items."

"I did, but they might not be the kind of interesting items you want to hear about."

Diane could feel her excitement drain away. "Tell me," she said.

"I did a careful check on a few of the items you mentioned. You're wrong about the San Diego trip. Lawson could not have been in Washington when Gordon Hardwick was killed."

"How can you be sure? According to the list of charges, he simply disappeared at that time. He could have been anywhere."

"On that list of charges you are right," said Nichols with a knowing smile. "But this list"—here he held up a sheet, like a magician pulling a rabbit from a hat—"shows the phone calls charged to the company on Lawson's credit card. On the two days that Reid Lawson was supposedly 'missing' from San Diego, he made three or four phone calls, on his company credit card, from Mexico City." He gave her the sheet. "See for yourself."

Diane's face fell. She could see her airtight circumstantial case beginning to crumble.

"And," said Nichols, "on the days he supposedly disappeared in Seattle—at the time Burns escaped—he made two phone calls from Vancouver."

"What about the other trips?"

"Pretty much the same thing. Phone records can verify his presence elsewhere." He shook his head in sympathy with her disappointment. "Pretty much gets him off the hook."

"Maybe someone else made the calls using his credit card," she said hopefully.

"Perhaps," said Nichols, but they both knew she was clutching at straws.

They both sat for a long time not saying anything. Finally Nichols broke the silence. "I'm sorry," he said. "I didn't really mean to destroy your story, but facts are facts. I can show you the rest of the company logs if you like."

She shook her head slowly from side to side. "No. That won't be necessary. I believe you."

He smiled. "If I were you I'd look for another suspect."

Diane's eyes widened. "No way," she said. "He's the one—I know it. I'm just not smart enough to figure out how he managed it. I'll just turn over the information I have to the CIA and let them figure it out."

Nichols shook his head sadly. It was obvious to him and to anyone who studied the evidence that she was making a mistake. He had tried his best but obviously she was determined to press on with this.

Despite her bravado, Diane was stunned. All of the carefully put-together pieces were coming apart. It seemed inconceivable that she was back to square one. She finished her drink. "Shit!" she said, then looked at Nichols, who gave her a small sympathetic smile. She held up her glass. "How about one for the road?"

Sixty-six

Carol was in a nail-biting panic. Something was wrong—terribly wrong. K.C. had suffered an obvious relapse. His condition had worsened. It was like Gordon all over again. He had the same paranoid fears, the same hysterical tone, the same groundless suspicions.

Groundless? Were they really groundless? she wondered. Even the paranoid do, sometimes, have very real enemies.

She tried to push the seeds of doubt that first Gordon and now K.C. had planted in her brain. It had been easy at first. Gordon was jealous and crazy. That had been his motivation for accusing Reid. But now K.C. K.C., who had been like a real baby brother to her. Why was this happening again? Why was this happening to her?

What was it about San Diego that had made Reid jump? She had seen it in his face. She thought back, and realized with a start that Reid had been in San Diego on business when Gordon had been killed. She remembered that she had tried to contact him at his hotel, but had been unable to do so until two days later. Reid had explained his inability to answer her messages by telling her how busy he had been. At the time she had been too upset to think about it.

"Where the hell was he?" she said aloud.

And why, she wondered, had he reacted the way he did when she told him of K.C.'s wild accusation? How would an innocent man react to such a statement? Wouldn't he just laugh it off and say, "Someone better call the men in the white coats"? Or would he decide to leave dinner, get in his car, and drive for half an hour to talk with his accuser?

How would a guilty man react? Would he turn evasive? Would he run for cover? Or—the thought hit her like the tolling of a bell—would he decide to eliminate his accuser and the evidence?

She remembered the gun. Reid had a gun hidden in the garage.

Carol ran to the stairs, taking the half flight to the garage level. She burst through the door, her heart beating like a captured bird's, and raced to the bench where he kept the gun. Even before she got there, she saw the separated boxes that had hidden the storage case from view, saw the space where it had been.

She ran to her car in the driveway and cursed when she realized her keys were in her pocketbook in the upstairs hall. She ran back up the stairs, then remembered she had a spare key in the glove compartment and started back down toward the car. She stopped herself, realizing she was running in circles, bordering on hysteria.

Call the police, she thought. But what if I'm wrong?

Now she was at the other extreme—immobilized. "C'mon," she snapped at herself. "Move!"

She jumped into her car and backed out into the street. Tires screeching, she raced off into the night.

Sixty-seven

K.C. had turned off the lights and sat in the living room, waiting in the dark. He had the portable phone next to him and every few minutes used the automatic redial to call Birdwell at his home. No answer. The sound of the control unit in the bedroom was inaudible, and he had to hold the phone next to his ear to assure himself that the unit was dialing.

He had a dull throbbing headache, but even in his semiconfused state it was obvious to him that he had made a mistake. He realized fully and for the first time the effect the drugs had had on his mind. He hadn't been thinking clearly. He shook his head slowly in amazement at his own foolishness. Anxious to catch Lawson, he had put his plan into operation too soon. Birdwell should have been here before Lawson arrived.

Without Birdwell, where would he be when Lawson incriminated himself? The answer to that was not comforting. He had to start thinking more clearly. He had to!

He had somehow imagined one of those old Hollywood gangster movies of the thirties where the real crook, gun in hand, admits to his crimes before killing the hero, who has tricked him into believing that his guilt is about to be revealed. At the last moment, of course, the hardworking but somewhat stupid police detective steps out from behind a curtain and says, "We've heard enough."

K.C. had even envisioned himself—in black and white—saying, "Take him away, officer." But he had forgotten one essential ingredient in the plan—the cop behind the curtain—Birdwell. Where the hell was he?

Next time, he thought, get the reinforcements here first, before the bad guys move in.

Next time? he thought with a start. Who said there was going to be a next time? He loosened the bulb in the light fixture by his chair.

Every time he heard a car door slam, he imagined he could hear Lawson's footsteps cross the courtyard, come up the steps, then pause outside his door. This usually caused him to press the redial button on the phone in a frantic effort to reach Birdwell. But, just as there was no answer, there was no sound of footsteps outside.

Lawson padded quietly up the stairs. His sneakered feet made no sound as he moved stealthily to the door of K.C.'s apartment. For a moment he stood there, undecided, then slowly turned the door handle. To his surprise the door was unlocked.

K.C. sat bolt upright in his armchair, the soft sound of the turning handle like a gunshot in the silent room. His fingers frantically probed at the phone, but in his haste he hit the reset button and listened in vain for some proof that the automatic redial was calling Birdwell.

The door swung open and a shaft of light swept the room. K.C. stayed quietly in his darkened corner.

Lawson called to him from the doorway, "Collins, it's me. Are you in there?"

K.C. said nothing.

"I know you're in there, Collins." The door was pushed open wider. "I think we should talk." Lawson reached inside and felt for the light switch, found it, and flicked it upward. Nothing happened.

"If you want to stay in the dark," said Lawson, "that's okay with me. We can talk in the dark." He stepped inside the room. K.C. could see him in the light from outside.

"Drop the gun," K.C. said quietly.

"Gun? What are you talking about? I don't have a gun." He turned toward the sound of the voice and held out his hands to show that both were empty. "What do I need a gun for? I came to talk."

K.C. thought for a moment, then tightened the bulb in the table lamp. The light came on, making him squint. "So, let's talk," he said, motioning toward the sofa.

Lawson smiled, relieved that K.C. was not armed. He sat across from K.C. The two eyed each other, wary like boxers in the first round of a fifteen-rounder.

K.C. broke the silence. "Talk."

Lawson shrugged. "Carol and I are concerned about you," he said. "You seem upset."

"You mean crazy."

"I don't mean that at all. I just mean—"

"Crazy like my brother."

Lawson could not meet the challenge of K.C.'s eyes. He looked at the floor. "I just found out this evening that you and Gordon Hardwick are brothers. There are certain disturbing similarities between you and your brother. That's why we're concerned."

"Concerned, my ass. Your only concern is your own neck." Perhaps it was the residue of the drugs, or the pent-up emotion of dealing with his brother's death, but K.C.'s anger was growing. And with the anger came a boldness that made him reckless. "When my brother got close to your little scheme you got rid of him, just like you planned to get rid of me."

Lawson's face was hard, like granite. "That's ridiculous."

K.C. picked up the phone and unobtrusively pushed the redial button. "I can have the police here in no time," he said, placing the phone on the table between them. The clicking sound of the redial was inaudible from the next room. He was counting silently to himself, knowing that after three rings, Birdwell's automatic answering tape would respond. He had timed it at least five times: four seconds for the ringing, eight seconds for the short message from Birdwell, and then the beep and one minute for the caller to leave his message.

He was counting, afraid Lawson would hear the muted clicks from the phone. It was difficult to listen to Lawson, count the seconds, and try to keep his wits about him. At twelve seconds he paused, straining to hear the signal from the tape machine.

He heard it and looked at Lawson to see if he had heard it too. Lawson only seemed wary of K.C.'s strange behavior.

"Okay, Lawson," said K.C. in a voice that he hoped was not noticeably louder. "I want you to tell me why you killed my brother."

Lawson shook his head. "This is your show—you tell me."

"He was onto your dealings with the Russians and you got rid of him."

Lawson nodded. Nodded! That wouldn't show up on the tape.

"Isn't that right?" he barked.

Lawson responded as if he had been slapped. "You've got your facts all wrong."

"Such as?"

Lawson was tiring of this game. "Look," he said, "you said you had proof of my guilt. I'd like to know what that proof is, and what you intend to do with it."

This was perfect, K.C. thought. Lawson was walking right into it. Even if Lawson killed him, their conversation would be recorded at Birdwell's. He almost laughed out loud, it was so perfect. Perfect? He'd be dead. How perfect was that? He tried to get a grip on himself, realizing that he was still not thinking clearly. "I've got proof of your guilt, all right." He peeked at his watch. He still had better than twenty seconds left to get Lawson to incriminate himself. Perhaps, he thought, when the time was up, he could push the button again, redial Birdwell's number, and start all over again.

Lawson would have none of it. He stood up, reached behind his back, and pulled out the pistol he had tucked into his belt. "Enough of this," he said. "What the hell evidence have you got?"

"A gun," said K.C. for Birdwell's benefit. "I thought you didn't need a gun."

"I'm very serious," said Lawson, pointing the gun at K.C. "If you've got some kind of evidence, I want it."

"Then what?"

Lawson's eyes narrowed. "Then I leave."

"Leave? Just leave me sitting here? Aren't you afraid I'd call the cops?"

"No one would believe a word you said about anything. You're a crazy man, remember? Even your sister-in-law will vouch for that."

K.C. picked up the phone. "Why don't we call her?" he said, smiling stupidly.

Lawson snapped at him and pointed the gun menacingly. "Put that damn thing down."

K.C. shrugged and put the phone back on the table. As

he did, he pushed the redial button. He smiled at his own crazy inventiveness.

They sat, staring at each other, while K.C. counted out twelve seconds. "Are you going to shoot me, Reid?" he asked.

Lawson's voice was icily cool. "If I have to. If I don't get what I want."

"Which is?"

"Stop playing games with me. What do you have?"

K.C. watched him sweat. "Somehow I thought you'd be cooler than this. You're unraveling, Reid. You look terrible."

"Dammit!" Lawson exploded. He jumped up and aimed the gun at K.C.'s face. "Tell me what you know. Show me your evidence."

K.C. stood up on wobbly legs. "It's not here."

Lawson eyed him carefully. "You bastard," he said. "You've got nothing. This is just some schoolboy prank." He raised the pistol and took aim. "This is your last chance."

The door opened and both men jumped. Lawson swung the pistol around and aimed at the figure in the doorway.

It was Carol. "Are you going to shoot me too, Reid?"

K.C. spoke first. "Carol, get out of here."

She looked away from Lawson to K.C. "Why, and let you two get on with this?"

"He killed Gordon," K.C. said.

She was calm, businesslike. "Is he right, Reid? Did you kill Gordon? I'd believe a lot of things about you, but I wouldn't let myself believe you were capable of murder."

Lawson's hands were trembling and his aim was unsteady. "I didn't kill anyone. I couldn't kill anyone."

Carol's eyes shifted to the pistol. "So what's that?"

He lowered the pistol and held it at his side. "I thought I could force him to give me whatever evidence he has. I wouldn't have used this."

"Wait a minute," said K.C. It was his turn to be baffled. "If you didn't kill Gordon—who did?"

Lawson shrugged. "I don't know." No one said anything and Lawson went on. "I'll admit that his death took a lot of pressure off me, but I didn't do it."

"But, if you didn't kill him, why are you here? What evidence are you looking for?"

Lawson's laugh was a choking sputter. "You mean you really don't know? This was all"—he searched—"for nothing?" He raised the gun again. "You don't have any evidence, do you? You can't prove anything."

K.C. decided that the time for the charade was over. "It's on tape."

"On tape?" Lawson was perplexed.

"Yes. You know those automatic answering machines? If someone calls and you're out, they can leave a message?"

"What the hell are you talking about?"

"You've been leaving a message with Birdwell of the CIA." K.C. picked up the phone and pushed the redial button again, then handed it to Lawson.

Still puzzled, Lawson took the phone and held it to his ear. When he heard the message his eyes widened. He dropped the phone on the chair. "They'll never hear what I said from this distance."

K.C. shook his head. "They'll hear me—I guarantee that. And with the sound-enhancement equipment available to the CIA and the FBI, I'm pretty sure they can pick up your voice."

Lawson's shoulders sagged and his face fell. He had the look of defeat about him.

Lawson sat down heavily, holding the gun in his lap as one might hold a toy. "It's over," he said. "I might as well finish it." He looked at both of them, hoping someone would say something.

K.C. looked down at the carpet.

Carol spoke first. "Don't be a damn fool. Give me that gun."

He looked down at the gun, slowly raised his shoulders, then let them fall and handed the weapon to Carol, who held it as if it were something slimy.

Lawson buried his face in his hands.

Carol turned to K.C. "Can you tell me what's going on? If he didn't kill Gordon, what did he do?"

"He's been selling secrets to the Russians. Diane and I thought he was the killer, but I guess we were wrong. Somebody else is covering for him. Doing his dirty work. Anyone who gets close to uncovering Lawson's secret is eliminated."

Carol lowered her voice. "Are you sure?"

K.C. looked at the pistol on the table. "He could have killed me easily. He could have killed both of us." He shook his head and looked at Lawson. "He doesn't have it in him."

"What do we do now?" asked Carol.

"Call Birdwell. Let him take care of it. We've found his spy."

"But not our killer."

He shook his head. "It looks like Diane and I have been barking up the wrong tree." He squeezed his eyes shut. He was still dizzy.

"Where is she?"

It came to him in a rush, and he smiled. "She's still trying to get the goods on Lawson." He let out a hollow laugh. "She was going to stop off at Ted Nichols's on the way home from the airport, to try to pinpoint Reid's whereabouts on . . ." He stopped. "It's wasted effort now."

"You shouldn't be disappointed," Carol said, sensing his mood. "You found the man they've all been looking for."

"Yeah, by accident," he said, then looked at her. "I'm sorry, Carol. I never thought what this might mean to you."

She touched a hand to his shoulder. "It's all right. Things could never have worked out for Reid and me anyway."

K.C. picked up the phone. "I'd better call Diane and let her know what's happened. No sense in having her waste her time."

As K.C. dialed, Lawson sat motionless, a dejected figure, his face still buried in his hands.

Sixty-eight

Ted Nichols had just finished mixing Diane's second drink when the phone rang. He ignored it as he squeezed a lime into the glass then brought the drink to Diane.

"Thanks," she said and looked questioningly toward the telephone. "Aren't you going to answer it?"

He looked at her and for a moment she thought he might say no. Instead he shrugged and said, "If you insist."

He excused himself and went to the kitchen. Diane sat

back, touching the cool glass to her forehead. Damn, she was tired. She was wishing that she were already at home or with K.C. She let the music flow over her, relax her, carry her away.

She could vaguely hear Nichols's voice coming from the kitchen talking to the caller.

He came back and sat across from her. "Why don't you tell me everything you know about this case. Maybe there's still something we can do."

"She's not there yet," K.C. said to Carol. "And she hasn't called him. She should have been there already."

Carol saw the troubled look on his face, and hoping to be helpful, said, "Maybe she just decided to go straight home."

He was doubtful. "She would have called." He began to dial Diane's number, then abruptly stopped and a distant look came over his face.

"What is it?" asked Carol.

He squeezed his eyes shut and shook his head as if trying to clear his thoughts. "Vivaldi," he said simply.

"Vivaldi?"

"He was playing Vivaldi. I could hear it in the background."

Carol looked at him strangely, then slowly a dawning realization spread across her face. She knew what he was thinking.

"She's there with him now," he said.

Carol's mouth opened and she quickly covered it with her right hand. "It's Nichols," she whispered.

K.C. took Lawson's pistol from Carol. "Stay here with him," he said. "I'm going up there."

Carol stepped between him and the door. "You're in no shape to go anywhere. Let me call the police."

He pushed past her. "Call the police and call Birdwell. Tell them I'm on my way to Nichols's."

She started to protest but he was gone before the words had left her lips. Carol went to the door and watched him race across the courtyard to the car, then she came back and picked up the phone. She was conscious that Lawson was watching her. It was the first time he had shown any animation in several minutes.

"What are you going to do?" he asked.

"I'm calling the police."

He stood up. "I think we should talk."

"It's a little late for talk, Reid."

"But I can explain everything."

"Not now," she said, dialing.

Lawson looked around, his eyes desperate. He ran to the bedroom and she heard something crash to the floor. The phone went dead in her hand. She held it to her ear for confirmation and said, "You're not going to stop me, Reid."

He was back. "If you'll just give me a chance to explain."

"Explain? How can you explain what you've done?"

"I leaked information to the Soviet Union because I believe that parity is the safest course for world peace."

"You *leaked* information or *sold* information?"

He ignored her question. "You don't understand," he pleaded. "If one side gets too big an advantage, the other might panic and launch a nuclear attack. The only sane course is parity. That's why I did it."

Carol's eyes went past him to the wall phone in the kitchen. He followed her eyes there and knew what she was thinking. He got there first and ripped the phone from the wall.

"Not until we talk," he said.

"You've talked already. There's nothing to say."

"You asked what I was doing when I was supposed to be in San Diego," Lawson said calmly. His voice was soft, but there was something in his eyes that made Carol wary. "I went to Mexico," he said, "to meet with a representative of the Soviet Union. He was—as always—interested in some of the high-technology items developed at TMK—items that I could provide. We'll wait for Collins to come back. I can talk with him. I can make him understand."

"If you don't let me get to a phone, he may not come back."

Lawson shrugged and Carol realized he had already thought of that.

"Then," he said, "I'd have only you to persuade."

"K.C. was right. You don't have the guts for it. Your 'guardian angel' takes care of all your problems."

Lawson's smile was part snarl, part sneer, part rueful grimace. "Up till tonight, I didn't even know I had a guardian angel. I just thought I was very lucky. Every time someone got close to exposing me, something happened—a suicide, a prison escape, someone else arrested for something I had

done. I should have known someone was watching over me."
He smiled now. "I really should have."

Carol made a dash for the door but he was too fast. He
caught her by the arm, spun her around, and flung her to the
floor. She tried to get up but he was on her quickly, his
hands around her throat.

Carol tried desperately to pry his hands away as he
squeezed harder and harder.

"If Nichols takes care of those two, you'd be the only
person who knows about me," he said, his voice soft and
carefully controlled to hide the strain.

Carol wanted to remind him about the tape, but she
could not speak. There was a loud buzzing in her brain that
turned into a roaring, as if she were on a train racing into a
deep, dark tunnel.

Sixty-nine

"Do you play chess?" Nichols asked.

"What?" asked Diane, surprised and puzzled at his change
of topic.

"Chess," he repeated.

"A little," she said. "I'm not very good at it."

"Pity. Kevin plays—fairly well. Not as well as Gordon
Hardwick did. Gordon was an excellent player. He understood the game."

Diane felt a sudden shiver, as if someone had lightly run
icy hands across her naked body. Had Nichols seen through
K.C.'s disguise from the start?

There was a perceptible change in Nichols's demeanor,
although she could not pinpoint exactly what that change had
been. He even looked different. The smile had slipped from
his face and his eyes had a vacant, almost glassy look that
frightened her. She had never liked his eyes anyway, some-

thing in them had never rung true for her. It was as if there was a shutter behind them that prevented light from penetrating.

"I'm not sure I'm following you," she ventured cautiously. "What does chess have to do with what we're talking about?"

"Chess," he went on, ignoring her question, "is much like life. We move forward, pushing others out of our way, planning our next move, calculating not only its immediate effect but what its effect will be years—or several moves—later. We make sacrifices to achieve our goals. Sometimes we allow our opponent to think he's nearing victory. We sacrifice an important piece, but it is merely a diversion. We never allow ourselves to be anything but relentless in the pursuit of our goal." He smiled. "The capture of the king."

He seemed somewhere far away, his voice soft and almost singsong, but without a trace of humor or emotion. It was a frightening transformation.

As he went on her nervousness increased. She was sitting with a man who was talking about a game, but for reasons she could not yet comprehend, she was afraid.

"Of course there are differences," he said.

She nodded, watching him with morbid fascination.

"Chess is much more honorable, more dignified, more . . ." he shrugged ". . . more honest. We know from the beginning the objective of the game and the nature and capabilities of the pieces." He looked at her, as if noticing her for the first time in a long while. "I mean, a bishop is always a bishop and moves as only a bishop can. A pawn is always a pawn and moves as only a pawn can. That is, of course, unless they can get to the eighth file—then a pawn can be anything you want. A queen, a rook . . ."

Diane felt her throat constrict. She was having trouble swallowing, and she fought to remain calm. "But," she said, "no matter what, a pawn can never change colors."

He shook his head, smiling. It was good that she was beginning to understand. "Of course not," he said. "That would never do. To have your own pieces turn on you would be unfair."

Diane took a deep breath. "And that's why chess is more honorable than life?"

434

"Yes," he said. "Life is dirty and dishonorable and insignificant."

"Oh, Nichols," she said, her voice cracking, but more from disappointment than fear. "Tell me it isn't you."

He ignored her question. "Tell me about Gordon's notebook."

She swallowed hard. An alarm was shrieking in her brain.

"Please tell me about the notebook."

She tried to think but the brain would not work. "It's . . . uh . . . It's a book where he put his thoughts, recollections, ideas, and . . . other things. It's mostly indecipherable mumbo-jumbo."

He raised an eyebrow. "But you were able to decipher it?"

"Some of it, maybe—not all of it."

"May I see it?" His voice was soft, soothing, almost reassuring.

"I don't have it anymore." Her eyes involuntarily went to her bag on the table between them.

He smiled and picked up the bag, then dumped the contents onto the table. He picked up the papers and studied them carefully. "Those are copies," he said simply.

She nodded. "I told you I didn't have the notebook."

He leafed through the pages. "There must be more than this?"

She found his calm tone hypnotic. It was as if he were willing her to cooperate, and she had no choice but to do as he bid.

"I gave it back to K.C.," she found herself saying. "He has it now."

He thought for a moment, then smiled. "A momentary complication. I can take care of him as soon as . . ." He looked at her with his strange blank smile and she knew he was going to kill her.

"Nichols," she said, "please don't do this."

He stood up. "I'm sorry. I really am, but what I'm doing is more important than your life—or mine for that matter."

Diane did not hesitate. She jumped up from her seat and made a sudden dash for the door. She heard him behind her but she made it to the door before he could catch her. Just as her hand touched the doorknob, Nichols grabbed her by the hair and violently snapped her head back. His other hand clamped across her mouth, cutting short the scream that had already started.

"I don't think anyone is going to hear you out here," he whispered into her ear as he pulled her back from the door. He was surprisingly strong, treating her efforts at struggle with disdain. With minimal effort he dragged her back across the living room, toward the bedroom door.

Inside the bedroom he threw her on the bed and then stood in the doorway watching her as she picked herself up. Diane sat up, straightening her skirt, watching how his eyes went to her legs. She ran her fingers through her disheveled hair, pushing it away from her face.

There has to be a way out of this, she thought. K.C. knows I'm here. If only I can hold on for a while. She had visions of K.C. bursting through the door, coming to her rescue, but she knew immediately that it would not happen. K.C. had no reason to suspect what was happening to her. Her breath came in short gasps as she struggled to hold on to her composure. If she was going to get out of this, she would have to do it herself.

Nichols crossed his arms and leaned against the doorway. She was surprised at how calm—almost detached—he was. His detachment terrified her as much as anything else. One thing kept running through her mind—"keep talking." She knew that when there was nothing left to say he would do whatever it was he had decided to do with her.

She took a deep breath. "Well, I didn't know we were going to wind up in the bedroom."

He didn't respond.

She decided to play it as if she was unaware of his real intentions. "This isn't going to be one of those messy rape scenes, is it?"

She waited for a word from him, but he remained adamantly silent.

" 'Cause if it is, I've got news for you—I'm not about to put up a fight." She started to unbutton her blouse. "Let's just get on with it." Her mind was racing. She had always sensed how much he wanted her, and now she was stalling him in the only way she knew. She slipped her blouse off and threw it behind her on the bed. She was naked from the waist up and felt a glimmer of hope as she watched his eyes roam appreciatively over her body. She wrapped her arms across her breasts. His eyes made her shudder.

Still he made no move or sound. She decided to be bolder. "Why don't you come over here," she said, licking her lips, "and let me take your pants off?"

She had to get him away from the door. The minute his trousers were around his ankles she would make a break for it. We'll see how fast he can run with his pants down, she thought.

He smiled. "It would be very nice," he said, "but I'm afraid I don't have the time. I also have to deal with Hardwick." He closed the door and moved to the lone dresser in the room. He opened the top drawer and removed a pistol.

Diane could hardly breathe. The room was suddenly devoid of oxygen and she took in air in great gulps. "K.C. knows I'm here," she managed to say.

Nichols shrugged. "No problem. He called just a little while ago. I told him I hadn't seen or heard from you." He smiled when he saw the defeat in her eyes. "Don't worry, I'll take care of him later. Just like I took care of Gordon and the others."

"It was you," Diane stammered.

"Yes, it was me," he said. "Lawson knows nothing. He's just a fool who sells his country's secrets for money and likes to think he's doing it for the betterment of mankind. My job is to see that no one gets in his way."

"Then he didn't kill Robert Tolbert?"

Nichols smiled. "I must again take the credit. That was my first job."

"But why kill him? He was a nothing."

Nichols shrugged. "It was an attempt to influence his father to deal with the Soviet Union." His grin was almost boyish. "Rather successful too, if I may say so. Of course, at the time we had no idea Lawson would become like a son to Michael Tolbert. That was just a lucky break. No amount of planning could have accomplished that."

"And you poisoned K.C.?"

As he talked, Nichols screwed a stubby silencer onto the barrel of his pistol. He nodded. "Yes. I didn't intend for him to wind up in a psychiatric clinic. I only meant to have him slightly disoriented." He smiled. "He must use a lot of salt. But perhaps this will make things easier."

Her fear turned to anger. "Why are you doing this? You bastard!" she screamed. "What have I done to you?"

He seemed genuinely moved. "I'm sorry. I really am.

But I've already explained." He smiled again. "Besides, very soon, most of the people you know will be dead anyway. You wouldn't want to be around to see that, would you? In a way I'm doing you a favor."

"What in God's name are you talking about?"

"Nuclear war between the United States and the Soviet Union." His face was cheerful, as if he were reciting last night's game scores. "It's going to happen—very soon," he said. "Within the next few days."

"You're crazy," Diane said. "Don't they read the papers in Russia? Don't they know about the Prometheus system?"

This time his smile was triumphant. "Prometheus doesn't work. I've seen to that." He knew he was talking too much, wasting time, but he couldn't help himself. He wanted her to know what he had done. He wanted her to know how important he was. It had been such a long time since he had been able to be himself. He had to tell someone. Someone had to know how successful he had been. "By this time next week the United States will be in ruins."

She shook her head disbelievingly. "They'll stop you. Someone will stop you."

"Who? Hardwick?" He shook his head from side to side. "I'll take care of him. Only I won't have to be as careful as I had planned. One more death will be totally insignificant."

He took a deep breath and Diane knew he was finished talking. She tried to think of something else, but her mind was completely blank. It reminded her of the time in college when she had frozen in front of her speech class, and she was amazed that she could be reminded of such an trivial event at the moment of her death.

"Why don't you put your blouse back on," Nichols said. "There's no need for you to be found half naked."

"Thank you," she said, picking up the blouse and slipping it on. Her hands trembled, and she kept fumbling with the buttons. She looked up at him apologetically.

"That's all right," he said. "Take your time. I want you to look nice."

She was crying now and hating herself for doing so. Huge silent tears ran down her cheeks, dropping onto her lap.

She finished with the buttons and was tucking the blouse into her skirt when she heard the tires squeal outside. Nichols's head snapped around toward the sound.

She jumped up, but she was slow. Nichols raised the pistol and aimed it at her forehead. "One sound," he said, "and I pull the trigger." He moved behind her, the gun touching the base of her skull.

Diane put her hand over her mouth, desperately trying not to scream.

They listened together to the sound of footsteps racing to the front door, the first pounding, the house-shaking crash at the door.

"Nichols!" screamed the voice from outside.

Diane's heart soared. It was K.C.

The front door opened and she heard him come in. As she struggled to yell a warning, Nichols clamped a hand across her mouth and held her against him.

"Nichols!" screamed the voice from the living room.

Diane heard him kicking in doors leading to other rooms. He was working his way down to them. She was glad she had put her blouse back on, then amazed at how her mind still focused on trivialities.

"He'll be here soon," whispered Nichols. "And all our troubles will be over."

K.C. was outside the door. They could hear him. Suddenly the door flew open and there he was, standing in the doorway, a gun gleaming in his hand.

Nichols had Diane crushed against him, the pistol to her head. "Come in," he said, his voice cheerful.

K.C. raised the pistol. "Let her go."

"Drop your weapon and we can talk about it."

Diane saw the doubt in K.C.'s eyes and tried to signal him with a shake of her head, but she could barely move against the force of Nichols's grasp.

K.C. raised the pistol and aimed at the only part of Nichols's body that was exposed, his head. "I mean it," he said. "Let her go, or I start shooting."

"I don't think you've quite recovered from the little doses of atropine that I've been feeding you. You look shaky."

"Bastard!"

Nichols took his hand from Diane's mouth while still holding her against his body. "Tell K.C. what fun we've been having," he said. "He'd like to hear all about it."

"Kill him," Diane said.

K.C.'s face was tortured. "I can't. I might hit you," he said.

"He'll only kill both of us."

Nichols was enjoying the cat-and-mouse game now. "Go ahead, K.C., give it a try. Take a chance."

K.C. raised the pistol, but Diane could see the hesitation in his face. His shoulders sagged and he lowered the pistol.

"Toss it aside," said Nichols.

K.C. threw it across the room. "You win," he said.

Nichols pushed Diane toward him. "Of course I win. I always win."

K.C. and Diane hugged each other.

"This is absolutely perfect," said Nichols. "The two lovers together at last." He laughed. "You've made everything so easy for me."

"He said he's disarmed the Prometheus system," said Diane. "He claims it won't work under nuclear attack."

Nichols seemed delighted. He shrugged modestly. "It's true."

"I don't believe you," said K.C. "How could *you* do something like that?"

"With Progano's help I altered the computer program. When the Soviet Union launches their strike the Prometheus will be immediately notified by satellite and go on war alert. Twenty-eight minutes later the Soviet missiles will reenter the atmosphere and Prometheus will begin tracking. Unfortunately, at the first signal for the system to fire, the entire Prometheus system will shut down, due to what will appear to be a malfunction. There won't be time to launch a retaliatory strike, so all United States missiles will be destroyed on the ground."

"That's why Progano is dead?"

"Yes. His mind was clearing—just as yours is now—and he wanted to report what he had done. Unfortunately for him, he didn't know I was the man behind his personality change. He made the mistake of contacting me before he went to the authorities."

"He killed Gordon," whispered Diane, and felt K.C.'s body stiffen.

Nichols bowed in acknowledgment. "A rather formidable foe."

"Tompkins?" K.C. asked between clenched teeth.

"He knew too much. He was getting too close."

"What about Burns?"

"At the bottom of a very deep lake."

Diane shivered and K.C. held her closer. "You're crazy, Nichols," K.C. said.

"Allow me to introduce myself," said Nichols. "Aleksei Karpenkov of Department 8 of Directorate S, KGB."

"You won't get away with killing us. Too many people know we're here."

"Nonsense."

"Birdwell knows." K.C. did not mention Carol.

Karpenkov shrugged. "Perhaps he will be the one to find you locked in an embrace in my bed. Victims apparently of a murder-suicide. It won't be too hard to figure out what happened. K.C. Hardwick, just released from treatment for some mental disorder, suffered a relapse and decided to kill his girlfriend, and then himself." He pointed briefly to the gun K.C. had thrown on the floor. "We can even use your own weapon."

"You'll never get away with it."

Karpenkov laughed out loud. "I've been getting away with it for almost twenty years. And now," said Karpenkov, raising the pistol, "I'm afraid it's time to say good-bye."

"What about the photograph at the Tea Garden," said K.C. hurriedly. He knew their only chance was to keep Nichols talking, in hopes that Birdwell or the police, contacted by Carol, were on their way.

Karpenkov was growing impatient.

"Merely a diversion so I could get you out of your apartment for enough time to drug your salt supply."

"Then why bother with the group photo with Greenwood?" said Diane. "Why not just let him wait in San Francisco?"

Karpenkov smiled. He was beginning to enjoy the explanation of what he had accomplished. "A little disinformation and misdirection. I thought I could keep you busy with Greenwood's nonsense about the CIA." He shrugged. "I didn't count on Tompkins being able to dig up as much as he did. I thought that he would merely regurgitate the drivel he was collecting from Burns and Greenwood. I underestimated him." His face broke into an almost maniacal grin. "And now he'll have to miss the coming fireworks." The grin slipped from his face. "And so will you," he said almost sadly.

There was a brief lull, and K.C. sensed that Karpenkov

was ready to act. "How about you?" he asked. "How do you survive this coming holocaust?"

"I leave for Tokyo tomorrow—a brief business trip. When the grim reaper arrives I'll be with old friends, following the accounts of the destruction of America in the newspapers. By this time tomorrow"—he stopped when he saw that K.C. wasn't listening, his attention elsewhere. Karpenkov heard it himself then, the distinctive chop-chop of a helicopter coming closer. The sound grew, until the craft was obviously hanging over the house.

K.C. looked at Diane, relief flooding his face. "Carol must have sent the police."

Karpenkov nodded. "Apparently so."

"It's over, Nichols. You'll never get out of here."

"I think you're probably correct. Unfortunately for you, you'll never know. You both know too much to live. I must stick to my original plan of disposing of you. Only now we can dispense with the subterfuge." He aimed the pistol.

K.C. threw Diane in one direction and dove to the floor in the other. Surprised by his sudden move, Diane tripped over the rug and banged her head against the small night table by the bed, knocking it over. Stunned, she landed heavily on the floor.

At the same time, K.C. heard a soft "phutt," as a bullet dug into the wall just above his head. He rolled over, hands grabbing at the gun he had thrown on the floor. His movements were smooth and fluid, as if he had practiced this maneuver for years. He found the gun, grasped it, then, in one perfect motion, rolled over and came up on one knee, aimed, and pulled the trigger.

Nothing happened.

Karpenkov shook his head with almost sad resignation. "Amateurs," he said disapprovingly. He looked briefly to his left at Diane, who was still slumped, dazed, in the corner, and then turned his attention back to K.C. "Perhaps if you had some acquaintance with weapons you would know enough to release the safety."

K.C. looked at the gun in his hand. The small safety catch was just above his thumb. He placed his thumb on the catch.

"Don't move an inch," said Karpenkov, as he aimed down the barrel of his pistol. The silencer unbalanced the gun and he had to steady his arm.

Diane, still confused by her fall, pulled herself up onto one knee and saw Karpenkov, one eye closed, aiming at K.C., who was balanced on one knee less than five feet from Karpenkov. Dimly she heard Karpenkov say, "Don't move an inch." Next to her lay a glass ashtray that had fallen from the night table. She picked it up, cocked her arm, and threw it as hard as she could. The projectile thumped against Karpenkov's shoulder, staggering him momentarily. His gun discharged and K.C. heard the whipping sound again as the bullet whirred past his ear and thudded into the wall behind him.

K.C. did not consciously aim the pistol—he merely pointed it in the general direction of Karpenkov. His thumb moved on the safety, his finger twitched reflexively on the trigger, and the room was filled with a deafening explosion. At the same time a small red splotch appeared on Karpenkov's chest, slightly to the left center. He jerked back as if pulled from behind, his face more surprised than anguished. The red splotch was growing rapidly. Karpenkov looked down at his chest and cursed softly, as if he had spilled coffee on a new shirt.

With his left hand he tried to stem the flow of blood, while with his right he raised the pistol again.

K.C. shot him again while Diane winced and covered her ears from the deafening noise.

Karpenkov spun around and slammed against the wall, then turned to face him. His hands at his sides, he dropped the gun and slipped down the wall to a sitting position, then slumped over onto his side. He was dead before his face touched the carpet.

K.C. dropped the gun and moved quickly to Diane, who was climbing slowly to her feet. "I killed him," he said in a trance, his face without expression.

She put her arms around him and they held each other. "It's all right," she whispered. "You had to do it."

In the distance there was the sound of yelling and running feet. When Birdwell burst into the room they were still clinging together, oblivious of the noise and confusion. It was enough for now that they were alive and had each other.

After a long moment, during which Birdwell stood over Karpenkov's body not saying anything, K.C. looked in his direction and said dully, "Carol called you?"

Birdwell shook his head. "No. I got your message on my

tape machine and tried to call you. When there was no answer, I called for reinforcements and rushed to your place."

K.C.'s face was blank for a moment as Birdwell's words began to register. "No answer?" he asked softly, his voice quivering. It suddenly dawned on him that he had left Carol alone with Lawson. He took a deep breath. "Carol? Is she all right?"

"When I got there she was okay," said Birdwell. "Lawson had almost killed her but I guess at the last moment he couldn't do it. She told us where you were."

Birdwell saw the guilt on K.C.'s face. "Don't worry," he said, "she'll be fine."

"I want to see her."

"Later," said Birdwell. "We've got other, more important things to worry about right now." He nodded in the direction of Karpenkov's body. "We've got to find how much damage this guy has done."

"More than you can imagine," chipped in Diane.

Birdwell's eyes widened. "Let's hear it."

Diane pulled away. "You'd better tell him," she said to K.C.

"Tell me what?"

"Nichols claimed he had reprogrammed Prometheus to shut down at full alert."

Birdwell seemed dubious. "That's not possible," he said.

"It *is* possible," said K.C. "He had access, and he told us that the chief programmer, Progano, was in on it, too."

"And," said Diane, "he said the Soviets are planning a first strike within the next few days."

Birdwell grinned. "C'mon," he said. "You can't be serious." The look on both their faces answered his question.

"Can you get through to the President?" asked K.C.

"I can get through to someone who can speak to the President at any time, night or day."

"Then," said K.C., "you'd better talk to him."

Seventy

The American was very familiar with the Moscow Metro. His name was Frank DeRosa and he was the first assistant to the cultural attaché at the American embassy in Moscow. At least that's what it said on his diplomatic passport. In actuality, DeRosa was the Deputy Chief of Station, CIA, Moscow.

He entered the underground at Sverdlov Square, riding the long escalator with the thousands of commuters who made this trek each day. The station was clean and well-lighted, the trains quiet and efficient, and the passengers orderly and courteous.

He rode out to the Dynamo Stadium Station, then turned around and came back. On the return trip he passed Sverdlov Square, then got off at Revolutionary Square. He was certain he had not been followed.

Vladimir Gorsky was waiting for him on a bench on the platform. He too had made a circular route to wind up in this place.

As DeRosa approached, Gorsky could feel his heart pounding in his chest. To have survived one trip to the basement of Lubyanka was a miracle. He would not be so lucky again.

DeRosa sat on the bench directly behind Gorsky. They were almost back to back. "Nice to see you again, Vladimir," DeRosa said in excellent Russian.

Gorsky coughed a greeting but did not answer.

"I hear there's been a big shake-up over at your office," said DeRosa. "We hear you came in for a very nice promotion."

"Yes," said Gorsky, thinking he was about to flush his career down the toilet.

"You said you had something big for me."

"You must guard this information with your life," whispered Gorsky.

DeRosa smiled. Russians were so dramatic. "I'll do that, Vladimir. You can count on it."

"It must be passed on immediately to the highest levels of government." Gorsky was agitated by DeRosa's casual attitude.

"No problem, Vladimir. Let's see what you've got."

If Gorsky could have changed his mind he would have. He felt like running. But he knew there was no place to run.

"Get on the next train," he said. "You take the first car, I'll take the second. We'll make the exchange at the next stop."

DeRosa got up and went to the edge of the platform to wait for the next train. Gorsky stayed where he was. Neither man looked at the other.

They boarded the next train and at the first stop, Novokuznetsk Street, both got off. Concealed by the crowd of disembarking passengers, Gorsky walked past DeRosa, handed him an envelope, and got right back on the train. DeRosa thought that Gorsky, with his head bowed and shoulders slumped, seemed strangely dispirited. He tucked the envelope in his pocket and headed for the escalator to the street above.

Back at the embassy, DeRosa took the envelope to the office of Moscow Station Chief Sam Bergman. They read the message together.

Bergman finished first and waited for DeRosa. "What do you think?" he asked.

DeRosa shrugged. "He said it was big."

Bergman chuckled. "Yeah, and this is just what the KGB would like us to think. They'd like to stall deployment of this ABM system for as long as they can. If they make us think they've penetrated and compromised the program, it would do exactly that."

DeRosa nodded. "You're probably right." He looked to his boss. "What should I do with this?"

"Circular-file it," said Bergman.

Later that evening, as DeRosa was clearing his desk, Bergman came in. DeRosa looked up. "You still here?"

Bergman nodded. "That message we looked at today. I've been thinking about it. I'd hate to be the one to disregard it if it turned out to be true."

DeRosa grinned. "Right, chief."

Bergman saw the grin. "What did you do with it?"

"I sent a flash copy to Langley this afternoon, and a copy of the original went in the diplomatic pouch that leaves tonight."

Bergman smiled. "Good thinking."

"Right, chief," said DeRosa.

Seventy-one

The President's face was grim. Even the California tan seemed to have faded, and the deep-etched creases in his face for the first time made him seem older than his years.

The men who had gathered around the oval table in the West Wing Situation Room of the White House watched him anxiously. For the first time, many of them were reminded that the President was an old man. He seemed distracted, nervously touching his fingers to his face, then clasping his hands together in an attempt to control the uneasy wanderings of his fingers.

The President said nothing. In fact, he had not spoken since giving his brief opening remarks at the beginning of the emergency meeting of the National Security Advisory Committee. Across from him at the table sat the Secretaries of State and Defense and the Director and Deputy Director of the CIA. To the President's left were the Secretary of the Treasury, the Attorney General, and the Chairman of the Joint Chiefs of Staff. To his right sat the Vice-President and the National Security Adviser.

All paid rapt attention, their grim faces mirroring the President's expression, as the Director of the CIA concluded the report he had compiled from, as he put it, "operatives in the field."

"And," said the Director in conclusion, "these are the reports we have received—one from the consulate in San

Francisco, and one from the embassy in Moscow. What we must decide now, is how much credence to give these reports, and then of course, what do we do about them."

Several members of the committee looked worriedly at each other, their eyes drifting back to the President, who seemed visibly shaken by the report, his usually bullish confidence gone. When he finally spoke, his voice, normally strong and firm, was soft and almost wavering.

"Is this possible?" he asked. "Could this just be a Soviet attempt at disinformation?"

Deputy Director Hanson spoke first. "The first report from Moscow, Mr. President, was regarded with great suspicion. This is just the kind of operation in which the Soviets excel. We saw it as a possible attempt to cause us to doubt the capability of our new ABM system."

"But now?" the President said.

"The first report was followed rapidly by a second, out of San Francisco. It was virtually a carbon copy of the first."

The President thought for a moment. "Could the second report be part of the same disinformation ploy?"

Hanson looked around the table. "It's possible, Mr. President, but I don't think so."

The President looked at every face. "Do we all realize what this means?" he said. No one answered. "If these reports are accurate the Soviet Union is preparing to launch a first strike against us sometime within the next day or so."

Again there was silence.

Webster Connolly, the National Security Adviser, broke the silence. "Both reports claim that the Soviets have compromised the Prometheus ABM system. If we can prove that false, then perhaps we can expose this whole operation as a Soviet fraud."

"We've already begun checking the programming," said General Gray, Chairman of the Joint Chiefs. "But without actually bringing the system to War Alert it could take weeks. The only way to check the system properly would be to raise our alert status to Defcon Two, and then actually bring everything up to launch readiness. That way we would know if the system is really programmed to shut itself down. If it does shut down, the reprogramming would identify itself and could easily be eliminated."

"Do it," said the President.

There was a shocked buzzing at the table.

"Mr. President," said the Secretary of Defense, "we have already raised the Defcon of all our armed forces in response to the Soviet military maneuvers in Poland and Czechoslovakia. The Soviet Navy is dispersed at sea, and their Rocket Forces are at combat readiness."

"Then our raising the Defcon could be considered a response to those maneuvers."

"The Soviets informed us of those maneuvers weeks in advance, Mr. President," said General Gray.

"And if we go all the way to Defcon Two," said Connolly, "the Soviets will know. They constantly monitor our microwave transmission, and their spy satellites would see our missile silo hatches open. They might misinterpret our testing procedure as preparation for a first strike." He shook his head and looked around the table. "Without prior notification of such a procedure, that's exactly what we'd think."

There were words of agreement around the room.

"The Russians are paranoid about being vulnerable to a first strike," said Gray. "If they get trigger-happy, they might go to launch on warning. Then we're into it."

"So," said the President, "you're suggesting that we sit and wait, hoping that these two pieces of information we have received are incorrect. We wait while the Soviets are on alert, conducting full-scale military maneuvers with all their forces at combat readiness. I don't like that one bit. Especially since we can no longer be certain that Prometheus can protect us. If Prometheus fails, a first strike could take out much of our retaliatory capacity." The President sat up at his chair, squaring his shoulders and looking from face to face. "It's time for ideas, gentlemen."

There was a brief silence, followed by a general round of suggestions.

"Tell the Soviets to cease and desist their provocative actions in Europe," said the Director of the CIA.

"And let them claim we are using Prometheus to force them to stop military maneuvers within their own borders?" Connolly asked. "The'd have a field day with that."

"Go to Defcon Two," said General Gray. "To hell with what the Russians think. We've got to test the system."

"A full-scale War Alert is out of the question at this point," said the Attorney General. "The Soviets would see it as a provocation."

"Perhaps a public repudiation of the 'no-first-strike—no-retaliation policy.' That will warn the Russians not to try anything," the Vice-President added.

"No," said the President, "that may be just what the Soviets want us to do. By renouncing these policies, we weaken our assertion that Prometheus is a purely defensive system."

"Go public," said the Secretary of State. "Tell the American people that we are having some technical problems with the system and that until it is on line, we must revert to previous defense posture."

"Forget it. I won't undermine the public's confidence in this system. That's all the Democrats need to block future appropriation or deployment."

Webster Connolly waited until the others had had their say. "Why not a little personal diplomacy? Talk with Ushenko. Tell him our concerns, and ask him to limit the scope of his military maneuvers."

The President nodded with a smile to Connolly. "Get me First Secretary Ushenko on the hot line," he said. "I'll tell him we're running a little test and explain that he shouldn't be concerned."

General Gray spoke again. "He might think it's a subterfuge—that you're trying to catch him off guard and get off a first strike while he thinks it's merely an alert."

"I think not," said the President. "Ushenko knows that we'd be foolish to try anything like that while his forces are on alert and in the field." He looked at Connolly. "Get Ushenko on the phone for me, Web. And get a translator on the line right away too." Now that he had made up his mind and was giving orders, the President was back in command. He seemed more relaxed, almost at ease. "I want you all to stay," he said. "I want everyone to hear this."

Later they all agreed it was one of the most remarkable performances they had ever witnessed. The President, who only moments before had seemed tired and enfeebled, was in complete control of the situation.

As soon as Connolly had returned with the news that the Soviet First Secretary was on the line, the President had taken two deep breaths and pulled himself erect in his chair.

"Good evening, Mr. Secretary," he said pleasantly, knowing full well it was early morning in Moscow. His voice was strong and forceful. "I don't want to make more of this than is really necessary, but it seems we have a little technical problem with our new defensive system." He nodded several times, smiling at Ushenko's response. "Oh I know you don't like that system, Mr. Secretary, but I can assure you, it is completely defensive in nature. I fully intend to leave it as my legacy to the American people."

He listened for a few minutes, his face a blank. "Let me tell you why I called, Mr. Secretary. We are having a test of our system and I don't want you or any of your people to misconstrue the nature or purpose of this test. We are moving to what our military calls Defense Condition Two, a full War Alert, Mr. Secretary, and . . ."

It was obvious from the President's expression that he had been interrupted. His eyes narrowed and his jaw jutted forward. "Well, you do as you deem necessary, Mr. Secretary. I think I would do exactly the same thing in your situation. But if both our countries are at full War Alert, we must be exceptionally careful not to do anything, whether by design or happenstance, to provoke the other. I know I intend to make certain that nothing of that nature occurs on this side, and I know that you'll do the same on yours."

He listened. "No, Mr. Secretary. I'm certainly not trying to tell you what to do. I'm just trying to give you fair warning"—his voice grew deeper and more menacing, but in an almost fatherly way—"that my promise of no retaliation is indefinitely suspended."

The President leaned back in his chair, one arm behind his neck as he listened.

"What that means, Mr. Secretary, is that we are prepared to respond, missile for missile, warhead for warhead, to any provocation in Europe or elsewhere."

The President listened, nodding and smiling jovially, as if he had not just threatened the Soviet Secretary with annihilation. "I knew I could count on your cooperation, Mr. Secretary," he said finally.

After a few more minutes of listening and smiling, the President engaged in a few superficial pleasantries and bid the Soviet First Secretary a polite farewell. He hung up the phone with a rather dramatic flair. "Well, gentlemen," he said, "we can go ahead with our test. I don't think we have to worry about our Russian friends interfering."

In dumb amazement, the men who had witnessed the

President's transformation shook their heads in wonder. Then the Secretary of State started to applaud, and in a flash they were all on their feet, applauding and laughing together.

MOSCOW—In a surprise move, the Central Committee announced today that Dimitri Ushenko has stepped down from his position as General Secretary of the Communist Party. Ushenko, who had assumed the preeminent position as leader of the Soviet Union only a week ago, resigned, it was said, for reasons of health.

In a related development, and one that was seen by expert observers of the Soviet system as having as much to do with Ushenko's resignation as his health, the Soviet military hurriedly canceled military maneuvers in Europe that in some cases were already under way. Observers maintain that Ushenko's strident rhetoric and combative personality, coupled with the immediate move to a massive show of military strength upon his selection as Party Chairman, had frightened much of Western Europe and caused dismay in his own country.

Even Soviet satellite states seemed distressed by the new militant stance. Articles appearing in the East German Communist daily, *Neues Deutschland;* the Czechoslovakian Communist party daily, *Pravda* of Bratislava; and the Budapest weekly, *Magyarors zag,* all called for the Soviet Union to moderate its recent strident tone. These defections were seen as significant in light of the fact that these newspapers generally adhere strictly to the Soviet Communist Party line.

It was not immediately clear whether Ushenko would maintain his former position as Defense Minister in the Politburo. Ushenko, whose health has always been described as good, has not been available for comment since the surprise announcement of his resignation. A new General Secretary is expected to be named within the week, with KGB Director Viktor Chebrikov and Agricultural Minister Mikhail Gorbachev prominently mentioned.

A surge of rumors earlier in the week had

Chebrikov discredited and removed from office, but today's speculation has laid that rumor to rest.

The next General Secretary will be the fourth in the little more than four years since the death of Leonid Brezhnev in 1982. Ushenko's resignation is seen by some observers as further evidence that the Soviet system is increasingly chaotic, and although mired in orthodoxy, seems paradoxically unable to steer a stable course.

Political observers await the emergence of the new Soviet leader before venturing predictions upon what course the Soviet Union might embark.

Epilog

It was a warm day for September, and K.C., Diane, Carol, and Birdwell were seated at the outdoor terrace of the Portofino Caffé in San Francisco's Ghirardelli Square. Just below them and to the right was Fountain Plaza, where afternoon shoppers and lunchtime strollers congregated around the circular fountain. Looking out across the square, they could see the Municipal Pier, and beyond that, San Francisco Bay.

"I guess," said Birdwell, "we'll never really know how close we came to disaster."

K.C. looked at Diane and made a face of displeasure. "I know how close *we* came," he said. "Too damn close."

Birdwell seemed contrite. "We never intended for you to get into that kind of situation, K.C. I'm sorry."

Diane nudged K.C. sharply with her elbow.

He sighed. "It was as much my fault as it was yours," he said to Birdwell. "I should have told you about the late-night phone call and the photograph. I knew someone was onto me."

Birdwell nodded. "And you should have stayed put like I told you to, instead of trying to do it all by yourself."

"If he had done what you told him," Carol said. "Diane might not be here now."

Birdwell looked down at the table. "I guess you're right. I'm sorry," he said softly.

They sat for a short time in silence, each trying to find some pleasant way to finish what they were trying to say.

Birdwell spoke first. "I guess everything worked out fairly well in the end."

"Except for Gordon," said K.C. He was determined not to make things easy.

Birdwell looked away in embarrassment. "I didn't mean . . ." His voice trailed away into nothingness. He tried again. "What will you do now that it's over?"

K.C. seemed uninterested. "I'm not sure."

Diane picked at an imaginary speck of lint on the tablecloth.

"How about that Stanford job?" asked Carol more cheerfully. "Is it still open?"

K.C. shrugged and Diane looked away. "I don't know," he said. "I didn't find out." He fidgeted with a napkin. "I don't think I want it anyway."

"What about TMK?" Birdwell asked. "With the shake-up they've had—Tolbert and Lawson out, and old man Whitaker taking over the company again—they'll be needing good, experienced people. You could do well there."

"It's not for me," K.C. said. "I'd like to get back to teaching. That's where I belong."

Birdwell looked at his watch. He seemed relieved that so much time had passed. "Well, I've got to get back to the office." He stood up and offered his hand to K.C., who took it only after a momentary pause. "We appreciate everything you've done, K.C. Your brother would have been proud of you."

K.C. nodded. "Thanks," he said, and then, almost as an afterthought he added, "Take care of yourself, and keep up the good work."

"Someone has to," Birdwell said, and with a brief nod to all three, he was gone.

"You were kind of rough on him, weren't you?" Diane said. "It wasn't his fault."

"Maybe not," K.C. replied in a tone of dismissal.

Carol jumped in in an attempt to change the subject. "Are you taking that job offer in San Francisco?"

Diane looked at K.C., then quickly looked away. "I think so," she said. "I might as well strike while the iron's hot. You never know if you'll ever be involved in a story like this again. This is my chance to capitalize on it."

"What about the network job in New York?" asked K.C.

Diane shrugged. "I don't think I'm ready for that yet."

They were all very quiet. The silence threatened to overwhelm them.

Carol stood up. "I think I'll get myself an ice cream at

Ghirardelli's. I'll catch up with you two later." No one protested, and she quickly made her exit.

K.C. and Diane sat for a few minutes, sipping coffee and trying not to look at each other. Finally he spoke. "You're not coming to New York?"

"I don't think so," she said softly.

"I think you should try it."

"It's not the right time," she said. "I'm not really ready."

"I think you're ready," K.C. said. "I know I'm ready."

Diane squinted at him. "Are we talking about the same thing?"

He went on, ignoring her question. "My place is too small. We could get a bigger place."

Diane swallowed hard. "Oh?"

"I thought we could live together."

Diane allowed herself a small smile. "I might like that."

"I thought we could get married."

"I'd like that better."

He reached across the table and took her hand in his. "You didn't think I was going to let you get away, did you?"

"I was beginning to wonder," she answered.

"Carol would never have spoken to me again!"

Diane laughed. "Neither would I."

They got up and made their way downstairs to the square, where they found Carol sitting by the fountain. She saw them approach arm in arm and smiled.

"We've got something to tell you," Diane said.

Carol embraced her and then K.C. "I thought you might," she said. "I just thought you might."

ABOUT THE AUTHOR

CHARLES ROBERTSON, who was born in Scotland, is a former high-school English teacher turned novelist. He lives with his wife and children in Stamford, Connecticut. *Red Chameleon* is his fourth novel.

Coming in Paperback!

The #1 *New York Times* bestseller
by the author of *The Godfather*

THE SICILIAN
by
Mario Puzo

Mario Puzo returns to the world of the Corleones in his riveting new blockbuster!

It is the end of Michael Corleone's two-year exile in Sicily. But before he returns home, Michael must carry out one final duty for the Godfather: locate and bring to America the bandit leader Salvatore Guiliano, a latter-day Robin Hood who dispenses his own brand of brutal justice to the corrupt powers-that-be. But his bloody crusade to defend his peasant countrymen locks Guiliano in a deadly combat with his most lethal adversary: Don Croce Malo, the ruthless *Capo di Capi* of the Sicilian Mafia. When Guiliano challenges the Don's iron-clad rule over Sicily, he unleashes a bloodbath of death and destruction.

Read *The Sicilian*, Mario Puzo's new masterwork on sale November 20, 1985, wherever Bantam paperbacks are sold.